Heart of Us

A Philosophical Romance

Emma Browne

This book is a work of fiction. Any resemblance to actual persons, living or dead, or events, is coincidental.

Copyright © 2020 Emma Wagner. All rights reserved.

No part of this book may be used, reproduced, or distributed in any manner whatsoever without explicit written permission from the author.

Scripture taken from the Holy Bible, NEW INTERNATIONAL VERSION®, NIV® Copyright © 1973, 1978, 1984, 2011 by Biblica, Inc.® Used by permission. All rights reserved worldwide.

Editing by Mary McCorkle & Rebecca Kremer
Cover design by Emma Wagner. Photo from unsplash.com

Made in Scotland.
Print edition

Dedication

To Stefan – you wonderful, kind soul. You were a hero, and I'm forever proud to have been considered a friend. Rest in peace.

And to all the others in my life that have struggled – or continue to struggle – with addiction of different kinds.

Chapter 1

Miranda

The day I saw Jack again started like any other Sunday morning.

I got up early, pulled on an old pair of leggings and an even older burnt orange t-shirt. I made a cup of herbal tea, started my laptop, and got the spreadsheets up. Spreadsheets on a Sunday morning are perhaps not everybody's cup of tea, but I find they bring a sense of comfort. I hear *some* people make decisions without first entering all the data onto a spreadsheet, but I'm not one of them. Spreadsheets bring logic, order and clarity to any issue, and help calculate risk. And how can you make any decision without first calculating the risk?

That morning I was running numbers for the social enterprise my friends Julia, Sophia and I were launching. We were still in the very early stages of starting up, but we had a plan and had decided to give it a go. Our idea was to sell period cups in Scotland to raise money in order to help fund women's health projects all over the world. Only a few years ago, I had never heard of period cups, but this project was quickly becoming something I felt passionately about.

I sat cross-legged, working on the spreadsheet, when the doorbell rang. I squeezed my eyes shut and ran my hands through my hair. I wasn't expecting anyone. Stretching my stiff legs and neck, I clicked 'save' and got up to answer the door.

'Hello?'

An old man in ripped jeans and hoodie stood on my doorstep. His dirty, grey hair hung in his eyes and his smile was wide as his eyes met mine. He swayed back too much and caught the door handle to steady himself. 'Miranda, luv.'

Smelling the alcohol and cigarettes on his breath, I sighed. 'Dad.'

'Well, are you going to let me in?' His words were slurred, and I wondered when he'd had his last drink.

I opened the door wider to let him in and he followed me to the kitchen. 'How about a glass of water to rehydrate?'

He chuckled merrily to himself. 'Water? I don't need any water. You got anything stronger?'

I shook my head as I filled a glass with water and set it down in front of him. 'Drink up,' I said in a stern voice. He rolled his eyes but drained the glass.

'Miranda darling, you're just like your mother.' He gave me a slow smile as his eyes were drooping, and he leaned back in his seat.

'Right.' I sat down opposite him and took him in. He looked – and smelled – like the binge he was on had gone on for quite some time, and I wondered how bad it had gotten. 'When's the last time you ate?'

'Dunno.' He yawned and made himself comfortable as though he was going to grab a quick nap.

I couldn't leave him to sleep it off at the table. 'Come on. You'll be more comfortable in a soft seat.' Helping him up from his chair, I led him to the couch in the living room, where he cuddled up with a cushion and promptly fell asleep. I covered him in a blanket and sat down in the armchair listening to him snore for a few minutes as I wondered how he had ended up like this.

Again.

Though I knew Dad's alcoholism was a disease, it still sucked that he – once again – was stuck on the drink. I shouldn't feel disappointed; Dad had been an alcoholic for as long as I could remember, and he always would be. There had been periods where he was sober – some lasted for a couple of years – but he had never broken the addiction completely. I doubted he ever would. At least the alcohol hadn't been too hard on him. He looked maybe ten years older than he was, his nose was red from overusing alcohol for too long, and he was in desperate need of a haircut, but he was healthy enough. He wasn't much of a role model, but he had a way of defusing arguments and bringing peace to situations, even as his own life was as chaotic as they come.

Still, it was hard to see him drunk.

I put my laptop away – spreadsheets might be comforting, but I was too sad to want to be awake this Sunday morning. Going via the kitchen, I made Dad a couple of sandwiches and another glass of water. I set them on the coffee table by the couch with a couple of pills for his head, ready for him when he woke up. Then I went back to bed and went to sleep.

When I woke up a few hours later, Dad was gone. The blanket was folded neatly on the couch, the sandwiches were gone, and – apart from a smell of cigarettes on the blanket – there was no evidence Dad had been there at all.

I rubbed my face as I wished he had stayed. He was probably feeling guilty about crashing at mine when drunk, but I would rather have him drunk on my couch than drifting around Edinburgh. I wished for the millionth time that he would get sober again and was wondering how long it would be until I would next see him when my phone pinged.

Soph: You coming to lunch at the Reids' today? X

Looking at the time, I saw I would just have time to brush my teeth before leaving. The Reids – or John and Karen – lived next door and were my friend Julia's parents. As I had been in their house more than I had been in my own growing up, they were family to me, so I didn't feel a need to get dressed up. My comfy old leggings and big scruffy t-shirt would do fine.

Me: On my way x

I brushed my teeth and pulled a comb through my hair before putting on my jacket and trainers and walking across the lawn. Sophia waved at me from the pavement as she hurried toward me. 'Hey!'

Wearing a blue casual dress with a thin belt and grey cardigan, as well as a black handbag and a pair of sunglasses, she looked well put together. I waited for her to get to the house before I said, 'You coming from church?'

She nodded, and we rang the bell before walking on in.

'In here!' Karen called from the kitchen, and I smiled at the feeling of being home.

'It smells lovely in here. What are you cooking?' Sophia took off her black flats and pushed her sunglasses onto the top of her head.

'It's nice to see you girls.' Karen gave us each a big hug, squeezing me tight as though she knew I needed it. 'We're having chicken, and there's lots of veg. You won't go hungry, Miranda dear.'

'Thank you.' I smiled, grateful that she cared enough to remember that I swung between being vegetarian and vegan.

I sat down to talk to Becky, their chocolate lab. Becky had lived at my house for months at a time over the years, and I would dare say nobody in the world knew me as well as Becky did. She had been there for me when Jack had left and Mum had died, giving me a reason to get out of bed in the mornings when I felt like giving up on life. Her velvet ears were soft on my cheek as I snuggled in for a hug. 'Oh Becky.' I sighed as I thought about Dad.

'Everything ok, Mir?' Julia asked.

I pulled my mouth up into an awkward smile and nodded. 'Yes, I'm ok.'

'You look like you've lost weight, darling.' Karen looked at me and frowned. 'You've got to be careful. We don't want any more of those dizzy spells you used to have back when Lisa was sick.' Lisa was my mum. She died from cancer in my third year of university, a few months after Jack left me. She had been Karen's best friend, and I knew she still missed her.

As did I.

'I don't think I've lost much weight.' I didn't want to talk about Dad, so I shrugged and redirected the attention. 'Julia has, though.' Julia had just spent a year on a teacher exchange program in Kenya and had come back about ten kilos lighter. And miraculously tanned, considering her fair skin and red hair. I didn't think I had ever seen her as tanned before.

'Yes, you look great.' Sophia nodded at Julia.

'Thank you.' She winked, clearly pleased with the way she looked.

'John, are you coming?' Karen hollered for her husband before turning back to us. 'Let's serve up. By the time we're sitting down I'm sure the boys will be here.'

The boys.

From the way Karen referred to them, you might think they were schoolboys. They were not. These *boys* were men in their late twenties, one of which was a site manager at a construction company, and the other worked at Edinburgh University. And both Nick and Michael looked nothing like boys. Except, perhaps, for the way their eyes still held a hint of the mischief they were planning.

Sophia grinned at me and I shook my head and snorted.

Sitting down, I nodded toward John at the other side of the table and wondered whether I should talk to him about Dad. Later, I decided as Sophia asked me to pass her some water.

We got our dinner, and – just as predicted – the guys walked through the door just as Karen said, 'Let's pray.'

'Hello!' Nick and Michael called, laughing as they came into the dining room with a familiar blonde coming up behind them.

All the air went out of my chest. I would know that voice anywhere.

'Hey,' Jack said, and my breath hitched as he came into view. His blonde hair was short and messy, and his eyes still sky blue. There was a bit of scruff on his cheeks, longer than a five o'clock shadow, but short enough to suggest he just hadn't bothered to shave since leaving Hong Kong. It further defined the sharp line of his jaw and made him look rugged.

His neck was strong, and there was a pair of sunglasses hanging from the loose white Henley which made his tan pop and showed off his muscles. To say Jack looked good was perhaps the understatement of a lifetime. He had looked *good* before he left. Now he was devastatingly beautiful.

Memories flew through my mind in a jumbled mess, and I watched as everyone got up to say hi. I would have found Karen's face comical had it not been for the emotional rollercoaster happening in my stomach as I watched her all but squeal at the sight of her long-lost son and throw herself into his arms. Jack squeezed her tight and rocked from side to side as he hugged her back and grinned.

'I can't believe you're here!' Karen said as she stepped back and ran a hand across his cheek. 'When did you land? Why didn't you tell me? Are you hungry? Of course you're hungry. Sit down.'

'Give him a chance to breathe, love,' John smiled at Karen as she fluttered around Jack. John pulled him in for a hug. 'It's good to see you, son.'

I stayed where I was, gave him what felt like a strained smile and a hi in reply to his 'Miranda.'

I had known Jack was coming home for good but, as far as I knew, he wasn't expected home for another few weeks.

As planning ahead was my thing, I had already planned how I would prepare myself before seeing him. I would dress in my best jeans and heels, blow my hair out and do my makeup. The plan had *not* been to wear old leggings and a big orange t-shirt with a smudge of… chocolate? at the hem, with my hair pulled up in a messy topknot to cover the fact I hadn't washed it.

Running a hand over my face, I wished for a sink hole to open and swallow me. To my distress, I found the Reid house was starkly short of sink holes.

It was six years since I last had seen Jack. At the time we had been engaged – planning to get married. But after a few weeks of living in Hong Kong, he had decided to break up with me, and I hadn't seen him since.

Around me, everyone sat back down and started dishing up, as I racked my brain for ways to escape. But it was futile. If I left too abruptly it would look like I still cared about him. Like his presence caused me to *feel* things.

And maybe it did. Maybe his presence brought up memories of the most painful time of my life.

Sure – there were feelings.

But any *romantic* feelings I had ever had for him were well and truly in the past. I had moved on a long time ago.

I struggled to pay attention to conversation as it turned to the camping trip the guys had gone on after picking Jack up at the airport on Thursday. Although I hadn't eaten since my cup of tea several hours earlier, I no longer had an appetite.

I was vaguely aware of Julia and Sophia trying to communicate concern for me with their eyes across the table. When Julia looked at me, I mouthed, 'Did you know he was going to be here?'

She shook her head; I was thankful this wasn't a set up.

'You ok?' she mouthed back, and I gave a sharp nod and looked away.

'It's just *wonderful* to finally have all of you together around the table here again,' Karen said, bringing her hands together over her chest. If she had been a cat, she would have been purring, she looked so delighted. And I would have been happy for her had I not been as caught up in my own feelings of embarrassment and wave after wave of pain as memories attacked me.

Seeing Jack and remembering our breakup brought back all the feelings of grief and sadness from back then. Everything within me was off kilter. Still, I sat through the meal and avoided making eye contact with Jack, whose eyes kept seeking me out.

I got the sense the girls did their best to distract him by starting a debate about camping and fishing and asking millions of questions, whilst somehow avoiding all the ones going through my mind. Like: *why was he here now?*

I picked at my food and tried to eat a little in order to appear unaffected, even as I felt as though everyone could see straight through me. As soon as we had eaten dessert, I escaped to the bathroom, where I washed my face and tried to cool down. It hadn't escaped my notice that Jack had jumped up to help with the dishes and offered to make his mum a cup of tea to keep her sitting down.

I found a clean hand towel and patted my face dry as I shook my head. I had a weakness for kindness. Facing my pale self in the mirror, I said sternly, 'You have dealt with this shit already. Pick yourself up and get over it.'

I pinched my cheeks and pursed my lips as I tried to believe that what I was saying was true, but I had a gnawing suspicion that I still had some dealing to do. An image of Jack in his henley shirt floated through my mind and I sighed, wishing there was a way to escape the attraction I still felt towards him.

I shook myself, trying to clear my head, and put a smile on my face before shrugging into my leather jacket, which made my outfit seem a little less hobo-ish. My smile looked strained, but it was the best I could do.

Then I took a deep breath and went with the others to the pub.

Chapter 2

Jack

Despite knowing I would see Miranda when I came home to Sunday dinner, I was unprepared for the way the sight of her hit me in the chest.

She was gorgeous.

Her thick dark hair was a mess on top of her head, and those moss green eyes and the freckles on her nose made it hard to breathe. She looked like she could use a few big meals, but her being just a little too skinny was nothing new. A memory of eating waffles together as children flashed by. Miranda had been maybe eight and had eaten eight waffles with cream and jam in one go without batting an eye. Her grin when she'd managed one more than I had had galled me at the time. Now I would have given anything for her to grin at me like that.

I blew out a slow breath and focused on being the returning son after being overseas for six years. Mum jumped up with a squeal when she first saw me, as she didn't expect me home for another few weeks. 'How come you're home already?'

I grinned at her as she wrapped her arms around me. 'The project I was working on finished up early, so I decided to come home. I need to go back out there for a few meetings in about a month, but until then I might as well be here,' I said through Mum's hair as she squeezed me.

Dad stood up more slowly and came over to slap me on the back. 'It's good to see you, son.' He wore a satisfied smile.

Julia was next, and I rubbed her head affectionately as I hugged her.

'You stink.' She pulled back at the smell of campfire and sweat.

'Camping.' I shrugged and grinned. 'It's good to see you too. I might have missed you. A little.'

'Yeah, I missed you too.' She grinned back at me.

Following Michael and Nick, who were dishing up food, I took in the scene. There were potatoes on the table instead of rice, and all the usual suspects sat around the table, talking over each other and smiling.

We had all aged a bit, but we were still the same people.

Sure, a few things had changed. Like Sophia and Michael had gotten married four years ago for Michael to get a visa to stay in Scotland. And Miranda, whom I had been engaged to six years ago, was now avoiding making eye contact with me. Still, Julia and Nick were the same – forever snapping at each other – and Mum and Dad still looked happy.

See? Still the same people.

I sighed. I was *home*.

'Mum, this all smells amazing.' I took a plate and started loading food onto it.

'I bet you guys are starving after camping these days.'

'Nothing beats your Sunday dinners, Karen,' Nick said, and I mentally rolled my eyes at how he was trying to act charming to Mum in order to irritate Julia. He needn't have bothered trying. Mum had always liked Nick, and he didn't have to do much more than breathe to annoy Julia.

Mum smiled at him before turning back to me. 'When did you arrive? Have you been camping, too?'

I nodded. 'Yeah. Nick and Michael picked me up at the airport on Thursday, and then we went straight up north. I'm pretty jetlagged still, but I couldn't miss camping.'

Michael slapped my back and smiled, whilst Mum shook her head. 'Boys…' She sighed. 'Anyway, it's wonderful to finally have all of you together around the table here again.' She looked thrilled.

'Wouldn't miss it.' Nick smiled and winked at Mum.

'Yeah, it's good to be home,' I said, as I looked toward Miranda.

'Jack.' Her eyes caught on mine and something passed between us. 'Long time no see.'

'Yeah.' I smiled at her. 'It's good to see you, Miranda.'

She gave a sharp nod before pulling her eyes away to look at her plate, where she was pushing some vegetables around.

'How was camping?' Sophia asked, clearly trying to divert my attention.

'It was great! Although Jack here slept for most of the time,' Nick said.

I leaned back in my chair and grinned. 'Yeah, yeah… you try going camping in a tent in the rain after travelling for 24 hours.'

'Did you catch any fish?' Sophia asked.

Michael nodded. 'Yeah. We did some fishing off the Isle of Mull yesterday and caught a couple of mackerels. Nick cooked them up for dinner last night.'

'Best mackerels you'll have ever eaten,' Nick said with a cocky grin.

Michael snorted. 'Might have been the only mackerels I've ever eaten, but sure.'

'You've never had mackerel before?!' Sophia put her hand on her chest and raised her eyebrows like she couldn't believe it.

'Oh come on, we're not all pescatarians, or whatever you call it when you eat a lot of fish.' Michael winked at her.

'Pescatarian?' Sophia snorted. 'A pescatarian is like a vegetarian that also eats fish. It's not someone that *eats a lot of fish*, you silly. Besides, you should eat more fish, it's good for you.'

'What was China like, Jack?' Julia asked, trying to get the conversation away from the Fish Versus Mac and Cheese debate we all knew was about to break out.

'Good.' I smiled. 'I missed you guys of course, but Hong Kong and China are amazing.'

'Well, it's good to have you back now.' Mum reached out and stroked my arm. 'How long do you have to go back for?'

'I'll just be away for a couple weeks or so in about six weeks. I've got a few meetings to do, but otherwise I'm home now. I've got a couple of weeks off now, and then I start work here.'

'Good to have you back.' Dad said.

I nodded and let the conversation going on around me wash over me. It was nice to be home. My eyes drifted to Miranda. She might have spent the meal avoiding looking at me, but I let my eyes rest on her. Her dark hair was pulled into a messy bun, showing off her slender neck, and her t-shirt hung off her shoulder, revealing the collarbone. As I watched her smile at Mum or pass vegetables to Sophia, I realised how starved of her I had been. Spending six years on the other side of the world, a part of me had missed her every day, and seeing her now made me wonder how I had survived staying away for this long.

I wanted to reach out and touch her, but I knew she was unlikely to want that, considering how things between us had ended. I cringed as I thought about how I had broken up with her.

She was still picking at her food, but not eating much. She wasn't talking much either, and seemed lost in thought. Unsurprisingly, she didn't seem thrilled to see me.

'Hey, are you coming?' Nick startled me out of my thoughts, and I nodded as I wondered where we were going.

***

As far as pubs go, The Sheep Heid Inn was a nice upscale pub, more of a relaxed and cosy living room than a seedy bar or a trendy club. It claimed to be the oldest pub in Edinburgh and had sheep heads on the wall, fireplaces, and tucked away little tables in corners with old-looking art on the walls.

Though there were plenty of places we could have gone for a pint on a Sunday afternoon, The Sheep Heid had been our place since we became adults, and it seemed fitting to go there. I ordered a beer, brought it out to the beer garden, and tried to follow the conversation, which centred on the social enterprise Sophia, Julia and Miranda were starting, and what to call it. Nick and Michael had talked about it some when we were camping, as they were both looking to partner or invest in the venture.

The plan to sell period cups in Scotland to fund projects for women's health issues around the world sounded like a good idea. Sure, the idea of a period cup grossed me out, but if I didn't think about the function of it too much, I could recognise the idea as having great potential. And, just like Nick and Michael, I was interested enough to consider investing.

If nothing else, it might get me a chance to work on something with Miranda. Because, after just seeing her again, I was more convinced than ever that I wanted her back.

And this time I wouldn't let anything keep us from staying together.

Chapter 3

Miranda

Going to the pub had always been somewhat uncomfortable for me. Dad being an alcoholic made my relationship to alcohol complicated, which meant pubs weren't my favourite places. I ordered a glass of lemonade when we got to the pub – not because I was a teetotaller (I wasn't. I could enjoy a glass of wine or the odd pint with friends from time to time), but because I had a strict rule not to use alcohol to handle my emotions – and sipped it slowly as I tried to keep my smile in place.

I was still reeling inside from seeing Jack again. He looked good. As though he could ever look otherwise. His blonde hair was longer and styled on top with the sides cut shorter. He had always put product in his hair, which made any of my attempts to run my fingers through it a sticky experience. Still, he had clearly run his fingers through it a few times today, which made me wonder if he might be as nervous about seeing me as I was about seeing him. Then again, perhaps it was just the left-over hair style from yesterday and he had run his fingers through it to make the best of it after camping in the wild with the guys. His blue eyes were as clear as ever, and I found myself avoiding them, as I knew they would only try to pull me in.

I couldn't afford to be pulled in.

Jack's relaxed attitude had me remembering what it was like back in the day when we would hang out all together. He would sit with his arm around me and laugh with the others, and I would snuggle in.

Glancing at his face, my hands itched to touch the scruff on his cheeks. In another life I would have reached out and felt it.

I sighed and pushed the memories aside, reminding myself that I was done with him.

And I didn't want him back.

I wasn't just *thinking* I didn't want him back whilst secretly hoping we would get back together. I knew people like that; Julia was one of them. She didn't get on with Nick at all, but we all knew she carried a torch for him.

Not me, though.

No: despite my obvious attraction to him, Jack and I were best kept in the past as a bittersweet memory. Any attempt to revive a romance between us would end in disaster. And since I was sure I couldn't live through that again, it was best to ignore the way my heart leapt every time I heard him speak. Memories of snuggling into him wouldn't be helpful going forward.

I bit my lip and looked away. It was best to focus on something other than Jack.

Anything else.

Around us, everyone was talking about our project. Jack seemed relaxed and happy to be back, and made a few period jokes with the guys, but he seemed interested in the idea of our social enterprise. I had a feeling the guys wanted in, even as I wasn't sure why. There would be nothing in it for them.

'Have you guys decided if you're going to go with an already existing product, or do you want to produce your own cups?' Jack asked, pulling me out of my thoughts.

'I've been looking into that.' My voice sounded strained. I cleared my throat in an effort to make it sound more normal. 'I found a company that produces things with medical grade silicone in China, which I would like to check out a little more.'

'Sure. Let me know if I can help with anything on that. I have a few contacts in China and Hong Kong that might come in handy,' Jack offered.

I stiffened. I didn't want his help. Not because I was mad at him – I wasn't. With so many years having gone by, I wouldn't have coped if I hadn't let go of the anger. I didn't want his help because I never again wanted to be in the position of having to depend on him for anything. 'I think we'll be fine, but thanks.'

Jack shrugged. 'Well, the offer's there.' He held up his empty pint glass. 'I'm thinking I've got to get home and shower.'

'I think you guys all need a shower,' Julia said, scrunching her nose. 'I bet you've washed by swimming in a loch this weekend.'

Nick shrugged. 'It's not camping otherwise.'

Leaving the pub, Nick offered Jack and me a lift home. I would have rather been anywhere other than in a car with Jack but walking home with him alone would have been worse. I nodded and got in the front seat of Nick's car, with Jack and Julia getting in the back.

Nick glanced at me and smiled. Then he – rather uncharacteristically – proceeded to talk to me about the weather for the whole journey home. Glad not to have to sit in what would otherwise have been a rather awkward silence, I answered with the odd 'Uh-huh' here and there, and thanked him when he dropped us off.

He shook his head and grabbed my shoulder before letting me get out of the car. I turned to look at him. He lowered his voice and said in his soft American accent, 'You'll be okay. But if you need anything, you call, you hear?'

I nodded. 'Uh-huh.'

Having decided the best way forward would be to avoid any interaction with Jack, I got out of the car and hurried up the path to unlock my front door. Opening it, I felt Jack's hand on my shoulder, and my stomach sank. Why couldn't he have just gone home to his parents' instead of continuing this awkward day?

'Hey, wait a minute.'

I concentrated on not letting my body tremble and stayed where I was, waiting for him to continue. When he didn't, I turned my face toward him. 'What?'

Letting go of my shoulder, he ran his hands through his hair, and I thought again of the product in his hair. 'Can we talk?' He gave me a cheeky smile and my stomach went all jittery as I remembered how I used to melt when he used the same smile on me before we broke up.

I snorted at the futility of trying to keep him away. 'Come on in, then.' Pushing aside the feeling that I would come to regret inviting him in, I told myself I would get better at ignoring the memories and the way they tried to tug on my heart strings. He had taken me by surprise showing up like he had today, but next time I would be more prepared. 'Are you having tea?'

'Sure, whatever you've got is fine.' He shrugged out of his denim jacket and followed me into the kitchen, where I went about making tea. 'I like how you painted the walls in here.'

I glanced at them. A couple of years after mum died, I decided the house was mine now and keeping it the way mum had kept it wouldn't bring her back or preserve any memories. So, I had a big clear out and painted the kitchen a light blue instead of the drab magnolia it used to be. It felt lighter now, and definitely more me. 'Thanks.' I gave him his cup and sat down. 'So... was there something you wanted to talk about?'

He stared at me his eyebrows knitted together. 'Right, yes.' He sipped his tea and smiled. 'So, this isn't awkward, is it? Is it awkward?'

Was he kidding? It was *incredibly* awkward. I scrunched my nose and held up my thumb and finger. 'It's a wee bit awkward, yeah.'

He twisted his mouth and his eyes sparkled. 'Yeah, I suppose. Does it have to be, though?'

I didn't know how to answer that, so I kept quiet.

'I mean, we used to be friends first. Then we were a couple, and then we broke up...' He waved his hands in the air when he talked. 'What I mean is, we were friends for years before we ever started dating, and I'm hoping we could be friends again?' He shot me another of his smiles and as my stomach flipped, I wondered how smart I was to let him back into my house.

Still, I was relieved he just wanted to assure himself we wouldn't fight. I didn't have the energy to fight or be awkward over something that happened years and years ago. 'Sure! Friends sounds good.' I gave what felt like an exaggerated smile.

His eyes sparkled with mischief. 'Unless you want to try dating...'

'No!' I shook my head and snorted. 'No, no, no. We're not going to be getting back together.'

He gave a soft chuckle that warmed my insides in a way that I was realising I would have to get used to again. 'Fine. Friends it is.'

'Friends.' I gave an enthusiastic nod and sipped my tea. 'So. Hong Kong, eh?'

He shrugged. 'Yeah. It was good for a time. Back now though.'

I took a deep breath as I tried to be okay with seeing Jack in my kitchen again. Searching my mind for friendly questions, I came up with: 'So. Were you transferred, or?'

'Yeah. It felt like it was time to come home. Started missing oatcakes, and ale, and haggis, you know?' His eyes danced over me, and I nodded, even as I doubted his transfer had anything to do with him missing Scottish food. 'How've you been?'

How could I sum up the rollercoaster of the last six years? I settled on, 'Alright,' even though they had been some of the worst years of my life.

It wasn't five seconds before Jack said, 'Bull.' His piercing blue eyes took no prisoners. 'Tell me how you've really been.'

I set down my teacup and looked him in the eye. 'Look Jacky, we can be friends, but you've got to give me some time to warm up to the idea. We're not going to pick up where we left off, and I'm not ready to have deep conversations. So yeah, parts of the last few years have been pretty crap, but I don't want to talk about it.' I tilted my chin up. 'Are we clear?'

His eyes were gentle as they looked at me, his smile crooked as he nodded. 'Crystal.' He stood up and took his cup to the sink. 'Do you still run?'

'Uh-huh.'

'What time do you go? I'll join you.'

I glanced at him. He had filled out since he left Edinburgh all those years ago. The lean physique he used to have as a result of running was replaced with muscles. So many muscles. 'Think you can keep up?'

He grinned. 'I guess we'll find out.' He whistled a song I recognized but couldn't place as he sauntered out of my house, leaving me in my kitchen chair staring after him for a long time.

I wasn't sure how I had gone from having decided to avoid him at all costs, to inviting him to run with me, in just a few minutes. And what was worse, from feeling indifferent towards him, to having shivers running up and down my spine whenever he looked at me. Scratch that – there had never been a time when I had felt indifferent towards him.

I dropped my head in my hands as I groaned. This would never work.

Chapter 4

PAST
Miranda

I was five when my Grandma died and left us a house in Edinburgh.

I hadn't known my Grandma, but I remember Mum being sad when we found out. A few months later, we moved out of our tiny, grubby flat in the South Side of Glasgow, and into a lovely detached house in Edinburgh. Not only did it come with more space, but it came with a new life.

Back in Glasgow, our neighbours had been single mums, rowdy youngsters, and people like us, on benefits. Mum had always worked hard as an industrial cleaner, but Dad couldn't seem to keep a job. Instead, he would be looking for work, staying sober and being around… most of the time. I was little and I don't remember much, but what I do remember is how happy I was. Mum would sing in the kitchen in the mornings before work and she would have a shy smile on her face whenever Dad would wolf-whistle his appreciation at how gorgeous she looked. At night they would dance in the kitchen as they prepared dinner, and Dad would tell Mum stories to make her laugh. Or he would play silly tunes on the old, clinky piano.

During the day, Dad would take me to the park, pushing me on the swings until I flew high in the sky, and he would laugh as he chased me around the park, pretending to be a lion pouncing on a zebra (me). I would run my fastest and fall in a heap of giggles as he would catch me in his arms and swing me over his shoulder, growling like a lion, as though he was about to dig into his meal. And on other, rainier days, he would play Uno with me for hours upon hours, or he would take me to the library and read me book after book. He would call me his little Mir-maid and tell me never to speak to boys, or they might get enchanted and ask me to leave him. I would pull an unimpressed face and say 'Daaadddyyy!' in an unimpressed tone. And he would wink at me and say, 'Just you wait and see.'

Then something would happen, and he would start waking up later and later in the day.

With headaches.

Dad wasn't a mean drunk, but he was unreliable and chaotic. Once he hit the bottle, he didn't seem to be able to stop and any money he could find would go toward booze. After a while, Mum couldn't take it anymore, they would have a falling out, and Dad would be gone for a while.

When Dad was away, the music left the house, and I would watch Mum sigh her way through the days instead. I ended up staying with the lady next door when Mum was at work. The neighbour was an older lady who smoked a lot and put me in front of the TV all day, except in the afternoons, when she used to force me to take long naps. I remember spending hours thinking up ways to escape to find my Daddy.

So, when Grandma died and we moved away, nobody was sad to leave. Instead we all felt like we were turning a new leaf, starting over somewhere new. I started primary school, Dad got a job stacking shelves at the supermarket, and Mum got a job cleaning at the hotel.

The area in Edinburgh which we moved to, Duddingston, seemed to house mostly bankers, lawyers and other upper middle-class people: it was clear from the start that we didn't fit in. Still, to begin with, everything was good. It seemed like things really had changed for us. There was a piano in the house, and Dad would play songs he had picked up over the years on it. Mum sang her out of tune songs in the kitchen again. We would take trips into town to see the sights, and we made friends with the next-door neighbours, the Reids. They had a girl my age, Julia, a boy, Jack, who was two years older, and baby Josie. Julia and I were in the same primary one class at school together and were soon best friends. And whilst it was obvious to us that the Reids were in a different social class from us, they didn't seem to notice, and we all became good friends. The Reids were good people, and, whilst they had their struggles like everyone else, there was a sense that you were loved and accepted in their house. I would go over and jump on their trampoline with Julia after school, and on weekends we would all go to the play park on Arthur's Seat or to the beach in Portobello together.

What Mum and I didn't know was that Dad had started drinking again. He hid it well this time. Then one day when I was six, he didn't come home, and when he returned the following day, head sore and with a bottle in his bag, Mum cried. Over the next few weeks, the singing stopped, and she pleaded with him to stop drinking before it was too late, but things only got worse and soon he lost his job. And then it wasn't long before he was gone for a few weeks.

Mum tried her hardest to pretend everything was fine to the world around us. And I think people believed us – at least to begin with.

***

Jack

The first time Miranda came to our house to play with Julia, I threw rotten pears at her.

It was Julia's first time having a friend over without parents and, though I was two years older, it bugged me that she wouldn't let me play with them. So, when they went outside with some dollies, I went outside too, and happened upon the rotten – and just mushy enough – pears under the tree.

It turns out throwing pears at girls wasn't a particularly effective strategy. Although I did get quite a few squeals out of them before Mum came out. With a long speech which mainly consisted of *you're bigger than they are and should know better* being repeated in different ways, she took away privileges and made me apologise to Miranda, who was crying.

I quickly found I didn't like it when Miranda cried. The tears coming down made little paths through the dirt on her face, which she had ended up with after being chased round the garden whilst being pelted with rotten pears. Her dark brown hair was frizzy and stood on end, making her look like a little troll with her small nose and freckles.

I felt a sting of regret. I hadn't wanted to hurt her – just to be included. Instead, Miranda ended up going home early, and Julia was so angry she wouldn't speak to me for the rest of the day.

The next time, I did better. Miranda showed off big blue bruises down her arms and legs where the pears had hit, as though they were battle wounds. I apologised again, and it wasn't long before we were all good friends.

And when I say *we were good friends*, I mean I was the leader, and they were my fan club and were up for everything I challenged them to. Honestly, nothing builds self-confidence like having a fan club.

Everyone should have one.

***

Miranda

After Dad started drinking again, there came a few years of him going backwards and forwards between us and the bottle. During this time, it felt like not much had changed since we had left Glasgow. We were still the same people with the same issues that never seemed to leave us.

The difference now was that in Edinburgh we were trying to fit in with the people around us. People that didn't have the same problems as we did, who easily earned five times as much as Mum did on her cleaning salary every month, and who seemed to live the perfect lives.

I don't know what we would have done without the Reids.

After trying to keep up the charade for a while, Mum broke one evening when Karen asked her if Dad was ok, as she hadn't seen him in a while. I overheard them talking in the kitchen as Julia and I were playing Uno in the living room, and that evening we stayed for dinner.

Mum's eyes were puffy when we went home, and I wondered what would happen next. Would Karen stop inviting us over? Would they start looking down their noses at us? But it turned out sharing with the Reids was the best thing Mum could have done. John started checking on Dad regularly, taking him on fishing trips during the summer months, and walking in the Pentland Hills. Dad had never been very outdoorsy, and I expect he struggled with the walking, but being around John seemed to ground him. And it was always clear the Reids had no expectations of him. Dad could take or leave their offer of help, and whether he took them up on it or not didn't seem to make them think differently of him.

Mum would go along to church with Karen, and brought me along, too. Sunday school was a new experience to me and I wasn't sure what to make of it, but I liked hearing the stories of how the big fish swallowed Jonah, or how Joseph's brothers threw him down the well and then sold him as a slave, or how David killed Goliath with his slingshot.

And as Dad wasn't working, Mum took on more hours at the hotel, and I ended up spending more time at the Reids'.

I didn't mind that at all.

Julia and Jack had the best games, and even their baby sister Josie was nice to be around. Julia and I would entertain her with peek-a-boo games, and we worked hard to teach her how to walk and talk and all the rest. But best of all was when Jack would play with us and we would pretend to be pirates or spies.

One day we were playing pirates. Captain Jack – we had to call him that or he threatened to stop playing with us – required that we show proof of how loyal we were to our captain. What would we do if we were in a shipwreck? Would we be deserters, or would we be prepared to eat anything in order to survive and stay loyal?

Captain Jack presented Julia and me with a worm each, which he had dug out of Karen's vegetable garden, and dared us to eat them.

'Do we bite it, or just swallow it whole?' Julia asked, equally fascinated and disgusted by the whole idea.

'I think we should swallow it whole. Otherwise we have to taste its guts.' I said, my stomach turning at the idea, even as I admired Jack for coming up with it.

'Then again…' Jack had a twinkle in his eye. 'If you don't bite it, then it will keep on living in your stomach.'

'Ewww!' Julia's face scrunched up. She put her worm in her mouth, took a quick bite, and swallowed before running into the house to get a glass of water.

I watched her run as I took a deep breath.

'You're not chicken, are you?' Jack taunted.

Chicken? *Chicken??*

Defiantly I put the worm on my tongue, crunching down on the slimy thing slowly, before swallowing it.

It was the most disgusting thing I had ever eaten – slimy and chewy – but I didn't let on. I licked my lips and raised my eyebrows. 'Where's your worm, Jacky? Are you not going to eat one, too?'

His smile grew into a grin and soon he was laughing so hard he struggled to stand up.

'What?' I asked. My stomach was still deciding what to do with the worm I had just swallowed, and I was starting to feel a little defensive.

Jack tried to pull himself together enough to speak coherently. 'Birds and fish eat worms. Do I look like a bird or a fish to you?'

Eyes narrow, I glared at him as he kept on laughing. 'You look like a chicken to me.'

But me calling him a chicken didn't seem to get the same rise out of him as he got out of me. Instead, he kept on laughing, and I went to get a glass of water. Then Julia and I spent long hours thinking up ways to get revenge.

***

Julia and I thought we'd never got our revenge. Instead life went on and we kept thinking up adventures to play, and soon the worm incident was just a memory Jack would rib us about occasionally, but mostly we handled it pretty well.

A few months later, it was August. We had spent the whole summer in each other's gardens, and we had noticed there were quite a few cats in our area. We would speak about them from time to time, and would try to engage them in our play, but most of the time they would run away when we tried to approach them.

Then, one day, I saw one of the cats lying on Mum's sun chair, and this time it let me pet it. After a while, I picked it up and carried it over to where Jack was sitting. 'Look!'

He glanced at me with the cat. 'Huh.' A calculating look came into his eyes. 'Did you know cats clean themselves by licking themselves?'

'Uh-huh, so?'

'They also lick their bums.' Jack scrunched his nose. 'So, they're basically just spreading their poo all over themselves.'

'Really?' It sounded more like Jack was envious of me after he had been trying to get the cat's attention all summer, than as though he knew what he was talking about. Still, I realised I could use this to my advantage.

'Yeah. Cats are disgusting.'

'Well, maybe it needs a bath then.'

Jack's eyes lit up. 'I'll get a bucket of water and we can wash it. Then it will be nice and clean for real.'

'Uh-huh.' I nodded, pressing my face into the cat's back to hide my smile.

A couple of minutes later, Jack had found a bucket of water.

'Here, give me the cat,' he said and held out his hands to me.

I gave the cat a last stroke, muttered a 'sorry' in its ear, before handing him the cat. Jack proceeded to try to dip it in the bucket, much to the cat's frustration. The cat, which had been docile and lovely whilst sitting with me, turned into a raging creature. Its hair stood up straight, and it gave an outraged meow as it scratched Jack's arms and tried to climb up and out of the water.

It was over in five seconds, and the cat escaped without injury. The tip of its tail might have gotten slightly damp, but otherwise no harm came to the cat. Jack's arms, on the other hand, were scratched up to the point of bleeding, and he looked at me as though it was all my fault.

I couldn't bring myself to ask about his injuries. Instead I laughed until I cried whilst he muttered something about mean little girls and went home to be bandaged up.

Chapter 5

PRESENT
Miranda

I was thankful I didn't see Jack for the next few days. Things were busy at work, and I spent most of my free time working on doing research for the social enterprise – Project Cup – Julia, Sophia and I were starting. I investigated about fifty different ways of sourcing period cups of different qualities and prices, and spent hours crunching numbers to work out what was feasible.

So, it wasn't like I was avoiding him. Not at all. It was just that things were *really* busy.

Then, early on Thursday morning, I went outside to go for a quick run before work and found him sitting on the steps to the house, like he had done lots of times before. He smiled as I came out, and my breath hitched. With the memories came all the feelings. Feelings I wished I had put to rest a long time ago. I gave my head a shake and bit out, 'What are you doing here this early?'

He stood up and raised his eyebrows at me. 'Good morning Jack, it's nice to see you. How are things?'

'Uh-huh.' I turned to lock the front door and tried to push the feelings out of the way in order to try to focus on being *friends* with my ex-fiancé. That was what I wanted, after all.

'I'm good, thanks for asking. Lovely morning for a run, isn't it?'

'Mhm.' Eyes narrow, I looked at him again. His hair was a mess, and his blue eyes twinkled as he looked at me. He was wearing a loose-fitting hoodie over a tighter shirt and tracky bottoms. He was dressed to lounge around the house, or… He didn't think he was coming with me, did he?

His smile grew wider, and my stomach sank.

He did.

I took a deep breath and stretched my neck, which was feeling more tense by the minute. I had not prepared myself sufficiently for this.

'Fine. You can come with me if you don't talk.' I avoided looking at him by making a show of putting my earphones in and checking my phone to make sure my running app was on.

I could feel the smile in his eyes as we set off at a comfortable pace, down the road toward Portobello and the beach. Running had always been a way for me to clear my head, but this time my mind was overwhelmed. Jack's long legs easily kept pace with me as we ran, side by side. We were silent, but on the inside my thoughts and feelings were tumbling around in a jumbled mess, getting louder and louder the further we ran. The two kilometres passed quickly, and soon we were on the prom.

Normally, I would head up or down along the beach for a couple of kilometres before going back, but I didn't have time today. Instead, I threw Jack a quick glance before speeding up and running through the sand down to the water, where I bent down to touch the sea before running back through the sand to where Jack stood waiting.

He bit his lip, as though to keep himself from smiling as he looked at me.

I could tell my running down to touch the water had triggered a series of memories for him, but I wasn't about to go down memory lane with him. 'I haven't got time to go further today,' I muttered.

'That's fine,' he said. 'Do you mind if I keep going?'

'Not at all!' I smiled for the first time that morning, relief flooding my mind as he gave me a knowing look before taking off down the beach toward Joppa and Musselburgh. I watched him leave – wondering how it was possible to still feel so much after six years – before shaking my head and heading back home.

I wasn't someone to bury my head in the sand, but this morning I was thankful for the spreadsheets I could immerse myself in at work. At some point I would have to come to terms with the fact that Jack – and all the emotions he brought up – were not about to go away, but that day was not this day.

***

On Saturday, Sophia rang my doorbell at nine o'clock – on time for once. She put a container of brownies on the counter, put the kettle on and proceeded to make us drinks as she talked about her week.

'I can't tell you how thankful I am it's finally the weekend. I'm already ready for a holiday, and I just came back from one a few weeks ago.'

'You've had a pretty intense workload recently, though,' I said as I put some bread in the toaster. 'You'll probably be alright if you get to sleep in and rest a little. Have you eaten?'

'Yeah, but you go ahead.' Sophia got a plate out for the brownies and set them on the table as I buttered my toast. 'I almost stayed in bed this morning. But then I couldn't stop thinking of all the progress we're making with Project Cup, so here I am.' She gave a quick shrug before turning back to the kettle and pouring water into the cafetière. 'What kind of tea are you having?'

'Ginger. I'll make it, though.' I got a grater out of the drawer and a ginger root out of the fridge and grated a bit of ginger over my cup before pouring over the hot water.

'Julia overslept, and is running late.' Sophia put her phone on the table as she sat down with her coffee opposite me.

'She's probably exhausted after the first few weeks of going back to teaching.'

'Uh-huh.' She looked me in the eye as I took a sip of my drink. 'So, are we going to talk about Jack being back?'

The tea burned my mouth and I winced. 'No, I don't think so.'

Sophia gave me an unimpressed look. 'Of course we are; don't be silly. You can't pretend he's not here, and he obviously meant a lot to you at one point. It's *got* to be difficult to see him again. Right?'

I ran my tongue over my sore gums. 'Yeah, okay, fine. It was a bit of a shock to see him last weekend, but it's alright. I got over him a long time ago, so I'm thinking we can be friends.'

Sophia's eyes narrowed. 'Friends?'

'Or acquaintances.' I cleared my throat. 'Whatever.'

'Acquaintances?' Sophia's tone held a lot of suspicion.

'Well, I'm sure Karen is hoping we'll get back together and everything will be right in her world again, but that's not going to happen. I'm sure we can probably be friends, though.' I wasn't sure at all. I had no idea how on earth a friendship with Jack was meant to work.

'Uh-huh.' The suspicion in Sophia's voice was still strong. 'Have you guys talked at all?'

As breezily as I could, I said, 'Yep, we had a little chat after we'd been to the pub last weekend, and then we went for a run on Thursday.'

She wasn't buying my blasé attitude. 'That's not what I meant, and you know it.'

'I don't see what there is to talk about. We broke up a long time ago. Anything we wanted to say about that has been said. No need to dredge up old stuff now.' There was probably loads that could be said. But what would be the point? I didn't want to cause any hurt, and I was done feeling sad about something that happened years ago.

'Are you sure that's how you want to play this?' Sophia frowned. 'I know it was a long time ago, but I saw your face as he walked through the door on Sunday.'

'Yeah, well, I thought about it, and there really isn't much to say. He had to do his thing back then, and I understood.' I tried to give her a reassuring smile. 'I got over him, you know.'

'Uh-huh.' Sophia seemed unconvinced but let it go as Julia came through the door. With rain streaking down her face, she looked as dishevelled as I felt.

I breathed a sigh of relief to not be the focus of attention any longer and got up to pour Julia a cup of coffee. 'Rough morning?'

She took a big sip and sighed. 'I slept in, missed the bus, had to wait in the rain, and then mum rang to tell me she needs me to come to church again. And I haven't had coffee yet.'

'Oh.' I scrunched my nose. Her hair was wet, as were her jeans. 'Maybe keep drinking your coffee?'

Sophia, being all kinds of nosey today, asked her about what was going on between her and Nick, and she told us that they had decided to be bury the hatchet after bickering for as long as they had known each other. That gave me some confidence. If Julia and Nick could be friends, then maybe Jack and I could too.

After a while, the conversation turned to what we were now calling Project Cup. I went over our agenda, and we got down to business. A few months ago, when Julia was still in Kenya, we'd decided via our Skype meeting that I had the better business head to bring to Julia's idea. I started chairing the meetings and even though we had a lot of logistics to get through, I didn't mind at all – in fact, I enjoyed it. Still, budgets, fundraising, branding and marketing weren't why any of us were involved with Project Cup. Instead, we all felt strongly about the cause.

It was mid-afternoon by the time Sophia and Miranda left and I was debating going for a run, when Jack came over. Strolling into my kitchen, where I was sitting with notes strewn all over the table and my laptop open to my spreadsheets, he pulled out the chair next to me and sat down.

I reminded myself that I did want to be friends with him, even as it irked me that he had just barged in unannounced. Why did he look so relaxed and *right* in my kitchen?

Couldn't he at least knock?

I raised an eyebrow at him. 'Hi?'

'Your doorbell needs to be fixed.'

I sighed. 'I don't have a doorbell.'

'Uh-huh.' He nodded. 'Exactly.

Chapter 6

Miranda

'What's all this?' Jack asked and picked up some of the papers on the table.

I took a deep breath, reminding myself that I wanted to be his friend. I *did* want to be his friend. 'Look, Jacky, do you see me barging into your house picking up random pieces of paper that seem important and reading them?'

His eyes glittered as he looked at me, but he put the papers back down. 'Nope, I don't. But if you did, you'd be welcome. Just saying.'

'Well, you're not.' I gave him a pointed look. 'Welcome, that is.'

'You want me to leave?' He sat up straighter. Although everything about him screamed strong and powerful, his face was kind in a way that made my pulse pick up its pace. It reminded me of how Mum used to tell me that when it came to picking a husband, the most important trait in any man was that he was kind. The kindness in Jack's eyes was new, and it confused me. The Jack I knew was a great guy, but also impatient, and he never had much empathy with anyone. He had never been good at handling feelings, and instead of showing compassion, he would avoid, attack or challenge people instead.

I shook my head. I wasn't looking to pick a husband, and even if I was, Jack wasn't ever getting back on that list. No matter how kind he was now. Tired, I blew out a deep breath. 'No, it's ok. You can stay.' Standing up and gathering the papers into a neat pile, I forced a smile. 'But leave the papers alone. I don't need you messing up my system.'

He relaxed back into his chair. 'Do you want a drink of anything?'

'Um…'

He got up. 'I'll just put the kettle on.'

I sat back down and watched him make himself at home in my kitchen. I had a feeling Jack and I had rather different ideas regarding what our new friendship was going to look like. Jack making tea in my kitchen felt a little bit too right. Like he hadn't been gone for the previous six years. Like he knew his way around my kitchen, even though I had changed it after Mum died.

Like he belonged there.

And that made me feel both safe and terrified. Safe, because it was nice to know that someone knew me. And terrified, because I wasn't sure I could handle falling in love with him again when I knew there was no future for us.

'What are you having?' He asked once he had put the kettle on and got two mugs out.

'Um…' I said again and cleared my throat. It was hard to make decisions about drinks when my thoughts were all jumbled by his smile.

'You have quite the tea collection here.' He rummaged through the cupboard. 'Ah! You have Chinese green tea leaves? Where did you get them?'

'Karen brought them back for me after she'd been out to visit you last time.'

'Oh yeah? Mind if I have some?'

I shook my head. 'Go ahead. I'll have some, too.'

He put three or four dried leaves into each of our mugs and poured on the boiling water. 'I love the smell of this. Brings me right back.'

I smiled. 'I bet it's got to be quite the change coming back here after all these years away?'

He put my mug in front of me and sat down. 'You have no idea.' He shook his head. 'Maybe the strangest part of it all though, is moving back in with Mum and Dad.'

'Yeah? I didn't realise you were planning on staying there permanently.'

He held his hands up and shook his head. 'I'm not. Definitely not. Just until I find my own place.'

'Uh-huh.' That was good news. Then maybe I wouldn't have to see him all the time. 'Have you been looking?'

'Just online so far. I have to go back to Hong Kong in October to tie up a couple of loose ends, and then I'm hoping to get it all sorted out when I come back.' He leaned back in his chair. 'Tell me about this social enterprise you guys are setting up.'

I sipped my tea slowly. 'What do you want to know?'

His head tilted to the side. 'Why are you doing it?'

I frowned. 'Probably a mixture of reasons, if I'm honest.'

'Honest is best.' His lips pulled to the side as he watched me. There was a lightness to his tone that made me feel as though I could be real with him without him making too much of it.

I shrugged. 'Partly I got involved because the thought of girls not being able to keep up with school because they don't have access to sanitary products is appalling. When Julia first told us about the girls at the school where she was teaching in Kenya, I wanted to help. I've never been the kind of person to jump at a new idea, you know. I prefer to sit down and work out the risks first.'

'Uh-huh.' Jack's smile grew and he nodded. 'I seem to remember that, yes.'

'Yeah, yeah.' I gave him a dry look as I remembered how we used to disagree on how to make decisions. Jack was all for jumping into things and working out the details later, whereas I was… not. 'But this time, I didn't need persuading.'

Jack's eyes narrowed and his eyebrows raised, even as the smile stayed in place. 'You didn't even do a pros and cons list before going for it?' He knew me too well.

'I've done plenty of risk calculations since.'

He nodded, pursing his lips as though to stop himself from smiling. 'Uh-huh.'

'But though there were still a whole bunch of questions that needed answers, I felt confident it was a good idea.' I scrunched my nose. 'And although there are an awful lot of things to do, I still kind of think we can make it happen.'

'Uh-huh.' Jack noted the hesitation in my voice. 'What's the plan?'

'We're in the test phase right now, so we're working on sourcing two thousand five hundred period cups to sell in Scotland and hope to make enough money to sponsor a project at a high school in Kenya.'

'The same school that Julia worked at, right?'

'Right.' I nodded. 'The period cups will be given to high school girls so they can stay in education.'

'What's your timeline?'

'Yeah, the timeline is somewhat unattainable.' I grimaced. 'Don't tell Julia or Sophia I said that, though.'

'How bad is it?' Jack sipped his tea, and I remembered my own cup. I took a sip, noting how the leaves at the bottom of the cup had expanded.

'Well, we need to sell about two thousand cups by the end of the year.'

Jack set his cup on the table. 'And you don't have the cups yet?'

'Nope.'

He frowned. 'Yeah, that *does* sound somewhat unattainable.'

'Uh-huh.' I smiled. 'What's life without a challenge though, eh?'

'Right.' Jack's eyes glittered as his smile reappeared. His smile reminded me of all the times when we used to step outside of our comfort zone and do something crazy together. He would smile at me like that then: like it was us against the world and he wouldn't have it any other way. It used to give me the biggest thrill. 'So, once you get through the test phase, then what happens?'

'*If* we get past the test phase…'

He waved his hand in the air as though my hesitation was superfluous.

'Depending on how the test phase goes, we then make a decision as to whether we want to plunge deeper and sponsor more projects, or if we are satisfied with what we might have achieved in Kenya. Although, every time we meet there are new ideas of how to help people in need of better menstrual health management, and I think we all feel we would like to keep going. If we can make it work, that is.'

'Course you can make it work.'

'Mm-hm, sure.' I laughed as I wished I had the same confidence in me that he appeared to have. 'Yeah, I guess though the timeline is crazy, we do have enough dedication that it might work.'

Jack scratched his jaw, which looked like it hadn't been shaved for a couple of days. He could probably grow a full beard now if he wanted to. It used to be patchier, but now the stubble looked fuller, and my hands itched to reach out to feel it.

'Who's doing what?'

Jack's question startled me out of my beard thoughts. I cleared my throat to give myself time to think. 'So, obviously it's Julia's idea…'

'Obviously.' Jack nodded.

'And Sophia's doing the marketing, and sales strategies, and things like that.'

'Uh-huh, makes sense, given her degree and experience in marketing.'

'And as I have a business with accounting degree and have been working with small businesses at the bank, I volunteered to do all the legal and finance bits.'

'Right, and who's sourcing the cups?'

'I am.'

Jack sucked his cheeks in and nodded. 'Where are you getting them from?'

'I'm still looking at options, but it looks like I'll get them from China.' After much research, I had found that Chinese companies could give us a much better price than any European company producing medical grade silicone products. But with a better price came all the questions of how the products were produced and by whom, and if the workers were treated fairly, and so on. Therefore, I had concluded a trip to China was in order – in order to check it all out in person.

I had wanted to visit China for a long time – ever since Jack and I had planned to go live in Hong Kong for a year – and this seemed like the perfect excuse to finally take some of the annual leave I had saved up. I hadn't booked any tickets yet, but I had my eye on some dates in October. That was only a few weeks away, but I figured we would need to sort out getting the cups as soon as possible, as Julia wanted to go out to the high school in Kenya in January.

'Sounds like you're doing a lot.'

'Yeah, but it's ok. We're all helping each other. It's not like we're expecting Sophia to somehow sell two thousand five hundred cups alone, you know?'

'Sure. Do you need any help with sourcing the cups?'

'Nope.' As much as I felt in over my head with the idea of sourcing the menstrual cups, there was no way I was going to put myself in the position of needing Jack's help. Been there, done that. Not going back there in a million years.

'Ok.' He bit his lip as if to keep a smile from slipping out. 'I could end up being useful, though. I've got a few connections in China.'

'Thanks for offering.' Maybe if I tried the polite way, he would get the hint? 'I'll be fine. I've got a couple of leads.'

I *did* have a couple of leads, but at this point I had nothing in stone, and it was starting to stress me out in view of our timeline. The stress reminded me of how, whenever Mum stood in front of a big task, she used to mutter *how hard can it be?* And then she would get on with it. That is what I intended to do, too.

How hard could it be?

Chapter 7

Past

Jack

They say that in Scotland, it only ever rains. And that might be true on the west coast, but in Edinburgh we see the sun quite a bit. And, for the most part, I prefer the sunshine. The week my sister Josie died, though, I would have liked it to rain.

Most of all, I would have liked some torrential rain, each drop hammering the pavement and making big puddles that would splash pedestrians as the cars went through them. Or a thick dreich mist, "the haar" as we call it in Edinburgh, which comes down so thick it's like wading through a cloud, and though there is no actual rain, you are soaked after spending two minutes in it. Even some random showers or just heavy clouds would have been preferable to the raging sunshine that seemed to have come to stay for good.

I wanted the angels to cry with us, but instead God sent the sunshine, as if he was gloating at how miserable we were, when he had been able to bring Josie home to be with him. And I may have taken a leaf from his book going forward. Empathy didn't seem important to God, and I swung between hating him for it and agreeing with him. Empathy was for wimps.

Josie was only four when she died. She was seven years younger than me, and though that might seem like a large age gap, I had very few memories of life before she was born. Josie was daring and adventurous, and where there was competition and sibling rivalry between me and Julia, I felt more protective of Josie. I would watch out for her, and she followed me around like I was her hero.

I mourned Josie, and it was a pain worse than any I had ever felt before. But worse still was everybody else's pain. I didn't know how to handle everybody around me grieving. Instead, I took my bike out and went to the park. Julia rarely came with me, she was stuck in her own shock, I think, and spent the summer doing chores, reading and watching TV. Miranda would come with me once in a while, though. To begin with, she seemed wary, and she was sad, too. But whenever I saw tears in her eyes, I would call her a cry-baby and challenge her to a race. She soon learnt, and the rest of the summer she provided a great distraction from all the grief at home.

We told our parents we were taking our bikes to Figgate Park, and they were fine with that – it wasn't far – and most of the time we did go to Figgate Park. But occasionally we took our picnic and bike to the steps of Duddingston Loch. From there, we would push and carry the bikes up the steps to Queen's Drive. It took us almost an hour, but Miranda was pretty scrappy and could carry her bike most of the way. We sat down and had a drink then, before getting on our bikes and biking round Arthur's Seat, stopping occasionally to look out over the city and further to the sea. Other times we stopped halfway up the hill and built a fort in the woods behind Dunsapie Hill, between the hill and the playpark. I was eleven and Miranda was nine, and though I would never have been caught alive playing with a nine-year-old girl at school, that summer I didn't mind.

***

Miranda

Jack and I shared our first kiss – a quick peck to see what the fuss was all about – when we were ten and twelve. None the wiser, we laughed it off and kept playing. On my thirteenth birthday, we tried again. If our first attempt had been half-hearted, our second attempt was anything but.

The dimples in Jack's cheeks had been causing tingles up my back for months by then. Still, I didn't want to be the girl who pined for a guy – Julia had that covered and was going through a stage of spending hours doing her make-up and telling me about how whatever guy she liked had spoken to her last week. The guys she had crushes on kept changing, and I suspected she was less interested in the guy and more interested in the feeling of being in love. For me, the feeling of falling in love was more uncomfortable. Jack's friendship meant a lot to me, and I didn't want to lose it just because I had a silly crush on him.

My thirteenth birthday was on a Monday. Mum made me breakfast in bed before school, but as she had to work all afternoon and evening, she had given me her present the night before. We had gone to see a film together, and Dad had been there too. He was living away at the time, but he had made the effort to be at the cinema. I can't remember what we watched; it didn't seem to matter as much as being there with both of them. Mum kept glancing at Dad, and he kept glancing at her, and by the end of the film they were holding hands. It made me hope that maybe something was about to change, and we could become a normal family again.

After school the next day, I didn't feel like spending my birthday alone. Instead, I went over to the Reids' house. Karen made me a birthday dinner and a cake, and I remember feeling that – though I wished some of my circumstances were different – I had it good.

When Karen set the cake in front of me and told me to blow out the candles, Julia said, 'Make a wish!'

'Oh Julia, we don't wish upon cakes or candles.' Karen tutted, and shook her head. 'We don't believe in superstition!' Karen wasn't into anything that she considered pagan or superstitious. There had never been a Father Christmas in the Reid household, as she didn't want to have her children confused about what she told them was true and what was made up stories.

I don't think Jack, Julia or Josie suffered from not having Father Christmas, but I did think it was somewhat strange that she wouldn't give them the chance to work it out for themselves. Also, I thought it was nice she wanted us to pray, but it wasn't as though God ever gave me anything I asked for.

Julia thought so, too. She rolled her eyes. 'Yeah, well it's also tradition, so…'

I glanced at Jack. He was studying me closely from across the table, and I wondered how obvious my crush on him was. Did he know? My stomach tightened as I thought of how mortifying that would be. He would tease me mercilessly for years. Still, his eyes on me felt electrifying, and wondering whether he could ever be interested in me was killing me. I gave myself a mental slap at how pathetic I was being over a boy, as I closed my eyes and wished for Jack to fall in love with me.

Then I blew out the candles, and Karen cut the cake.

'What did you wish for?' Julia asked.

'I can't tell you, or it won't come true, right?' I took a bite of the cake, hoping my hair covered my face enough to conceal the way my cheeks were turning red. There was no way I would share my wish with anyone.

I left the Reid's at nine that evening, and just as I was about to unlock our front door, I heard Jack call, 'Hey, Miranda! Wait up.'

I held the door open for him, and he ran across their lawn and up the steps to the house.

'Are you coming in?' I asked when he hesitated.

He swallowed, as though unsure of what to say. 'Is that ok?'

'Uh-huh.' I nodded, suddenly aware that we were alone. He came in the hallway and stopped.

'Did you want something?' I asked.

'Yeah.' His dirty blonde hair was messy on his head, and his blue eyes pierced me. 'I've been thinking…' He took a step closer and reached for my hand.

'Okay…?' My cheeks were heating up, and I felt electric. Like I was on fire or would combust at any minute. My mind was racing with all the possibilities.

'Can I… kiss you?'

I pulled in a sharp breath and gave a slow nod. 'Yes.'

The hesitation in his eyes gave way to a smile. 'Good.' He kept hold of my hand and his other hand slipped round my neck and cupped the back of my head. I closed my eyes as he brought his lips to mine for a quick peck. Then he did it again, staying longer this time. All thought fled my mind, and I put my free hand on his upper arm, holding on to him as my legs grew weak. His tongue swept out and licked the top of my lip before he nipped it lightly with his teeth. My eyes flew open, and the grin on his face was everything.

He pulled me closer, wrapping his arms around me as he breathed me in.

I think we were both surprised at how different this kiss was compared to the previous one. And, as both of us liked it, we figured we would keep doing it.

So began my teenage years. And my romantic relationship with Jack.

Chapter 8

PRESENT
Jack

Settling back into Edinburgh after being away was harder than I had expected. I still worked at the same company, and much of my job remained the same, but there were lots of new people to get to know and the office culture and politics were different. There had been office politics in Hong Kong too, but I was used to them. And, though I was working for the same company, which was meant to work on the same systems, I found the secretaries in Edinburgh had their own rather finickity ways of doing things. The longer I was there, the more convinced I became that the head secretary, Liz, had been in the job for too long and needed to be replaced. The bureaucracy she implemented was driving me crazy. It wasn't just me; the other secretaries couldn't stand her, and several of my colleagues would just shake their head whenever I asked about how the system worked. Still, she probably had another ten years left before retirement, and the department boss seemed fond of her.

I resigned myself to learn her ways and conform.

Maybe hardest of all though, was moving back in with Mum and Dad. They were great, and I was thankful to have a room to return to, but after living on my own for six years, I had come to appreciate my own space.

It made sense to wait to get my own place until after I returned from going Hong Kong to tie up the last strings, but since coming home I had spent many hours online looking for flats or houses to move into.

Mum seemed happy to have me home again. She made sure to cook all my favourite foods and invited me to come to church with her. I hadn't been much of a churchgoer before going to Hong Kong, and my time away hadn't changed my stance on God. I had heard my whole life – and especially after Josie died – that God was in control. I think people at church took comfort from this. They kept saying that God had a plan and he knew what he was doing. For me, though, the concept of God being in control didn't bring comfort.

At all.

If God was in control, then the pain and suffering in the world were his doing. He sent people to hell and, worse, he made people live through hell on earth. And though I should perhaps try to live a life that would appease an all-powerful God that appeared to like to put his so-called children through suffering, I couldn't bring myself to want to. Instead I felt disdain for him, and I wanted nothing to do with him. Some might say I was throwing the baby out with the bathwater, and maybe they had a point. Christianity did seem to bring a lot of people a lot of peace in life – and I knew God meant a lot to my parents. But I couldn't seem to separate a baby from the bathwater – it all seemed too jumbled up to try to work out which bits to keep and which to throw out. It was easier to just throw it all out.

So, though I knew Mum was only doing what she thought was best for me in asking me to come to church, it soon started getting on my nerves. I had only been home for a few weeks, and already I was reaching for the techniques I had learned in counselling in Hong Kong. I counted to ten, took deep breaths, reminded myself that *Mum is trying to show me she cares*, reminded myself of my values, and so on. Still, it was clear I needed my own place.

So, when Nick texted and wanted to play squash, I dug out an old racquet that had seen better days and went. I got a strange text from Julia on the way over telling me to 'be nice to Nick'. It was strange mainly because Julia had made no secret of the fact that Nick wasn't her favourite person. So, she had either broken him, or something had changed.

It all became clear when Nick got in my car. He didn't look broken at all. Rather the opposite. Unable to hold back my smile, I said, 'Julia and you finally decided to go for it, huh?'

He shook his head. 'Something like that, yes.' It looked like he had won the lottery – which was unlikely as he would say the lottery was a tax on stupidity – or like he had found a pot of gold at the end of a rainbow.

I slapped him on the shoulder. 'About time, man.' I knew Nick had always been interested in Julia, and I was happy they had finally decided to give it a go. Besides, Nick was already family – this would only solidify that fact.

My squash game was rusty, and Nick won three straight sets. I don't think I could have beaten him that day even if I had been at the top of my game, though. Besides, I was distracted by thinking about Miranda. If I was honest – and I was learning how to be – I spent most of my time thinking about Miranda. It seemed impossible not to. I couldn't explain exactly why – maybe it was her clever brain, or her kind heart, or just her beautiful eyes – but I was entirely wrapped up in thinking about her.

After talking to her a few times over the last few weeks, it had become clear to me that though she had agreed to be friends, she would rather be acquaintances. I didn't want to cross any boundaries, but I was starting to get frustrated with her lack of wanting to go beyond the surface of anything. And after not seeing her for six years, it was clear we had a lot of time to catch up on. Only she didn't seem keen on catching up at all.

Once in a while I would catch her looking at me. Her eyes seemed to say she still cared about me, and that gave me some hope. Still, as soon as I would meet her eyes, she would look away and start talking about something mundane.

Like the weather.

I had forgotten how much of conversation in Scotland circled around the weather. In Hong Kong the weather was whatever it was. Mostly it was warm. In Scotland, on the other hand, the weather seemed to be the only thing people ever talked about. Not because it was such a riveting topic of conversation – although, to be fair, we'd had a few very nice weeks since I got home. No, people talked about the weather because they wanted to be acquainted and polite, but they didn't want to be vulnerable and talk about things that actually mattered.

That was fine when I was at the office. At the end of the day, who really wanted to know the thoughts and feelings of the people there? Not me.

But when it came to Miranda, it grated on me. We had never had the kind of relationship where we wanted to talk about the weather before. And who cared about the weather when we could be talking about things that mattered?

I think Nick could tell my focus wasn't on playing squash, but I didn't want to burden him with my confusion and frustration when he was so obviously happy. Instead, after dropping Nick at his flat, I turned up the music as The Black Keys' *Howlin' for You* came on the radio. Trying not to think about Miranda, I sang along with the music at the top of my lungs. When even the music couldn't get me out of my head, I decided to stop in to see Michael.

Michael and Sophia shared a nice two bedroom flat in Newington, which was close to both Arthur's Seat and the University, and I laughed when I saw the tag on the doorbell – The Huxleys. How they had managed to convince us all that they were 'just friends' – after being married and living together for five years – was anyone's guess.

Michael was in the kitchen making dinner when I got there. Passing me a beer from the fridge, he asked, 'You staying to eat?'

'Sure, if there's enough?'

'Yeah, I'll just make some extra rice. I think we have another pack of naan bread in the freezer too. Let me check.' He opened the freezer and rummaged about until he found what he was looking for. 'I take it you survived squash with Nick.'

I snorted. 'Just. He won three straight sets.'

'Yeah, he's upped his game since we all first started playing.' Michael had rice on the stove and chicken frying. He stirred the chicken quickly before going back to chopping vegetables to add to the pan.

'That, or maybe it was because I haven't played since moving to Hong Kong. I'm a bit rusty.' I took a sip of the beer.

'Yeah?' He smirked. 'I can imagine you'll be feeling rusty all round being back here. Takes a while to settle back in after being gone for that long, eh?'

I nodded. 'Yeah.'

'It's the same for me whenever I go back to Canada. Man, I love Canada, but it's different from here, and it takes some getting used to.'

'Yeah, everything is different, but it's okay. It's mostly nice to be back.' An image of Miranda sitting across from me at her kitchen table floated through my mind, making me smile. Her determination to make Project Cup work despite everything being against them struck a chord deep inside me. And her thorough plans and assessments of what needed to happen – watching her amazing mind go into action to create something – was inspiring. Her spreadsheets made me believe that the world could be changed.

She had changed in the years I had been away. She was always one of the most real people I had known, and that part of her had intensified. Her realness used to scare me, but now I wanted it. Now it felt like I would never be able to breathe without it. And now every time she withheld her honesty from me, I felt deprived. Like she didn't trust me with it. I knew she had every reason not to trust me, and though I had only been back for a few weeks, I already knew I would give anything for her to trust me again.

'Uh-huh.' Michael shrugged. 'What's up with Miranda and you? She seemed a bit... prickly towards you last night.' He was referring to how we had all been at Nick and Julia's flat the previous evening. Nick had remodelled the kitchen in their flat and had made us all ribs to celebrate it being done.

'Yeah.' I winced. *Prickly* was the right word. Like she didn't want me to get to close. 'She swings between being polite and a wee bit passive aggressive.'

'Huh.'

'I don't really know what's going on. I'm trying to give her time to get to know me again, and to sort out anything that needs sorting out from the past. I think there's some unresolved hurt around how I left and then broke up with her, but she's very reluctant to go there. Last week I got her to tell me about the social enterprise, and she seemed fine to talk about it then. She's amazing, you know? She's got the whole business plan, and if Mir is in, then that social enterprise is going to be successful, no matter what they're selling.'

'M-hm.' Michael twisted his lips as if hiding a smile.

'But this week she's been like a clam about everything.' It was driving me crazy.

'Maybe she's trying to tell you to back off?'

'Do you think?' I rubbed my stubbly cheek and leaned against the kitchen counter.

'I don't know. Maybe.' He waved the spatula he was using to stir the pan as he answered. 'Or maybe she's feeling confused and doesn't know how to handle the situation. It's got to be a bit weird for her – that her former fiancé who left her at a really crappy time in her life now is back and wants to be friends. Don't you think?'

'Well sure, I get that it's weird.' I nodded. I *did* get it. 'It's weird for me too, you know?'

'Uh-huh, sure. Still, it's different for you, though. You decided now is the right time to come home, whereas she just has to react to your decision.' Eyes narrowed, he scanned my face. 'None of this would be a problem unless you want her back. Right?'

I met his eyes and cleared my throat. 'Right.'

'Are you serious?' Sophia's eyes were wide as she looked at me and entered the kitchen.

'Hey, where did you come from?' I asked, as I tried to keep my stomach from sinking over how one of Miranda's best friends had just heard me say I wanted to get back together with her.

'I was in my room packing for… Never mind that.' She waved a hand in the air dismissively. 'You were saying you want to get back together with Miranda?'

'Um…' Leaning against the kitchen counter still, I hung my head, trying to think of how to get her off my back.

'Yes or no, Jack.'

I braced myself as I looked at her. 'Don't tell her.'

'I don't think you get to decide what I tell anyone.' Sophia bit the inside of her cheek as she studied me.

'True.' I nodded. 'Still. She's reluctant to want to hang out, even as friends. If she finds out I want more at this point, she'll freak out completely.'

'She has reason to, though, doesn't she.' Sophia was stating facts, not asking questions.

I sighed and looked away. 'Yeah.'

'Tell me why I shouldn't let her know.'

I pressed my lips together as I considered my words. I didn't want to share anything with Sophia, but if she was going to keep this between us, I would have to give her something. I shrugged. 'Back then, I wasn't good for her. She went through a whole lot of crap, and I couldn't handle it. She wanted to get married, and I did too, but it would have been awful for her. Breaking up with her then was the right decision.'

'And I suppose you explained all this when you broke up with her, so she could weigh in and you could make such a decision together?' Sophia's eyebrows were high on her forehead, her eyes narrow as she tilted her head to the side.

'No, I didn't.' I pushed my hand through my hair and hung it behind my neck as I focused on her. 'Look, I agree with you. I did everything wrong back then.'

'Huh. *You think?*' Sophia nodded, her words dripping with sarcasm. She took a deep breath, as though she was reminding herself to be patient with me. 'Why do you think now is going to be different?'

'I can't know that anything is going to be different this time. But I *have* changed. I was immature and irresponsible back then. I've spent the last six years working on becoming a better person. I'm not done – I never will be – but I'm ready to try again.'

Sophia studied my face for a long time. She must have found whatever it was she was looking for, because then she nodded. 'Ok. I'll help.'

Michael smirked. 'I didn't hear anyone asking for your help.'

'Oh Michael, Michael, Michael…' Sophia muttered and shook her head as she got some cutlery out of the drawer. Turning to face him, she waved the cutlery in the air. 'If he's ever going to get Miranda back, he's going to need help. I bet he doesn't even have a plan.'

Michael looked at her as though he didn't believe his ears. 'He hasn't asked for you to meddle, though.'

'But-'

'Hey.' I waved my hands at them. 'Still right here.'

Sophia glanced at me before turning her attention back to Michael. 'I'm just saying he's going to need help.'

'Uh-huh.' I sighed. 'I hesitate to ask this, but why do you think I need help?'

'Tell me your plan, and I'll tell you if it's any good.' Sophia's eyebrows were raised as she waited for me to speak.

'Uh…'

'See!' She turned to Michael, her hands in an *I rest my case* gesture. 'He *doesn't* have a plan.'

Michael pressed his lips together and shrugged as though he was giving in to her madness. 'Mhm, yeah.'

I shrugged. 'Ok, fine. My plan is to be friends with her and let her see how I've changed. And as she sees who I am, and gets to know me again, I hope she'll fall in love with me. Again.'

'Uh-huh. That's a great plan.' Sophia nodded as though she agreed, then raised her hands and eyebrows as she said, 'If you want to spend the next *fifty years* pining away for her.'

I frowned. 'Why do you think it would take that long?'

'With a plan like that, you'll be dead before she ever decides she wants to be with you.' Sophia shook her head. 'Men!'

Michael turned the cooker off and got plates out. 'Dinner's ready. Let's eat.'

'Look, I'm not saying I'm Don Juan or anything…' I caught Michael's amused look and I winked at Sophia. 'But I think she'd come around quicker than that.'

Sophia took a plate and filled it up with food before passing it to me and doing the same for Michael and herself. 'Unsurprisingly, Miranda has massive trust issues when it comes to men. You've got to by-pass her distrust if you're to ever have a chance of her falling in love with you again.'

'Huh.' That made sense. I frowned, surprised I hadn't thought of that myself.

She sighed but turned toward me. 'Here's what to do…'

Chapter 9

Miranda

Though things had been awkward at first, Jack's easy way soon made me feel less on edge and more able to relax.

I had concluded that I would probably always have feelings for him. But I also knew that, for my own sanity's sake, we could never get back together again. Still, he lived next door, was my best friend's brother, and he had been my friend since I was five. And if I wasn't going to have him back, the next best thing was to be his friend.

Yeah, his clear blue eyes still threw me off from time to time. They had a way of sneaking past my barriers and making me feel too much – vulnerable. And there were few things I hated as much as feeling vulnerable. But I had decided I would rather have his friendship and put up with the occasional wave of feelings, than have to cut him out of my life.

Yeah, it was more than an occasional wave. It was more like every few hours.

Or, maybe, every hour.

It was all the time.

But still, I would get over it. Besides, it was my problem, not his. Why should he lose a friend just because I couldn't get my feelings under control? No, I was an adult and I would handle my feelings.

Still, it was awkward.

To distract myself, I immersed myself into setting up Project Cup, checking budgets, following up on emails and working on my itinerary for my visit to China.

Jack and I had fallen into a routine of going for a run in the morning before going to work. If I avoided looking at him, I could focus on running and handle having a surface conversation about the weather and food fairly well. It was when my eyes accidentally wandered, and I took in his well-defined thighs and arms, that I struggled not to jumble my words.

That rarely happened, though. Only maybe once or twice per run.

Or slightly more often.

Still, on the whole I managed to stay focused. And though I had been running for a long time, it was clear Jack was holding back as he matched his stride to mine.

We were running on Arthur's Seat, when he said, 'Sophia gave me the dates you're going to Hong Kong, so I booked onto the same flights. That's ok, right?'

'Sophia did *what*?' I asked. Surely, I had misheard. Sophia wouldn't do such a thing without talking to me about it first, would she?

'Sophia gave me the dates—'

'Yes, I heard you.' I kept running, but my breathing was all over the place. 'Why would she *do* something like that?'

I glanced at Jack after going up the south side toward the pond at the top of Queen's Drive. He wasn't even winded. He kept running, staying silent as I tried to make sense of what was happening to me. Just the thought of going to Hong Kong with Jack made me feel nervous, as it reminded me too much of how our plan had been to get married and live there together. And as far as I was concerned, going to Hong Kong together to pretend all these years hadn't happened wasn't a good idea.

I frowned. 'And why would you want to go to Hong Kong together now?'

'I had to go anyway, and I figured it would be nicer to go together,' he said.

I wasn't sure I liked the sound of that. I shot him a look. 'Really?'

He slowed down and came to a stop, and I stopped, too, and looked out at the sea as I waited for him to reply.

'Well, yeah. It *would* be nicer to go together. It's a long journey.' He shrugged. 'But also, I figured I can show you around and stuff. You can stay at the company apartment where I'll be staying.'

My lungs were burning, and my body was aching from pushing it too hard whilst not breathing properly, and the suggestion of staying together with Jack in Hong Kong didn't help. It sounded far too much like Jack was planning for us to have another chance at playing house in the Far-East together.

Then again, maybe I was making a mountain out of a molehill. It wasn't like I was going to take a year out to explore Hong Kong as Jack's wife. This time, I was going because I had business in China, and there was a whole heap of things I needed to sort out.

Ignoring Jack, I stared at the sea and focused on taking deep breaths. When my lungs were breathing easier and my body felt cooperative, I started running again.

Jack shook his head at me and ran beside me, his long legs eating the pavement. He threw me the odd glance, but let me think in silence, and as we ran, I felt able to think again.

Though I had been in contact with the companies in China for a while now, I was painfully aware of how out of my depth I would be. As much as I hated to admit it, I would need help with travel arrangements, and I would have to work out where to stay and find someone to translate for me. Jack had lived in Hong Kong for a long time; maybe he could end up being useful. And likely much cheaper than having to pay somebody to help.

We had just passed Dunsapie Loch and were about to start going downhill again. I would usually take a minute to look at the view, but today it didn't even register. It wasn't often I made big decisions without spending some time with a spreadsheet first, but I decided this wasn't really a very big decision. I had known Jack for most of my life, and surely it would be safer to travel with him than it would be to pay some random person to help me. Besides, if he was going anyway, what was the harm in making use of him?

Still, I had some choice words for Sophia next time I saw her.

We were almost home again by the time I said, 'Fine, Jacky. How good is your Chinese?'

'What? You're asking for help?' His hands were on his chest and his eyebrows were high on his forehead. He did a good job of the shocked Southern American accent.

'Oh, shut up.' I rolled my eyes. 'Will you help out or not?'

He gave me a smug look, his dimple on display as he raised his eyebrow. 'Course I'll help. Just let me enjoy this moment first.'

'Yeah, yeah. Just…' I tried to steady my breathing again. From his reaction, I realised I hadn't been very clear about what I meant. I felt panic rising at the thought of him reading more into this than I intended, and stared him straight in the eye, waving my hand in the air. 'This doesn't mean anything. We're not getting back together or anything. Ever.'

He winked at me. 'Who said anything about getting back together?'

I sighed. 'Uh-huh.'

***

Once home, I pulled out my phone, not even checking my running stats before dialling Sophia.

'Miranda, how's it going?' Her voice was cheery as she spoke.

I had no time or energy for social niceties for someone who had just betrayed me. 'Uh-huh. Did you give Jack my flight details for Hong Kong?'

Sophia cleared her throat. 'Well, you see… What happened was _'

'What?' I bit out. 'What happened to make you do this to me?'

Sophia caught a nervous laugh and said, 'Do you think you're maybe exaggerating just a wee bit now?'

'Exaggerating?' What was she *thinking*? I took a deep breath and sat down at the kitchen table. 'Exaggerating. Uh-huh, sure.'

'I don't mean you don't have reason to feel a little worked up, it's just…'

'Uh-huh, it's just what?'

'So, remember how we spoke about Jack, Nick and Michael being part of the board?'

'Right.'

'Well, Jack was really keen to be involved and said he would be happy to invest money, too, but he insisted on going to China with you. Basically, he blackmailed me.' She sighed. 'Think of it as taking one for the team.'

'You didn't think it would be a good idea to talk with me about this first?' I rolled my lips between my teeth to keep from saying more.

'Um, yeah. I should have done that.' She groaned. 'I'm sorry.'

'Uh-huh, sure.' I pinched the bridge of my nose and squeezed my eyes shut. 'You know, whatever. It'll be okay.'

'Yeah.' Sophia put a little too much enthusiasm into her words as she said, 'I'm sure it will be great. I know you guys broke up, but you're friends, right?'

'Right.' It sounded hollow, even to my ears, and I wondered what on earth I was thinking agreeing with her then.

'Right! Then, he'll help you with whatever you might need help with, and you'll have a great time together.'

'Yeah.' Having a great time with Jack was exactly what I was afraid of. I wanted to be friends with him, but maybe not the *travelling across the world together* kind of friends. It seemed that kind of friendship was likely to bring up feelings towards him that I didn't want to feel. My shoulders slumped as I resigned myself to the fact that I was going to Hong Kong and China with Jack. 'Next time, you check with me first, okay?'

'Sure.' Sophia said. 'I really didn't mean to upset you, Miranda. I'm sorry.'

'I'm not upset.' I was upset.

'Mhm, yeah okay.'

I decided the way to deal with the prospect of Jack and I going to Asia together was to pretend it wasn't happening. That way I couldn't stress about it. Instead, I immersed myself in my spreadsheets at work, and I spent my evenings working on the legal side of getting Project Cup set up properly.

A week before I was due to go to Hong Kong, Miranda, Sophia and I met up at a little Greek lunch place in the Old Town.

'You alright?' Julia asked as I sat down at her table. Sophia wasn't there yet.

'Not bad.' I smiled. 'I booked my tickets for Hong Kong! I'm going on Saturday for three weeks.'

'Yay! What did they say at work?'

'It was fine.' My manager seemed surprised when I asked for the time off but seemed happy to sign off on my request. 'I have most of my annual leave still to take, so it wasn't a problem.'

'Great. And what's this I hear about Jack going as well?'

I might have rolled my eyes. 'Aye. He says he's got to go anyway, and he's waited to book his tickets until he found out what dates I was going. I didn't even tell him. Sophia the traitor told him.' I wasn't bitter. Not at all.

'Ouch.' She frowned. 'She was probably just trying to be... kind?'

'Nah, he blackmailed her. She asked him to come onboard as an investor, and he said he'd do it on the condition that she told him the dates I would be in Hong Kong, and that I stay with him when I'm there.'

She seemed embarrassed her brother would behave in such a way. 'Well, that's awkward.'

'Aye, no kidding.' I took a deep breath and tried to put Jack out of my mind as Sophia burst through the door. 'Speak of the devil.'

Sophia narrowly avoided crashing into an older man as she hurried towards us. She pulled off her jacket and made some lame excuse about being late because she had left late. I might have glared at her as Julia got up to give her a hug. Sophia was never on time for anything, and she didn't seem to have any respect for other people's time either.

'What?' Sophia asked when she saw me.

'That is the worst excuse ever. No wonder you're late if you left late.'

'Yeah, yeah, ok. Sorry.' She chuckled to herself but gave me her best serious face as she pretended to take me seriously. 'I'm sorry. Did you guys order yet?'

'Not yet.' We ordered our falafel wraps, and we got out our note pads and tablets as we waited for the food to arrive.

'Right.' Sophia got down to business. 'I spoke to Jack, Nick and Michael, and they are all happy to come on board with funding and promotion.'

I sneered. 'At a price, of course.'

Sophia sighed and dropped her pen on the table. 'Are you going to be passive aggressive this whole meeting, or can we have it out and be done, do you think?' Her eyebrows grazed her hairline as she looked me in the eye.

I scowled at her. Though she had explained why she had told Jack, the more I thought about it, the more nervous I felt. And the more nervous I felt, the more annoyed I was with her for telling him in the first place. 'If I wanted a trip to Asia with Jack, I'd have gone a long time ago. Like, for instance, when he asked me to marry him and move out there with him six years ago…'

Sophia rolled her eyes. 'Oh come on! You totally *wanted* to go with him! The only reason you didn't was because your mum was sick. So don't give me that.'

I cringed at her words. Biting my lip, I peered at her through narrowed eyes. She was right. I had wanted to go with him.

At the time, we were engaged, and when he got the job in Hong Kong, he had asked me to come with him. I had two years left of uni but had decided to take a study break in order to go with him. All our plans were prepared when I found out my mum had terminal cancer. I decided to stay home in order to take care of her and spend the last few months of her life with her.

Jack still went.

He had a job waiting for him, and an adventure to hunt down. His fiancé's mum dying of cancer maybe *should* have been enough for him to change his plans, but I didn't want to be the one to hold him back. And I didn't want him to stay out of guilt. We told each other it would be good for us to have time apart, and that our relationship would have a chance to mature and grow stronger. *Absence makes the heart grow fonder* and all that. So, we set out to do the long-distance relationship thing. We video called a couple of times, and we private messaged each other a lot. Still, it was only three weeks after he left that Jack broke up with me.

Via email.

At the time, I was hurt. Nothing in my life made sense any longer. Julia told me Jack seemed to like Hong Kong, and as much as I wanted to be spiteful and wish he would rot somewhere, I also was envious of him. My life was consumed with dealing with sickness and death and I wished so many times that I could have left it all behind and gone with him. Instead, the next six months brought one devastation after the other as I cared for my dying mum and waitressed. Mum needed more and more of my time, and I had less and less time to miss Jack.

Still, I did miss him. Every day, I was sick with missing him.

I missed his smile, the adventure of being around him, his enjoyment of life. And I missed having his shoulder to cry on as death seemed to be everywhere I turned, and I watched my mum get frailer and frailer as she went through months of treatment.

'Listen, I don't want to hurt you; I know that year was the most horrific year of your life, and I'm sorry about that.' Sophia reached out to put her hand over mine, her eyes sad. 'I can't pretend that you didn't want to go, though. You did.'

I looked away as I remembered how every fibre of my being had longed to go with Jack to Hong Kong back then. And for months after Jack left, I had daydreamed about how life would have been different if I had gone with him.

I swallowed to try to get rid of the lump in my throat. 'Yes. I did.' I sat up straight and looked her in the eyes as I said in a determined voice, 'But that ship has sailed, and going down memory lane with Jack for three weeks is not going to be helpful to my mental health.' That I was sure of.

'What if this is the ship coming back for you? Maybe you should give it a chance?' Julia said hopefully.

I glared at her. No matter how many times I had told Julia that Jack and I weren't ever getting back together, she still hoped I would change my mind. She had wanted us to be sisters in law ever since I first moved in next door, and as nice as that was, it was also delusional. 'Yes, because *heartbroken* is my favourite state to be in, and I can't wait for that to happen all over again.'

'Right.' Sophia rolled her eyes. 'At this point the plans are that you will travel to Hong Kong with Jack and stay at his flat there. And when you go to China, he'll go with you. So, whatever does or doesn't happen between the two of you is up to you. But those are the plans.'

'Great.' Sophia was right; the plans were in place, so I might as well make peace with the whole thing. I closed my eyes. I wasn't sure it was possible to feel at peace about it, but I would try. 'Has he booked his tickets already?'

'Yes, he booked the same flights as you,' Sophia confirmed with a nod. 'I'm sorry, you know. Jack was pretty clear about his terms, though, and he wouldn't budge no matter what I offered instead. So, there we are.'

'Did Michael and Nick have terms as well?' Julia asked as the food arrived. The two halves of a falafel wrap over a green salad with a side of hummus here was to die for. I sighed as I bit into the wrap.

'No, they were both pretty eager to get involved. But Nick did say he was interested in going with you to Kenya, if you're up for that, Julia?'

'That would be fine,' Julia said. I smiled as I thought of how Julia had been hostile toward Nick for years, but now she was planning a trip to Africa with him. It was nice to see them getting along for once.

It struck me that with all these people coming onto the board, we would need clear expectations and agreements in place. I wasn't about to end up in any more awkward situations or be blackmailed into doing anything else I didn't want to do.

I glanced at Sophia and said, 'If you give me your notes, I'll work on writing up some contracts for all of us, so we have it in writing.'

'Really? Do we need contracts?' Julia asked. 'I mean, we've known the guys for years.'

I took a deep breath. That was exactly why we needed contracts. The clearer things were up front, the less likely things were to spiral out of control. 'It's not to make things awkward; rather the opposite. It's a way to protect our relationships. I'll write up a contract for all of us to sign, with our different commitments laid out from the start. This way, everyone knows what we're all agreeing to.'

Julia didn't seem convinced but nodded. 'Ok, sure.'

'We don't come here often enough. This is amazing.' Sophia sighed. 'We might have to do some fundraising later, but for now, with Jack and Nick coming on board, we should have our start up costs covered.'

'Great,' I said. At least there was one upside to travelling with Jack. 'I'll adjust the budget.'

Sophia took a sip of her water. 'I've got a few ideas about fundraising, as well. But I think we should talk about your trip first. Am I right in thinking that you're going to visit two different companies and their factories and, based on what they can offer, put in an order?'

I nodded and proceeded to go over the details of my trip. Then we talked about Julia's trip to Kenya, where she would work with the school we were giving the cups to, and we looked at my budget. It balanced, and Sophia and Julia seemed happy enough, but there were still too many contingencies for my comfort.

'If you let me know all the bank details, I'll make sure to pass them on to Jack, Michael and Nick, so they can deposit the money they're putting in quickly,' Sophia said and looked at me. 'That way, you can pay for the cups.'

I nodded and made a note to send her the details.

'We're cutting things pretty close here, aren't we?' Julia frowned as she looked at her calendar.

'Yes, but I think we should be fine.' I tried to exude confidence as I spoke, even though it was obvious to me that our timeline was way too optimistic. I turned to Sophia and asked about the website she was designing for us. Everything was on track, and we soon wrapped up our meeting.

Julia, who lived close to the university, left for home, whereas Sophia and I walked down the steps and through Waverly Station together to catch our buses.

'Are you still mad at me?' Sophia asked, as we took the escalator up from the platforms toward Prince's Street.

I shook my head. 'I was never mad at you.'

She gave me a dry look.

'Okay, fine. Maybe I was a little annoyed that you wouldn't consult with me before giving Jack all that information, and agreeing I would stay with him, but whatever.' I shrugged. 'It's not really that big of a deal.'

She glanced away, and I wondered what she was thinking. 'Uh-huh, for sure.'

'Like you said, we're friends, so a little trip to China should be no problem. Right?'

Sophia nodded. 'Right. I think you guys will have a great time. It'll be like old times.'

I cleared my throat. 'Uh-huh. Sure.'

'And if something was to happen…' She elbowed me gently and shot me a cheeky smile.

'Nothing will happen.' I grabbed her arm and made her look at me as I said again, '*Nothing* will happen.'

She nodded and gave me a kind smile, as though she was trying to reassure me. 'But if it did, that would be okay too.'

I flinched. Would it?

Chapter 10

Miranda

Sitting at the gate at Edinburgh Airport waiting to board the flight to Helsinki, I picked at my nails. I had obtained my visa for China a couple of weeks earlier, and, whilst I was looking forward to experiencing Hong Kong and China, I was also – just a little – anxious at the thought of flying. I stared out the window, looking at the plane that had just started disembarking, whilst ignoring the hum of energy given off by Jack who was sitting next to me.

Or I tried to ignore it.

His long legs were stretched out in front of him, one foot resting on the other and rocking from side to side. If I didn't know better, I might have thought he was nervous. I kept my eyes focused on the plane to keep from asking Jack to keep still. Again.

Last time his answer had been to put his hands on my cheeks and place a big smacking kiss on my lips. I had reared back, my eyes going wide in surprise as I slapped his hands away. 'Ever heard of consent, Jacky?'

He shook his head at me and reached out to pat my back. 'It's going to be ok Mir; we're not going to crash.'

Thankful I didn't blush easily, I shook my head at him and looked away. The butterflies in my stomach were fluttering, and I had a suspicion Jack had more to do with that than my nerves about flying did. Travelling with Jack was a bad idea. Still, here I was, having bought tickets to go to Hong Kong with him for the second time in my life. And this time, I was going to get on the plane.

Still, if Jack didn't stop bouncing his leg soon, I would strangle him in his sleep.

I got my phone out and sent a text to the group text thread I had with Julia and Sophia.

Me: How important is your brother to you? You won't mind if he never comes home again, would you? xx

My phone buzzed and I checked the message thread.

Jules: Nah, he's not that important. Do what you have to do xx

Me: Great, coz I'm already feeling my patience wearing thin, and we're not even in the air yet. Why did I agree to this??

Soph: Think of the money. You'll be fine! Enjoy yourself and if things start back up with Jack, what's the harm, amiright? Xx

I snorted and shook my head.

Me: Sure, it's only my heart that's at stake... Also, that sounds like you're pimping me out.

I glanced at Jack, who stood up as they started calling people sitting in rows fourteen to twenty-five. 'You coming?' he said, taking his carry-on off the floor and getting his passport and boarding pass out.

'Uh-huh.' I stood up and gathered my things as my phone buzzed again.

Soph: Stop! I'm not pimping you out – all I'm saying is you could take the opportunity to have a fling with him

Yeah, that was *not* happening.

Jules: So long as I don't have to hear the details! xx

Me: Got to go, they're boarding our flight now. X

I turned my phone off, joined the queue to board the plane, and found my seat next to Jack's. Stuffing my carry-on underneath the seat in front of me, I took a deep breath as the aircraft started taxiing down the runway. I glanced at Jack and he smiled reassuringly. I was clearly doing a terrible job pretending not to be nervous. He reached for my hand, which was clenched tight on my lap. Bringing my hand to his lips, he kissed the back of it. 'It'll be ok.'

Anxiety gave way to a sense of dread. This was the second time he had kissed me since we arrived at the airport. I pulled at my hand, and he let it go. 'Jack...'

'Yeah?' He tilted his head toward me.

I cleared my throat but managed to look him in the eye as I used my firmest voice to say, 'You've got to stop kissing me.'

My serious eyes and firm voice had little effect on Jack. His eyes glistened as though he was up to something. 'Let's make a deal.'

Deals with Jack had rarely turned out in my favour. I sighed and eyed him warily. 'What kind of a deal?'

His eyes were gentle, even as they sparkled with mischief. 'Seeing as it's just you and me for the next few weeks, how about we decide that for these weeks, we're allowed to kiss?'

I sat up straight. 'What kind of logic is that?' I shook my head. 'Why do you think I want to kiss you? I thought I'd made myself clear in saying that we're not going to be getting back together. I'm not just playing hard to get here. I mean it.'

'I've understood that you don't want to get back together. And that's not what I'm suggesting.' He held his hands up as if to say he was innocent. 'I'm just saying that for these weeks, we could allow ourselves to pretend that we don't have a complicated history. We could decide we won't talk about the past, and we won't expect anything from each other beyond these weeks. It'll be a sort of holiday from the issues of the past.'

I know I should have turned him down straight away, but his suggestion intrigued me more than I might have liked to admit. I paused. 'And when we go back?'

He shrugged. 'Then we talk about it, and if we want to just be friends again, then that's what we do, and if we want to start going out–'

'That's not going to happen.' That much I was unwaveringly clear on.

He put his hands up again with the innocent gesture. 'I've heard you. I'm just saying, in three weeks you might feel differently.'

I snorted. 'Not a chance.'

An eyebrow lifted, and he bit his lip as if to hide a smile. 'Well, then. What have you got to lose?'

Innocent, my foot. 'I don't have anything to lose, but that doesn't mean I want to be kissing you.' I looked away, avoiding his gaze in the hope he might not see the truth in my eyes.

I felt him scan my face. 'Prove it.'

Caught off guard, I glanced at him. He had raised his chin in challenge. I chuckled. 'Why should I have to prove a negative? Do you also need me to prove I don't like to eat worms?'

He smirked. 'I believe you've already proven that.'

'I was eight years old and didn't know better!'

The smirk grew into a wide grin. 'Uh-huh. The thing is, you're telling me you still don't like to eat worms, but you've changed your mind about wanting to kiss me. You used to love kissing me. So, forgive me if I'm a little sceptical.'

'I'm allowed to change my mind.' I folded my arms across my chest.

'Sure, you are. I just don't believe you have.' He rested his head against the headrest and closed his eyes as though the conversation was over, before saying, 'There's a way to prove me wrong, though.'

I huffed, and even as I wondered how he had managed to manoeuvre me into this corner, I knew I hadn't needed any manoeuvring at all. He was right. I did want to kiss him.

One little kiss couldn't hurt, right?

Right?

'Oh, go on then.' I tilted my face toward him.

He grinned, clearly way too pleased with himself. 'You sure?'

I raised my chin back at him. 'Kiss me.'

Thoughts like *what was I thinking agreeing to this?* melted away as I looked at the lips I had dreamt about for years after we broke up. He leaned in until he was about an inch away, and I could feel his breath on my skin. I took a sharp breath, and his familiar scent made my head feel lighter. As my lips tingled in anticipation, my heart beat like a drum. Then, instead of touching my lips with his, he hesitated and pulled back. He pursed his lips and he scanned my face. 'Wait. If we're going to do this, we do it properly.'

I gave him an exasperated look. 'Yeah yeah. Are you going to just talk or…'

My breath hitched as he slid his hands around my neck, cupping my cheeks gently. His thumbs stroked my cheeks once whilst his fingers slid underneath my ears.

I shivered, and my eyes flew up to his. He glanced at my mouth before meeting my gaze. His piercing blue eyes were full of desire and determination, and I got the feeling they hid something else. Something deeper.

Then his lips touched mine and I felt myself melt. Just a little.

His lips were gentle, his tongue darting across my lips, and I opened to let him in as the kiss grew hungrier. The longing I used to feel for him back when we were dating came rushing back, and my heart lurched. His hands were in my hair and I reached for his face. His cheeks were stubblier than they used to be, and still they felt familiar.

He pulled back when the air hostess came around, offering drinks, and I caught my breath and looked out the window. The clouds were now below us.

'Tell me again how you don't want to kiss me.' His voice was soft, barely above a whisper, and the feeling of his lips against mine still lingered.

I cleared my throat. I wasn't a liar and wouldn't pretend I didn't like kissing him. 'So, you're a good kisser.' I shrugged and tried to appear unaffected. 'Doesn't mean I want to get back together.'

Jack nodded. 'Still, we could enjoy having a holiday fling together.' He leaned back in his seat and picked up his magazine, as though he was entirely unaffected. 'Think about it.'

As if I could think about anything other than kissing him now. I got my knitting out and focussed on getting the pattern on the sock right. I had brought wooden knitting needles that I could take through airport security, and I was thankful I had my knitting then. My hands needed to be busy as my mind tried to make sense of Jack's mad idea. Thankfully, I had knit the same pattern lots of times before, so I didn't have to concentrate too hard. Instead, my mind was playing *What If*. What if he was right and we could have a no-strings fling in Hong Kong without anyone getting hurt? Would I want that?

Was the Pope a Catholic? Of course I wanted a no-strings fling. I hadn't kissed many guys since Jack, but none of them had come close to the way he kissed. Maybe it was because he knew me. Or maybe because we had spent our teenage years practicing with each other. In any case, if there really were no strings, then why would I opt out of having a fling with him? The only reason I could see would be if a fling brought the possibility of making me want more. Would I fall for him again?

I shook my head. That wasn't going to happen.

Turning it over and over in my mind, as I knit round after round of the sock's leg, I came to the conclusion that he was right. I really had nothing to lose. I never wanted to be in a long-term relationship again, and I would never marry. It dawned on me then that an opportunity like this might not come along again. This trip might be my only chance to be an item with somebody who – mostly – knew me.

I put my knitting down, confident I had thought through all the possibilities from every angle. There was no risk involved and, as Jack had all too easily proved, I would enjoy a short relationship with him.

I reached out and took hold of his hand. 'Ok, I'm done thinking.'

He looked up at me. 'Yeah?' The hopeful smile on his face reminded me of when we had been teenagers, and he had suggested some outrageous adventure like rock climbing up castle hill or biking through the night to St Andrews. Back then, saying yes had been easy.

I had grown up since.

I hesitated before throwing caution to the wind and giving him a weak smile. 'Yeah.' I cleared my throat. 'But if this is going to work, we have to agree not to talk at all about the past. And when we arrive back in Scotland, we go back to being friends, no questions asked.'

Now it was his turn to hesitate. His eyes searched mine, and, upon seeing my determination, he nodded. He stroked his thumb across the back of my hand, causing my whole arm to tingle. 'If that's what you want.'

'Yes.' I nodded decisively. 'Also, no sex.' That was a line I wasn't going to cross with him again.

He shrugged. 'That's fine with me.'

I sat back in my seat. 'Okay then.' Unsure of where to go from here, I avoided looking at him by studying the safety instructions on the seat in front of me.

'Come here, then.' He lifted the armrest between us and wrapped his arm around my shoulders, pulling me close. He leaned in and kissed the top of my head. 'Snuggle in.'

I took a deep breath, filling my lungs with the familiar scent that was Jack and just a hint of masculine cologne. I relaxed, soaking up the feeling of his arms wrapped around me. It had been a long time since I felt as safe and at home as I did right then.

Despite being in a tin tube somewhere over Sweden.

Chapter 11

PAST

Miranda

Jack, Julia and I all went to the church youth group together. Not because *we* wanted to, but because *Karen* wanted us to. To be fair, it was a good youth group, and we had a great youth leader who organised fun things and really cared about us and about us getting the opportunity to explore who God is.

I was fourteen when our youth group went on a weekend away to a missionary centre in Oban. Having not travelled much, I wanted to take in the scenery, so I sat next to Julia at the front of the bus where we could take it all in. The scenery was amazing as we travelled along rocky hillsides and along the lochs up the west coast. We stopped once, just to stretch our legs, at the iconic Rest and Be Thankful. As others took the chance to climb the sides of the hill and have a laugh, I spent the time gazing over the valley. *Rest and Be Thankful* was exactly right.

I had all kinds of crap going on at home. Dad had been gone for a few years now, the longest he had ever stayed away, but recently he had been in contact more, showing up at the house crying. I wasn't sure what was going on, but it sounded as though Dad had hit a fairly low point. Also, with the end of the school year coming up, I was feeling the pressure to perform at school.

But as I stood there, soaking in the beauty of the rugged mountains with the yellow gorse bushes just bursting with colour, I felt like I could breathe again. Jack's arms encircled me from behind, and I leaned against him as he brushed a kiss to my ear.

'Pretty, isn't it?'

I nodded. 'More than pretty. It's… everything.'

A couple of hours later we arrived at the manor house in Oban where we would be staying. We were met by the YWAM missions team there who showed us our rooms. Then, we gathered in the big living room, where a fire was burning in the stove, and they gave us a short introduction to the weekend before starting a time of worship.

I sat on the floor in a corner of the room and listened to them speaking about how we cannot love a God we don't know, but once we get to know him it's difficult not to fall in love with him. I wanted to believe that what they were saying was true, but so much in my life said the opposite. And God wasn't someone I loved, but rather someone I kind of feared. One of the YWAMers took out a guitar and started singing. People around me started joining in with the familiar songs, but I sat there in my corner, wondering if I would ever be able to love God.

After the first song, one of the YWAM team girls said, 'I've been thinking about what it looks like to know and love God, and sometimes it can feel a bit daunting. It's a big step to commit your whole life to God. But maybe you'd like to give it a go for just this one weekend? You could try it out, search him out and let him find you this weekend. Let him show you who he is. And if at the end of the weekend that's that and you don't want to take it any further, then that's ok.' She shrugged. 'Still, what's one weekend?'

I remembered the peace I had felt at Rest and Be Thankful, and I decided that, for this one weekend, I would give God a proper go. Not because I felt obligated to – I didn't – but because I wanted to find out for myself if there really was something to the whole God thing.

I stayed in my corner until late that night. I read the Bible, journaled, and sang along to the songs. The fire was fizzling out in the hearth and most of the rest of the youth group had left by the time I crept into bed that night. There was a deep sense of peace that enveloped me as I put my head to rest.

The next morning, the bell rang at seven, and by nine we were back on the bus, waiting in line for the ferry that would take us across to the Isle of Mull. The sea between Oban and the Isle of Mull was choppy, and though I hung out and had a laugh with everyone, I felt somewhat queasy. I was thankful the ferry crossing only took about an hour. We all got back on the bus, and I sat next to Jack, who had convinced me I would be able to see the scenery just as well from the window seat further in the back as I would at the front of the bus.

Going along the windy roads from Craignure to Fionnphort, we passed mountains I itched to explore, and beautiful beaches, even as I was feeling more nauseous by the minute. Once in a while, we passed a village or a lonely house, but mainly there were sheep scattered across the hills. Not that I got to see much of the scenery, as a game of *steal the hat* was going on around me. The game seemed to get rowdier and rowdier, until it ended when I stole Jack's cap and proceeded to vomit in it.

I hadn't meant to end the game, but by that point I was so nauseous I had no alternative than to throw up. And Jack's cap seemed a fitting container.

You might think Jack would have rubbed my back, or held my hair out of my face, or offered me a drink of water when I was done. But Jack wasn't one to be sympathetic.

'Miranda!' He groaned, before calling for the bus to be stopped so I could get off.

Doing my best to stop retching, I walked carefully, keeping a hand under the cap to catch any leaks. Thankfully, the cap was surprisingly watertight. Once out of the bus, I vomited again by the side of the road, before our youth leader, Molly, came up behind me with a bottle of water and a plastic bag for Jack's cap.

'I don't think Jack will want this back, eh?' she said as she took it from me.

'Probably not.' I wiped my face with the end of my sleeve. I tended to cry whenever I threw up.

'Are you ok?' Molly rubbed a hand down my back.

I cleared my throat and wiped at my face again. 'Uh-huh.'

Once I had taken a few deep breaths and another few sips of water, I felt better. Molly and I swapped seats on the bus so I could sit in the front for the rest of the way. It wasn't much longer before we got to Fionnphort, where we got off the bus to take the ferry across to Iona. The crossing only took about ten minutes, and the fresh sea air made me feel better. Jack came to find me and Julia as we stood by the railing staring towards the horizon.

'So… I take it you threw out my cap?'

Annoyed he cared more about his cap than about how I was doing, I said, 'Did you want it back?'

He scrunched his face in disgust. 'I guess not.'

'I didn't think so.'

'Honestly, Jack!' Julia cut in. 'You've got the sensitivity of a brick. Miranda is clearly feeling out of sorts, but all you care about is your stupid cap.'

Jack's shoulders went stiff, and he pulled a hand through his hair. 'Right,' he muttered, clearly unsure of what to say.

'No, it's ok.' I sighed. Sometimes Jack seemed completely closed off to me, but I didn't want to start a fight with him over something so trivial. 'I'm feeling better, and I'm sorry about your cap. I'll see if I can find you one to replace it.'

'Don't worry about it. It's just a cap.' He ran a hand through his hair, still unsure of himself.

'Well, it came in very handy. Thank you.' I smiled as I reached out for him and pulled him in for a hug.

He relaxed against me and hugged me tight for a minute before saying, 'Just don't kiss me. I'm sure you have puke-breath.'

Pushing him away, I snorted. 'Mhm.'

The ferry was docking, so I took his hand in mine. Together with the rest of the group we walked off the ferry and toward Iona Abbey.

I spent the rest of the weekend allowing myself not to think about what was going on at home. Instead, I revelled in the beauty that was the Inner Hebrides and Oban. The peace that seemed to rush towards me as we stepped onto Iona would have made me consider becoming a nun had it not been for my relationship with Jack. The windswept island with its Celtic crosses spoke of an ancient history of God's peace flowing gently, and part of me wanted to stay there forever. I never wanted to leave the peace.

We did a lot of walking, and explored the island that day, all structured around a Celtic rhythm which was led by the YWAM team. They took us through short devotions, and easy songs, and we read through a few of the Psalms together. And, deep inside, I acknowledged that though there were many things I didn't understand about God, the love and peace I felt that day made me want to know him and be known by him.

When we returned home on the Sunday evening, we were all exhausted and happy. I felt like, though it had only been two days, I had become a different person somehow.

That's why, when I came home to find out arrangements had been made for Dad to go to rehab, I felt it was God answering my strongest yearning and most heartfelt prayer. It felt as though God was finally coming through for our family.

Chapter 12

Present
Miranda

Being in Hong Kong was... amazing. We spent the first couple of days staying in a flat provided by the company Jack worked for, as he was technically there for meetings. He had to put in a couple of full days of work in the first week, and I was glad I had brought my knitting, but mostly we did sight-seeing, whilst trying to get our body clocks to adjust to the time change.

Hong Kong is beautiful, lying as it does on the sea with big mountains to contrast the busy city, and I enjoyed experiencing the culture. We took the tram up Victoria Peak to take in the views of the city and went to Victoria Harbour at sunset. We took in the night lights that lit up the sleek city buildings, and went to beautiful, tranquil gardens that seemed in such contrast to the busy city life but, somehow, still fit. And then there was the food. Though there was much meat on offer, as a vegetarian I had no problem finding lots of delicious food to eat. Jack took me to his favourite places and ordered food until I couldn't possibly force another bite down.

One day, after he finished work, he met me at the harbour. The grin on his face when he saw me made my heart race. I wondered how I would ever survive seeing that look directed at someone else, but reminded myself not to think about the future, and let myself enjoy this break from reality. For this trip I could pretend he was mine.

I grinned back. 'How was your day?'

He pulled me close, sending tingles down my spine, and dropped a kiss on my lips. I sighed as he pulled away, and the pleased look on his face grew. 'Better now.' And I knew that whatever kind of day he had had, that would have been his response to seeing me then.

As far as flings go, it couldn't have been better. I had given up on any notion of holding back a long time ago, and whilst I knew it would hurt to end this side of our relationship forever after we landed in Edinburgh, I also knew I would forever regret it if I wasn't fully engaged whilst I had the chance. Because I knew I would never have this opportunity again.

One morning, after we had been there for a few days, I woke up as I heard Jack getting himself ready for work. I wrapped myself in the robe I had picked up when shopping, tied it at the waist over my sleep shorts and tank top, and went to put the kettle on.

'Good morning,' Jack said, as he entered the kitchen area a few minutes later. His white shirt was tucked into a blue pair of slacks, and his tie was hanging untied around his neck. Jack had left after years of being a student, but since leaving he had become a professional, and the suits were a good fit on him.

Too good.

It was impossible to stop the spread of a smile on my face. 'Sure is.'

He smirked. 'Last full day of Hong Kong. Got any plans for the day?' He took a banana off the counter and stuffed it into his bag with his coffee mug.

'Maybe I'll just go downtown and soak up the atmosphere.'

'Oh yeah? Maybe we could meet up somewhere once I've finished with work?'

My toast popped up, and I pulled my attention away from him to get it out. 'Sure. Text me.'

I took a deep breath as Jack came up behind me and wrapped his arms around my waist, dropping his head to take a deep breath at my neck. The butter knife fell out of my hand as he pulled at the loose neck of my robe to expose my shoulder. The scruff of his shaved chin scraped against my skin as he placed gentle kisses along my shoulder up my neck. His hands scooped my hair and, tugging it to one side, he tilted my face to his so he could trail soft kisses along my jaw. Then, he waited for me to open my eyes to meet his before lowering his head and devouring my mouth. His lips were soft, even as his teeth nipped at my lips and his tongue soothed his bites. Still tugging on my hair with one hand, his other hand wrapped around my waist, pulling me close to his chest as his lips stayed on mine.

Then, he pulled away.

Catching my breath, my eyes flew to his.

'Have a nice morning.' He looked just a little too pleased with himself.

I pressed a hand to my lips as I fought to find my balance. 'Uh-huh.'

He took his bag, waved his hand and shot me a grin as he left the flat.

Turning back to my cold piece of toast, I sighed. Jack had been great at kissing when we were teenagers, but kissing Jack the man was different.

It was raw. Enchanting.

It was like living a dream.

***

By the end of the day, Jack had finished up his work project and we grabbed the front seats on the top deck of a tram and went to Kennedy Town, where we got off and had a celebratory dinner before going back again. The tram ride took just under an hour, and it was lovely to watch the city go by in the night. I wondered if this was what life would have been like if I had gone with Jack back when I was meant to, but quickly put the thought out of my mind. There was no point in going there. Instead I forced myself to live in the moment. And the moment was pretty good. Holding on to Jack's hand as I experienced Hong Kong had made it all a thousand times better than going alone would have been.

Late that night, I video called Julia and Sophia about our plans, and the next morning Jack and I put on our backpacks and left the apartment early to get to the Hong Kong – China border at Lo Wu. We went through Security and Passport Control upon leaving Hong Kong, walked across a corridor, and went through Security and Passport Control again to enter China. Having grown up hearing stories about people being caught at the Chinese border for smuggling Bibles and then put in jail for the rest of their lives, I was nervous. It was an irrational anxiety, as Jack so helpfully pointed out, as I wasn't smuggling anything, but I still breathed a sigh of relief when were cleared to go.

And despite Jack being annoying like that, I was thankful he was with me. He had spoken to some friends and sorted out our travel to Guangzhou. There we would meet with Mr Chen, the guy I had been put in touch with when I had done my research on sourcing medical grade silicone products. I had originally intended to visit two companies, but the second company had stopped responding to my emails, which meant I had decided to drop them and hoped this one would work.

We got back on the metro, and were soon in Shenzhen, where we got on a high-speed train to Guangzhou.

Though it was a few years later than I had expected, it was thrilling to sit on the train with our backpacks together, looking out the window as we sped past all the places. Jack took a selfie of us, but I convinced him not to post it to Instagram, as the stars in our eyes as we looked at each other were too evident. We had decided our fling would be an Asia-only deal and, frankly, I could do without the questions a picture like that would cause.

Instead, I took a picture of him, which I posted with the caption *Craziness with this guy in China! #Adventuretime*. And he took a picture of me and posted it on his account with the less ambiguous caption, *Everything is better with this girl #Loveofmylife*.

There went my hopes to keep our fling under the radar. My heart both took flight and dived in dread as I wondered if this fling was really a very bad idea after all. I commented on his picture with a simple *#JustFriends*, but I resigned myself to getting all the questions.

The train station in Guangzhou was heaving with people trying to catch a train or arriving from other cities. I was thankful to have Jack there as he seemed to know where to go. Coming out of the station, we walked across the big square, also full of people. After a quick meal at KFC (because: western style toilets), we got a taxi through the busy city to a nice-looking business district. We found the right building and went to find Mr Chen. Dressed in a neat suit, he was waiting for us in the foyer, and took us to his office, where we took off our heavy backpacks before sitting down. My back would have wept for joy had it been able to.

'Would you like some tea?' Mr Chen spoke softly and showed no emotion.

Jack had told me always to say no to anything offered the first two times, as saying yes straight away might be perceived as rude, so I smiled gratefully and shook my head. 'No, thank you.'

'Are you sure?' Mr Chen tilted his head.

'I'm fine, but thank you.' I glanced at Jack, and he agreed.

'How was your trip?'

'Not bad,' Jack said. 'It's nice to be in China again.'

'Ah, you've been before?'

'Yes, I used to live in Hong Kong.'

'Ah. And yourself?' He looked at me.

'It's my first time. I've wanted to come here for a long time. I love the food, and this is such a beautiful country.'

'Thank you.' Mr Chen nodded. 'I went to university in Manchester, so I know it is very different from the UK.'

'Oh, really? I thought your English was very good!'

Mr Chen laughed. 'Thank you.'

'I had a friend from China when I was at university in Edinburgh. We studied Business and Management together. Her English name is Eva.'

'Oh.' Mr Chen nodded. 'Will you visit her now you are here?'

I shook my head. 'No. She married an English man, and they live in London now. She came back here for the wedding, though, and her wedding photos are amazing. There's this one photo of them standing on a bridge over a pond. Only, there are so many fish below the bridge, you can hardly tell it's a pond.'

'For luck.' Mr Chen gave a smile.

'Yes, that's what she told me.' I smiled back at him.

'Let me get you some tea.' Mr Chen stood up and looked at us in question. When we nodded, he left the room briefly to get us some cups of green tea with leaves at the bottom of the cups.

'Now. About these silicone cups.' Mr Chen sat down and leaned back in his chair. 'You are here to work out if you can get them for a fair price, and to see if they will be produced in an ethical way. No?'

I gave a startled laugh. 'Yes. How did you know?'

'Why else would you be here? You would have ordered them online if you weren't concerned about the ethical side of things.'

I nodded. 'Yes.'

'How much time do you have left in China?'

I looked at Jack and answered. 'We have flights out of Beijing in ten days.'

'If you want to see the factory where the cups will be made, you will have to go to Yunnan province. The factory is outside of Kunming. You can fly from here or take the train. It takes thirty-six hours from Guangzhou station. Then you will have to take a bus out to the smaller town where the factory is.' He shrugged. 'Or you can take my word that the workers are treated well.'

I smiled. 'With respect, Mr Chen, I think I'd like to see if for myself.'

He tilted his head and smiled. 'Of course.'

We talked about the size of the order and looked at prototypes of the two models I had selected, before he gave us all the directions we would need for the visit to the factory.

After our meeting with Mr Chen ended, we stepped outside with our backpacks again. Jack said, 'I guess we've changed our plans from taking the train to Beijing now to going to Kunming instead?'

I grimaced. 'Is that ok?'

'Of course.' His whole face beamed at me. 'It's an adventure.' My heart skipped a beat as he winked. I had always loved how he was up for anything.

Instead of trying to find a hostel for the night, Jack rang a friend in Hong Kong who arranged for us to stay at his company's apartment in Guangzhou. And, somehow, we managed to get train tickets for the train that left early the next morning. The apartment was close to the train station, which made getting the train the next morning easy. We pushed through the crowds and found our train a few minutes before it was due to leave. We were in a sleeper coach with six beds in each alcove, and we had the top bunks. I climbed up the beds to get to mine, and Jack passed me our backpacks before climbing up himself, softly whistling that tune I couldn't place.

Below us was a couple in their thirties, and on the bottom bunks were two girls in their early twenties. Their English wasn't great, but Jack was able to communicate a little with them in a mix of

Chinese and English. None of them smoked, for which I was thankful, as many of the other passengers spent the whole journey smoking. Slowly the whole carriage filled with smoke.

I resigned myself to getting the black lung, and Jack laughed. 'I think getting the black lung takes a little more than breathing smoke for thirty-six hours. Besides, the pollution in Guangzhou is probably just as bad for your lungs as the air on the train is.'

Part of me wanted to spend the journey just looking out the window, taking all of China in, but Jack took out a deck of cards, and we played cards for hours. Once in a while, a lady with a very shrill voice would come through the carriage with a food cart, and we would get some packs of noodles, which we poured boiling water from the urn at the end of the carriage on, before slurping them down with our chop sticks. Jack was a pro at the chop stick thing, but I felt like I was starting to get a hang of it, too.

Every few hours, the train would pull in at a station, and people would get on and off, and Jack would get off the train to buy some treats at the platform snack trolleys. My heart was in my throat the whole time he was off the train. I worried he wouldn't make it back before we took off again, but he always did. And the treats he got us were worth it. Forgoing the Hundred-Year-Old Eggs, which Jack told me were fermented using rather questionable processes, we opted to buy nuts and crisps, and jujubes instead. Jujubes were fruit similar to pears in taste and consistency but had a big stone like a plum on the inside. He also bought tea leaves which we put in our travel mugs and filled up with hot water from the urn.

Travelling for thirty-six hours had sounded incredibly boring when Mr Chen had first mentioned it, but it turned out to be amazing. Hanging out with Jack like this felt like a dream. There were no expectations to make anything happen – it was like a break from reality. At ten, the carriage lights were turned out, and things quietened down. At that point, we were sitting on my bunk listening to music on Jack's phone, with an earphone each. His arm was wrapped around me, I was knitting, and Oasis was in our ears.

'Are you tired?' Jack lowered the volume on the phone, and I nodded. 'I'll watch our stuff if you want to go to the toilet first.'

I scrunched my nose. I wasn't keen on the toilets with a hole in the floor which appeared to go straight onto the track. 'Ok. Great.' Putting away my knitting, I kissed his cheek before untangling myself from the earphones and heading for the toilet. When I came back, I found him asleep on my bed. Unsure if I would fit next to him, I decided to sleep in his bed and let him get his rest. It was dark outside, so I let the train rock me to sleep.

I woke up a few hours later, as the train had stopped at a station and new people were getting on. The cold night air was a nice break from the smoke, but it also made me feel wide awake. Looking over at my bunk bed, I saw Jack was still fast asleep. His messy hair was standing on end, and after having been clean shaven during our time in Hong Kong, his cheeks were now sporting some scruff. Watching him sleep, I thought about all the smiles, and the ways he had kissed me during the day. The sting of longing in my heart made me wish our history had been different and that we could be together for real.

I swallowed the lump in my throat and turned onto my other side. Putting all thoughts of Jack out of my mind, I turned my thoughts to what I wanted to get out of my visit to the silicone factory.

Soon, the train had rocked me to sleep again, and the next time I woke up it was light out and the lady with the shrill voice was announcing her presence. Jack quickly climbed down the bunks and dashed after her, coming back with oranges and more noodles to have for breakfast.

The day passed quickly, and soon we arrived at the busy train station in Kunming.

Chapter 13

Jack

Being in Hong Kong with Miranda was better than I could have hoped, considering our history. When I moved to Hong Kong six years earlier, we had video called a few times in the first few weeks of me being there. It had started off ok, but the distance between us felt so tangible and deep that I soon knew I had to break off our engagement. Still, I couldn't break up with her on a video call. I couldn't cope with seeing her crumble as I tried to explain why.

So… I wrote her an email.

Yeah, I know. It wasn't my finest moment. But she sent me a nice reply a few days later, and things seemed fine. She seemed sad, but she understood what I was trying to say.

I'd done the right thing in breaking up with her.

As days turned into weeks, and months turned into years, however, breaking up with her *via email* seemed less and less clever. I realised just how stupid it was when I told my shrink about it a few months later, and she struggled to keep from wincing.

I wanted to bang my head against a wall when I thought about how stupid that had been. But though Miranda still wouldn't talk about the past, she seemed more and more comfortable around me now. Having this little window of being just us, away from everything, seemed like the best gift.

After spending the previous six years apart, a small part of me had worried we would have changed and were no longer compatible.

And we *had* changed. We both had.

We were no longer the innocent couple with no worries. Life had happened to us, and where she might have jumped before, now she seemed to hesitate. Still, she had – somewhat uncharacteristically – agreed to have a fling with me, and I counted that as a win.

Now I only had to convince her to keep it going after we returned home.

She had spent hours poring over her spreadsheets before we left, trying to work out all the details for the trip, and I had worried we would get there and she would freeze when things didn't go as planned. Consequently, I was relieved to find that she wasn't married to her plans, but was open to adjusting, even when major parts of her plan needed to change. Like when one of the businesses she was going to visit didn't pan out, or our spur of the moment trip to Yunnan province became necessary.

After spending most of the train journey snuggled up together on a single bunk bed, it felt like we were closer than we ever had been – even when we had been engaged. Miranda's eyes seemed to shine when she looked at me, and I was sure she could see my love for her in my eyes too. We both avoided telling each other though, and I wondered if Sophia's idea of a fling in China was genius, or if it would come back and bite me later.

We arrived into Kunming at the end of the day and got some food. Sitting next to each other on stools close to the ground, we ordered lots of different dishes, which we tried with rice.

The food in Yunnan province was spicier than the Cantonese food we had been eating in Hong Kong and Guangzhou, but every bit as good. Miranda fell in love with the spicy deep-fried beans, but for me it was the meats that were most exciting. I tried everything from kung-pao chicken to deep-fried grasshoppers, and even some dog meat.

When I offered Miranda a taste of the dog meat, she laughed and put on a Northern Irish accent to say, 'No, thank you.'

I smiled and shook my head. 'Such a shame you're a vegetarian. You'd love the taste of this.'

'Yes.' Her eyes sparkled as she returned my smile. 'Regrettable indeed.'

With a sudden need to touch her, I reached for her face and gently wiped my thumb under her lip. Her lips were full and soft, and I wished we were somewhere more private so I could have kissed her. 'You've got something there.'

Her eyes grew suspicious. 'You know, you're the only one I've ever met who does that. Nobody else will wipe food off my face or tell me I've got food stuck. So, I'm thinking either everyone else is letting me down – letting me walk around with food all over my face – or you're making it up.'

I was totally making it up. 'Or maybe you eat more sloppily when you're around me?'

She elbowed my side. 'You calling me a sloppy eater?'

'Ouch.' I tried to keep a straight face. 'It's okay. Really, you're not that bad.'

She tutted, but wiped at her lips, as though she was self-conscious despite herself.

I laughed, and she reached over and rubbed my hair.

'Whatever.'

After eating, we took a taxi to the bus station to catch the bus, which left at midnight, as Mr Chen had instructed us to do. The sleeper bus had bunk beds, and again we found top bunks next to each other. Here, though, there was less space, so we each lay on our own bunk and held hands as the bus rocked us, rather violently, to our destination. The bus stopped at five am, an hour before we were meant to arrive, and we wondered if we had arrived at the right place, but as everyone else got off the bus, we got off too. We took our bags and went to find a place to have breakfast.

The town smelled like dust and food. Scruffy looking dogs lay in the alleys, and noodles were hanging from frames on the pavements.

We found a little restaurant and had spicy noodles for breakfast.

'You awake?' I smiled at Miranda as she yawned.

'Didn't get much sleep on that bus, but this soup is helping clear my head. That man in the bunk under yours snored like an asthmatic buffalo the whole trip.' She laughed. 'I've never heard anything like it.'

I snorted. 'Yeah, that's some talent.'

We sat in the restaurant for a few hours, trying to warm up, and playing cards to stay awake until it was late enough in the morning that we could take a taxi to the factory.

They were expecting us, and we were showed around the factory as Miranda asked all the questions she had about how it all worked. It seemed like a good place, and Miranda seemed happy enough to sign a contract for the order.

By the time we were done at the factory, it was only eleven am, and we had hours before the bus would go back to Kunming.

'What do we do now?' Miranda asked. 'Should we try to find a hotel and get some sleep?'

'Psht. Sleep is for babies.' As much as I wanted to spend the day cuddling with her, I also saw the opportunity for an adventure. I grinned at her. 'I vote for taking a bus out to some little village and seeing the countryside.'

She frowned. 'Are you not tired?'

'Exhausted. But we've only got today to experience this. We can sleep some other time.'

She studied me, and I saw the moment she decided to throw caution to the wind. Her eyes changed from uncertain and suspicious to resigned, and then excited. 'Okay, show me.'

Putting my very broken Mandarin – and plenty of Google Translate – to use, we found a bus that would take us three hours west, to a little village in the mountains. We found seats next to each other toward the back of the bus, and Miranda took the window seat.

Soon, we were out of the city, and rolling hills became steeper mountains as straight roads turned narrow and windy. The bus climbed the steep mountain roads faster than what seemed safe, considering the sharp drop on the side of the road.

I glanced at Miranda. She was taking deep breaths and appeared to studiously ignore looking out the side window at the sharp drop. Instead, she was sitting as straight as she could, trying to see out of the front window.

'You okay?'

Without looking at me, she held out a hand and said, 'Can I have your cap, please?'

Knowing what to expect, I rushed to pull it off my head and handed it to her. She nodded her thanks as she sat herself up straighter and took a couple of deep breaths before the retching started.

'Oh, Miranda.' I winced at how ill she was and reached for her hair to hold it away from her face.

People around us started to notice what was going on, and soon the bus driver had been alerted. He pulled to a stop and let us off the bus so Miranda could finish puking her guts out.

Once she was done, I took the cap and threw it in a plastic bag to be binned, before handing her my bottle of water.

'Thank you.' Her voice was frail as she wiped her face with her sleeve. 'I'm sorry.'

I flinched. 'It's only a cap. Come here.' I pulled her in for a hug, rubbing her tense back gently. I wished she would relax. 'Take a few deep breaths, and you'll soon start feeling better.'

The bus driver had taken the opportunity to have a cigarette, but now that Miranda was done puking, he made a show of throwing the butt on the ground and putting it out. He gestured toward the bus, and I nodded.

'We've got to get back on now; will you be ok?' Why couldn't I have agreed when she had suggested getting a hotel room and resting? Why did I always have to push us that bit too far?

'Yeah. I feel better now.' She wiped at her face again. 'Thank you.'

I grabbed her hand and tugged gently. 'Come on. Let's get back on the bus before they leave without us.'

I spent the rest of the journey glancing at Miranda, passing her water and sweets and a pack of biscuits out of my backpack. As we came closer to our destination, the road straightened and widened, and Miranda perked up again.

It was only when we got to the little village at the end of the bus route that we were told there was no return bus until the following day. I glanced at Miranda, relief flooding me as her eyes sparkled, and she elbowed me in the side.

'You come up with the best adventures.' Her whole face shone.

I couldn't help grinning at how delighted she seemed, despite obviously being way outside her comfort zone. 'Yeah. I planned this, you know.'

'Uh-huh, of course.' She bit her lips, trying to hold back her smile. 'So what do we do now?'

I cleared my throat. 'We find our hotel of course.' I looked around, hoping there would be a place we could stay that night.

From what I could see, the village had a petrol station, a primary school, and a little shop. Not sure at all what to do, I smirked at Miranda and said, 'I'm sure they'll be able to help us at the shop.'

At the village shop, we found out there was only one hotel in the village, but fortunately it was just across the road and very cheap. At ten Yuan per person, our overnight stay only cost the equivalent of one British pound. We soon discovered that the reason for the bargain price was that our bedrooms were above the pigsty, which was also next to the hole in the ground that functioned as a toilet.

I tried breathing through my shirt as we dropped the bags in our room, but the stench was invasive, and I wondered again why I had thought going for an impromptu trip to the countryside had been a good idea. 'I'm willing to accept that this wasn't one of my brighter ideas.'

'You what?' Miranda sat down on her rather dirty looking bed. She swiped at her hair as her shoulders shook with laughter. 'Y'wanna go fer a walk?' Her words came out slurred around her cackles. 'Or do y'wanna sit here fer a bit?' She was writhing on the bed now, her giggles bursting free.

I shook my head at her and wondered how I had ever spent six years apart from her. How had I lived without her for all those years? 'Um… let's go explore the area. Let's do anything other than sit here with the pigs.' I shook my head.

'I gotta pee so bad.' Miranda wiped at her face as she tried to sit up.

'Come on, you can stop by the facilities on our way out.' I chuckled at the thought.

'The facilities…' Miranda bent over in another fit of giggles.

I took her hand and pulled her in for a hug before we left the building. Smiling down at her, I nodded. 'This wasn't exactly what I had in mind when I suggested going for a nice walk in the countryside.'

She shrugged and grinned at me. 'On the upside, I don't think the pigs can possibly snore as loud as that man on the bus last night, so there's that.'

I bent down and kissed her forehead as I remembered the earth-shaking snores we had listened to all night. 'At least there's that.'

Our walk took us along the hillside trail, where we discovered banana plants and rice fields, and across the river we could see what people we met told us was Myanmar. We ate jujube as snacks, and at dinner time we ended up back at the hotel, which was the only restaurant in the village.

We were the only customers apart from a group of men playing mah-jong in the corner. There wasn't a menu; instead, you ate what you were served, and that night, they served rice and chicken and leafy greens.

Miranda filled up on rice and the leaves, but I lucked out and ended up with chicken feet. I took a deep breath and made sure to keep the smile on my face as we thanked the waiter.

Miranda's eyes gleamed with delight when she watched me attempt to keep my facial expressions in check as I gnawed the meat off the feet of the chicken. It didn't taste as bad as the idea of it seemed, and I was thankful to have ended up with the feet rather than with the head. Still, it wasn't something I would order again.

After dinner we went back to our room – pushing through the stench of the pigs below us – to have an early night, as we were both exhausted after not sleeping much the previous night. Miranda couldn't stop the tears from leaking from her eyes as she laughed at the way our day had turned out. 'I can't believe you ate those chicken feet!' She wiped at her face. 'And then when they brought more…' The laughing started again. 'Best trip ever.'

I smiled as I watched her from where I was sitting on the stained mattress on my bed, until she eventually quietened down. I could have listened to her laugh all day. I lay awake for a long time after Miranda had fallen asleep, wondering how I would ever go back to being just friends with her if she followed through on her decision to end our fling at the end of our trip.

The following day, we travelled back to Kunming, and we spent the next few days sight-seeing there before flying out to Beijing, where we spent a day going to The Forbidden City and visiting Tiananmen Square, where Mao Zedong still lies in formaldehyde as a visitor's attraction.

The Forbidden City and Mao were amazing, but I found it hard to look anywhere other than at Miranda. Her eyes were soft and full of light as she looked at me, and her smile made my heart sing.

I listened to her talk about Project Cup, and her commitment to making a difference in the world stirred something deep inside me. In the six years we had spent apart, she had only grown more attractive, and walking down the street with her, I felt like I had won the lottery. How I had managed to convince her to have a fling with me, however short, was a mystery and a dream, and I didn't want to wake up.

We were both anxious, because our trip was about to end, and we still hadn't talked more about what would happen to us when we landed back in Scotland. This time, though, I was determined not to let circumstances or difficulties pull us apart.

Then, we flew back to Edinburgh via Helsinki, and our trip was over.

And, as it turned out, our fling was over, too.

Chapter 14

PAST

Miranda

After Dad left for rehab, the mood in our house shifted. Mum seemed more hopeful, and even school felt easier. Dad was away for six months, and we went to visit him a couple of times. He seemed to be doing well and looked like a different person. The grey skin, shaggy beard, and long hair were gone, and in their place were a neat haircut and a smile. He looked at least ten years younger.

I asked him if he missed the alcohol, and he told me there were reasons for why he would drink, but he was learning to find alternative ways to handle those reasons. It wasn't the answer I wanted to hear, but I respected him for being honest and for doing the work to be able to stay sober.

Mum and I were given some pamphlets about addiction, and the main thing that struck me was that Dad would never be cured. Instead, he would have to do one day at a time for the rest of his life. That made me feel somewhat anxious, and it made me want to try to protect him from anything that might trigger a potential fall off the wagon.

Dad came home just before Christmas. Mum prepared for it by spending ages cleaning the house and cooking food. The tiredness she had carried for so long disappeared, and instead she seemed to dance across the kitchen, and a smile was never far away.

John went to collect Dad at the rehab, and when the door finally opened and Dad stepped in, Mum wore a shy smile. 'Welcome home.'

Dad's eyes found hers, and I watched as a thousand questions raced between them, as though he wasn't a hundred percent sure he was welcome. He cleared his throat nervously. 'Hi Lisa.'

Mum's eyebrows rose, and she walked towards him and shut the door behind him. Stepping up to him, she put her chin out and looked up at him. 'Can I have a hug?'

Dad searched her face before taking a deep breath and raising his arms tentatively around her. Her arms circled his waist, and she stepped into the hug, resting her head on his shoulder. And as awkward as it had seemed at first, the longer it went on, the more it seemed right. Dad seemed to breathe her in and slowly relaxed, and by the time Mum kissed his cheek and pulled away, they were both smiling.

Dad lifted his chin toward me. 'Hey, Mir-maid.'

I gave him a crooked smile. It was weird seeing my Mum and Dad hug for the first time in months. 'Dad.'

He took his jacket off and hung it up before coming over to hug me too. He hadn't hugged me in years, but as he did, I felt a deep sense of belonging. Looking back, I don't understand why I would associate my Dad's hugs with feeling secure and at home – so much of what he did gave me a sense of insecurity and anxiety. Still, his hugs were grounding in the rawest of ways. Maybe Dad was so real that there wasn't room for any questions – I don't know.

Instead of going to the Reids' for Christmas as usual, this time we had them over at ours, and I think we all felt a sense of pride in being able to host Christmas as a family. We were no longer just the leeches that were always being invited over to their house – this time we could contribute something as well.

Karen had got us all year-old ugly Christmas jumpers from the church charity shop, and we ate, and played games, and listened to each other tell stories, and laughed.

At night, we all went to church. I sat between Mum and Jack, with Jack's arm around my shoulders, and as we sang Christmas carols and listened to the reverend go on and on, I felt I had everything I could ever wish for. There was even a slight dusting of snow as we came out of church.

Dad's next task was to try to settle back into a normal lifestyle. That turned out to be quite difficult, as nobody wanted to employ him, and instead, he ended up with the options of volunteering or doing college courses. Not knowing whether the courses would ever lead to any work made the investment into his education seem somewhat risky, but despite all the alcohol, he had a good brain and wanted to study. Still, the courses he ended up taking were only part-time, and he struggled to fill the rest of the time. Every day was a test, and Mum and I tried our best to keep him occupied. And though there were many days I anxiously called out 'Dad?' when I came home from school, we found a routine that seemed to work.

It wasn't until a year and a half later that the first big test came.
***
Jack

I met Michael and Nick during fresher's week at university. They were studying other degrees, but we ended up sitting next to each other at some cross-programme orientation to the university.

As neither of them was from Edinburgh, I offered to show them around the city. Nick was from the US and Michael from Canada, and both were in awe of the old buildings and all the history. Michael brought his camera and took pictures of things I would never have thought to take pictures of. It was all a bit funny to me – I liked Edinburgh, but I dreamed of travelling. I wanted to experience new cultures, eat different kinds of food, and see the world. The old, damp Edinburgh buildings were just old to me. Still, Michael and Nick seemed to like them, and from then on, we were friends. Nick and I joined the same football team, and we all joined the same gym and started working out together.

After a few weeks, I invited them to come over for Sunday lunch at my parents' house. They both glanced at each other, as though they weren't sure, so I told them about how we would fill the house on Sundays, and that they wouldn't be the only strangers there.

Nick shrugged, and said he wouldn't mind a hot meal, and Michael appeared to relax, and said he would come too.

That Sunday, Mum had made lasagnes before going to church, leaving Miranda and me in charge of making salads. Julia offered to help, but we soon had her setting the table instead of helping with the food. It was better for everyone that way.

Mum and Dad brought a bunch of people home from church, and soon the house filled with kids I had never met running around chasing our dog, Becky, and people talking awkwardly to each other.

Miranda's parents, Lisa and Jimmy, came over too – Lisa brought a big tray of apple cake for dessert – and just as Dad was about to say grace, Michael and Nick rang the doorbell. I let them in, and chuckled as they held out a box of chocolates and a sad-looking potted plant.

'Give them to Mum and she'll love you forever.' It was true – the way to Mum's heart was kindness in whatever form. Chocolate and flowers, no matter how wilted, qualified.

Nick straightened his spine as though he was feeling uncomfortable. 'Okay.'

Nick and Michael looked awkwardly at each other but followed me into the kitchen where people had started helping themselves to food. Mum held on to Becky's collar as she was speaking to Lisa.

Becky, who had more heart than manners, struggled to contain her excitement over all the people gathered in the house, and when she saw Michael and Nick, she started pulling to get loose. Mum was jolted out of her conversation and dragged toward us as Becky tried to jump up and greet them.

'Let me put her away, and I'll come and say hi.'

'It's okay,' Michael said as he reached for Becky, who started licking him as her tail wagged and she kept trying to jump. 'She's a good dog.'

I laughed. 'She's not really. She's spoiled and lazy and doesn't listen…'

Mum put a hand across her chest, looking aghast at my words. 'She is *not.*' She turned to Michael and Nick. 'Don't listen to my heathen son.'

I snorted and watched Becky, who was struggling to try to get away from Mum. Scrunching my face, I held up my thumb and index finger, showing a small space between them. 'She is, though. A wee bit.'

Mum ran a hand down my arm and tutted. 'Aw, Becky's a lovely dog and don't you say otherwise.'

'Uh-huh.' I smiled and grabbed onto the dog's collar. 'I'll put her in the garden so she can calm down.'

Mum straightened, rubbing her hands on her jeans. 'Okay.' I pulled Becky along as I heard Mum say, 'You must be Nick and Michael.'

Once Becky was shut outside with a chew-toy, I returned to the kitchen to see Mum hugging Michael as though they were long-lost friends. Judging by the bewildered look on Nick's face, he had already had his hug. Michael seemed relaxed when he stepped out of her arms, though, and she took in the plant and the chocolates. 'Thank you. I'll put these out with dessert later, and we can all enjoy them.'

'Join the queue and get some food. We can sit in the garden if you want.' I grimaced. 'It's a bit crowded in here.'

I introduced them to Miranda and Julia, and I watched the girls do the eye-thing girls do when they're talking to each other without using words.

We took our food out onto the patio, and Becky came and sniffed us all, before lying down under the table.

Julia started chatting to Michael and Nick, asking them both a hundred questions, and soon there was a discussion about the nature of truth going on. Julia had a way of turning the most normal conversation sideways and finding something to debate.

Miranda and I mostly watched as the three of them discussed whether truth is always true and how culture or experience can impact a person's perception of truth. Miranda bit her lip a few times, as though she wanted to say something, but shook her head and listened instead. Then the conversation turned more personal as Michael asked, 'Would you rather be told a harsh truth or live a sweet lie?'

Now Miranda couldn't help herself. 'Are you asking if we would rather live a fantasy than in reality?'

Michael gave her a lopsided smile. 'Maybe?'

'I mean, I understand that we all want to escape reality sometimes, but I would rather know the truth than pretend everything is always okay.' She frowned. 'Wouldn't you?'

'Well, I guess it depends on what the truth is,' Julia leaned back in her chair, angling her face toward the sun. 'Some truths might be unnecessary.'

'You think?' Nick frowned.

'Well, I don't know.' She glanced at him. 'I'm sure I've told a white lie or two. Not because I wanted to be lie, but because it seemed kinder.'

'Do you really tell white lies to be kind, though? Don't you tell them to avoid feeling awkward?' Nick smirked at her. 'I reckon people that tell white lies like to think they're being kind, but they really just don't want to feel uncomfortable.'

'I'm sure you're maybe partly right,' Julia tried to cover her reddening cheeks by burrowing into the collar of her jacket, but then she sat up and looked him in the eyes as if in challenge. 'I take it you don't ever tell lies then?'

Nick shrugged. 'Didn't say I'm perfect.'

Julia snorted and mumbled a snarky sounding 'oh really?'

'What do you think, Jack?' Michael asked.

'Well…' I cleared my throat. 'I reckon truth is good on a need to know basis. I mean, some truths don't add anything to our experience of reality – they're just hurtful.' I shrugged. 'Why hurt others unnecessarily?'

'I would rather know. Fantasies might be nice for a time, but they will eventually end, and then everything falls apart.' Miranda shook her head. 'I'd much rather live a flawed – even harsh – reality I can trust, than a blissful fantasy based in lies.'

'You would *always* tell the truth? Even if the truth would kill someone?' Michael bit the inside of his cheek as he studied her.

She frowned. 'I don't know. But I know *I* don't want to be deceived.'

I ran my hand down her shoulder, cocking my head to the side as I looked at her. I wanted to tell her that some pain was just pain, and pain for pain's sake was pointless. I wished I could create a cocoon of happiness for her, so she could always escape the pain life seemed to continuously throw at her. 'It's not exactly deception though, is it? I'd say it would be kindness to save your life by telling a lie.'

'Kindness is speaking the truth, even when the truth hurts.' Her eyes were gentle as she squeezed my hand. 'Nobody can escape reality forever.' And it felt as though she stopped herself from adding, *'Not even you, Jack.'* Her comment struck me as pointed, but I wasn't sure what she meant – or even if I wanted to know.

I winked at her. 'Maybe not forever, but for as long as it lasts, I'd rather enjoy life than suffer.'

She rested her head on my shoulder and gave me a wry smile. 'You would say that, wouldn't you…'

'Not all suffering is bad though,' Michael said. 'Maybe suffering caused by truth is actually good for us?'

I snorted. 'Uh-huh, well I'm willing to forego that goodness.'

'But aren't we talking about different things here?' Julia asked. 'I mean, there's a difference between not telling someone that their hair looked better before they had it cut, and lying about big things, don't you think?'

'No!' Miranda sat up straight, and her hands were in the air as she spoke. 'Sure, keep some things to yourself, but if I ask you whether you like my hair, you better tell me the truth. Otherwise, how can I trust you on anything at all?'

'Okay, but whether I like your hair or not is irrelevant to whether your hair objectively looks nice.' Michael cut in and smiled. 'Opinion isn't always truth, is it?'

Mum came out on the patio with a tray for our dirty dishes. 'Are you all okay out here?'

'Yeah, this was great, thank you,' Nick said with a smile. 'Best lasagne I've had in ages.'

'Oh, I'm glad you liked it.' Mum returned his smile. 'You're welcome to take some leftovers home. I've put out some lunch boxes on the counter. Just help yourself.'

'Really?' Nick looked at Mum as though he couldn't make sense of her.

Mum patted his shoulder. 'Really, really.' She set the tray on the table. 'Julia, will you bring the dishes inside when you're ready? If you guys want dessert, it's been put out now.'

'*If* we want dessert…' Michael looked at me with a grin, then turned to Mum. 'What do you think truth is, Karen?'

Without missing a beat, Mum said, 'Oh that's easy. Truth is a person, and you can know him.' Her face lit up as she smiled. 'His name is Jesus.'

I cringed and glanced at Julia, who had scrunched her face in a pained expression.

'I'll make sure to bring the tray inside, Mum.' I stroked her arm.

'Great. You'll want to hurry up if you want any dessert. Some of the children inside are hoping for a second helping already.'

'Nice save,' Julia snorted, as Mum left and we gathered up the dishes.

'What do you mean?' Michael asked.

'She was about to start evangelising you guys.' Julia shook her head as Michael gave a surprised laugh. 'No, really.'

'I would have liked to have seen that.' Michael seemed fascinated. 'I can't remember the last time somebody tried to evangelise me.'

Chapter 15

Miranda

I was sixteen, and it was mid-autumn when our next challenge came along. I say "challenge" because I have been to therapy since, and there I was encouraged to think about it in as positive a way as possible. A challenge is something you can rise to or overcome, whereas *all hell breaking loose* has a somewhat different connotation. But if I were to be honest, the next few years were the worst.

It was a sunny autumn day when I got a text from Mum asking that I come straight home from school. I had planned to go over to hang out with Jack – who now spent his days at uni – but sent a message with Julia to tell him I would catch up with him later, instead.

Both Mum and Dad were in the kitchen when I got home, which was unusual as Mum worked late on Wednesdays, and Dad would be on his way home from the garage where he was working part-time as an apprentice. Their faces were ashen, though Mum tried to pretend everything was fine. 'How was school?' she asked.

'Fine.' I sat down. 'What's going on?'

Mum looked at Dad, and he took her hand across the table.

'Your Mum had some bad news.'

'Right..?' I waited.

'Right,' Mum said, in a brisk tone. 'So, I've been to the doctor's today, and he says I've got breast cancer.'

'What?' I frowned. 'How does he know that? Does it not take a while for them to do tests and things?'

'Yeah.' Mum nodded. 'I've been a few times and the test results are all in. It's cancer.'

I took a sharp breath, which hurt my throat as I tried to process what she was saying. 'Cancer.' It sounded so final.

'Uh-huh.' Mum reached for my hand and I grabbed on to hers. 'I've got to have an operation, and then, depending on how much of it they can remove, I'll have to have chemo and/or radiation.'

'How long will that take?'

'We don't know yet. It all depends on how everything goes.'

'Oh.' I didn't know how to process this. I had never had to worry about Mum before, and even now, I felt like I knew she would be able to handle this. She could handle anything. I was less sure of how Dad would cope. Would this cause him to start drinking again?

'It's going to be okay. We can do this. It's just a matter of trusting in God one step at a time.' Mum gave a determined smile.

A few weeks later, that was still Mum's attitude. She had her operation and started chemo. When her hair started falling out, Karen came over, and they shaved the rest of it off. She said the anti-nausea medication she had been given helped a lot, but I could tell she continued to have the occasional bout of nausea. Nonetheless, whenever I asked her about how she was doing, she would smile that same smile, and give me a Bible verse about not being afraid.

Karen came over a lot, bringing food and keeping Mum company which meant Dad could keep his internship at the mechanics'. Dad handled things better than I had expected and stepped up to the challenge. As much as he was able to, he took Mum to appointments and was there for her. And he kept in contact with his sponsor and saw John at least once a week.

But once in a while, when he didn't see me watching, his face would look haunted, and I spent the next few months worrying that Mum's cancer would cause him to go back on the bottle, or that Mum would die.

***

Though watching Mum go through having cancer was tough, not everything was awful.

One morning in the spring, I had been feeling particularly stressed. Mum had had chemo the day before, and the effect had kicked in today, which meant that she spent most of the day exhausted. She had slept most of the evening after I got home from school, and when I went in to check on her, she seemed disoriented. She hadn't eaten much and was clearly losing weight.

All she wanted was ice chips to crunch on, so we had made sure the freezer was full of them.

Seeing Mum – who was usually full of life – struggling like this was painful, and when I went to bed that night, it took me a long time to fall asleep.

I woke just after 4am, when Dad knocked on my door. 'Miranda?'

Instantly awake, I sat up. 'Yes. What is it?'

Dad put his head round the door and said, 'You coming with us, or what?'

'Where? What's going on?' I rubbed my face. Had I forgotten something? Was everything ok?

'Everything is fine. We just need to go do this thing. Come on.' He left my room, and I got up and went after him.

'What thing?'

'Get dressed – you'll want something warm.'

I returned to my room, pulled on jeans and a warm jumper over my pyjama shirt, and tied my hair into a ponytail. Mum and Dad were standing by the front door when I came back. I put my coat and boots on, and we went out to the car.

'Where are we going?'

Mum shook her head. 'He won't tell me either.'

It was still dark outside, but on the horizon the sky was starting to brighten slightly. Dad drove us to the Dunsapie Loch car park on Arthur's Seat, and I realised he wanted us to go up the hill.

'Do you think this is a good idea?' I frowned. 'I don't think Mum can walk all that way.'

Mum was struggling to get out of the car. 'I'll be ok. We'll go slow, right?' She smiled and I knew this kind of thing was part of what she loved about Dad. Still, I would have been surprised if she could walk across the car park, never mind up the hill.

'You'll have to carry the picnic.' Dad handed me his rather heavy rucksack. I slung it onto my back, and he went and squatted in front of Mum. 'On you get.'

Mum smiled. 'Are you sure? I'm sure I can walk it.'

There was no way she could have walked it.

'Why walk when you can ride, though?' Dad said, and Mum put her arms over his shoulders and hopped on, wrapping her legs around his waist. Dad stood up and let out a loud 'Neeeiiiggghhh!' and Mum's embarrassed smile melted into a laugh.

I shook my head at them, and we started our walk. Dad sang silly songs and Mum joined in. I wondered how many of my class mates had ever been woken at 4am because their Dad wanted to carry their cancer-sick Mum up a hill to watch the sunrise, and thought I was the luckiest girl in the world to have parents who loved each other so much.

By the time we got to the plateau, the sun was starting to push its way over the horizon. We decided not to scramble our way up the last bit to the top. Instead, I set out the blanket I had carried, and Dad set Mum down onto it. Out of the rucksack, I pulled out the coffee he had packed for himself, ginger tea for Mum and me, three small bottles of water, a freezer bag filled with slowly melting ice chips, a container with sandwiches and a big tub of cut up fruit.

'Aw, Jimmy.' Mum sighed, and though she had big dark circles under her eyes, she looked happy.

'Now then.' He rubbed his hands together before sitting down on the blanket behind Mum for her to be able to lean on him. Dad wrapped his arms around her and pulled her close, and she closed her eyes and settled in. He muttered something in her ear, and her eyes flew open with a laugh as she slapped at his leg.

'Jimmy!' Mum's cheeks took on a more healthy-looking tone.

'Uh-huh.' His eyes sparkled as he looked at her. 'Be a dear and pass me my coffee mug, Miranda, would you?'

We ate, mostly in silence, as we watched the sun rise. Mum had half a sandwich and some fruit along with her ice chips, and Dad and I both felt better for it.

I was late for school that morning – it took us quite some time to get home – but I didn't mind. That morning was a slice of heaven for me.

Later, when I told Julia about it, she suggested we start a tradition of going up Arthur's Seat to see the sunrise once a year. Going up Arthur's Seat with Julia and, later, Sophia, was different than going up with my parents, but it still became one of the highlights of my year.

***

Jack

When Miranda first told me that Lisa had been diagnosed with cancer, I said, 'They can cure cancer now though, can't they?'

I didn't mean to be insensitive, but I couldn't handle the worry that was in her eyes, so I figured I would play down the scary bits and help her see things from a more positive perspective instead. Crying about things that couldn't be changed had never helped anyone, in my opinion.

She nodded. 'Yeah, but it sounds like the treatment might be pretty intense. She's likely to lose her hair, and she'll be sick for a long time.'

I shrugged. 'I'm sure it'll be a challenge, but she'll be ok. It's Lisa, right?'

Miranda nodded again. I could tell she wanted to cry, but I couldn't have that. Instead I set out to distract her, so we went into the city for an evening at a comedy show. There was an age restriction on the show, but we snuck Miranda in, and we had a great time. And for the next few months, whenever Miranda seemed down, I came up with a new adventure for her. We didn't talk about the cancer, or anything related to it. Instead, I insisted everything was fine, and tried to make sure that she would relax when she was with me.

We started running together. At first, we did a couch to five kilometres program, but soon we were going further, and signing up for races. I enjoyed running, but Miranda caught the bug – and soon it was she that kept insisting we go for runs. Even on days when we didn't have time, we would run down to the sea and turn at the edge of the water before running home again.

If it was hot, or Miranda seemed particularly down, I would chase her down the beach, pick her up as we got to the edge of the water, and keep running into the sea as she would squeal and giggle in my ear. Then we would run back home, sopping wet but happy.

I think the reason her parents didn't have a problem with us hanging out that much was that they saw how her mood was lighter when she had spent time with me. They could see she needed to be away from the cancer at home.

Still, they must have worried about us and all our hormones. And they would have been right to worry. I was a year and a half older than Miranda, and she was *hot*.

Really hot.

We became an item when Miranda turned 13. I was still 14 then, and at that point we were happy to hold hands and kiss. We stuck to the rules set out by our youth leaders – and though I can see why they talked to us about boundaries in relationships, I also wonder what on earth they were thinking. Considering the level of power they held in our lives at the time, one might think they could have been more careful to invite us into conversation – instead of setting down a bunch of rules none of us were that committed to keeping in the long run. Even so, we did stick to their rules for a few years.

As we grew older, though, we both found it harder to keep our hands off each other, and we were both starting to question a whole heap of the rest of the things they were telling us at church.

By the time I started uni, we weren't far off sleeping together. If we had still cared about what God thought at that time, the rules and the resulting guilt from breaking them *might* have been a big enough deterrent.

I doubt it, though.

Keeping our hands within the boundaries had become increasingly difficult. And seeing as we'd had plenty of conversations by then about how we were coming to the conclusion that God was actually not somebody we wanted much of a relationship with, we weren't all that affected by the guilt involved with breaking the rules. Particularly, the idea of how God appeared to enjoy inflicting all kinds of hardship and pain on us in order to *grow our character* was disturbing to us both.

No, breaking the rules wasn't a deterrent, but it was important to me that we only did what we were both comfortable with. I never wanted to pressure Miranda in any way, especially as I knew she had a load of crap going on at home.

It wasn't until my second year of uni – when I had moved out of my parents' house and in with Nick and Michael – that we actually slept together.

By then, Lisa was finished with her chemo, and had been told the cancer was gone. She was free.

And, as we all breathed a big sigh of relief, Miranda turned seventeen and I moved into the new flat. I decided that, when the opportunity next presented itself, we should hold off so we could talk about it. I didn't want our first time to be something that *just happened*. We had waited a long time and I wanted it to be special.

Talking led to Miranda going for an appointment at the Family Planning clinic, where she got birth control pills and condoms. Then, we decided on a date when we knew Michael and Nick would both be away. After all the planning and anticipation that went into it all, we both had high hopes for the evening.

Way too high hopes.

But even though our first time was terrible in many ways, it was also special. And things got better as time went on.

***

Miranda

When Mum was diagnosed with cancer, it felt like the world fell out from under my feet, and though we got through it one step at a time, I spent the whole year worrying. I worried about Mum dying or reacting negatively to the chemo, and about Dad starting to drink again.

Any peace I had felt when Dad went to rehab and came home in recovery dissipated.

Karen saw that I was worried and kept telling me God was in control and I didn't need to worry, giving me Bible verses and telling me she was praying for us.

And as thankful I was for all Karen did for us, her words also frustrated me.

If God really was in control, it was within his power to fix Mum, and help Dad stay sober and dependable. Then why didn't he fix things? Did he want us to suffer? Was he sitting on a cloud laughing as we went through this hell?

If so, he wasn't someone I wanted to have anything to do with.

Or, if our suffering wasn't for his enjoyment, then was he making us go through this in order to show us that we could depend on him?

If so, how very insecure of him.

Or, did he make us go through this suffering in order to grow our characters? Or so we would have an amazing testimony of his faithfulness at the end?

If so, his plan was flawed and failing. My character wasn't getting any better. And if we got through the whole ordeal, then I would thank the doctors who had treated Mum, not God.

Though Jack switched off or changed the subject every time I tried to talk about how I was feeling, hanging out with him did help take my mind off things.

We explored parts of Edinburgh I hadn't known existed, started running, and hung out with his friends from uni.

And we made out.

A lot.

I would have slept with him a lot earlier, but though I knew he was eager to be with me too, he was a lot more principled than I was, and kept us from going there for a long time. He didn't want us to sleep together whilst Mum was sick, because he wanted to be sure I didn't sleep with him because I was feeling upset about something.

Mum finished her chemo about nine months after her initial diagnosis, and then we spent the summer holding our breath, before receiving the news that the cancer was gone, and she was in the clear. Finally, we could relax, and life could go back to normal.

By then, Jack, Nick and Michael had moved into a flat closer to the university and were about to start their second year at uni. I had just started my last year of high school.

Jack and I planned the evening we were going to make love for weeks before it happened.

I was on the pill, and we also had condoms, because you couldn't be too safe, right?

We told my parents I was going on a youth group trip.

Then Jack took me out for dinner, and afterwards we went back to the flat he shared with Nick and Michael, who were both in North America for a few weeks before their school year started.

Jack had cleaned the flat, and there were rose petals scattered across the bed.

I smiled when I saw them, and he blushed and rolled his eyes.

'So...' He closed the bedroom door behind us. He seemed nervous. 'I know we said we would make love tonight, but we don't need to do anything you don't want to do.'

My smile grew. 'Uh-huh.' I grabbed his belt and stepped up close to him, looking into his eyes. I ran my hands up his strong chest and behind his neck. 'It's ok. It's just us. Let's just be together and see where things go.' I pulled his head down and kissed him gently before nipping his upper lip.

Soon we were on the bed, and clothes were coming off.

Afterwards, as I lay with his arm wrapped around me, and my head rested on his chest, I wondered if there could be anything better than being together with the person you loved.

Chapter 16

PRESENT
Miranda

Jack had, predictably, been disappointed when I had told him I hadn't changed my mind about the fling ending when we landed back home in Edinburgh. He told me he was thankful for the time I had given him and spent the remainder of the flight from Helsinki to Edinburgh with his arm wrapped around me as I pretended to sleep.

I couldn't *actually* sleep – I was enjoying being close to him too much and wanted to soak up the last few hours of him before we landed, and I had to return to reality. But I was worried that Jack would try to convince me to change my mind if I appeared to be awake, hence the pretending to sleep.

Whilst I hadn't changed my mind about wanting a long-term relationship with Jack, I knew I would miss the companionship and excitement that came with this type of relationship. I would miss feeling close to somebody.

All this did give me pause, and I wondered if my determination never to have a long-term committed relationship was realistic. I knew a relationship with *Jack* was out of the question – that had been established a long time ago – but maybe I could find somebody a little safer? Someone I could live a nice enough life with, and have all the benefits of a relationship, but without the risk of falling in love or, God forbid, having children.

I shivered as Jack stroked his hand over my arm.

A few minutes later, we started the descent, and I had to fake wake up before putting my seat belt back on. I glanced at Jack, who was smirking knowingly at me.

'Nice nap?'

I gave an embarrassed laugh as I stretched my arms over my head. '*So* nice.'

He smiled wryly. 'Come here. We still have ten minutes before we're on Scottish ground again.'

I leaned close, and he wrapped his hands around my neck, thumbs stroking my cheeks, and fingers under my ears – much like the first time he kissed me properly on the way to Hong Kong.

He took a deep breath. 'I won't push, Miranda, but the offer to keep going like this will always stand.'

My eyes flew to his. 'Jack…'

His eyes were steady and determined. 'There will never be anyone other than you for me.'

'Don't say that. You'll find a nice girl to marry some day and have lots of little adventurous children with messy blonde hair and gorgeous blue eyes.'

His eyes narrowed. 'Are you done? 'Cause I'm going to kiss you now.'

I gulped and nodded.

Leaning in, he kissed me as though his life depended on it, pouring himself into every bit of it.

And I couldn't help but reciprocate.

Whilst I hadn't allowed myself any wistful dreams of *what if*, I was uncomfortably aware of how right it felt to be with Jack.

Later, I told myself I got so involved because of our history, but I knew it was more than that.

I knew I would always love Jack.

Love just wasn't enough to base a long-term relationship on.

Chapter 17

PAST
Miranda

When Mum finally got the all clear, we all took a deep breath and thought we could relax. Life could go back to normal again. After the summer of not being in treatment, she was starting to look healthier again, and her hair had started to grow back.

I came home late one night, a few days after getting the test results, and found Mum sitting alone in the living room. Dad still hadn't come home. She had texted him and left messages on his cell phone, but so far, she hadn't had any reply.

We later found out Dad had met an old friend at the bus stop after work, and when he told him about Mum's recovery, the friend wanted to take him out to celebrate.

And that was that.

Dad couldn't stop after one drink, and he couldn't handle the shame of coming home drunk. So, he stayed away for ten days. When he finally came home, he found out he had lost his internship at the mechanic because he hadn't shown up for ages. With Mum back at work and all the extra time on his hands, it wasn't long before it happened again.

And again.

The relief and celebration of Mum being cancer free turned sour, and now coming home either meant Dad was home and hung over, or he was out drinking. Money started being tight as Dad spent what money there was on alcohol, and I knew it wouldn't be long before things would start going missing.

It became clear things weren't going to change.

I came home one day and found Mum with John and Karen in the kitchen. Mum wiped her hands across her face as I came in.

'Hi Miranda.' Karen stood up. 'Cup of tea?'

'Sure.' I set down my backpack. 'I'll make it.'

When Mum had been in treatment, I had cut out caffeine – I was already stressed enough – and had started drinking herbal teas instead. I found a camomile tea I liked and poured hot water over the teabag as I took a deep breath. I knew what was coming, and still I cried as Mum told me.

Dad moved out a week later. John had found him a little flat in Leith, and we got him some things to make it nice. Nobody was happy, but we could all see that things weren't working any more. Dad needed time to sort himself out, and I hoped this would help. Mum still cooked for him. She would take his meals over once a week and clean his flat. I wanted to go with her, but she kept asking me to wait. Give Dad a bit more time.

I didn't see him for nine months. I missed the twinkle in his eyes, the outlandish ideas he would come up with, and the atmosphere he brought when he was himself. He could always coax a smile out of Mum, find time to dance her round the kitchen, or play us a tune on the piano. And now that he wasn't there to do those things, the house felt cold and lonely.

I next saw him at my high school leavers' ceremony. Mum had told me he had been sober for a couple of months by then, and he was seeing John every week again. Still, he had stayed away from our house, and I wasn't sure why. Mum seemed to think he wanted to be sure he wouldn't relapse before coming back, and maybe that was true.

It felt like he had abandoned us, though.

But he came to the leavers' ceremony, and I felt relief over him being there – as well as shame at how insecure and obviously out of place he seemed. He had made an effort to look tidy, but it was clear to anyone looking that he was an addict. His hair was long again, his clothes were too big, and he smelled of cigarettes.

But he was clean and sober, and I chose to focus on that.

After that, he started coming round more regularly. He still didn't move home – and though part of me wanted us to be a family again, I also didn't want the drama of not knowing what it would be like when I came home at the end of the day.

***

I started studying business at Edinburgh University after the summer, and that's when I met Sophia. Sophia did the marketing track of the business degree program, but we had many classes together, especially in the first year, and ended up hanging out a fair bit.

Julia was doing teacher training, so we didn't see as much of her during the day, but at night we would all hang out together, and we all went to family dinners at the Reid's house on Sundays.

Family dinners had always been a thing at the Reid house, and there were always more people there than their family consisted of, and more food than anyone could eat. My family was always invited, and there was often a scattering of random people there as well. When Jack started university, Nick and Michael started coming along, and after meeting Sophia, we started bringing her along, as well.

After dinner, Karen would pack the leftovers into lunch boxes, and anyone that wanted them could take them home. I had been too embarrassed to take food home for a long time, but after watching Michael and Nick go home with lunch boxes, I started taking them too.

It didn't feel like charity as much as it felt like Karen being thoughtful and caring.

During that first year of uni, I lived at home, but I wasn't home much. Mum was still a shell of who she used to be, and I found I needed to be away from the constant reminders of how messed up our family was.

Instead, I focussed on school, and on Jack, and on hanging out with my friends. I think everyone knew my Dad was an alcoholic, but we didn't talk about it, and I was thankful for that.

After his first year at uni, Jack got an internship in Hong Kong for his summer breaks, and I spent summers waitressing at a cafe in town. Sophia spent her summers in Cumbria, staying with her parents, and Julia travelled, visiting Jack and going on summer mission trips for a few weeks. I worked as many hours as I could, trying to keep busy to avoid the feelings of loneliness, and to save up money to move out of the house.

The summer between my first and second year at uni was difficult, and I was thrilled when Julia finally came home so I had somebody to hang out with. She worked at the same cafe for the month of August when the Festival Fringe was on, and we were run off our feet with all the tourists in town for the festival.

By the time uni started again, I started to look for a flat, and I asked Julia and Sophia if they wanted to move in with me. They were both open to the idea, but a few weeks after we started looking, everything changed.

Again.

***

Jack

Spending the summers between my years of uni doing an internship in Hong Kong was amazing. I loved the city, and the atmosphere at the company I interned for was great. They started me off gently, but I got to work on interesting projects, and I loved the challenge. Dressing in a suit every day made me feel like I was doing the adult thing, and that sparked a whole bunch of new thoughts for me.

One of the only things I didn't like about Hong Kong was that Miranda wasn't there. The time difference made it difficult to have regular conversations, so our communication mainly consisted of a long thread of messages about how we missed each other. I sent her pictures of landmarks I went to, and she told me about her customers at the café.

As time went on, it became clearer and clearer that I didn't want to spend my life away from her. I wanted to be with her, and I wanted her to be with me.

At the end of the summer when I came back home, about to go into my last year of uni, I came back with a plan, and spent the next few weeks trying to set it all into motion. I spoke with Lisa – not to get permission, but because it seemed important that she wasn't blindsided – and tried (unsuccessfully) to get hold of Jimmy.

Then I went ring shopping.

I didn't have much money, as the internship had only covered the living costs involved with being in Hong Kong, but I found a gold ring with a solitaire that I thought Miranda would like. I paid for it out of my very small savings account.

It was early October by the time I took Miranda to a restaurant in Portobello, and then for a late walk on the beach. I wasn't nervous – I knew there would never be anyone for me other than Miranda, and I was certain she felt the same; we had both told each other that for years.

Instead, I felt fortunate to be with her again. Fortunate to have her glittering eyes look at me as we walked along the beach and shared about our day.

But the little box did seem to be burning a hole in my pocket.

'You know you didn't have to take me out for a meal tonight in order to get laid, right?' She had her arm wrapped around me as we walked along the beach. 'You don't have to spend money on seducing me – I'm pretty much a sure thing.' She gave me a teasing smile.

'Who says I'm trying to seduce you?' I grabbed her and lifted her into my arms. 'Maybe I was setting you up for a swim in the sea?'

'I don't think so.' She laughed nervously and started to wriggle as I started toward the water. 'Come on, Jack. Put me down!'

I laughed, but set her down carefully, keeping hold of her hand. 'No, but I did have something else in mind.'

'Oh?' She pushed some hair behind her ear.

I nodded. 'I've been thinking that this arrangement we've got of living separately isn't working for me anymore. Being away from you this summer was torture, but so is living in the same city and knowing you're just a few minutes away, but still not with me.'

'Mhm.' Her eyes narrowed, and she tilted her head to the side in suspicion.

'And I've been thinking we need to do something about that.' I pulled the little box out of my pocket, fiddling with it to get it to open, and held it up to her. 'When I think of the future, I think of you. I love you, and you're who I want to be with for the rest of my life.' I went down on one knee. 'So, I was wondering if you'd be open to marrying me?'

Miranda took a deep breath and beamed at me as she pulled me back to my feet. 'Yes!' She slid a hand up my chin and pulled my face close. 'Yes, I want to marry you.' She pressed her lips to mine as her arms circled my neck, and my arms found her waist. 'Yes, yes, yes.' She punctuated each yes with a kiss.

I grinned, my heart growing as I looked at her. 'You sure?'

She pulled at my hair to keep me from kissing her again and gave me a stern look. 'You better not be joking right now. Show me that ring again.'

I loosened my hold on her in order to show her the ring. 'What do you think?' I cleared my throat. 'I can take it back and you can pick a different one if you don't like this one. You've got to wear it for a long time.'

She frowned at me. 'No. Don't be silly – it's beautiful.'

I took it out of the box and, finding her hand, slid it on her ring finger. It was a little bit big. 'I didn't know your size, but we can take it back to have it resized tomorrow. They said it doesn't take long.'

She curled her hand closed so the ring wouldn't slip off but kept looking at it. 'I love it.' She sighed and gazed up at me. 'And I love you.'

'I love you too.' Nuzzling her cheek, I breathed her in before kissing her soft lips again. Pulling back, I looked down into her eyes and said, 'So, I was thinking: I haven't got much money right now, but if we both work this year, we can save up and get married in the summer. What do you think?'

She nodded, her face beaming at me. 'Sounds like a plan.'

We had the ring resized the next day, and everything was fine.

In hindsight, though, the ring being too big maybe should have been a sign. We were too young – with too many issues that we hadn't figured out – to be making commitments for a lifetime.

***

Miranda

When Jack proposed, it felt like life was finally changing for the better. Even though we had been an item since I was thirteen, I still felt tingles up my spine when his eyes would find me from across the room. And feeling his hand at the small of my back whenever we went anywhere still made me feel cherished.

I had wondered if Jack would be less interested in little old me after seeing the world, and if things would be different after spending our summers apart, but those worries turned out to be unfounded. We slotted back to being Miranda and Jack – I was his, and he was mine, and that was that.

Throughout our relationship, we had barely ever fought or had disagreements. There was enough drama going on around us. Looking back, though, I wonder how healthy that was. There were things we should have talked about. Things that bothered me. Though we liked being together and would have long philosophical conversations, our conversations stayed on a theoretical level and never involved our real experiences or our feelings.

Jack didn't like talking about feelings or hard stuff, and I learned to avoid bringing things up by going for long runs or distracting myself in other ways. But there were things I would have liked to have been able to talk to him about without being worried that he would try to shut me down or make light of the difficult feelings I was having. I still struggled with anxiety over Mum's health and over Dad's sobriety and wellbeing.

But though there were things I would have changed about our relationship, on the whole I loved being with Jack. He was constant, and caring, and wouldn't be dragged into drama when things around me fell apart. *Of course* I wanted to marry him. Being his wife had been on my future to-do-list for years, and I had filled notepads practicing signing my name as *Miranda Reid*.

After speaking to our parents, we started planning a June wedding. By June, Jack would be finished with university, and though I would have two years left to go, the school year would have ended. And when Jack was offered a job in Hong Kong to start in August that year, we decided we would go for a year. I would take a study break so we could explore the Far East together.

Consequently, apart from saving up for the wedding, we were also saving up for our big move across the world. I made a budget and it became clear that although our parents would help pay for the wedding (and we weren't planning for it to be a massive function), we still had a lot of saving up to do. I decided not to move out of Mum's house, in order to save on rent. I had kept my job at the cafe and asked for more hours, and Jack found a job as a barista in town.

Winter passed in a blur with uni, wedding planning, and our jobs taking most of our energy and time. By the time April and exam time came around, we were both exhausted but giddy with how close our adventure was starting to feel. Then Mum went for a routine check-up and was told the cancer was back.

It blindsided us completely.

Mum had emergency surgery, and they found it had spread to the breastbone. It wasn't 'just' cancer.

This time, it was terminal.

Dad, who had started coming round the house again and had been sober for almost a year, fell off the wagon and wasn't heard from for two months. By that time, we had decided to postpone the wedding. It would be too much to get married, and I wasn't going to go to Hong Kong whilst Mum was dying either. I decided to follow through with my study break, though, and would spend my time caring for Mum and working at the cafe.

As much as postponing the wedding was hard, harder still was that Jack decided to go to Hong Kong, anyway. He spent a long time deciding whether to go or to stay, but in the end a combination of him feeling useless in Edinburgh and the great job offer he had in Hong Kong made him opt to go. It was only a year, he said, and then he would come and marry me, and we could get on with our lives.

Or so we thought.

Chapter 18

PRESENT
Jack

A couple of days after we came back from China, I went to see Miranda again. After spending the last few weeks together, it was weird not to see her every day, and I missed her.

A lot.

I figured I would go over there and see if I could charm her into changing her mind. Her resistance to getting back together didn't make sense to me. She had clearly enjoyed our time in Asia, and her choice to go back to being just friends seemed contrary and… wrong. She wouldn't tell me her reasons, and I wondered what she was hiding. Or if she was just scared.

When I got there though, she had a crying Julia on her couch.

'Oh, hey Jules.' I frowned, confused at the sight of the mountain of used tissues next to her. 'What happened?'

Miranda looked at Julia. 'Do you want him to leave? I can get him to go if you want?'

I shook my head at the hope in Miranda's voice that she might have an excuse to get rid of me. She clearly knew exactly why I was there. I sighed. I would have to change tactics and play the long game instead. Pushing now would get me nowhere.

'Nah, it's ok.' Julia faced at me, tears still streaking down her face. It was painful to watch. 'Nick came back from America and broke up with me.'

Oh, crap. I ran my hands through my hair and down my face. 'Are you sure?'

'Pretty sure.' She gave me a dry look through her still very wet eyes, as if to say I was being stupid. 'He told me he wasn't cut out for relationships and he wanted to end it before it was too late.'

'The little idiot!' I shook my head and groaned as I thought of all the implications of this. 'Ah, no! Now I have to go kick his arse.'

'Wimp.' Miranda snorted.

I loved Nick as a brother, but I didn't want to fight him. He worked in construction and lifted weights. I worked in an office and might go for a run occasionally. 'Seriously? Have you seen his arms?'

'I'm sure a strong guy like you can take him.' Miranda's voice dripped with sugary sarcasm.

'Of course.' I ignored her sarcasm and gave her my most charming smile before turning serious. 'Still, I was hoping he'd straightened himself out and wasn't going to make a pig's ear out of it when he finally pulled his finger out and started going out with *my sister.*'

'Well, you were wrong,' Miranda said pointedly.

I narrowed my eyes and raised my chin.

Was that a challenge in her eyes? What else did she think I was wrong about?

Feeling more convinced she had broken things off because she was scared, I squared my shoulders. I had spent six years preparing myself to get her back. I wasn't going to let her fears win.

'I'm still here, you guys.'

Miranda turned back to Julia. 'Yes, so why didn't anyone tell us that he bought the flat?'

'I don't kn-'

'He didn't tell you?' I frowned, pushing thoughts of Miranda out of my mind and focussing again on Julia.

Nick sent me a message over a year ago, when he first bought the flat off my dad, and we talked about it then. At the time, he asked me to keep it quiet, and as I figured that had to do with him not wanting people to know that he had money, I agreed.

'You knew?! And didn't tell me?' Julia blushed with anger. She clearly took issue with being the last person know. If Julia had known Nick owned the flat, she would have been paying rent. Finding out that she was essentially squatting in what she had thought was her own apartment would have been humiliating. Especially if that piece of information came as Nick was breaking up with her.

'Yeah.' I winced and tried to downplay Nick's stupidity. 'He told me not to say anything – probably because he wanted to surprise you or something.'

'Uh-huh, and what a surprise it was.' Her dry tone said it all.

Resigned, I zipped up my jacket and pulled out my phone. 'I'll see you later,' I said, and left the house whilst scrolling through my contacts. If I had to talk with Nick about breaking up with Julia, I would need Michael there.

***

'Nick, you in there?' I waited a few minutes before the door was opened.

'Hey.' He folded his arms across his chest, and leant against the wall, giving the appearance that he was relaxed. Upon closer inspection, though, the frown on his face and the apathy in his eyes were evident. He wasn't relaxed.

He was hurting.

I pushed past him and toed off my shoes before going to get a couple of beers out of the fridge. I opened the bottles and handed Nick one where he sat on the couch. I sat down, taking a sip as I looked at him.

'You look like someone killed your puppy, man.'

'You here to insult me?' He lifted an eyebrow. 'Or beat me up?'

'Dramatic much?' I snorted. 'Look, I don't know what you're thinking, breaking up with my sister, but do you really think I could beat you up?'

He hung his head in his hands. 'Figured I'd have to give you a chance to try at least.'

I pursed my lips as I scanned him. 'Nah, you're miserable enough. No need for me to break my hand on you.'

'Glad my misery serves some purpose.'

'Yeah, well, maybe stop buying cat piss for beer and you'll start feeling better and start making better decisions.' I narrowed my eyes. 'Like *not* breaking things off with Jules.'

He ran a hand down his face, as if to cope with the exasperation he was experiencing. Then he bit out, 'Glad we could have this talk.'

'Uh-huh.' I set my Budweiser down on the table as the front door opened, and Michael came in.

'Hey.' He glanced at us as he sauntered into the kitchen to find his own beer, before sitting on the couch. 'You both ok?'

He looked like he had run over. 'Miranda texted Sophia, and Soph wouldn't leave me alone, so…' He opened his bottle. 'What did I miss?'

I nodded toward Nick. 'Nick here was just telling me about why he stupidly just broke up with Jules.'

Michael winced. 'Man…'

Nick looked from me to Michael and back, then shook his head. 'No. I'm not doing this. I've made the right decision.' He glanced at me when he heard my snort. 'Jules might be a bit upset now, and I'm sorry about that…'

'A bit upset,' I muttered.

'But she'll get over it.'

I looked at him in disbelief. 'You're such a bloody idiot.'

'Hey-' Michael tried to cut in.

'I may be an idiot.' Nick nodded. 'It's a risk I'm willing to take.'

I rolled my eyes and went to call him stupid again, when Michael sent me a look to shut me up. 'No need to call him names, Jack.'

'Yeah.' I set my empty beer on the coffee table. 'Nick, I think you've made a mistake, but I'm here for you. Let me know if you need anything.' He nodded and I slapped his shoulder as I stood up. 'I'll head on out, then.'

Michael stayed a few minutes longer, but, knowing he wouldn't be long, I waited for him in the car. A few minutes later he came out of the building, saw me, and got in.

'He's going to regret breaking up with her,' I said, as I pulled away from the curb.

Michael sighed. 'He's already regretting it, but he's too stuck in his head to do anything about it.'

'And when he finally works it all out, he's going to have to work so hard for her to trust him again. And that's if she hasn't moved on by then.'

Michael bit the inside of his cheek. 'Sounds like you know what you're talking about.'

Stopping at a red light, I looked out the window. I cleared my throat before saying, 'Yeah, well any idiot can see he's making a mistake here.'

Michael smirked. 'Sounds like you've got more insight than some, though…'

I scratched the back of my neck. He was obviously fishing. 'If you're asking how things are with Miranda, just come out and say it.'

His smirk grew into a grin. 'How are things with you and Miranda?'

'Not great,' I bit out.

'Which means you've decided you want her back, but she's not so sure?'

'Oh, she's sure alright…'

'Really?'

'Yeah, she's sure we're never, ever, ever, getting back together.' I sighed. 'Ever.'

'Smart girl.' Michael chuckled, but went quiet when I glared at him. 'So, is there a plan?'

Chapter 19

PAST

Miranda

The night before Jack left for Hong Kong, we went for a long walk on Portobello Beach.

Mum was still doing okay. She was doing chemo and her hair had fallen out again, but she was coping, and it felt like – though her diagnosis was terminal – she might live for a long time still. She kept saying, 'We all have terminal diagnoses; I'm just going to die sooner than I'd expected.'

Everything in me wanted to say *hasta la vista* to life in Edinburgh and go with Jack on an adventure. But I had made my choice to stay, and I knew it was the right choice. Even so, doing life in Edinburgh without Jack would be torture, and it took everything in me not to ask him to stay. I didn't want to *ask* him to stay, but I wished he would wait and go later.

Maybe in a year.

In a year, life would be less complicated, and I would be free to go with him.

But most of all, I wished I was enough to keep him in Scotland.

And I worried about how we would change over the next year. He would meet lots of interesting people – people without cancer-sick mothers and alcoholic fathers that were free to do what they wanted and go across the world on adventures. Maybe he would realise that, though his high school sweetheart was nice, there were so many women without crazy issues in the world, just waiting to be explored.

Part of me knew that our relationship would never be the same after this year, and that the best thing would probably be to break up. To give him the freedom he probably needed.

But I couldn't do it.

It seemed unfair that Dad would disappear into alcohol, Mum would die of cancer and Jack would leave for Hong Kong – all at the same time. Therefore, as much as I wanted Jack to be free, I also couldn't go through with giving him the ring back. I needed to keep some form of reassurance that my life wasn't falling apart completely.

Jack and I spent the evening walking along the beach, and around nine we started the walk home. We had decided I wouldn't come with him to the airport to see him off – too much drama – so this evening was goodbye.

'You know, Christmas will be here soon enough,' Jack said when he noticed my decidedly wet eyes after kissing me at my door.

I nodded. 'I know.'

'So, let's not do the cry-thing. We'll talk in a couple of days, once I've landed, and everything will be fine. We love each other, right?'

'Right, yeah.' I wiped at my eyes and gave a weak smile. 'Better make this quick then, eh.'

He shook his head. 'Always with the tears…'

'I know.' My voice was shaky, and the tears wouldn't stop. If only he knew how many tears I had spared him over the years.

'Come here.' He pulled me in for a hug, nuzzling my neck before trailing a row of kisses along my jaw and to my mouth. He nipped my bottom lip before pulling away. Chasing his mouth, I rose onto my tiptoes, and ran my hands though his hair as I pulled him toward me. He slid his hands up my sides, grabbing onto me as he deepened the kiss.

Tears forgotten all my senses were awakened.

He pulled back and smirked. 'See you later.'

Then he left me standing on my front step as he sauntered across the grass to his parents' door, whistling a silly tune as though he didn't have a care in the world. He stopped at the door and sent me an air kiss. Before the door closed behind him, he whisper-shouted, 'See you at Christmas.'

I opened the door to Mum's house and went inside. Mum was already in bed, and the house was dark, so I made a quick camomile tea and went to bed.

The next morning, Jack sent me a message.

Jack: Just about to take off. Let's go together next time. I love you. X

I saw the message before taking Mum to hospital for her chemo appointment. That day she had a bad reaction to the chemo and ended up staying in hospital overnight. Thankfully, it turned out it wasn't as serious as we had first thought.

But I knew then I had made the right decision to stay with her, instead of getting on an airplane with Jack.

***

Jack video-called me a few days later. He showed me his flat, which was beautiful, and told me everything was going well thus far. The team he would be working with appeared to be a good fit – at least as far as he could tell at that point – and he seemed excited to be there. Before finishing the call, he asked how things were at home.

I told him briefly about Mum's hospital stay, but I didn't want to bring him down, so I kept things breezy. He was still jet-lagged, and I noticed how he struggled to pay attention as I talked.

The next time we spoke, he told me about how he had spent his weekend doing some sightseeing. He said he missed me.

I missed him, too, but I had been kept busy after Mum's hospital visit. As soon as I mentioned Mum, though, he changed the subject, and I understood why. I didn't want to be the depressing girlfriend back home that he was shackled to. Instead, I told him a customer story and we had a laugh.

For the next three weeks we had another couple of video calls, and otherwise we sent each other messages with pictures. He sent me pictures of interesting new foods he had tried, and I sent him pictures of his favourite Scottish things, like ale, fish and chips, oatcakes, and me on Portobello beach.

Jack living away was weird, but I was getting used to it, and looked forward to the messages and calls. So, when I got an email quite out of the blue, I was shocked as I realised the email wasn't a love note. Instead, he was breaking up with me.

Miranda,

After thinking more about our relationship, I've come to the conclusion that I am not ready to be in such a serious relationship at this point. I need time to grow up and to become the person I want to be, and this seems like a good

time for it. For that reason, I think it is best if we call things off now.

I realise this will be rather unexpected for you, and I am sorry for any hurt I am causing. Know you will always be precious to me, and whatever happens, I'll always be your friend.

Jack.

I read the email over and over again, trying to make sense of it. It was so stilted, and not at all in line with the messages he had been sending a couple of days earlier that week where he told me how much he missed me and that he was thinking of coming home.

I had told him he would soon get used to Hong Kong, and to stick things out because he wasn't a quitter. I hadn't heard from him since, and I guessed he had taken my message to heart.

Just not in the way I had meant.

I floundered for several days as I tried to process it all before writing an email to send back. I didn't know what to write and everything ached as I deleted length drafts. When I finally sent my reply, I felt it held all I had to say.

Jack,

Though I admit I am disappointed, I understand and wish you all the best.

Miranda.

Then I took off my ring. I wasn't sure what I was meant to do with it. Should I give it back?

Everything in me hurt and I wished for what could have been. Still, a little part of me held on to the hope that Jack would come back and tell me this was all just a bad dream. That part of me found a long necklace, put the ring on it, and wore it underneath my clothes from then on.

***

After replying to Jack, I was a mess.

I felt anxious and sad throughout the day. I would wake up in the morning wondering why my pillow was damp. Then everything would come back to me, and I would feel a wave of nausea trying to get me to go back to sleep. Maybe if I slept more, I could wake up to a different reality?

My left hand felt too light, like it was missing something, and my thumb would trace the place where the ring used to be.

I had to get up to take care of Mum and go to work, though, so I battled through the nausea, putting it down to not eating well enough. I had no appetite left.

After Mum had seen me be sick twice in one week, she watched me sip my ginger tea from across the kitchen table and said, 'It's probably time you took a pregnancy test, isn't it?'

The tea went down the wrong tube, causing my eyes to water. 'What?' I spluttered when I could talk again.

She said nothing but gave me a weak smile.

Panicked, I got up to get my piece of bread out of the toaster. I spread butter on it as I did the maths and realised Mum might have a point. I spent the day at work obsessing about it. What would I do if I was pregnant? How would I tell Jack? After getting his email, this would seem like a manipulative ploy to keep him attached to me. I wanted him back, but I didn't want him to come back out of obligation. Still, I couldn't exactly hide a pregnancy from him. Not when his family lived right next door.

Touching the ring through my clothes, I tried to ground myself – I was borrowing trouble now. Better wait to worry about anything until after I had taken a test. Besides, I probably wasn't pregnant – it was probably just a bug.

I picked up a test kit after work that day and peed on the stick after Mum was in bed. Laying the stick on the sink, I waited the two minutes with my heart in my throat. My skin was clammy when I looked to see the result.

Positive.

Positive??

My heart skipped a beat, even as my mind wondered how this could be *positive*. This was *not* how things were meant to go. I was supposed to be happily married in Hong Kong, and any potential children were to wait until after I had finished my degree and settled nicely into a job.

Could it be a false positive? That happened, right? The tests were meant to be carried out in the morning, so that was probably the reason it showed a positive result. Good job I had bought two test kits. I would take another in the morning.

And somehow, despite it all, it *felt* positive.

Like maybe there were still good things in life.

Like maybe God wasn't just out to get me.

I put a hand to my tummy. 'Hello?' I whispered. 'Is someone in there?'

I didn't sleep well that night; there were too many thoughts and feelings running through my mind. And when I finally did sleep, I had weird dreams about telling Jack about the baby, only to find he wanted me to have an abortion.

Waking up the next morning, I wasn't sure what was up or down. The nausea was overwhelming, and I was exhausted. But as I peed on the stick again, I knew that if I was pregnant, then I was keeping it. My body, my choice, right?

The test confirmed the previous result. I was definitely pregnant.

Two weeks later, I had my first midwife appointment and an initial scan. My periods had been so irregular since Mum got sick that I had overestimated how far along I was, and the first scan ended up being at nine weeks. The picture showed a little bean, just over two centimetres long. My determination to keep the baby grew as I watched the ultrasound technician explain what was what. Up until that point, I had known I was pregnant, and I certainly was sick enough to prove it, but seeing the little bean on the monitor made it *feel* real.

On my way home from the hospital, I stopped at a yarn shop in town and bought some soft merino wool. Then I spent the evening showing Mum the ultrasound picture and searching for knitting patterns online. Though Mum worried about me and the baby, she saw the baby as a blessing. We both found some patterns to knit and started knitting that evening.

Mum looked like she was dying to ask, but somehow, we avoided speaking about Jack. Still, he was constantly on my mind. I kept touching the ring through my clothes, hoping despite everything that things would be alright.

I had to find a way to tell him about the baby and, seeing as he had broken up with me via email, I figured maybe writing him an email would be best. I could send him a copy of the ultrasound picture so he would understand I wasn't just making the whole thing up. Still, I realised this wouldn't be the email he was hoping to get.

I wrote three drafts, which I deleted before going to bed. Maybe the words would come to me if I got some sleep first.

Four days later, I still hadn't sent him the email. I was sitting at the breakfast table nibbling at a rich tea biscuit and slowly sipping my ginger tea, when I felt Mum look at me across the table. She was eating a piece of toast with her tea.

'Did you tell him yet?'

I pushed my fingers through my hair and scrunched my face. 'Not yet.'

'I guess you've got a few weeks before you start showing.' She shrugged. 'I don't see it getting any easier, though.'

I sighed. 'No. I'll tell him tonight.'

Mum nodded.

It was later that day when my stomach started cramping and bleeding. Terrified, I rang the midwife from the staff bathroom at work, and she arranged for an ambulance to come pick me up. By the time we got to hospital, though, there was nothing they could do to save the baby. They talked me through my options, and I was sent home later that afternoon.

Mum and I were quiet as we drove home. There was nothing to say.

I spent the night and next few days bleeding and cramping, and it was awful. In every way.

Mum kept looking at me with sad eyes, full of empathy. As kind and supportive as she was trying to be, though, I knew her grief wasn't helping her health. She still had chemo to do, and I wanted us both to spend her last few months enjoying life instead of grieving. So, telling myself it was for Mum's sake, I decided to push my grief on the future.

We put away our knitting, and spent the next few months watching films Mum liked. We probably watched *Grease* fifteen times and *Wedding Date* about twenty. On days she could handle it, I would put on Carol King or Queen and we would dance in the kitchen as I cooked.

I say *we*, but Mum didn't do much dancing.

Or eating.

Instead, she sat on a chair and watched me.

Though she knew I was putting on a brave face, she never pushed me or questioned me. She let me escape, and she let me use her as an excuse not to have to wade through all the grief I was feeling. Maybe it would have been better for me to face reality, but right then that was all I could handle. Later – once Mum was dead – the memories of those times reminded me that though life sometimes sucked, there was goodness to be found.

And if there was any silver lining to all the grief I was experiencing, at least now I wouldn't have to tell Jack he was going to be a dad.

I wouldn't have to be the one to close the door on his adventures and trap him into growing up.

Chapter 20

PRESENT
Miranda

A couple weeks later, our fling was a thing of the past and we had established a new routine. Jack would come over most nights after work to hang out as friends would, whilst Julia and I sewed little bags for the period cups (as we didn't have money to pay for packaging).

Julia had moved in after her breakup with Nick. She kept apologising and told me she was looking for somewhere else to live, but I was happy she was there. It made it easier not to have any conversations with Jack about the past. Instead, we could focus on talking about Project Cup, and on helping Julia keep her mind off Nick.

One Friday night in late November, Julia and I were sewing the last bags, and Sophia sat with her laptop updating the Project Cup website and social media.

The following week, we would be selling period cups at the Edinburgh Christmas Market, where we would time-share a market stall with another company as an experiment. Our period cups didn't exactly scream Christmas, but we wanted to see what the market was like, and we would try to sell as many cups as we could. We hoped they would fund a Kenyan high school's project to give period cups to all the girls at the school after Christmas.

Jack sat at the piano, fiddling with the keys and pulling silly tunes out of it. It reminded me of how Dad would play jazz or Beatles songs on the piano when he used to live with us. Neither of them had taken lessons, but they both had an ear for it, and though I couldn't play – or sing for that matter – listening to Jack play piano made sewing bags for the period cups a little less tedious.

I finished pulling a drawstring through the top of a bag and stood up to stretch. Hunching over like this for hours made me thankful I had a yoga class I could go to tomorrow. 'Does anyone want a cup of tea?' I asked.

'I'll make them.' Jack stood up and took orders.

When he came back, I was working on another bag, so he set the tea down on the table next to me. 'I meant to ask: your dad was over when I came home from work today. How's he doing?' he asked.

I hadn't seen Dad since the morning of the family dinner at the Reids', which wasn't a good sign. When he was sober, I saw him often, but when he was drinking, I could go months without seeing him. And as he didn't have a phone, it was hard to get in touch with him. I worried about him, but there was nothing I could do to make him stop drinking.

I frowned. 'Was he drunk?'

Jack hesitated, clearing his throat before he answered. 'I wouldn't say he was *drunk* drunk.'

Julia looked up. 'When did he start drinking again?'

'Oh, he's been at it for a few months now.'

'I'm sorry Mir. That sucks.' Julia reached out to stroke my arm.

I shrugged. 'It's good he went to see John. I should talk to him about seeing if we can get Dad some help again.'

As much as I appreciated her caring about me, I never knew how to respond to people's caring. Dad had been this way for as long as I could remember, and whilst I found his alcoholism difficult to deal with, sometimes it felt as though *all* other people saw in Dad was his alcoholism. And, largely, they tended to think he was an alcoholic because he chose to be one.

I didn't think so. Not anymore. For me, the alcoholism didn't seem to have much to do with choice. Instead, I saw it as an illness. Did Dad have free will, and could he stop drinking?

Yes.

For months at a time, he was able to stay away from the bottle, and during those times he was an incredible person. He was kind and had a way of bringing peace to all kinds of situations.

But then something would happen, and he would have a drink. And when other people would stop drinking, he couldn't. Instead of stopping, he kept drinking for months, unable to get away from the clutches of the alcohol. There was no reasoning with him to get him to stop. And instead of coming round to play the piano and talk about *War and Peace* or whatever other literature he was reading, shame would keep him away. For months.

To me, my dad's alcoholism meant he was unreliable. And whilst I would always love him, I knew I couldn't trust him. Not because he didn't want to be trustworthy, but because he was ill.

The conversation around me turned to something different, and I nodded along though I wouldn't have been able to tell you what we talked about. Instead, I thought about Dad. I wondered how he was doing and what it would take to get him help this time. Tiredness seeped into my bones and I yawned.

Julia must have seen me, or maybe she was tired, too, because it wasn't long before she started putting things away and told Jack and Sophia it was time to call it a night.

Thankful not to have to kick people out, I sent her a tired smile as Sophia packed up her laptop and she and Jack left.

Exhausted, I went to bed, hoping I would feel better in the morning.

I woke up when I heard the front door close, and realised Julia had left. I turned over onto my other side and tried to go back to sleep, but, though I was tired enough, sleep wouldn't come. Instead I just lay there feeling all the feelings.

All the miserable feelings.

Triggered by the thoughts of my Dad the previous evening, deep sadness had wrapped itself around me like a cloud, and I was thankful it was a Saturday and I had nothing pressing on my schedule that day.

During the year when Jack broke up with me, I had the miscarriage, and then my Mum died from cancer, I spent a good few months in a fog of grief. As time passed and life went on, the fog had slowly lifted, and now it had been a while since it had last descended over me. But today, there was no escaping its clutches.

Jack breaking off our engagement had broken my heart. He was it for me, and the prospect of facing life without him was… hard. Still, I put on a good face to his family, and only cried in the shower or when I went for runs in the rain on the beach.

Then, when I miscarried, nobody apart from Mum knew about the pregnancy. Telling Julia or John and Karen then would have only made them tell Jack, and I saw no point in him knowing at that stage. There was nothing he could do about it and telling him would just cause him grief. Instead, I pushed my grief to the side and did my best to distract myself with caring for Mum. Still, once in a while, I would have one of those black dog days – days where nothing felt right, and all I wanted to do was curl up in a ball and sleep my feelings away.

And this day was one of those days. This day, there was nothing I would rather do than hide from the world. I didn't want to see anyone or do anything. I didn't want to have to stand up. Wrapped up in the fog of sadness, all I could cope with was the idea of lying underneath my duvet.

So, when Jack opened my front door and called out for me, I stayed where I was.

Undeterred by the lack of reply, he came in the house. 'Miranda? You here?' When he came to my bedroom door, he knocked. 'Are you decent?'

I sighed. 'Uh-huh.'

He pushed the door open, gave me a once-over, and came in. 'Oh, Mir...' He sat down at the foot of my bed.

Unsure of what he was doing, I looked at him. If I had ever shown him any signs of not being happy back in the days when we were dating, he had tended to respond by ignoring the feelings or just disappearing for a few hours, until I was back to being my usual self again. Expecting him to do the same now, I was surprised when he instead reached out to stroke my feet over the duvet.

He sat there, just stroking my feet for twenty minutes before lying down on top of the blankets next to me. Making a space for me to lie on his arm, he motioned for me to snuggle in, and though our level of relationship no longer technically allowed for physical contact like that, I couldn't help myself. Still under the duvet, I snuggled up to him and he wrapped his arm around me. I breathed in his familiar scent, and felt his heart beat steadily as I lay there quietly with my head on his chest.

Thinking of my dad the previous evening had brought back all the reasons for why I never wanted to be married to Jack. When he broke off our engagement all those years ago, he told me he couldn't cope with being in a relationship right then, and that we both needed time to grow up before either of us was ready for marriage. He had been right: we were young, and life was crazy. But *I* had been ready to get married. All I wanted was to be Jack's wife, because I knew he would never leave me like Dad had.

Only, I had been wrong.

Jack had left me at the point where things in my life were the hardest they had ever been, just like my dad had done over and over again. And when Jack left me, it wasn't because he had an illness like alcoholism. No, Jack left me because he *chose* to. And, though I knew Jack loved me, I would never again be able to trust that he wouldn't turn around one day and leave me.

If there was one thing Dad had taught me, it was that love isn't enough to keep a relationship going. There also needs to be consistency and trust. And when you love somebody but can't trust them, the hurt you experience over and over again when they are unable to live up to what they have promised soon becomes too much.

It was one thing to have a dad like that – I had no choice or power there. But I wasn't going to have the same kind of relationship with a husband. And, though I had known that in my head for many years, it was only now, lying as I was on his arm, that I finally let myself feel the pain of it. Overwhelmed with grief, I couldn't keep my tears in, and though I tried to do the silent cry, it wasn't long before I was sobbing.

He hugged me closer and let me cry.

When I was finally out of tears, he said, 'Do you want to tell me what's going on?'

How could I tell him I was grieving the end of our relationship? I couldn't.

I shook my head. 'I'm sorry.' Wiping my face on my sleeves, I sat up and saw the wet stain on his shirt. 'I'm sorry about your shirt.'

His eyes were steady as he lifted his head and met mine. 'Don't be sorry about your feelings around me ever again.' Laying his head back on the pillow, he sighed. 'Do you know why I broke up with you back then?'

Startled, I froze. How did he know I had been thinking about our breakup?

'No?' I hesitated. 'I think your email said something about not being ready to get married?'

He rubbed his face and sat up, leaning against the headboard. 'Yeah, I wasn't ready. But do you know how I knew I wasn't ready?'

I shook my head.

'I knew because if I'd been ready, I wouldn't have gone to the other side of the world just so I wouldn't have to watch you face the pain of your mum dying.'

Chapter 21

Jack

When I was eleven, my sister Josie died in a traffic accident during a family holiday in the Trossachs, on the West Coast of Scotland.

Josie was four, and though she was much younger than me, she was my little Josie Posie. She lit up the room and seemed to have an endless supply of energy – until it was suddenly gone, and she would curl up wherever she was and have a nap. She could fall asleep anywhere, and despite her short life, we had lots of pictures of her asleep over her dinner, or on the floor, or in someone's arms.

When awake, she would follow Julia and me around, and we often got her to do things like steal food from the kitchen cupboards for us. Mum knew what was happening, but she hardly ever got us into trouble for it.

Then Josie died, and the grief was all-consuming. For a long time, her absence was felt as strongly as her presence used to be. And, as time went on, her absence changed us all.

Julia went from being full of life to pretending to be full of life. It was as though she thought she somehow had to make up for Josie being dead.

Mum fell apart for a few months, and then she found Jesus. She had always been a Christian, but now things went to another level, and she got involved with everything at church.

Dad withdrew inside himself for a long time, and he too threw himself on God, although his style was less evangelical and more contemplative.

Mum took comfort in how Josie's death, whilst shocking to us, wasn't a surprise to God. But for me, knowing God had known Josie would die – possibly even orchestrating her death – was no comfort.

As I grew older, this concept bothered me more and more, and I spent many hours talking to Miranda about it. She too had found it increasingly difficult to deal with the thought that God predestined people to go through awful experiences.

If God was so loving and he had the power to stop the suffering in the world, why wouldn't he? Why would he instead predestine people to go through pain and hardships?

The more we thought about it, the clearer our conclusion became: God was not loving at all. And neither of us wanted anything to do with him or his kind of *love*.

Losing Josie was the worst thing I had ever experienced, and just as bad was seeing how we as a family coped with the pain. As I watched Mum and Dad and Julia go through their grief, I saw how it changed them, and I would have given anything to be able to take away their pain.

Their despair emphasised how helpless I was and, in order to cope with feeling so utterly powerless, I started resenting their pain. The more they hurt, the more frustrated and powerless I would feel, and as a result I became less and less able to handle other people's pain.

Even other people's physical pain became too much for me. I found it so hard to deal with other people's suffering that I would start an argument or make insensitive comments instead of showing compassion. I might tell someone they needed to toughen up or ask why they didn't fix their problems instead of crying about them. And I would mock people that were struggling, calling them weak for letting things get to them.

So, when Miranda's mum, Lisa, was diagnosed with cancer *again*, I didn't handle it well. I realised Miranda needed somebody to lean on, but it couldn't be me. I tried to help her with practical things, and I would remind her to keep positive, but I knew that wasn't what she really needed.

I just couldn't give her more.

Knowing I couldn't take Lisa's illness away was physically painful to me, and I chose to focus on *anything* other than that.

I threw myself into uni – getting the best grades I ever had – and got a part time job in order that I would have less time to spend with Miranda. I told her I got the job so we could pay for our wedding, but I already knew the wedding wasn't going to happen. And when we decided to postpone the wedding, I told her we would put the money toward our Hong Kong adventure, even as I knew she wouldn't be coming to Hong Kong with me – though she didn't know that yet.

When she, understandably, decided to stay home and care for Lisa, my choice was to either stay in Edinburgh with Miranda or go to Hong Kong and be free.

I picked Hong Kong.

Not because I didn't *want* to be with Miranda, but because I *couldn't.* The pain of not being able to take her pain away was killing me. Every time I saw her, I spent the time trying to make sure she had a good time, but I knew it was like trying to repair a torn-off limb with a band-aid.

'And that's why I broke up with you.'

'Oh, Jacky…' The tears were back in her eyes, and I mentally kicked myself for putting them back there when she had just finished crying.

'When I was in Hong Kong though, I decided it was time I sorted myself out. I couldn't keep running from pain like that, you know?'

She nodded, wiping at her cheeks with her sleeves.

'I started seeing a psychologist out there. And, though it was a long process, I started making some progress.'

'How long were you in therapy?'

I took a deep breath. 'A long time.' I shrugged. 'That's why I stayed out there so long. I didn't want to come back until I knew I'd be able to handle my emotions.'

She sighed. 'Why didn't you tell me?'

'What would I have said? I didn't even know what my problem was until I started counselling.'

'I don't know.'

'Yeah.' I shook my head. 'I'm sorry I was a jerk. I realise I broke up with you when you probably most needed somebody to lean on.'

The tears kept filling her eyes, and they were in mine, too, now. She leaned forward and reached for my face, where she wiped at my tears.

'It's ok, Jack.' She nodded. 'It's ok.'

Chapter 22

Past

Miranda

Despite the awkwardness of Jack breaking up with me, I still hung out with Julia. She and Sophia were sharing Jack's former flat in town. They were both busy with university, so we didn't hang out as much as we used to, but we still had Sunday lunch at the Reids' and an active thread on Messenger. With Julia being Jack's sister, I couldn't tell her about the miscarriage. Instead, everyone thought I was sad because of the breakup and Mum's illness.

Both Julia and Sophia tried to get me to come out with them on weekends, but mostly I didn't feel up to it. Besides, I wanted to spend most of my free time with Mum, taking advantage of the time I still had with her. Julia, Sophia and I went up Arthur's Seat at the end of September, though.

When we got to the top, I found myself overwhelmed by how beautiful the sun rising over the sea was. How could there be such beauty in the world when I had just lost my baby, been broken up with, Mum was dying, and Dad was wasted somewhere?

It didn't seem right or fair.

'Men, eh.' Sophia looked out toward the sea with a sigh.

I smiled through the tears. 'Ugh.'

'No kidding.' Julia slumped against the ground. She glanced at me. 'I'm still stunned you and Jack broke up.'

I gave a dry laugh. 'As am I.'

'So, it came entirely out of the blue? No warning at all?'

I shook my head. 'Well, I didn't see any signs of it coming. And honestly, after seven years of dating, and almost marrying the guy, I didn't expect him to break up with me via email.'

'What?!' Julia's eyes looked like they were about to pop out of her head. 'He broke up with you via email?'

I nodded. 'Uh-huh.'

Julia lay back down on the ground. 'He's such an absolute pillock.'

'All men are the same, though.' Sophia shrugged. 'Totally clueless.'

'Well, as much as I'm not feeling particularly impressed with Jack right now, there are good men out there.'

She looked at me, eyebrows high. 'Oh really? Then you won't mind if we set you up on a date?'

'Ugh.' I grimaced, and my hand reached to find the ring under my clothes. 'Maybe give me a little while to recover first.' I didn't ever want to go on another date, but I didn't want to tell Sophia that. She had enough issues with men and didn't need mine added to her own.

Julia gave me a sceptical look. She had been around Jack and me for long enough and could see through my facade.

'I bet you'll need longer than *a little while*,' Sophia said. 'Did he give any reason for breaking up with you?'

'He said he'd come to realise he wasn't ready to be in such a serious relationship. He did the *it's not you it's me* thing, but it doesn't really matter. The outcome is the same, whatever reasons he might have.'

'Mum said he's already saying he's going to stay in Asia for Christmas, so at least you won't have to see him for a while.'

I nodded. Karen had told me.

I had avoided going over to the Reids' for a few weeks after the breakup. There had been too much going on for me to also have to deal with the fallout of Jack's break up with me on my other relationships. So, when Karen had come over and sought me out to clear the air between us, I had wanted to hide. She told me nothing had to change between her and me just because Jack's and my relationship was over, and she had mentioned that he wasn't coming home for Christmas. That had been a relief.

'Anyway, tell me something that isn't depressing.' I said. 'How is uni?'

Julia smiled. 'I'm starting placement in a couple of weeks, which feels a little overwhelming, but I'm trying to prepare for it.' Julia was doing her third year of teacher training to be an English teacher.

'Oh, yeah? Do you know where? Do you have to travel for it?'

'It's actually a school in Bruntsfield this time, so I can walk.'

Despite her placement being close by, Julia going into placement would mean she would be even busier than normal, and I knew I would miss her.

'We started a pretty intense statistics course just now,' Sophia said on the way down the hill. 'I know you're on a break from uni, but if you want to have a look at it, I could really use your input. You've always been better at stats than me.'

'Sure.' I was always happy to look at numbers – they made sense to me even when nothing else in life made sense. I thought everybody should be required to take a basic statistics course – it might help people understand the world better.

But most of all, I was thankful Sophia was reaching out to me. Though I wanted to make the most of my last few months with Mum, I knew I needed friendships.

Some days, the extreme exhaustion I was feeling – coupled with the sadness I felt over so many things – was overwhelming. Maybe that's why Julia and Sophia's friendship meant so much. They had a way of containing all the sad I was feeling. They were safe.

***

Dad showed up drunk a few days before Christmas.

Though I could see how he wished everything was different, a part of me wondered why he didn't just make a choice to be sober. If not for himself, then for Mum and me. If there ever was a time to man up and do the right thing – now was it. But instead, he squandered the little time he had left with Mum, lost in a bottle.

I tried speaking to Mum about it the next day. At this point, she had her breakfast in the living room, as moving around needlessly seemed like a waste of precious energy. I sat on the couch next to her, watching as she slowly ate her piece of toast. Her hands looked old, and the skin was loose and transparent. She had lost a lot of weight, even though she was taking steroids, and physically, she looked like a frail shadow of her former self.

I wondered how much longer she had left – she had already lived longer than the doctors had estimated when she was given her diagnosis.

'What was going on with Dad last night?' I asked.

She looked at me over her cup of tea, eyes narrow as she scanned my face. 'Your Dad is ill, Miranda. No amount of wishing differently will change that.'

'No, I realise that, but surely he can see that now isn't the time to be binge drinking?'

'Of course he can see that. Doesn't make a difference, though. Some things are what they are, and all we can do is pray for him. This alcoholic person isn't who he is on the inside. You know that. It's just his way of handling the pain.' She looked away. 'We've all got our ways of dealing with pain, don't we?'

I nodded, though I wasn't sure what she meant.

'I used to think like you,' she went on. 'If he can't sort himself out for himself, then couldn't he at least try for our sake? But all that will give you is bitterness. Instead, you've got to remember who he is – he'll need you to remind him later. He's a good man, your Dad is.'

Throat clogged, I could only nod. Mum looked out the window, lost in her thoughts. We sat there for a long time, neither of us talking.

I tried remembering who Dad was without the alcohol, and though I had many memories, I found it difficult. So many of my childhood memories of him were clouded by the alcoholism and by the mental health problems he had struggled with. To be fair, I had been relatively sheltered from it all, as he tended to leave when he drank.

And yet, the memories rushed through me of Dad being hung over, or a little merrier than normal, or of the times when he was slurring his words and clearly didn't have a handle on himself.

I sighed.

Mum tilted her head and gave me a thoughtful smile. 'Your Dad loves us as much as he is able to.'

I snorted. 'He obviously loves alcohol more than he loves us, so that's not saying much, is it?'

'I think of it more like the alcohol has made him its slave. He's bound there until he next is able to escape.' She smiled. 'And in the meantime, we can be resentful, or we can keep loving him – as hard as it might be – and showing him that escaping will be worth it. That life is worth living and that there is hope. Even for him.'

Chapter 23

Miranda

A couple of months later, when Mum died, people told me it was probably for the best, and at least now she didn't have to suffer any longer. I would nod and smile stiffly, while everything in me wanted to scream at how insensitive they were. I would have given anything to have her for just a few more days. Looking back, I can see that perhaps they were right. Maybe it was a relief for her to die. But at the time, as far as I could see, there was nothing *for the best* about my mum dying.

I just missed her.

Jack sent a note a couple days after she died. I read it over and over again, hoping the note would change into a sensitive, kind – even loving – note.

It didn't.

Miranda,

I don't know how to express how sorry I am about your mum. She was always such a big part of my life and it kills me to know she is no longer around to tell me off, offer unasked-for advice, or cook spaghetti. I'm sorry I wasn't around for her this year and that I'm not able to come to her funeral. Lisa always meant a lot to me, and I will miss her always.

Jack

I hadn't read the note in years, but I remembered every word of it. The formal tone of it was so far away from the Jack I knew, and I had wondered why he would send such a stilted note. Julia had told me he couldn't come home for the funeral, and I was thankful he didn't. Jack being formal and distant with me to my face would have been way worse than him not being there at all.

Instead, my Dad was there. He had been drinking for days, throughout the funeral preparations, but he managed to be sober for the day of the funeral. And John and Karen, Julia, Sophia, Nick, and Michael were there too. Mum didn't have sisters or brothers, but people from church and from the hotel where she had worked were there.

When it was over, I took the necklace with Jack's ring off. Any hope of us ever getting back together was gone. I hung the necklace on the mirror in my bedroom as a reminder not to open myself up to the pain of relationships ever again. Then I went to the supermarket and bought weeks' worth of tinned tomato soup, noodles, and bread rolls for the freezer, went home and locked the front door, closed the blinds and went to bed.

I didn't feel like eating, but I forced down a tin of soup, a pack of noodles and a bread roll every day. I spent my time sleeping, crying, and reading old books, curled under a blanket with Mum's pillow, which smelt like her. At least to begin with.

Julia and Sophia texted every day, but I didn't want to see them. I didn't want to see anyone at all. I needed to be entirely wrapped up in my grief.

After a week, Julia and Sophia came by and made me shower. They cleaned the house whilst I sat, broken, on a chair, watching them. They talked about anything that wouldn't make me think of Mum and took me to Portobello for ice cream on the beach, even though it was February and freezing cold.

We sat huddled together, our backs against the cement wall, facing the sea, as we ate our ice cream.

'Do you think sadness existed in the Garden of Eden?' Sophia asked.

'Is that the same question as, *does sadness exist in heaven?* Julia replied.

I sighed. How did they have energy to have a philosophical conversation about God?

Sophia bit the inside of her cheek in thought. 'I guess so.'

'Then no, I don't think so.' Julia sounded decisive.

'No?'

'No. I think heaven is a happy place where emotions like sadness are superfluous.'

'Really?'

'Yeah, how would it be heaven if people were sad? Doesn't sound like heaven to me. At all.'

'Huh,' Sophia frowned. 'Maybe my question was wrong then. Maybe I should have asked, *how do you define heaven?*'

My head was tired – the grief overwhelming to the point where thinking hurt – and here they were *defining heaven*. I wasn't sure heaven existed at all. If it did, it felt far far away. Out of reach.

I hoped it did exist.

I hoped there was a place where Mum was happy, free from pain and full of joy.

I did know hell existed though. Whether it was an actual place you could be sent to after death, or not, I couldn't say. But there existed hell on earth. And as much as I ached in pain and grief then, I knew I was barely scratching the surface of the hell some people went through.

'Oh, I know the answer to this one,' Julia smiled, and I sighed at how simple everything seemed to her. 'Heaven is where God is.'

'Okay, in that case,' Sophia frowned as she talked, as though she was working out what Julia's answer actually meant. 'You don't think the Garden of Eden and Heaven are the same? Because there were times in the Garden of Eden when God was not present. So much so, he had to go looking for Adam and Eve when he wanted to spend time with them.'

'Huh.' Julia narrowed her eyes. 'I guess?'

'Also, if you say Heaven is where God is – and I guess you'd say God is here – then would you say Heaven is here too? Or where is Heaven?'

Julia brushed at the hair in her face before licking her ice cream. 'Yes, I think Heaven is here too.' Julia seemed to have no idea what she really thought – she was just regurgitating a bunch of pat answers she had been told in church. Or by her Mum.

I scrunched my face into my scarf and tried to ignore the annoyance I felt at her glibness.

'But we have sadness here, so...' Sophia pushed back again.

'Okay, maybe I mean that Heaven is *available* to us here.'

I rolled my eyes and, unable to stop myself, I joined the conversation. 'Then how do we access Heaven here? By dying?'

Julia frowned. 'No, I think...'

'Huh. Actually, maybe you're both right,' Sophia cut in. 'Maybe Heaven *is* available to us here, but only if we're truly dead.'

I snorted. 'Well, I feel pretty dead, but it doesn't at all feel like what I imagine Heaven might feel like.'

Sophia smiled wryly. 'No, I don't think that's the kind of dead I mean. What if the way to access Heaven is to truly die to ourselves, and allow Jesus to live through us?'

'Huh,' Julia said. 'I'm not sure, though. I'm a Christian in that I've given my life to Jesus, but I still don't know how to access Heaven. If it actually *is* available to us here.'

'Hmm, I've got to think some more about that.' Sophia said.

We sat in silence, eating our ice creams and watching the waves. Julia agreeing that she didn't have a clue made me relax a little. I had found that people liked to give me simple, unthought-through absolutes since Mum became ill. As though a glib sermon heading could come close to providing any comfort.

Instead I wished people would be a little more real. A little more willing to see me and my feelings, rather than paint over them with an *at least Lisa's in heaven now.*

I leaned my head back against the wall and closed my eyes. Maybe this defining heaven conversation wasn't as stupid as I had first thought – at least it reached below the surface.

After a while Sophia shook her head and said, 'I like what you're saying, Jules.'

'About Heaven?'

'Yes,' Sophia frowned. 'But I also like the idea of sadness existing in Heaven. I want for sadness to exist there. I think in Heaven we will be capable of holding our emotions in a way where we can feel enormous sadness, and therefore we will also be able to experience utter joy.'

'So, you're saying you don't believe joy can exist without sadness? Because I think it's the other way around. I think joy is the absence of sadness.'

'Huh.' She frowned. 'No. Or yes. No, I'm not sure what I believe about that.'

'Sounds like you've got it all figured out, Soph,' I said with a smile that felt weird on my face. I hadn't smiled in a long time. But as weird as it felt, it also felt relieving to know that I wasn't alone in having nothing figured out.

She snorted. 'I wish.' She shook her head. 'No, I don't know what I think about that, but whether sadness exists in Heaven or not, I like the idea of *God* experiencing sadness.'

'Does he, though?'

'How could he not?'

I turned my face to the sea, staring unseeingly at the waves. She continued, 'His infinite sadness when he sees our pain must be heart-breaking for him. I think he cries when we cry, and I think there's nothing he'd rather do than take away the pain.'

I wasn't sure what I thought about God in general at the time. I hadn't been too impressed with him and his way of predestining me for all these hardships lately. But her words touched something deep in my soul, and I found myself wishing – hoping – that what she was saying was true.

'I like that.' I said and wiped at my damp cheeks. 'And I'm thankful for how you guys have taken care of me today, but can we go home now? My butt is sore, and I can't feel my fingers.'

Julia smiled and tucked her hair behind her ears as she stood up. 'Yeah, it's freaking cold here. Let's race to the car.' She reached out and pulled Sophia and me up before taking off at a run.

Sophia shook her head and smiled at me. 'She always cheats.'

'Ever since we were kids.' I agreed, and we followed Julia back to the car at a slower pace.

They dropped me off at my house after I convinced them I would be fine to stay on my own.

And I *was* fine that evening.

I had a cup of tea as I wrote in my journal and listened to David Bowie's Sound and Vision on repeat. It was one of the songs Mum used to have me put on in those last few months of her life to dance to in the kitchen. At the time, I had danced to make her last few months mean something to her, but now I wondered if maybe her song choices had been more about reminding me life was worth living than about her. There was something deeply comforting about the song, and though I felt sadness and grief, I also felt an enormous peace. It was as if I was covered not in sadness, but in comfort. Then I went to bed and slept the whole night for the first time in months.

The following months were rocky. There was more grief fog than there were good times, but as time wore on, I found that not everything in my life was wrapped in grief anymore. I redid the kitchen and had a clear out of the contents of the house. I saved special things and gave away things I no longer needed. Soon the house wasn't just Mum's house, painfully full of memories of her, but it was mine, and I started to enjoy being there again.

When autumn came, I went back to university and – with some adjustments – I taught myself how to live again.

Chapter 24

PRESENT
Miranda

Jack's reasons for breaking up with me made sense. And seeing how painful it had all been for him made it easy to forgive him. Maybe I had forgiven him a long time ago.

Still, forgiveness was one thing, but trust was another. And though I no longer held anything against Jack, I knew I would never trust him again.

It was great that he had gone to counselling, but if I knew anything about people, it was that they don't change. If I had a pound for every time Dad had stopped drinking, apologised and told us this was it – he would never drink again – only to see him fall off the wagon a few months later… I might have been able to afford to put him into rehab now.

No. People didn't change.

Still, Jack's eyes went hopeful when I told him it was ok and, though I had gone on to tell him this wouldn't change anything, I knew he thought it was a matter of time before he would be able to change my mind.

I didn't know how to be clearer about where I stood without being unkind. Instead, I just told him to leave me alone so I could have a shower and get dressed.

He was back a few hours later and spent the rest of the day doing little projects around my house whilst I sewed more bags for the period cups. And as much as I wanted to tell him to go away, I also wanted to keep him around for as long as he would let me. Not just because of all the odd jobs he did, but because I let myself pretend that he belonged there.

Because I realised it was a slippery slope, I decided I would spend the next few weeks weaning myself off. I would spend a little less time with him every week. That way my heart could get used to life without him again in a healthy way.

As it turned out, that plan was great in theory, but not nearly as great in practice. It might have been easier had he not lived next door, or if he hadn't been part of the board of Project Cup. Or if he hadn't been so nice to hang out with.

He turned up after work most nights and would help me cook dinner. Then he spent the evenings helping with the business side of Project Cup or fixing things in my house whilst whistling songs under his breath.

And though I realised it wasn't exactly normal for friends to spend every evening together like that, he never pushed for more than friendship.

I told myself it was all good.

I knew I was lying to myself. But it was a comfortable lie.

***

A few weeks later, Julia and I were at Sophia and Michael's flat. We had just finished a Project Cup meeting planning the stall for the Edinburgh Christmas Market, which would be starting a couple of days later. Despite the challenges, things were coming together nicely.

'What's going on between you and my brother?' Julia asked as she dried the dishes I had stacked up in the rack after washing.

I dropped the glass I was washing in the sink.

After Nick had broken up with Julia a few weeks earlier, Julia had been so wrapped up in her own heartbreak that I had assumed she was oblivious to what was going on with anyone other than Nick.

Apparently, I had been mistaken.

I glanced at her and then at Sophia, who was waggling her eyebrows at me.

'Yeah, I'd like to know that too!'

I gave them both a dry look. 'There's nothing going on with Jack and me.'

'Are you sure?' Julia frowned as though my answer confused her.

'Yeah.' I looked her in the eye and nodded. 'I'm sure. We're friends.'

'Right.' She nodded, too, and I turned back to the sink and fished out the glass I had dropped. It hadn't broken. 'It's just...'

Sophia cleared her throat. 'Are you *really* sure?'

'Yeah.' I raised my hands to emphasise how sure I was. 'I'm sure.'

'Huh.' Julia's frown deepened.

'Huh, what?'

'Does Jack know there's nothing going on between you guys?'

I became aware I was dripping water all over the floor, so turned back to the sink again and sighed. 'Why?'

Julia glanced at Sophia. 'Just the way he looks at you.'

'And how he's always hanging out wherever you are,' Sophia said.

Julia nodded, and continued, 'And you guys went to China together.'

'He's my friend!'

'Yeah, well Michael's your friend too, but I don't see him...' Julia bit her lip. 'Oh.'

'Oh, what?' Sophia asked.

Julia's hand flew to her chest, and her eyes went wide as though she had just discovered a secret. 'Are you secretly in love with him, but you're afraid he's going to turn you down?'

'No!' I rolled my eyes. 'No, no, no!'

'Because you really don't need to worry.' Julia shook her head to emphasise her point and gave me her most reassuring smile. 'He's so in love with you...'

'Gah! Stop!' I turned to her again, and, not caring about the drippage, I held up my hand. 'First, we only went to China together because we both had business there at the same time. And yeah, I know he wants to get back together, but I'm not interested, and I've told him that.'

'What? Why?' Julia straightened and her eyes narrowed. 'What's wrong with him?'

'*Nothing's* wrong with him. He's just not right for *me*.' I took a deep breath. 'I don't want to get married to anyone. At least not yet. Maybe in ten years or so, who knows? But not anytime soon.'

'So, are you suddenly against marriage as an institution?' Julia frowned.

'No.' I clenched my teeth and tried to summon some patience with her. 'I'm just saying I like being single. And whilst Jack is a nice guy, I don't want to be in a relationship with him.'

'Yeah!' Sophia cheered. 'Singles unite! We don't need marriage to be happy; we're the authors of our own happiness.'

I smiled. Maybe Sophia would help get me out of this awkward conversation after all.

Julia tutted. 'Sophia, *you're* married.'

She snorted. 'It's a *fake* marriage. You know I'm just doing Michael a favour, and when he gets his citizenship, we'll get a divorce and I'll never get married again.'

Eyes wide, I looked at Julia and put on Sophia's northern English accent. 'Yes Julia, you see, it's a *fake* marriage.'

'Uh-huh.' Julia laughed. 'Let's talk about something else. You guys are impossible.'

Sophia put her towel away and took out some bowls. 'Ice cream, anyone?'

We had ice cream and drank tea, and I put the whole Jack situation away until later that night when I was in bed, unable to fall asleep.

If Julia, who was wrapped up in her own heartbreak over Nick, was asking what was going on between Jack and me, things were getting too sticky.

I would have to talk to Jack. Somehow.

***

Running a market stall had been an exciting idea, but I was pretty sure it would have been nicer to do it in the summertime. December in Scotland is dark and wet, and the temperatures were just above freezing most days. Still, our little stall had walls, which meant it wasn't too bad, and there were lots of people milling around, so we had plenty of opportunity to talk about the period cups.

Sophia and Julia were naturals at engaging people, and when they were at the stall, we would sell quite a lot.

When I was on my own, it was more of a struggle. I had never been a salesperson and speaking with so many people made me feel uncomfortable. All I wanted to do was to sit in a corner with my knitting and pretend I was somewhere else.

Sophia told me I didn't smile enough, and that's why people weren't all excited to buy anything from me. She may have had a point. She sighed when I told her I didn't smile at people because if you did, they – especially tourists – had a way of thinking you were their new best friend.

'What's wrong with being friendly?' she asked as she rearranged the display. 'You're as bad as Michael.'

Michael looked at me over his coffee cup, a smile in his eyes. 'It's called having boundaries. And there are few things in life that are worse than having to make conversation with somebody you don't know.'

She gave him an exasperated look and waved her hand in the air. 'Yeah, well it sells no period cups and makes for a life with no friends.'

He shrugged. 'I've got all the friends I want.'

'Me too.' I nodded.

'Well, if you want to sell more cups, you can try smiling.' Sophia looked at me. 'Or we could try to make sure there's someone here with you as much as we can.'

I shook my head; it wasn't fair on everyone else to have to babysit me. 'Nah, I'll be alright.' I put on a smile, decided I could be an adult too, and went on to talk to some new customers.

***

I left Sophia and Michael at the stall around nine that night, exhausted after a long day at work and then a few hours at the market stall being friendly to strangers. I got to the bus stop opposite Waverly Station just as my bus left, so I checked the screen for how long it would be before the next one came along.

Sixteen minutes.

There were lots of people waiting for their buses, but I snuck into the shelter to get out of the wind.

'Miranda? Is that you?' I turned to see Angus from work standing next to me. He worked with statistical analysis, the department next to mine, and we had taken some of the same courses at university. At university we hadn't hung out together at all, but once we both started working at the same firm, we would talk in the break room from time to time.

'Hi Angus.' I nodded. 'What are you up to?'

'Just been to the gym. What about you?'

Angus had a nice lean physique, and I knew he was into running. 'The gym sounds nice. Are you training for anything specific?'

'No, I'm not doing another race until April. Do you run?'

'Yes, but not when it's icy. In the spring and summers, I try to run 10K twice a week, and I've done a few races, but nothing like a marathon.'

'Huh. Maybe we should sign up to do a race together.' He adjusted his glasses and smiled, showing off the dimples in his cheeks. His nerdy cuteness was endearing. I smiled back at him. 'We could do *Edinburgh's Toughest* for charity or something. Get the office to sponsor us. It's just over five K, but it's to the top of Arthur's Seat and down again, so it's pretty intense. Good way to start the race season.'

Surprised, I nodded. 'Uh-huh. Yeah, maybe that's an idea.'

'So, what have you been doing tonight?'

I shrugged. 'I've been freezing my behind off at the market all evening.'

'Christmas shopping?'

'No.' I shook my head. I had done my Christmas shopping months ago. 'A couple of friends and I have started a social enterprise, and we've got at stall here at the Christmas Market.'

'Really?'

He seemed genuinely interested, and I went on to briefly explain the whole story. He didn't even flinch when I told him we were selling period cups.

'Huh. I would buy one but I'm not sure I'd get much use out of it.' His smile grew and I chuckled. 'But maybe we could do our run to sponsor your Project Cup then. Are you registered as a charity?'

'Yes, a social enterprise,' I nodded. I got my phone out to make a note of it so I wouldn't forget. 'That's a great idea. I'll bring it up with my friends and we can see if there are others who would like to join us, too.'

He nodded. 'Are you going to the office Christmas party?'

The office Christmas party was a dinner out where I was expected to make small talk with people I normally never spoke to, whilst they drank too much and said inappropriate things. As soon as I had the date for it, I had made sure to make other plans. When people asked, I would pretend I wanted to go but – *unfortunately* – I had this other thing that had got in the way. 'No, I'll be at the market stall that night.'

'Shame.' He pursed his lips. 'Maybe we could go out for dinner another night, instead?'

Surprised, I felt like a deer caught in headlights. 'Uh… Maybe.' I cleared my throat as I saw my bus pull up to the stop. 'Oh look, there's my bus. I'll catch you later!'

'Have a good night!'

'Uh-huh. Yeah. You too!' I waved and got on the bus and went up the stairs to find a seat. I sat down and took a deep breath as the bus pulled away from the stop. I leaned back against the seat as questions flooded my mind.

Had Angus just asked me out?

Still buzzing an hour later as I lay in bed, I methodically sorted through the questions, and decided it was all a non-issue. I wasn't going out with Angus – or anyone else – any time soon. Still, if I ever changed my mind and decided it would be nice to have a safe, committed relationship with a guy, then Angus would fit the bill. He was easy to look at, we had lots in common, and he was a good guy.

I snuggled in to my blankets and closed my eyes. Maybe one day it would be nice to be in a relationship with a guy, provided my feelings weren't involved beyond a friendship level. It might be nice to have some company.

Chapter 25

Jack

By mid-December, I felt I was making progress with Miranda. I had made sure to respect her decision to end our fling but had taken every opportunity to hang out with her as friends. I made myself useful around her house and spent most evenings in November on her couch working on stuff for work, as she prepared for the Christmas Market. I was on the dinner rota Julia and Miranda had going, and cooked dinner for the three of us twice a week.

When Julia asked if I cooked rice every time because I missed Hong Kong, I shook my head and caught Miranda's eyes. 'No, but it reminds me of good times.'

Miranda looked away, hiding her face behind her long hair.

I went on to tell Julia about the time when we ended up staying in the room above the pigsty and had rice and chicken feet for dinner.

Julia, who had been rather sombre since Nick broke up with her, laughed.

I caught Miranda stealing glances at me, and it was nice to know she wasn't immune to me, despite her insistence that we just be friends.

'So, have you found a place to live yet?' Julia asked me as we were clearing the table one night in early December.

Living at my parents' next door was convenient, but now that I was settling back into Edinburgh for the long haul, I needed to get my own place.

'I'm not sure, but I'm going to go look at some places on Saturday,' I said.

'Really? Where?'

'There's one on the other side of the park, one in Portobello and there's a place in Leith. Why? Are you looking, too, or are you going to stay here for the rest of your life?'

Julia shrugged. 'I was just looking the other day, but I've decided to leave it until I'm back from Kenya at the beginning of February.'

Miranda frowned. 'You don't have to move out, Jules. You're always welcome to stay here.'

'I know, and I love that about you. But at some point, I need to stand on my own two feet and not rely on people around me.' She smiled at Miranda. 'You know?'

'Well, I like having you around, so no stress.'

'Still, it would probably be good to start looking at what's available.' Julia eyed me, a question in her eyes.

'What?' I asked. 'You want to come with me to look at the flats on Saturday?'

'Sure!' Julia nodded and looked at Miranda. 'Let's all go!'

'Uhh…' Miranda gave her a startled look. 'I'm sure Jacky doesn't want us there.'

'Of course he does. Don't you?' Julia gave me an exaggerated nod. 'You'll need us to make sure your new place has everything on your list.'

'Uh-huh, yeah.' I narrowed my eyes as Julia tried to communicate something through hers. 'Of course.' Whatever Julia was trying to tell me, it might be nice to have company when looking at the flats. I cleared my throat. 'Yeah, you should both come.'

Julia looked satisfied. 'Great!'

Miranda and I looked at each other and she shook her head. Julia was clearly up to something, but as Miranda and I had both worried about her, we let it go. Julia had been a shell of her real self since Nick had broken up with her a few weeks earlier, so it was a breath of fresh air to see her excited about anything. She spent the rest of the evening questioning me about what I was looking for and wrote a long list on her phone of what she called *essentials* in order for us to refer to it later.

When Saturday morning came around, Julia and Miranda met me outside at nine thirty, and we got into Mum's car. 'Morning,' I said as I took them in.

'Uh-huh,' Miranda answered. She looked as though she had just woken up. Her winter coat wasn't zipped up and under it she wore an oversized jumper over leggings.

Julia, on the other hand, seemed almost chipper. Her red hair bounced as she said, 'Good morning! Where are we going first?'

'First stop is here in Duddingston,' I said, and drove the short distance to the cul-de-sac where the ground floor flat was located, as Julia chattered on about how exciting it all was.

I parked in the parking bay just outside the house and we got out and met the landlord, Dave. We shook hands, and he led the way through the front door.

'The previous tenants are moving out in the first week of January, and the flat will be available from the eighth of January. They're out just now, so feel free to have a look around.'

Julia got her phone out and started going through her list as we looked through the apartment.

'Ooohh!' Came Julia's voice from the kitchen. 'It has a dishwasher.'

I sent Miranda a knowing look and she smirked back at me. Julia tended to end up doing the dishes whenever we ate together, as her cooking was somewhat of a health hazard.

We joined Julia in the kitchen. It was small, but with Mum and Miranda just a couple of blocks away, I wasn't expecting to be doing much cooking there, so that was fine.

Looking round the rest of the flat, it seemed like a good place. It was nice and fresh and came furnished – which was a plus as I didn't have much – and it was spacious for being a two-bed. There was a shower and bath in the bathroom, and the only downside Julia could find there was that the bathroom sink didn't have a mixer tap.

'You'll scald yourself on the hot water and then freeze on the cold.' Julia shook her head. 'It's a stupid system.'

I had never given sinks or taps much thought, but I guessed she had a point.

'Mir, will you flush the toilet?' Julia asked.

'Sure.' She pushed the handle, and the toilet flushed. 'Seems to be in working order.'

'Good.' Julia nodded. 'And again.'

Miranda gave her an amused look but complied. The flush was weaker this time, but good enough. Julia narrowed her eyes at me in question.

'The toilet works.' I gave her an exaggerated thumbs up. She seemed to be taking this apartment hunt a little seriously, considering *she* wasn't planning on moving in.

She shook her head and went to ask Dave a bunch of questions about the utilities, and I couldn't help but think she was trying to make herself scarce.

With Julia chattering away to Dave, it became clearer how quiet Miranda was being. She looked around, but seemed withdrawn – almost insecure – and it made me wonder what was going on.

When we were done, we all got in the car. I looked at my watch – we didn't have much time to get to our next viewing. 'What do you guys think?' I asked, mainly interested in Miranda's opinion.

'Well, apart from how there's carpet everywhere except the bathroom and kitchen, and how there isn't a mixer tap in the bathroom, I think it's a great place.' Julia nodded. 'I loved the dishwasher. Honestly, that flat could have been an absolute den, but with a dishwasher it would still be a winner.'

'Uh-huh. Sure.' I supposed it wasn't a bad thing to have a dishwasher. 'What do you think of it, Miranda?'

She shrugged. 'Yeah, I think it would suit you well.'

Julia's phone started ringing as I turned the key to start the car and Oasis came through the speakers. Julia turned the music down as she answered her phone, and, after a short conversation, she turned to me and said, 'Sorry, but you guys will have to do the other two without me.'

'What's going on?' Miranda asked.

'Oh, it's nothing. Someone from church. I need to go though.'

'Oh? Should I come with you?' Miranda glanced at me and sent Julia a look I couldn't decipher.

'Definitely not.' Julia shook her head. 'You should stay and help Jack. I'll text you the list of essentials.' She gathered her things and got out of the car. She waved, and then winked at me before saying, 'See you both later!' and slamming the door shut.

'Uh-huh.' I turned to the backseat where Miranda was sitting. 'I wonder what that was all about?'

'Who can know the mind of Julia?' Miranda sighed. 'I don't have to come with you to the other places if you don't want.'

'You don't want to come?'

'No, I mean, sure. I'm happy to come along, but no pressure.'

'Then you should come with me.' I nodded and gave her a smile in the rear-view mirror. 'But come sit in the front with me.'

Once Miranda was in the passenger seat, I pulled out of the parking space, and we waved at Julia as we passed her running toward the bus stop at the top of the street. She gave us an enthusiastic wave back, and I shook my head at her. Miranda spent the next few minutes staring out of the passenger window. She sat straight and stiff in her seat.

'Are you going to tell me what has you this quiet?'

She glanced at me before quickly moving her eyes away.

'No pressure.' I pulled a face as though I didn't care that much. 'Up to you.'

'Gah!' She said and dragged her hands through her hair. 'Sophia and Julia cornered me the other day, and now it feels like Julia is trying to set us up.'

I smirked. 'Yeah, I was getting those same vibes. I wouldn't worry about it. You know what she's like. She gets an idea in her head, and suddenly she's made nothing into something.'

'I know,' Miranda groaned. 'And some of her ideas are great, but I wish she would have some boundaries and not barge into other people's lives...'

'Uh-huh.' I bit my lip to keep from smiling and took a left towards the sea and Portobello, where the next flat we were going to look at was.

'I see you laugh, but just wait. It's going to spiral out of control if we don't do something about it.'

I cleared my throat and gave her a more serious looking nod. 'Sure. Sure.' Frowning I asked, 'And what would this spiralling out of control look like exactly?'

Miranda glared at me. 'It would look like everything we don't want to have happen, that's what.'

I wasn't so sure about that. In fact, I had a feeling the opposite would be true. But seeing how distressed Miranda was over it, I decided now was not the time to push. Instead, I would continue to play the long game and hope it would pay off in the end. 'Uh-huh. You know she's probably just getting herself invested in the idea of the two of us together again in order to distract herself from her breakup with Nick, right?'

Miranda nodded. 'And it *is* nice to see her smile again. I was starting to think she'd lost her smile for good.'

'Yeah.' It was hard to watch both Julia and Nick go through what was obviously painful to both of them. I shook my head. 'I still can't make sense of why Nick broke up with her. It just seems stupid.'

Miranda's eyes narrowed and she bit her lips. 'Yeah, well I hope he finds some sense.'

The landlord of the next flat, Steve, was standing outside the house waiting for us when we pulled up, so we quickly got out of the car.

Portobello was a nice area, and the proximity to the beach was a definite plus, but as the landlord led us up the dark staircase to the little flat, I knew this wasn't where I wanted to live. The smell of pets was evident as he opened the door, and as we entered the little hallway and Steve turned the light in the living room on, the fuse blew. He cleared his throat and tried a different light which seemed to work. 'Of course that would be fixed before you move in,' he said awkwardly.

'Of course.' I agreed, not sure if he meant the electrical problem or the pet smell. It didn't matter; I wasn't going to live there anyway.

Having made up my mind about this flat already, I spent the viewing watching Miranda instead. She wore a neutral expression as she took in the worn couches in the living room, and the stained mattress in the bedroom. When we opened the door to the bathroom though, she shook her head. 'Carpets. In the bathroom.'

I smiled at how offended she sounded. 'I take it you don't approve.'

She gave me a dry look. 'If you never want anyone to come visit you, I think you might have found the perfect place.'

We quickly looked at the kitchen before I shook Steve's hand and told him I would have to think about it.

He made a clicking sound with his mouth as he winked in a way that made him look like a shady car salesman. 'Better be quick though, I've got another five people coming to view it today.'

'For sure.' I shook his hand again, before steering Miranda out of the flat and down the steps to the car.

Miranda glanced at me as she put her safety belt on. 'Just in case you have some strange idea about actually moving in to that place…'

'Such a nice area, though.' I sent her a wink and clicked my mouth in the same way the landlord of the flat had done to us as I started the car.

'Oh, stop. What was that man thinking? The smell, the light bulb that went out, the mattress…' Miranda held up a finger at a time as she went through her list. 'And the carpet in the bathroom! Who thinks having carpet in the bathroom is a good idea? Honestly.'

I laughed. 'Yeah, I don't think I'll go for that one.'

Miranda was still shaking her head. 'Where to next?'

'There's this little flat up in Leith. The pictures look great, and it's right by the sea.'

'The sea would be a big draw. What's the price like?'

It was double what the Portobello flat was. I shrugged. 'I could afford it.'

'Of course you can.' Miranda was a little touchy when it came to money. 'Why aren't you buying instead of renting if you're that well off?'

I winked at her and clicked my mouth again. 'Who says I'm not?'

Miranda took a deep breath as though fighting for patience, then raised her eyebrows at me and gave me an annoyed smile. 'Are you?'

I took a right turn at the traffic lights. 'It depends.' I sucked my cheeks in as I thought about it. I hadn't made any decisions yet. I wanted to be near to Miranda so she could get used to having me around again, but mostly because there was nowhere I would rather be. And I was hoping she would soon catch on to how right we were for each other and want to be with me again.

But until then, I had to live somewhere, didn't I? And I didn't want to throw money away.

'On what?'

'Couple of things,' I said evasively even as I knew it would annoy her. 'I think you'll like this next flat, though.'

She narrowed her eyes at me and turned the radio up as The Offspring's *The Kids Aren't Alright* came on, and she started singing along. Off key. I smiled at her random taste in music, and at how she knew every word of the punk rock song.

When we got to the flat in Leith, I texted the landlady to let her know we were there, and got a text back telling us she was waiting inside. Having been here before, I led the way to the old-looking building and up the stairs at the back of it. Heather, the landlady, was waiting for us at the door.

I shook her hand, and she smiled when I introduced Miranda. Heather gave us a quick walkthrough of the flat before her phone rang and she excused herself.

I followed Miranda into the living room, where she smirked at me and said, 'A little on the stereotypical side, don't you think?'

I glanced around the room, taking in the hardwood floors, white walls, black leather couch, big flat-screen TV on the wall, and all the chrome details. 'Perhaps.' I gave her an amused look. 'You should have a look out that window, though.'

She went to pull the curtains apart and gasped as she saw the view. 'I didn't realise we are right by the sea! If I had this flat, I'd get rid of the curtains. Nobody can see in anyway, and there's no reason to cover that view. Ever.'

She was right; the view of the sea would always be different and always beautiful. Still, as much as I liked the sea, Leith felt too far away from Miranda. If I lived here, I would have to make a conscious choice to go to her house, and she would never come see me. That settled the issue for me. There would never be a view as beautiful as Miranda; no sea could compare to her, and I wished then that I could tell her. I wished I knew how to convince her to take another chance on us. I rubbed my hands over my face to clear my mind of the wishful thinking that led nowhere, and smiled. 'Yeah, I imagine it would never get old.'

Miranda turned her head to me, and I realised I was in her space as I looked down on her face. She didn't move away, though. Instead, she tilted her face closer, her eyes on my lips, as though she was waiting for me to kiss her.

She startled when Heather said, 'Sorry about that. Do you have any questions?'

Quickly jumping away from me, Miranda's cheeks reddened as she glanced at Julia's list. She cleared her throat and proceeded to ask a bunch of questions, making notes on her phone as Heather answered.

I sighed but let her escape into her list. I wondered what that moment had been all about. Since coming home from China, it felt like Miranda was sending out some mixed signals. On the one hand, she had told me she didn't want any kind of romantic relationship with me. But then she would look at me like she was about to kiss me. Or I would catch her sniffing me when I was close by.

When Miranda was done asking all the questions, I told Heather I would have to think about it, which she seemed fine with. I had nothing to think about – I wasn't going to get this flat.

On the way out, Miranda gave me a thumbs up. 'You should take it.'

I scrunched my nose. 'Nah… You're right, it's too stereotypical.'

Miranda winked at me and clicked her mouth like Steve had done. 'That view, though.'

I smiled and went about making arrangements to rent the first flat we had looked at in Duddingston.

Chapter 26

Jack

Once the Christmas Market started, I saw less of Miranda, as she would go there straight after work during the weeks they had the stall and not come home until late. So, one afternoon in mid-December, I stopped at a falafel bar after work, ordered a couple of wraps, and took them to the market.

Miranda was sitting in the stall with her knitting, ignoring the shoppers going by the stall. Her hair was covered by a warm hat, and her scarf was tucked into a thick winter coat that came down to just above her knees. Her nose and cheeks were rosy from the cold, and her chin snuggled deep into the scarf as she counted stitches, seemingly lost in her own world.

Everything in me wanted to reach out and warm her cheeks with my hands.

'Hey,' I said, and she gave me a startled look.

'Oh. Hey.' She hurried to put her knitting away – as if embarrassed to have been caught – and stood up.

'Busy?' I grinned as she picked up a bunch of leaflets and re-arranged them.

'Very. As you can clearly see.' She gave me a sheepish smile as she waved her hands at the stall.

'Want company?' I could see she was on the verge to say no, so I handed her a cup of green tea.

'Thank you.' She wrapped her hands around the cup and took a tentative sip.

'How many cups have you sold today?'

She looked away but answered truthfully. 'None.'

I bit the inside of my cheek as I let my eyes sweep over the stall and the surroundings. 'How many hours until you pack up?'

She checked her phone and sighed. 'Six hours and thirty-seven minutes.'

I smirked. 'Let me in the stall and I'll help you.'

She narrowed her eyes as if unsure of what I meant. 'Are you for real?'

I nodded and held up the carrier bag. 'I also brought falafel wraps.'

She tutted. 'Now you're just trying to score points.'

'Can't a guy bring his favourite girl some falafel wraps out of the goodness of his heart?'

She gave me an unimpressed look. 'No.'

'Huh.' I shrugged. 'Maybe I'll have to keep your wrap, then.'

'I don't think so,' she scoffed, and waved at the carrier bag. 'Here, hand it over.'

'Oh, did you mean to say, *I'm sorry, my favourite Jack, please can I have a wrap?*'

She snorted. 'I'm sorry, my favourite Jacky, please can I have a wrap.'

I grinned and handed her the wrap. 'There. That wasn't so bad, was it?'

'I haven't eaten properly today.' She unwrapped it and took a big bite as she groaned. 'It's delicious.'

I leaned against the stall and unwrapped my own food to keep my hands from reaching for her. 'Then can I come in the stall?'

She looked up from her wrap. 'Uh-huh.' Finishing her mouthful, she carefully set her food down before unlocking the side door of the stall. 'Come on in.'

I smiled and stepped in next to her, causing her to take a step back.

She looked up at me, her eyes wary, as though she had suddenly become aware of how close we were.

I wanted to step closer still, reach out and cup her cheek, breathe her in, drop soft kisses along her jaw... I caught myself before doing any of that. Instead, I let myself keep gazing into her eyes, until she flinched and looked away, breaking the charge of the moment.

I cleared my throat and took a step away. Pretending there wasn't enough electricity to power the city between us, I tried to be casual. 'Do you have a strategy for how to get any cups sold tonight?'

'Yeah. I was going to try to be friendly to people.' She grimaced. 'I tried that for a while, but I was tired, and hungry, and cold, so I think my *friendly* might have accidentally scared some people off.'

'Huh.' I bit my lip to hide a smile. 'Have you thought of doing some kind of give away?'

'Like what?' She wiped her mouth with her fingers and flicked her tongue over her lips.

I tore my gaze away from her lips and tried to remember what we were talking about. 'Like sign up to our mailing list for the chance to win a period cup? It might create a bit of interest in the stall, which might lead to some sales.'

'Sure. Let's try it.' She took another bite of her wrap before she stuffed the serviette into the carrier bag and ducked under the counter. Bringing out a big sheet of paper and a red pen, she quirked her eyebrow. 'How's your handwriting?'

I shook my head.

'Never mind. I'll do it.' Miranda started writing just as a group of women came up to the stall. She ignored them, which I took as my cue to start chatting.

By the time the ladies left, they had all signed up to the mailing list, and I had sold two cups. I turned to Miranda, who had just finished writing the sign, and grinned.

She stared at me, clearly unimpressed. 'You think you're so cool.'

I laughed. 'Maybe we should have a competition. Who can sell the most cups tonight?'

'Fine. We both know who'll win, though.' She waved her hand at my face. 'You'll just use those pretty blue eyes…'

'Ah, but you know I only have eyes for you.' I winked at her.

She snorted. 'We should work together instead. You can charm the ladies and I'll handle the sales?'

It turned out we made a good team, and by the time we packed up the stall for the night, we had smashed the record for sales in one evening. Miranda had passed tired a long time ago, gone through a giddy stage, and now, as we locked everything down and headed to the bus stop, she yawned. 'Thank you for helping out tonight.'

I smiled and looked down at her. 'I had fun.'

'Yeah. Me, too.' Her eyebrows dipped into a hint of a frown before smoothing out and she smirked. 'Jules and Soph will be shocked to see who holds the record for most sales in one shift.'

When we got on the bus, I made sure she got a window seat, and sat down next to her. She leaned against the window and was asleep by the time the bus pulled away from the stop. I watched her as she slept, wishing I could put an arm around her and snuggle her up with me. But I didn't think that would go over too well, so I let her sleep in peace and only put my hand on her shoulder to wake her when we got to our bus stop.

Stepping off the bus, the cold night air woke us both, and we walked the short distance to her house. I stopped at her gate, handing her the bag I had carried with her knitting in it.

'Thank you,' she said, looking me in the eye. 'For everything.'

I smiled. 'Sleep well.'

She nodded, her eyes on my lips now, and I wondered if she, too, was thinking of all the times I had kissed her good night. 'You, too.' She waved her hand toward her house. 'I'll just…'

I nodded and smirked at how awkward she was being. 'On you go.'

She left me waiting at the gate as she walked the steps up to her house and let herself inside.

Chapter 27

Miranda

It was almost a month later by the time I finally spoke to Jack properly about things. I would have talked to him about it earlier, but I could never get time alone with him, and I didn't think it was the kind of conversation we should have in front of others.

It was late at night one Sunday a couple of weeks before Christmas, and Jack and I were packing up the market stall, as it was the last night of our turn at the stall. The following week, the other company would have the stall, and then we would have it again in the week leading up to Christmas. Packing the stall down and setting it up again every other week was a little tedious, but it was nice to have breaks from the busy Christmas Market.

Selling period cups at the Edinburgh Christmas Market had seemed ludicrous when Sophia had first floated the idea by us. But now I was thankful we hadn't thrown the idea out. In fact, I was surprised by how well we had done. Our mailing list was growing, and though lots of people were disgusted by even the thought of our product and had given our stall a wide berth, the majority had been encouraging and interested.

We had sold more cups than I had expected – so much so that we had broken even on the cost of the cups during the week we had just finished. Now all the rest of the sales would fund a Kenyan high school's project to give all their teenage girls a free period cup. Julia was going out there in early January to partake in the project, which was headed up by the school's head teacher.

I had never done anything like this before. Sophia had done a gap year before starting university, and Julia had done her year of teaching in Kenya the previous year. Both had come back talking about how there is a world out there that needed us to help. And whilst I had been excited for them, I felt unable to leave Edinburgh for any longer periods of time because of Dad. I wanted him to know that I would be there for him, even when he wasn't reaching out. I didn't need to go anywhere else to find *the world that needed help*.

Still, it was exciting to be able to help make a difference for the girls who might otherwise drop out of school because of the shame associated with not being able to afford sanitary products. It made me feel as though I was part of something bigger, and that was more motivating than I had expected.

Up until then, I had seen Project Cup as a short-term project, but now – for the first time – I started to consider the possibility of making it a long-term thing. I wanted it to go beyond being just a one-off project that helped one school in Kenya, and make it into a business that impacted women's lives all over the world.

So, when I did the accounts, I looked at what it would take for Project Cup to grow. I came to the conclusion it needed investment and whole-heartedness – also known as *risk*. It needed somebody to have to guts to jump with both feet and put everything they had into it.

I started toying with the idea of quitting my job, or at least significantly reducing my hours, in order to invest my time into Project Cup instead. I just hadn't worked out how to pay my bills, and take care of Dad if he needed it, if I didn't work a proper job. Yet.

'Are you almost done there?' Jack asked.

I gave a startled laugh. He had taken a couple of boxes to his car as I packed up the last things. 'Yes. This is the last box now. You can head on home; I won't be long.'

He raised his eyebrow at me and gave me a look as though to say I was being ridiculous to suggest he leave me alone in the city centre in the middle of the night. 'Uh-huh.'

I gave him a dry smile back.

The summer when I was eleven, Dad had been sober, and lived with us for a few months. I had a lot of good memories from that summer: one of them was how he had taught me how to defend myself if I ever needed to. As an eleven-year-old, the techniques he taught me probably wouldn't have gotten me very far, but I had put on some muscle since then. I felt fairly confident I could put up a fight should I need to.

Still, it was nice of Jack to keep me company.

'Here. You can fold the tablecloth.' I passed it to him and yawned.

He tucked the tablecloth under his arm and reached to take the box from me. I stepped out of the stall, locked everything, and then his hand found mine as we walked through the market under the Christmas lights back to our cars. Jack whistled that familiar song I couldn't place, and I told my sleepy self it wasn't romantic, but – again – I was lying.

By the time we got to the cars, it had started to snow. It was just a few flakes sailing slowly to the ground, but it was snow.

Jack put the box in the back of his car – still holding onto my hand – before taking me to my car. There he turned toward me, pressing his warm lips to my cold forehead before opening my car door for me. He closed my door and ran over to his own car.

Flustered by his kiss, it took me longer than it should have to start my car. Despite having been tired and cold all evening, I was now wide awake, and warm, and tingly all over.

What had just happened?

Would a friend give you a kiss on the forehead? Would Michael or Nick kiss my forehead? Would Angus?

Then again, I told myself, Jack and I were *very* close friends. So maybe it was ok?

No. We couldn't be that close. It was too dangerous. I would have to say something. I cringed as I thought of how to bring it up, but I couldn't let this go on.

It took me longer than usual to drive home. I pulled my car into the drive and opened the garage, as Jack pulled his car up behind mine and started unloading the boxes. The snow was coming down heavier now, though the ground wasn't cold enough for it to stay.

When the last box was put away and the garage closed, I turned to thank him, and found him standing closer than I expected.

'Jack,' I said, as he looked down at me. My neck tingled, knowing he was about to kiss me again. 'We need to talk.'

He was still standing so close I could feel his breath on my face. I watched, mesmerised, as the side of his mouth pulled up slowly. 'Do you want to go inside? It's pretty cold out here.'

'Uh-huh.' I shook my head and fumbled to get my keys out. 'Right. Yeah.'

Once in the kitchen, I went to fill the kettle, stepping awkwardly around Jack where he was leaning against the counter.

'What's going on, Mir?'

It was now or never. I steeled myself, put the kettle down and looked him straight in the eye. 'I'm thankful for your friendship, but I can't help but feel as though you see more here than I do. You kiss my forehead or hold my hand, and that isn't what I want our friendship to be like.' I waved my hand in the air. 'People are asking questions, and it's all making me feel uncomfortable, because I don't *want* anything more than friendship from you.'

Jack was still leaning against the counter. 'I'm sorry.' He rubbed his forehead before dropping his hand with a sigh. 'I've tried so hard not to push you. It's hard though.'

'I feel I've tried to tell you several times that I don't see a future for us, but I know we've been hanging out a lot lately, and maybe you've misinterpreted…'

Jack held his hand up. 'I'm sorry I held your hand and kissed you earlier. I can see you weren't ready for that.'

Ready? *Ready?*

Oh no. I pulled my hands through my hair, tugging at it in frustration. 'It's not that I'm not *ready!* When will you understand?'

He frowned. 'What do you need me to understand?'

I put my hair behind my ears and looked at him. 'That we aren't getting back together.' I swallowed. 'It's not ever going to happen.'

He bit the inside of his cheek and looked away as though deciding what to say. 'Yeah, I've heard you say that, but I can see that you feel this too.' He motioned at the space between us and spoke gently, as if to express that he cared about me, even though he was clearly frustrated. 'I don't want to pressure you. You know I love you, and I always will. I wasn't ready to get married back then, but that doesn't mean our relationship has to be doomed forever. I-'

'Let me stop you there.' I held up my hands. Listening to his hopes for our relationship was painful. 'I don't know how to say this to you, but I need you to stop talking about us getting married. I'm *never* getting married. Least of all to *you*.'

He flinched as though I had slapped him. 'Why?'

'*Because!*' I took another deep breath to calm down. 'Don't take it personally. I'm not going to marry *anyone*.'

'But why? I thought we talked about what happened, and you said you understood why I broke things off with you back then.'

I shook my head, wishing it was as simple as that. 'Yeah, it's not about that.'

'Then, what? What is it about? What aren't you telling me?'

'I-' It was on the tip of my tongue to tell him about the baby then, but I stopped myself. What good would it do him to know now? 'Look Jacky, all you need to know is that I will always be your friend.' I cleared my throat. 'Always. But that's all I can give you. And I need you to stop hoping for more.'

He looked at me, as if trying to figure out what was going on. 'I wish you would tell me what this is about.'

I almost laughed, because the thought of telling him brought both relief and terrible anxiety, and there was no way I could see how it would help him to know. Instead, I took a deep breath. 'It's probably best if you go now.'

He sighed and buttoned his winter coat over his scarf. 'Yeah.' He nodded and left me standing in the kitchen with the kettle that still hadn't been put on, staring after him as he let himself out.

Again, I felt a stab of deep sorrow, and I struggled to see anything out of my eyes for quite some time. But I shook it off, made some camomile tea, and went to bed.

So what if I didn't sleep very well that night. I had done the right thing.

I had definitely done the right thing.

Chapter 28

Jack

I have always believed in respecting what people say, and have never been the kind of guy to push or coerce a woman who had said no. Consequently, on the airplane, when Miranda said our Asia fling was over, I respected her wishes and stepped back. We'd had a great time in Asia, and I thought it would be a matter of time before she would want to make our relationship real and permanent. I had made no secret of the fact that I wanted us to be together. I would marry her in a heartbeat if she gave me the chance. And over the following weeks, she seemed more and more open to me. We spent lots of time together, as *friends*. But I thought we both could see that we were headed towards being more than friends. Therefore, her pulling back again hurt.

I would respect her wishes and back off again, but it *did* hurt.

I couldn't do much about loving her. She was everything for me, and no matter what she said, she didn't decide what I felt or hoped. But I wouldn't push her, and I felt terrible that she felt like that's what I was doing.

And still, I wanted to know what was behind her refusal to let us be together when it seemed at least part of her wanted to. I was sure now she was hiding something, and the less she wanted to tell me, the more intrigued I became.

She texted me early the next morning.

Miranda: Is everything going to be awkward now?

Me: Of course not. I'm sorry I pushed when you'd said no.

Miranda: I probably could've been clearer.

Me: Your words were clear enough. I was hoping for more, but I can respect your choice.

I was still confused, as her words didn't seem to match what I had seen in her eyes. That confusion made it harder to come to terms with Miranda's mind being made up. It hurt like nothing else, but I could only blame myself for not taking the chance when I had had it back in the day.

Miranda: Thank you. Wanna come over tonight? You still want to be friends, right?

Being her friend without there being any hope of getting back together again would hurt more than being stabbed in the gut. But if *friends* was what she could give me, then I would be the best friend she had ever had.

Me: Sure, I'll swing by after work. You cooking? Course I still want to be friends — don't be daft

***

A couple of evenings before Christmas, I was at her house helping her decorate her Christmas tree, making sure to stay well and truly inside the friend-zone.

It was only a little tree, so didn't take long to dress, and afterwards, she brought out a handful of plastic zip lock bags. She also had little packs of soap and hand sanitizer, tins of beans, beautiful pairs of wool socks, ordinary socks, packets of crackers, energy bars, chewing gum, a few period cups, and so on.

'What's this?' I asked, as she sat down on the couch and started stuffing items into the zip lock bags.

'I like to make up little care packages for Dad to give his friends at Christmas.' She looked at me. 'Do you want to help?'

I nodded. 'Sure.' I bit the inside of my cheek to keep from asking one of the millions of questions that were on the tip of my tongue, hoping she would tell me without having to ask.

'You probably think this is weird.'

I opened a multi-pack of energy bars and started putting them in the bags. 'Why?'

'I don't know.' She took a deep breath. 'Dad has a lot of homeless friends, and most of the time the kinds of gifts he would give them aren't the kinds of gifts that are actually helpful to them, even though they might be the kinds of gifts they want most.'

'Are you saying you give your dad a bunch of care packages to give to his friends for Christmas?'

She nodded. 'Mum started doing it a long time ago, and I've been doing it since she died.'

'I like these socks.' I had seen her knitting socks all autumn and had wondered who would wear them, as I had only ever seen her wear two different pairs.

She gave an embarrassed laugh. 'Well, they're not all pretty, but hopefully they'll be warm.'

'I'm sure they'll love them.' I helped her make the care packages up and didn't think too much more about it. It was a long time since I had seen Jimmy, but every time I asked about him, she seemed to close up, so I decided not to go there.

When Christmas came around, I had done my best to be more friendly and act less… interested in her. I made myself stay away more and ask questions less, and, though there was still some tension after our late-night chat when she had told me to back off, things were going well.

Too well.

She continued to be reluctant to share anything beyond surface level information, and I was getting increasingly frustrated with how well she was avoiding talking about whatever it was she was hiding.

I was still trying to work out how to get it out of her when Christmas Day came around. Everyone was gathering at my parents' house for a traditional Christmas dinner, and Sophia, Michael, and I had been put to work in the kitchen. Mum had given us all jobs to do to help get Christmas dinner on the table, and my job was to peel about three kilos of potatoes, a kilo of carrots, and some other root vegetables.

Michael and Sophia were bickering about how to say aluminium, or whether macaroni and cheese could be considered a meal. I didn't feel bad staying out of that one. They acted like an old married couple, even though they were both adamant they were just friends that happened to be legally married.

I shook my head when Sophia tried to get me to get me to side with her over whether olives were nice to eat or not. 'I'm staying out of your marital spat,' I said, and Sophia threw me an annoyed look. 'What? You guys are married and are having a spat. Hence, it's a marital spat, no?'

'No!' Sophia shook her head as Michael rolled his eyes, I wasn't sure if he was rolling them at me or her.

'Uh-huh, sure. Keep me out of it, in any case.' I winked at her and she sighed.

A few minutes later, she said, 'When the Bible talks about women being quiet at church, how do you interpret that?'

'Yeah, I'm definitely staying out of that one.' Though I wasn't sure how she had ended up on that subject, it sounded like a recipe for disaster. I glanced at Michael.

He looked amused.

I shook my head at him and went to turn up the Christmas music, when Miranda and Julia walked through the door. They were both wearing ugly Christmas jumpers. As was I. Ever since we were kids, Mum would go round the charity shops after Christmas to buy up any Christmas jumpers, which she would give us the following year.

And as ugly as Miranda's jumper was, she was still the most beautiful girl in the room.

'Oh, good morning girls,' Mum said, her hands deep in the turkey as she tilted her cheek toward them for a kiss.

'Happy Christmas,' Miranda said cheerfully.

'Oh good, the little elves are here,' I said, and smiled as Mum had Miranda pull out a chopping board to chop the vegetables I had peeled.

'What do you want me to do?' Julia asked Mum.

'I've got the perfect job for you, dear. Would you set the table?'

I chuckled. 'That's because she doesn't want to take any risks with Christmas dinner this year.'

Julia threw me a dark look, and I got the feeling she would have said something had Mum not been there.

'Now, now Jack,' Mum said, working hard to hide her smile, as she finished rubbing the turkey with oil and herbs. 'Be nice to your sister.'

Julia went to get cutlery and said, 'Uh-huh, that's fine. I don't mind setting the table.'

Ignoring the others, I turned to Miranda and said, 'I like your jumper.'

'Uh-huh. Yeah, it's high fashion, this is.' She smiled as though she was holding back a laugh. 'I like yours too. And your pinny.'

I looked down at the frilly apron I had on over my reindeer jumper with bells. 'I jingle when I walk.' I glanced at Mum, who was talking to Dad. 'I don't know how she finds these ugly things.'

'She has a gift for sure.' Miranda chuckled, and I made sure to concentrate on peeling the potato.

'Hey. Merry Christmas.' Nick came in the kitchen and handed Mum a box of chocolates.

'Aw, thank you dear,' Mum said and gave him a hug. 'Merry Christmas to you too! It's good to see you.'

'Hey man.' I tilted my chin up at him. He hadn't been round much since his breakup with Julia, and I could tell he was feeling uncomfortable. I had been clear with him that nobody was picking sides and told him he couldn't skip out of Christmas.

'You guys look like you've got this under control,' he said as he looked around the kitchen, tensing when Julia came in to get plates for the table.

'Nick,' she said, as though trying to be on her best behaviour.

'Jewel.' He nodded.

She disappeared into the dining room again, and he cleared his throat. 'So how can I help?'

'Well, we're all set in here, I think,' Mum said. 'But maybe you could find some chairs for the dining table?'

He stared at her before nodding. He took a deep breath and left to face Julia in the dining room.

Miranda glanced at me. 'He looks miserable.'

'Yeah.' I didn't say that he looked as miserable as I felt, because it was Christmas, and I didn't want to scare her off. It was the truth, though. 'Hey, did you see your Dad this morning?'

She nodded. 'Yep.'

When she didn't say anything else, I decided to leave it for now and try again later. Something told me her reluctance to get back together with me might be related to her relationship with her dad.

We ate and ate, and spent the evening playing games and talking about different ways of understanding Jesus and the cross. It got a bit heated, as it always did when we discussed God, but I enjoyed it. It was a long time since I had thought much about God at all. But seeing as it was Christmas, I guess it was fitting to think about him.

As we ate nuts, talked theology and played games, it struck me how much I had missed celebrating Christmas at home all those years when I was away. I had celebrated Christmas in Hong Kong as well, but whilst it was nice to go to a Japanese restaurant and have sushi, it didn't *feel* like Christmas.

Now, though, surrounded by family and friends, dealing with the tension and challenges that were real relationships, and having deep discussions about theology, Christmas somehow felt complete.

We walked to church that night. Not to the charismatic evangelical church Mum and Dad usually attended, but to the more formal Presbyterian Church just up the road. They had a candle-lit midnight service we had attended ever since I was a baby, and walking there in the dark together was part of the Christmas tradition. Nick had left after our discussion about God, and though that was a shame, I figured the day had probably been intense enough for him. Nick's leaving seemed to make Julia a little less on edge, too.

It had rained during the day, but now the sky was clear again and the temperature had fallen. Though going to church on Christmas Day was part of the tradition, I did struggle with the idea of it. It seemed hypocritical of me to go to a place dedicated to the worship of God when I had no desire to worship him myself. It may have been a long time since I had thought much about it, but I was still clear on the reasons why I didn't like God.

Miranda ran home to get a warmer jumper, and I waited for her whilst the others started walking.

'Hey, you didn't have to wait for me,' she said as she hurried towards me.

I shrugged, and we started up the road together. 'Maybe I'm not waiting for you. Maybe I'm just reluctant to go to church.'

'Yeah, I know the feeling.' She nodded and pulled her hair out of her coat. 'The Christmas service is usually nice, though.'

'Sure.' I said, and she smiled wryly at my sarcastic tone. 'How's Jimmy doing?'

She looked away, but I was surprised when she didn't ignore my question about her dad. 'He's been worse.' She snorted. 'But he didn't seem great, no.'

'How do you mean?'

'He was still a bit hung-over from last night, although he did his best to act sober.' She shook her head. 'He was happy to see me, though, and he lit up when I gave him the gift bags.'

'Oh, yeah?'

'Yeah.' She nodded. 'I didn't stay long.'

'Did you go to his flat, then?'

'No, we met up for coffee. He doesn't like me to come to his flat. I don't know if he's embarrassed because it's always a mess, or if he doesn't want me to run into his friends.'

'Why? What's wrong with his friends?'

'There's nothing *wrong* with them.' She frowned as she thought of how to continue. 'They all have pretty… colourful lives. Some of them have some form of mental health diagnosis, and most of them have some kind of addiction.'

'They're not criminals, then?'

'What? *No!* She looked offended, but then softened. 'I mean, of course there's a bit of criminal stuff that goes on; there always is when there are drugs involved. A few of them have been to jail, but on the whole, they are good people.' She sighed. 'They're people that got dropped between the sofa cushions of society.'

I glanced at her. 'Is that what you believe? That it's society's fault they're the way they are?'

She nodded. 'Not one hundred percent, because everyone has some level of choice. But overall, yes.'

'Some people have more choices than others, eh.'

'Well, yeah.' She met my eyes, and I got the sense she had strongly held beliefs about why some people ended up on the fringes of society but was unsure whether it was safe to share them with me. She glanced away. 'Still, Dad doesn't want his friends to give me any trouble.'

I wanted to ask her to tell me more about her thoughts but decided not to push things now. 'Would they?'

'Not when they're sober. Not most of them, anyway. It's different when they're on stuff, though.'

We were at the church now and went inside. Miranda sat down next to Sophia and Julia, and I took a seat next to Mum. The church was warm, and decorated with candles and poinsettias, and there was a nativity scene set up at the front. Classical music was playing gently in the background, and it all made for a cosy picture. The reverend stood up, and the service began. The service consisted mostly of carols and a short message – none of which I heard. I was too distracted by what Miranda had told me.

Though I had always known Jimmy was an alcoholic, and that her upbringing had been different than mine, it hadn't hit home until now how different from mine her life had been. She never used to talk about the alcoholism with me, and because she was so well adjusted, I guess I thought things hadn't been too awful.

No, that wasn't it. I wouldn't lie to myself.

I didn't know much about Jimmy's alcoholism because I had been afraid to ask. I had been afraid she would tell me awful stories that I could do nothing about, and instead I had pretended there was nothing wrong. And at times, that had probably been fine. But I could see now how selfish I had been. Not just in how I had broken up with her, but also in how our relationship had functioned.

And now I didn't know how to tell her how sorry I was. I worried that would just make everything worse.

Was this the reason why she wasn't willing to get back together with me? Did she think of me as someone that was fun to be around, but who wouldn't be there for the hard things in life?

I stood up as everyone around me stood to sing *O Come All Ye Faithful*. I hid an inward snort. Mum elbowed me in the side and gave me a look, so I sang along, albeit half-heartedly. *Faithful* suddenly meant a lot more than not sleeping with someone else.

I shook my head. I might not have been a very faithful person back then, but I had changed. All those years in therapy had helped me become a better person. Someone who wasn't afraid of pain anymore.

But how did I tell Miranda that?

Chapter 29

Miranda

As I attended the midnight service on Christmas Day, I thought about Dad. After calling and texting him for weeks to arrange a time to meet up, he had finally texted me back a couple of days earlier. I had told Jack that Dad and I had met up for coffee, and that was true, although he probably thought that meant we had gone to a coffee shop. Instead I had stopped at Starbucks on the way and picked up a coffee for him and a tea for me. Then, I went to meet him in Regent Road Park, where we had sat on a bench overlooking Arthur's Seat. That was where we tended to meet when he was in one of his drinking periods. When he was sober, things were different. Everything was different then.

I had told Jack that my dad was a bit hung-over. It might have been more truthful to say that Dad was still drunk from last night, but I had never seen the need to be that frank when people asked about Dad. The only person who knew what Dad was really like was Jack's dad, John, and he had never judged. Instead, he had been a stable friend for Dad. Other than John, though, I found people had their own understanding of alcoholism, and the less I told them about Dad, the less likely they were to judge.

I didn't think people generally were judgemental and cruel, but I had heard my fair share of: *if they really want to get sober, they could just stop drinking*. And whenever I had tried to talk about Dad with Jack back in the day, he was never very interested. Instead, it had seemed he would rather talk about anything else. So, when Jack had asked about Dad tonight, it surprised me. I wasn't sure what to tell him, or how frank to be. And it was awkward talking to him about it, because Dad was a good reminder of why I couldn't get back together with Jack.

Dad was amazing in the good times, but he never had been able to handle the bad times. Watching Mum go through the heartbreak of loving him – and consistently being disappointed by him – was the main reason I didn't want to be in a relationship with somebody I loved.

My heart wouldn't be able to handle that again.

Julia smiled at me when the service ended, and after making some awkward small talk with the people around us, we made our way outside. I took a breath of fresh air, pushing my thoughts to one side, as Sophia said, 'I love Christmas services. There's something reassuring about them. Does it bother anyone else, though, when the reverend talks about Jesus entering our world, *our time*, as a baby?'

I frowned. 'That *is* how the story goes though, isn't it?'

She laughed. 'Sure, he was born into the world like all the rest of us, but saying it in a way where he enters our *time* suggests that he was somehow outside our time before. That God somehow stands outside of time.'

Julia shook her head. 'Honestly Sophia, haven't we had enough of theological discussions for one night?'

'Never!' Sophia said in an ominous sounding voice before giving the widest grin.

Julia huffed and gave her a gentle push. 'Come on, let's walk back.'

I frowned and followed them, walking next to Michael. 'Do *you* not think God lives outside of time?'

'How would that work, exactly?' Michael looked at me as I thought about it.

'I don't know, but I guess maybe God sits in this big room, and what we do here on earth – from start to finish – is like a movie to him. It starts when he hits play, and ends when he hits stop?'

'Then, would he experience all these thousands of years as thousands of years? Could he fast forward? Go back and change things?'

'I guess to him our whole existence might seem like the wink of an eye.'

'Uh-huh.' Michael nodded. 'And what is his role?'

'He's the director? The author?' I shrugged. 'I don't know.'

Michael squeezed his eyes shut and rubbed his face. 'Oh, there are so many ways I disagree with you on all of what you've just said.'

I laughed. 'Of course there is.'

Julia turned around and gave Michael a firm look. 'But because you're such a nice person and understand that we've had enough theological discussion for one night, you will refrain. Won't you?'

'You're no fun, do you know that?' Sophia sent Julia a playful frown.

Julia snorted. 'Since when are theological discussions considered fun?'

Michael held up his hands and smiled. 'Right. I'll just say one thing.' He looked at me again. 'What *is* time?'

Julia groaned. 'That's *not* what refraining means!'

Michael and I both ignored her.

I gave Michael a dry look. 'Well, time is made up of seconds, minutes, hours…'

'No, that's one way to *measure* time. But it isn't what time *is*.' He shook his head. 'Time is just *before and after*.'

'Before and after?'

'Yeah. If nothing ever happens, then is time really a thing? But, as soon as an event takes place, there becomes a before the event, and an after the event.'

'Huh.'

Michael smiled at the frown on my face and gave me some time to think.

'What does that mean, though?'

Julia turned again, squeezed in between Michael and me, and looked up at him. 'Michael, do you ever miss Canada?'

He frowned at her. 'Why?'

'I've been thinking of going for a visit. What are the sights not to be missed?'

'Yeah, yeah, fine.' He put his arm around her shoulders and gave her a squeeze. 'We can talk about something else.'

'Oh, yay!' Her face lit up and she clapped her hands in an exaggerated show of excitement.

As we walked home talking about trivial things, I wondered why Sophia and Michael both seemed to think the concept of whether God existed inside or outside of time was so important. I had never considered the idea that God might not exist outside of time, but as I started thinking about it, it struck me that there was a whole heap of assumptions I had made about God.

I wondered how many of them were true.

Chapter 30

Miranda

After Christmas, I spent the days in the office working on reports and thinking about the nature of time. I also thought a lot about Jack.

After I had spoken to him about our relationship again, he had backed off, and we had gone back to a more comfortable friendship. Or it should have been comfortable. I no longer felt the pressure of him wanting more out of our relationship, and all our interactions had been only friendly.

He helped me put care packages together for Dad's friends and asked about how things were with Dad in a way he never had before. Or he would come over, and we would cook dinner together after work. Or he would go over the Project Cup accounts with me, and he spent hours reading up on the laws around social enterprises.

It was all very friendly. Which was exactly the way I wanted it to be.

Except it *wasn't*.

Because the longer this charade went on for, the clearer it became that I would forever love Jack. I had loved Jack the teenager, but after spending so much time together over the last few months, I realised that Jack the teenager had nothing on Jack the man.

Jack the man was kind and considerate, and full of adventure and ideas. And after spending the last six years in a daze in which I had decided to give up on hoping for anything other than a boring life, I was starting to dream and think in possibilities again.

And though I knew that there could never be anything more than friendship between us, now that the pressure was off, I wished I could go back in time so things could be different. I wished we hadn't postponed our wedding, and that Jack had stayed in Edinburgh instead of going to Hong Kong back then. I wished I had told Jack about the baby when I had first found out. And most of all, I wished there was a way of erasing the past and rewriting our story.

But there wasn't. And even as everything about Jack made me love him more, I also knew I had to start looking for ways of doing life without him.

I had told Jack I wouldn't ever marry anyone, but I wondered if maybe it would be nice to marry somebody my heart would be safe from. Somebody that could be a companion rather than the love of my life. I liked having my own space, but I wasn't sure I wanted to live alone for the rest of my life.

In any case, I had to do something to get away from all these feelings I had about Jack. Maybe if I dated somebody that wasn't him, I might get the message that Jack and I really weren't getting back together.

That's why I agreed to go out with Angus.

I had seen Angus in the lunchroom a few days earlier, and he had asked me out again. Not knowing how to get out of the situation, I nodded and said yes. He pushed his glasses up his nose and looked a little taken aback that I had agreed. 'Really?' he said, and then I really couldn't get out of it, so I nodded. He beamed at me then and told me he would check his calendar and we could arrange an evening the following week. I didn't know any other twenty-six-year-old men who would want to consult their calendars before making arrangements to date somebody, but that was Angus.

A few days later, it was Hogmanay, and we were gathered at my house. After going to the street party in the city centre for a few years, we had decided we would rather spend New Year's Eve inside than freezing to death in the rain with thousands of people. Sophia had instigated an annual monopoly game. She was a ruthless player and won most years, but the rest of us had a more relaxed attitude to the game. This year Nick had opted to go to the street party with some work friends, and it was the first year Jack was there.

I had played Monopoly with Jack and Julia when we were kids. It tended to end with Julia throwing the board across the room after accusing Jack of cheating – which he vehemently denied doing. I don't think Jack cheated as much as she thought he did – he was just better at playing the game and was therefore more likely to win.

I made sure everyone had drinks and snacks easily accessible before sitting down in my assigned seat next to the cash Sophia had dished out for me.

'Do you want to be the shoe, as usual?' Sophia asked.

'Go on, then.'

The game began. Jack gave Sophia a run for her money, and within an hour they were taking over the board, making alliances with the rest of us to force each other out of the game. Sophia got me on her team, but Jack managed to persuade both Michael and Julia to be on his side. When Jack started building houses on Mayfair and Park Lane, Sophia already had three houses each on the green streets. She landed on Go and smiled as she replaced the houses with hotels. 'You're all most welcome to visit my hotels,' she said, and gave a smug smile.

'Yeah, yeah.' Michael took a sip of beer before rolling the dice. He landed on Fleet Street, which belonged to himself, and passed the dice along to Jack. 'This game is such an awful picture of how the world works.'

'What?' Jack frowned and rolled the dice. 'Yes! Free Parking.'

I sighed and helped him scoop the money up from the board. He would have to make some big mistakes in order to lose this game.

'Yes, exactly like that,' Michael said. 'The rich get richer and the poor get poorer. And it's all down to whatever luck one happens to have.'

'Luck?' Sophia snorted. 'This isn't about luck. It's all about strategy.'

'That's what all the rich people would tell you.' Michael shrugged.

Sophia tutted. 'You're just a sore loser.'

'Uh-huh. And so the world keeps turning.'

'Is it my turn yet?' I asked.

'Uh-huh. Go ahead.' Jack leered at me as he gave me the dice. I was down to my last hundred pounds, and as far as real estate went,

I had mortgaged everything except Bow Street and Piccadilly. If I rolled a five or a seven, I would land on his hotels on Park Lane or Mayfair. An eight would take me to Go, though, and I could do with the extra money.

'Eight, eight. Please let me roll an eight.' I rolled the dice.
Five.
'Ouch.' Jack grinned.
I sighed. 'Yeah, yeah. Just tell me how much you want.'
'That'll be one thousand five hundred pounds. Please.'
'*What?*' There was no way I could pay – I was out now. I held out my hand, wrist up, to him. 'Do you want my blood, too?'

He laughed. 'Nope, but I'd be happy to relieve you of those streets you've got there.'

Michael gestured. 'And this is where monopoly is actually kinder than the world is. At least when you lose monopoly you're out of the game. When you lose all you've got in real life, you still have to keep going. Somehow.'

Julia nodded. 'It's really tragic.'
'Yes. Tragic. Awful. Horrendous.' I sighed. 'It's an *evil* game.'
Sophia sighed. 'Oh, shut up. Michael, nobody will want to play if you keep going on like that.'

'Oh? Really?' He smirked. 'Wouldn't *that* be a shame.'
Jack laughed. 'Maybe we should call it a draw, Sophia?'
'A *draw*?' Sophia glared at him. 'There is no such thing as a draw in monopoly! If you don't want to play anymore, we count up our money and see who won.' She shook her head and muttered 'Call it a *draw*? I've never heard such nonsen-'

Jack shrugged. 'Fine.'
It turned out Sophia had won, and she shook her head as she put the board away. 'Sore losers. Wouldn't even let me win fair and square.'

I took up drink orders and went to put the kettle on. Midnight was only a few minutes away now, so I took the champagne and sparkling grape juice out of the fridge and got some glasses, leaving the tea for later.

'Hey.' Jack came into the kitchen and put a bunch of dirty glasses on the counter. 'They're suggesting we play poker, instead.'

'Huh.' I smirked. 'I bet Michael suggested that.'

Jack frowned. 'He did. Why?'

'He loses every board game to Sophia, but she can't beat him at poker.' I pulled a tray of cut up fruit I had prepared earlier out of the fridge and passed it to Jack. 'Drives her crazy.'

Jack laughed and took the tray into the living room. He came back with more dirty dishes, and started loading the dishwasher.

Watching him, I sighed. He would make some woman a wonderful husband one day. Maybe, just maybe, it could be us. Maybe it was the happiness of the evening, but I let myself imagine it was me – for way longer than I should have.

The dishes banged, snapping me back to reality. My fanciful imagination was out of control tonight, and when I saw the growing smile on Jack's face, I realised I had been staring. Annoyed at myself, I searched for a way out of being alone with Jack.

'You can just leave the dishes. I'll sort them out later,' I said. 'Take these glasses in instead. It's almost midnight.'

'I'm just about done here,' he replied as he put the last plates in the washer, before taking the tray with champagne glasses off the counter.

I followed him into the living room with the champagne and sparkling grape juice. Julia was passing around party hats and streamers whilst Michael was shuffling playing cards. I passed Julia the champagne bottle to open and poured myself a glass of the juice.

'You'll have to remind me of the rules of Poker again,' I said as the champagne was poured.

'Oh, sure. Later. It's 23.58 already.' Sophia said. 'Are you all ready?'

I smiled and nodded. There were some traditions I liked more than others. Counting down to midnight on New Year's Eve was one of them. Maybe the irrational part of me hoped that with the new year came new beginnings. A chance to leave the past behind and to start over. It was a part of me I worked hard to keep in check, but on New Year's Eve it tended to come out.

Glancing round the room as Sophia started counting down, I held up my glass. 'Eight, seven, six…'

Julia blew her whistle and popped a party popper, her eyes glittering with laughter. My eyes circled round to Jack and found him watching me. A shiver ran up my spine as his eyes held mine.

'Three, two…'

He clinked his glass to mine.

'One. Happy New Year!' Sophia cheered.

I raised my glass closer to Jack's, clinking it again and stepping closer. Wrapped up in the moment, I took another step and wrapped my arm around his waist. 'Happy New Year!' My words were muffled into his shirt.

He bent his head down toward me to hear over the noise around us. 'What did you say?'

Bringing my face up from his shirt to look at him, I said it again. 'Happy New…' He was so close, and warm, and the thoughts in my head jumbled as the awareness of being so close to him hit me in the gut. My New Year optimism wrapped around the wish that life could be different, and I found myself thinking that maybe with a new year could come new beginnings. Maybe things *could* be different if we tried again. Maybe…

I stretched onto my tippy toes and now he was only a breath away. He stood, entirely motionless, watching the indecision in my eyes as I decided what to do.

Kissing him would be so easy.

An accidental bump by Sophia pushed the arm I held my glass with, and without warning the glass tipped out of my hand, pouring its contents down Jack's shirt.

The surprise on his face as he took a sharp breath in pushed any thoughts of kissing him out of my mind. Stepping away, I let out an embarrassed laugh. 'I'm sorry! I'll get a towel.'

I ran to the kitchen, finding a towel on the counter. I took a deep breath to steady myself, then shook my head. Burying my face in the towel, I squeezed my eyes shut as I reminded myself that New Year's Eve was a construct people had made up. A new year did not mean a clean slate. It just meant another day. Nothing changed just because there was champagne and party poppers.

Jack continued to be Jack, and I continued to be me. And no matter how nice it would be if we could change our past – the truth was that we couldn't.

Consequently, it would have been a disaster if I had kissed him. A disaster.

And if my heart twinged a little at the missed opportunity, I reassured myself that it was definitely best to have avoided that.

Chapter 31

Miranda

The following day we had a Project Cup fundraiser at the beach. Sophia had volunteered to raise money by doing the Loony Dook – a dip in the sea on New Year's Day. We hadn't raised loads of money, and Nick and Jack had ended up throwing Julia into the sea too. Afterwards, the three of us girls went home to my house, and I made them warm drinks. They sat on the couch, wrapped up in all my blankets, still shivering, and we talked for hours. Julia and Nick were leaving for Kenya in a few days, and I wondered how that would go, as Julia seemed rather murderous when she spoke of him.

'So,' Sophia looked at me and wiggled her eyebrows. 'Have you made any decisions about Angus from the bank?'

'Angus at the bank?' Julia sounded intrigued. 'How come I live with you, but this is the first I hear of Angus at the bank?'

I cleared my throat as I felt my cheeks go warm. 'I think I've decided to go out with him.'

'Oh, yeah?' Sophia grinned widely.

'Yeah, I think so. I mean, I can give it a go.' I shrugged. 'It's not like I'm agreeing to marry him by going out for dinner once, right?'

'Right.' Sophia nodded. 'Absolutely.'

'Wow, it's been a while since you dated anyone.' Julia stroked my arm, and I gave her a tentative smile. 'How do you feel about it?'

Awkward. I felt mainly awkward about this whole situation. I took a sip of my tea and said, 'I guess I'm nervous? He's a good guy, you know.'

'Yes.' Sophia nodded. 'And also, hot.'

I blushed again. Sophia was right. There was nothing about Angus that was unattractive. 'Yes, well, there's that.'

'If this is the Angus I think it is, yes, he *is* hot.' Julia smiled. 'It's nice that you're dating again.'

After having been engaged to Julia's brother, speaking with her about dating other people felt a little strange. I ran my hands through my hair and peered at her through squinty eyes as I grimaced. 'I decided it's a new year, and it's time to move into a new phase.'

'Not a minute too soon,' Sophia said. 'I can't remember the last time you had a date.'

Julia seemed thoughtful, but not hurt. 'Uh-huh. It's been a while.'

'Probably at least a year,' Sophia said.

'Something like that.' I wasn't about to tell them about my fling with Jack in China. They would never drop it. 'I think I decided to take a break after that guy, Edward, stuck me with the bill in the restaurant after he left with a girl he used to date. I never heard from him again.' It still annoyed me, more than a year later.

Sophia sighed. 'Honestly, men can be such…'

'But now, here you are,' Julia cut in, saving us from a rant from Sophia. 'About to date Angus. And he's a good guy.'

'I think we need alcohol,' Sophia said. 'To toast the New Year and your date, and also to warm me up. I'm still cold from the sea.'

The next morning, we went into town to set up our stall for the last few days of the market. We sold cups and gave out flyers until it felt like there couldn't be a person in Edinburgh that hadn't heard about Project Cup. And when Angus texted, I replied, and we arranged to go for our date after work the following Thursday night.

That Thursday, I struggled to concentrate at work. I almost cancelled the date with Angus ten times but kept reminding myself that it was time to move on. Besides, if I didn't want to end up alone, I had better get back in the dating pool.

I freshened up my make up in the ladies' room before gathering my things and walking to the lobby, where Angus had asked me to meet him. He wore a grey coat, and his scarf matched his blue eyes, which lit up when he saw me.

'Miranda!' He kissed my cheek. 'It's good to see you.'

I gave a nervous laugh and nodded too enthusiastically. 'Yes. I'm sorry I'm late.'

'Oh, no worries.' He waved my apology away. 'We have plenty of time.'

We walked down the steps of the Mound, and through the Christmas Market. My heart sank as I realised his idea of a date was probably a bratwurst at one of the Christmas Market stands and a ride on the Ferris wheel. At this point, I had spent about as much time at the Christmas Market as I ever could want to spend there. Still, I had decided to date him, so I would give him a chance. Maybe he could find a way to make it interesting again.

'I bet you spend enough time here, if you've got a stall here, eh?' He said as he scanned the busy market.

'I don't mind.' I gave him a weak smile. 'Although I must confess, selling isn't my forte.'

He scrunched his nose. 'I don't know how you do it. All the people...'

I laughed. 'That's what I said, but my friends insist all these people are a good thing. I think they call them *customers?*'

'I know.' Angus cringed. 'But you would have to *speak* to them? And make *small talk?*'

I nodded, still smiling. 'I know. It's awful.'

We walked past the National Gallery, but instead of turning into the Gardens, Angus led me up Hanover Street to a little Mediterranean and Middle Eastern restaurant I hadn't been to before. A lady ushered us to a table in the corner and took our drinks order.

'I hope this is okay,' Angus said, once she left. He seemed a little nervous, but smiled, flashing his dimples at me.

He was cute, and there were no sparks. None at all. In fact, though it was a bit awkward at the start, it had started to feel... nice.

Perfect.

Nice was just what I wanted. Nice meant comfortable, and convenient. Reliable. My heart was in no way in danger from getting broken.

'It's great.' I smiled back. We got out the menu and ordered a few dishes each to share from the meze section. It turned out

Angus was vegetarian too, which again was nice, and would be convenient in the long term.

He asked me about Project Cup again and I told him that Julia had just left for Kenya with the cups we were giving the high school in Mombasa. He seemed interested and asked a whole bunch of questions about how we had started up, so I told him the story as the food was brought to the table a few dishes at a time.

'It sounds as though you guys have some choices to make as far as the future goes. But whether you go on and grow the whole thing, or end it after this shipment has been paid for, it's a great idea. So, are you planning to continue, or is this it now?'

I cleared my throat. 'I've actually been running the numbers, and we would have to change how we run things if we were going to take this much further. We would need to take some significant financial risks to keep going. This first time we're basically making ends meet – the cups we are giving away are being paid for by the ones we're selling here – but none of us are taking a salary. And in the long term we would have to make the business side of things here work better.'

He nodded. 'Is that something you want to do?'

'Well, yes.' I bit my lip as I thought about it. 'I would like to make it work. It's just that the risk feels quite big. It would require us working without pay for a few months. And I'm not sure if I can afford that. You know?'

He looked at me as though he was desperate to say something but held back. Instead he shrugged and said, 'Well, we could try raising some money.'

I wished it was as easy as that. 'I'm just not sure how much money we can raise. We did the Looney Dook at Hogmanay just now, and raised about three hundred and fifty pounds, which isn't exactly enough.'

His eyes narrowed. 'It sounds as though you need a few proper investments, as well as a team of people that would be willing to do a whole bunch of smaller fundraisers.'

'Uh-huh.'

'I think we should do that run up Arthur's Seat in April I was telling you about. We should get the office to sponsor us. They're all in banking, so I figure we should be able to raise some money off that. And I'll do the Edinburgh marathon in May too. You can join me if you want?'

'I've never run a whole marathon before,' I spluttered. I wasn't sure what to think about how he was this eager to help.

He shrugged. 'You could do the 10K or the half instead. In any case, I'm sure we could raise some money that way. And by then, you guys will have figured out whether you can make the business feasible in the long term.'

'Huh.'

He let me stew on that for a while. 'What are you thinking?'

'I don't know what to think.' I frowned. 'Why do you want to help like this?'

He bit the inside of his cheek as he looked at me. 'I think there are some ideas that shouldn't be given up on too quickly, don't you agree?'

'Sure.' I nodded. 'In any case, I would like to do the run in April with you. I run round Arthur's Seat all the time when it's not this cold, so I don't think the distance should be a problem.'

'Ah, but do you run up and down the hill?'

I laughed. 'No, not exactly.'

'It's not that intense – people run up Ben Nevis after all – but it's a good little starter race for the season.'

'I bet.' I was mopping up the last of the hummus with a piece of pita bread. 'This food is amazing.'

'Yeah, I like this place.'

I smiled. There were loads of things that were nice about Angus. He was kind and interesting and nice to look at. I could see lots of reasons why a relationship with him would fit me perfectly.

Or so I thought, until we walked to the bus stop. He told me he would wait with me for my bus to take me home.

'I had a nice time tonight,' I said as we came to the empty bus shelter.

'Me, too.' He turned toward me. Stepping closer, into my space, he looked down at me, his eyes roaming my face and focusing on my lips. My heart sped up and I felt a wave of nausea as he dipped his head, bringing his lips towards mine. Panicked, I turned my head, letting his lips touch my cheek instead of my lips, and quickly pulled away. Shivering, I wondered why on earth I had put myself in this situation.

He gave an embarrassed laugh, and, even as I was mortified, I knew it would be a long, long time before I would ever want to kiss anyone other than Jack.

'I'm sorry.' Now that there was a little distance between us, I felt able to breathe again.

'Don't apologise.' Angus shook his head and took a further step back. 'I misread the situation. Obviously.'

'No, I'm…' I ran my hand through my hair as I tried to think. 'I don't know. You're a great guy and I'd like to see you again. It's just I'm still feeling a little raw from a previous relationship, and…'

'I understand. It's totally fine.' Angus held his hands up.

I sighed. 'I'm sorry. This is awkward.'

He shook his head and flashed his dimples at me again. 'Don't worry about it. Oh, look, here's your bus.'

Relief flooded me as the bus pulled to a stop. 'Well, thank you for tonight. I had a good time. I'll see you tomorrow.'

Finding a seat, I took a deep breath and wondered what had happened. Why did I panic? Why couldn't I have just let him kiss me?

How long was I going to keep being *raw* from being with Jack?

Chapter 32

Miranda

Walking home from the bus stop, I saw somebody sitting on my front steps. I got my phone out in one hand and my keys in the other, and decided to walk past and pretend to be on the phone – just in case. But walking past my gate, I realised the person on my front step was Jack.

He sat hunched over, his chin dipped into his coat and his hands in his pockets.

I walked up to him and gave him a soft kick. 'You awake?'

He sat up straight. 'Hey.'

'What are you doing here?' I asked, as I went to open the front door.

He got to his feet. 'Just wanted to make sure you got in alright,' he said, looking away.

I narrowed my eyes at him. 'Sure. Well, I'm home now, so-'

He stayed on the step as I walked in, waiting until I turned to look at him. 'Why did you go out with what's-his-face?'

I wasn't sure how he had found out about Angus, but I suspected Julia had told him. Avoiding his eyes, I took my coat and boots off. 'I wanted to try dating again, and Angus is a nice guy-'

'What?' Jack took a deep breath, making steam against the cold night-time air as he blew it out slowly. '*I'm* a nice guy. Why would you date *him* and not *me?*'

My hand went to my rub my eyes, forgetting I had make-up on. 'Look, Jacky, I've already told you, we're not getting back together-'

'Uh-huh, and you told me that's because you don't want to get married and have kids. But if that's true, what are you doing dating some-'

Putting my hands on my hips, I turned to him and looked him in the eye. 'Maybe I changed my mind about getting married. Maybe I *don't* actually want to live alone for the rest of my life. Is that *allowed?* Also, you don't get to be possessive of me anymore. That ended when you broke up with me. Six years ago.'

'You're right. You're right. I'm sorry.' He held a hand up. 'Of course it's allowed. I just don't understand why you would pick someone like that over me. He's clearly not the guy for you.' He pulled his fingers through his hair. 'What's wrong with *me*?'

I looked away. I didn't want to have this conversation. Not now or ever. But I knew how persistent Jack was – he wouldn't settle until he had all the details.

Taking a deep breath, I opened the door wider. 'You'd better come in if we're going to have this conversation.'

He stayed where he was, jaw squared as he looked at me. Then he seemed to make his mind up and gave a sharp nod as he entered the house, closing the door behind him and toeing his boots off. He sat down on the living room couch and raised his eyebrows at me.

Unsure of the wisdom of what I was about to do, I hovered by the door. I wasn't ready for this conversation. At all.

'You want a drink?'

'No, I want you to tell me what's going on.'

'Well, *I* need a drink,' I said, and turned on my heel, leaving Jack where he was. I wished for alcohol for the first time in years as I waited for the kettle to boil. Camomile tea might be relaxing, but I doubted it would take the edge off the nerves I had.

Returning to the living room, I set my tea down on the coffee table, still not sitting down. My stomach hurt as I avoided his watchful eyes.

'Do you need the toilet now, or are you done procrastinating?' he asked drily.

'Do you want to hear this or not?' My eyebrows lifted, but I sat down.

'Sorry, yes.' He looked away, taking a deep breath. 'I do.'

'I'm asking because once you know, you'll never be able to unknow it, and it's not a nice story.'

'Gah…' He dragged his hands through his hair again. 'You're driving me crazy, Miranda. Just tell me!'

'Fine.' I took a sip of my too hot tea and winced before setting it down on the table. Looking at him, I decided there was no good way of saying this. 'I didn't know it at the time, but I was pregnant when you moved to Hong Kong and broke up with me.'

His eyebrows drew together, and he tilted his head toward me as though sure he had misheard. 'What?'

'I was pretty broken up after you left, and then you broke up with me and I felt sick all the time. I thought it was because I wasn't eating properly, or because I was sad about us and anxious about Mum being sick. But after a few weeks, Mum suggested I take a test, so I did.' I held my hands out. 'It was positive.'

Jack sat frozen in his seat, staring at me. Not sure if he was listening, I kept going, 'Part of me was thrilled. I had your baby growing in me, you know? The other part of me was terrified because Mum was dying, Dad was lost in a bottle, you had broken up with me and gone to Hong Kong, and there I was, pregnant. I never wanted you to feel manipulated to be with me, but I had a feeling you'd come home if I told you.'

I paused, and he said nothing. Seeing the confusion written all over him, I looked him in the eye. 'I went to see a midwife. Mum went with me to get a scan, and we saw the baby. I have pictures. I'm not making all this up.'

'Uh-'

'They said I'd have to come back four weeks later for another scan, as I was only nine weeks along. I went and bought yarn, and Mum and I started knitting little clothes for the baby.' My hands were shaking, so I set the teacup down and wiped my hands down my jeans. 'I knew I had to tell you, and I was trying to work up the nerve. I tried writing, but the words wouldn't come.' I remembered the feeling of seeing my baby on the monitor and knowing I was going to be a mum. And the fear that came along with it. 'A few days after the ultrasound, I was at work when I started cramping and bleeding. By the time I got to the hospital, there was nothing they could do.'

My hands went to my cheeks and came away wet. I might have been terrified of what it would mean to have a child, but I had loved that baby. 'I was devastated to lose the baby.'

Out of words, I leaned back in my seat, eyes still leaking, and waited for Jack to respond in some way.

Just as I was about to give up on getting any response, Jack cleared his throat. 'Did you tell anyone?'

'Just Mum.' I wiped my face with the sleeve of my cardigan, not caring that the mascara was smearing. 'I was taking care of her, and you had just broken up with me, so I had an excuse when I wasn't feeling up to going out and doing things. I didn't think it was right to tell other people when you didn't know. And I didn't want to tell you because...' I sighed. 'Do you remember that time when we talked about truth over a Sunday lunch? Someone had asked about whether we'd rather live a sweet lie or a harsh truth? You said then that you thought unnecessary truths were just hurtful, and you would rather not know. And it's not like you could have changed anything by knowing. That's why I figured it was better not to tell you.'

He cleared his throat again, but I kept going. 'A few months later, Mum died, and I got your very polite email of condolence. It seemed clear to me then that you had moved on, and I knew I'd done the right thing not to tell you.' Shrugging, I looked him in the eye again. 'But that was the crappiest year of my life, and I'm not ever going to put myself in a position where I might have to go through any of it again.'

I sipped my drink, leaning back against the couch as I waited for Jack to take it all in and respond to me. It felt good to have told him. I felt unburdened – free even. I had carried the pain alone since Mum had died, and now there was another living person who knew.

Still, I knew all this wouldn't be easy for him to process, and I felt a sting of doubt over whether telling him had been the right thing to do.

My tea was almost gone by the time Jack rubbed his face and looked at me, his whole being radiating sadness and hopelessness. 'I don't know how to process this.'

I nodded, wishing there was something – anything – I could do to take away the pain I saw on his face.

'We made a baby?' It was like he couldn't quite believe what he had heard.

'Yeah.' I remembered feeling as shocked as he looked. 'It was a surprise to me, too.' I hoped he believed that it hadn't been an elaborate plan to make him stay with me.

'We made a baby.' Confusion gave way to wonder.

'Yeah.' I had been so worried over his reaction to hearing about the pregnancy but seeing the wonder on his face almost brought tears to my eyes in relief. The thought of having a baby with Jack had been such a positive thing for me, and it would have been devastating for him to be sad or angry about it. 'Wait here,' I said, and went to get the three ultrasound pictures I had.

'Here. These are the pictures.' I sat down next to him and put the pictures on the coffee table. 'The baby was only nine weeks old, and only about the size of an olive or a grape. But you can make out the head, and on this picture, you can see its little legs.'

Jack leaned forward to look for himself.

'I can take a picture of them for you. That way you can look whenever you want.' I didn't want to give him the pictures themselves – they were all I had left of the little life we had made together.

He got his phone out, passing it to me, and I turned on another light so the picture would come out better on his phone. When I had taken a couple of pictures, I gave him his phone back and glanced at him.

'Are you okay?' I asked.

Rubbing his face, he sat back in the couch. 'I don't know.' He shook his head. 'I don't know.'

I took a deep breath and shrugged. 'Well, now you know.'

He nodded and it looked like he wondered whether he would ever recover. 'Now I know.' His face twisted in pain.

'I'm sorry,' I blurted, not sure what to say or do to ease the hurt he was feeling.

He closed his eyes, and when he spoke again, it was more like a whisper. 'Me too.' Then he looked at me, his eyes swirling with emotions ranging from grief to disappointment and betrayal.

Though I had known our relationship was doomed for years, watching him leave that night felt like having my heart ripped out of my chest.

Chapter 33

Jack

I left Miranda's house and spent the next few hours walking blindly around Edinburgh. It was below freezing out, but I didn't feel the cold. I was plenty wrapped up in my thoughts and in the sense of betrayal and grief I felt.

I had known there was more to Miranda's story about not wanting to be more than friends with me, but I would never have guessed she had kept this kind of secret from me.

For six years.

I ended up on a bench in Figgate Park and sat there, lost in my thoughts in the darkness, until I was tired enough to go home and go to bed.

The next morning, I called in sick to work and rang Michael. He was able to get out of work, so we went camping. We stayed in a pod by Loch Tay and spent the days in the mountains.

The trees by the campsite – which were full of life during the rest of the year – were bare now and, as we got higher up, there was snow scattered across the hills. The sparse landscape and stony hills which had stood there for thousands of years were a contrast to Edinburgh, where it was easy to get swallowed up in the busyness. Here, the only activity necessary was to breathe.

After doing a shorter walk on the Friday, we spent the Saturday walking up Ben Chonzie. We had done that before, albeit in better weather, so we knew where we were going. The cold air stung as it blew in our faces, and for the last few hundred meters there was snow.

We were mostly silent, and I was thankful Michael wasn't the kind of person I needed to make small talk with.

It was already dark by the time we got back to the pod, so we made a fire and spent the evening having sausages and beer and trying to warm up. I was about to call it a night, but I saw Michael looking at me as though he was deciding whether to leave me to stew or ask what was going on. It didn't take long before I found myself talking. Out spilled the whole story, and Michael listened without saying much. I showed him the picture of the ultrasound, and, though he hadn't known about the baby, he didn't seem surprised.

'That's a lot to take in. How are you doing?'

'I don't know. I keep wondering how she could keep something like this from me. *For six years!* Did she not think I deserved to know that we were going to have a baby together?' I blew out a deep sigh. 'I don't see how I could ever trust her again. You know?'

Michael sipped his beer. 'Uh-huh.'

'I thought we were moving in the right direction. She was warming up to me again, and I know we had something precious, but then she drops this bomb and all I can think is that I can't trust her.' I looked away. 'But maybe what hurts most is that even after spending the last six years trying to become a better person, that isn't good enough.'

'What do you mean?'

'I've always known Miranda deserves better than me, and when I left for Hong Kong all those years ago, I left because I couldn't be who she deserved. She deserved to have somebody stable that she could trust to be there for her when she was going through the worst time of her life. I just couldn't handle it. So I left.'

Michael frowned. 'Go on...'

'When I got to Hong Kong and realised that I had chosen Hong Kong instead of her, I wondered if that was because I didn't love her enough.'

'Did you?'

'I loved her more than I could express. I just wasn't able to face all the feelings of powerlessness over everything she was going through.' I shook my head. 'I started going to counselling, and I spent the next six years working on becoming a better person.'

Michael snorted. 'Did it work?'

'Yes!' I glared at him.

He laughed. 'Great!'

'Yeah. It was *great*. I'm a *good* person now.' I frowned. 'But Miranda doesn't seem to care how much I've changed. All she can remember is how I'm the person who deserted her when she needed me most.'

Michael sipped his drink and stared into the fire.

'And because of that, she decided it was best not to tell me about our baby.'

Michael shrugged. 'Maybe she thought she was doing you a favour.'

'Uh-huh.' As frustrating as it was, I could see that her intention had been to protect me. 'It's a favour I didn't ask for, though.'

'Perhaps it was a bit high handed, but don't you think she kept her secret from you because she cares about you?'

'Maybe.' The cold was getting to me, so I picked out another log from our little pile, put it on the fire, and watched as the flames started licking it. 'It still hurts, though.'

'What hurts?'

'It hurts that we lost the baby. And that she didn't tell me about it back then. And that she kept it all secret from me for over six years. And that – no matter how much I've changed – Miranda will never see me as anything more than untrustworthy and unstable.' I slumped. 'And now every time I think of her, I feel hopeless.'

'Uh-huh.'

'Like I spent six years trying to become somebody that was worthy of her, and then I find out that not only will she never think of me as anything other than who I was, but she is also a liar.'

'Liar? Don't you think that's taking it a little far?'

I shrugged. 'To lie by omission is still to lie.'

Michael winced. 'Look, I can see that you're angry and hurt, and that's allowed. But I think you'll end up lonely and depressed if you're going to react like this to everyone who omits to tell you anything.'

'Anything? This isn't *anything*. This is omitting to tell me that I was going to be a *dad*.'

'Yeah, I hear you.' Michael sighed. 'Still, you have some pretty high expectations of Miranda.'

'I don't think it's too much to expect honesty.'

Michael set his drink down and leaned his elbows on his knees, pinning his eyes on me. 'Do you know what I think? I think it's great you went to counselling.'

'Yeah?'

'Yeah.' Michael nodded. 'You probably learned things about yourself and about how to handle life in a healthier way.'

'Right.'

'So, you might have grown and learned and matured, and that's all great, but you didn't become a good person by going to counselling. You're still the same Jack. You're a person that will make mistakes and mess your life up in all kinds of ways. If you rely on you being such a good person, then I reckon you're in for some disappointment.'

I frowned. 'Why?'

'Because nobody is that good.' He smiled. 'Not you and not anyone else. People make mistakes.'

'Uh-huh.'

We both stared into the fire for what felt like a long time, before Michael set his bottle on the ground and leaned forward, placing his elbows on his knees. 'Did she say why she didn't tell you?'

'She said something about how there was nothing I'd be able to do about it, anyway.'

Michael frowned. 'That doesn't sound like the whole truth.'

'And she said that she didn't want to be the reason that I ended up stuck in Edinburgh.' I sighed. 'She had a whole bunch of crap reasons.'

'You know, it's okay to be sad about the miscarriage. And it's okay to be disappointed about the past.' Michael looked me in the eye. 'But don't make Miranda out to be a villain when she was trying her best.'

I hung my head. 'Yeah.'

We put out the fire soon after that and went to bed. For a few moments, I looked at the ultrasound picture. I couldn't tell which part of it was baby and which part was anything else, but when I looked at it, my throat constricted, and I struggled to breathe. I put it away and stared at the camping pod ceiling for hours, listening to Michael snore and thinking about how unfair life was.

Michael was right. I was angry and sad and disappointed and hurt. But if blame had to be apportioned, it should be placed on me.

Not on Miranda.

As much as I hated that she hadn't told me about the baby, I hated even more that I hadn't been there for her. And I hated that the choices I had made back then still continued to haunt me.

I needed help.

The following Monday morning, I called a counsellor and set up an appointment.

Chapter 34

Miranda

After telling Jack about my miscarriage, I locked the door and went to bed. I fell asleep quickly but had weird dreams all night and woke up with a headache. I spent the day at work going through the motions and trying to distract myself from all the thoughts of Jack, whilst also trying to avoid seeing Angus. I didn't want to see him when I was so confused, especially after the awkwardness of the cheek kiss.

When I got home to my empty house, I warmed up some lentil soup for dinner and took a cup of tea to bed. I tossed and turned, and tried counting sheep, but although I was exhausted, sleep wouldn't come. Instead, all the thoughts and feelings caught up with me.

I thought of Jack's reaction to my telling him about the miscarriage, and I felt increasingly confused. I remembered the look of pain on his face when he realised that I was telling the truth, and I wished then I hadn't told him. I wished I had spared him the knowledge.

Even so, another part of me felt relieved at finally having told him, as that part of me had thought all along that he had a right to know. I also felt relief at the thought of there being someone else in the world that knew. For so long, I had carried the miscarriage as a secret. I had been afraid to let it go. It had come to represent all my dreams dying, and by clinging on to it, I remembered that life – and God – were not on my side. It reminded me not to take risks, because the outcome would only lead to heartbreak.

And now Jack had backed off, perhaps forever. And that was a good thing. If telling him about the baby was what was required to get him to finally give up on the idea of us getting together, then I felt justified.

The problem with that was that I missed him. I missed knowing that he believed in us, even though I had always known our relationship was doomed.

Now he knew, though, and knowing he finally accepted that we were never getting back together... *hurt.*

I told myself that I had gotten over him once, and therefore getting over him this time would be easier. But a part of me knew that I had never really gotten over him. And I wondered if I ever really would. Maybe some people, like swans, were bonded for life.

Though I wasn't sure exactly why, I dug out the necklace with the engagement ring from the drawer of my bedside table, where it had laid for years. I pulled it over my head again and looked at the ring, remembering all the hope I had felt when Jack had given it to me. I tucked it under my clothes as a reminder of how foolish I had been. Maybe wearing the necklace would stop me from doing something stupid, like calling Jack and...

No. I patted the ring under my clothes. It was best we stayed away from each other.

I spent the next few weeks avoiding people, mainly Jack – which wasn't that hard, as he had moved out of his parents' house and into the flat in Duddingston we had been to see – but also everybody else. I didn't know who Jack might tell about the miscarriage or how they would react. Jack's parents had been like parents to me, especially after Mum died, and I worried they would feel hurt by me.

Instead, I stayed away and put my head down at work, spending my evenings doing overtime or swimming in the Commonwealth Pool. Despite the awkward cheek kiss, I was still planning on doing the Edinburgh Toughest race with Angus in April and needed to keep fit. Or so I told myself.

But instead of pushing myself to perform better in the pool, I found myself in the slow lane, thinking.

Though I had enjoyed the idea of dating, I now felt it was better to wait, and Angus had seemed fine with the idea of just being friends. I didn't want to spend my life alone, but the idea of a relationship with anyone other than Jack no longer held any appeal. So, I threw myself into work and exercise and little else. By focussing on my job, I ensured job security, and I convinced myself that was enough.

Project Cup was a nice project to have on the side, but now I knew I couldn't throw my job away to invest my time into it. I didn't need to take risks in my life. I just needed stability and security.

Sophia had been over quite a bit in the last few weeks, and I knew she was wondering what was going on. I hadn't told her much, except that Jack had finally realised we weren't going to be getting back together. So far, she had allowed me to pretend everything was fine. But about two weeks after my date with Angus, we were having dinner when she raised her eyebrows in expectation. 'Are you ready to tell me what's going on with you and Jack yet?'

Though part of me wanted to deny that there was anything going on, I wondered what it would be like to be free of the secrecy. Maybe it was time. I put down my glass of water and decided to just come out with it. 'If you're wondering why Jack never comes over anymore, it's because I let him know about how I was pregnant when he left for Hong Kong and miscarried a few weeks later.'

Sophia dropped her fork into her food. 'What?'

'I said, if you're wondering why...'

'No, I heard you. I just...' She frowned. 'Why didn't you tell us?'

Avoiding her eyes, I said, 'I found out after Jack broke up with me, and I didn't know how to tell him without seeming like the manipulative ex who got herself knocked up in order to keep the guy around. But I miscarried before I could tell him, and then I figured there was no point in telling him at all. And if I wasn't going to tell him, it didn't seem fair to tell anyone else either. You know?'

Sophia's frown deepened. 'You didn't tell anybody?'

'Mum knew. But otherwise, no. I didn't tell anyone.'

'And then your Mum died just a few months later.'

'Uh-huh.' I snorted. 'It was a shitty year.'

'Yeah, no kidding.' She shook her head. 'I'm sorry you went through all that. And I'm sorry I wasn't there for you better then.'

I busied myself with my food. 'Don't worry about it. You were busy and you couldn't have known.'

Sophia reached across the table and took my hand until I looked up at her. 'No, I'm really sorry. You shouldn't have had to go through all that on your own.'

'I didn't go through it all alone. You guys were there for me in lots of ways that year, and I'm so thankful for that. I was okay.'

Sophia took another bite of salad before putting the fork down. 'I'm confused, though. Why doesn't Jack come over anymore?'

I pressed my hand to my chest, finding the ring, which was there somewhere under my shirt, and looked at her. 'Well, I think maybe he finally realised there is no future for us.'

'And why is that?'

'Well…' I tilted my head. 'I think he was pretty upset that I didn't tell him about the baby. And then I think he realised that there wasn't ever the level of trust between us that made us able to handle things like this. And the truth is, that no matter how much two people love each other, if there's no trust there, then it's not going to work. Is it?'

Sophia's eyes narrowed. 'Surely it's about more than *is the trust there or is it not?* Surely there's a level of taking risks and choosing to believe the best about the other person?'

'Of course, but we also have to take into consideration the person's character and their history. If they've already proven they're not trustworthy, it would be stupid to take risks with them. Don't you think?'

Sophia nodded. 'Sure, but people change.'

'Do they?'

'Yes! We've got to believe people can be better than what they were. That there is redemption available for us all.'

'Uh-huh. Sure. I'm just saying I can't take any more risks with Jack.'

'That's fair. But don't then say that you're through with him because he's given up on you. He hasn't. In fact, I saw him when he came back from Hong Kong, back in August - September. He wanted to show you how much he cared about you, and how he had taken the time and put in the effort to become someone he could be proud of. Someone who would be there for you.' She threw her hand in the air, laying it out as though displaying evidence. 'I think you have seen that he's changed. Haven't you?'

I closed my eyes and thought about the ways Jack had surprised me over the last few months. How he had talked about how he felt or asked how I felt about things. How he had sought me out, instead of hiding from emotion. 'Sure. It's obvious he's grown up since then. But that doesn't mean he won't go back to being who he used to be again. My dad is constantly swinging between being an alcoholic no one can rely on, and being the kindest, most fun person to be around. And I love my dad, but I can't be in a relationship with someone like him.'

'And Jack is like your dad because he didn't stick around six years ago?'

'Yeah.' I bit my lip. 'I guess so.'

Sophia pulled her hands through her hair, stopping halfway through to tug at her roots. 'Well, I guess you've got to make your choices. I'm just saying that you're happier when you're with him. Sometimes life is better with a little bit of risk.'

'And sometimes, life is chaotic and depressing, and you end up full of anxiety because the person you love is unreliable, and you don't know what he might do.'

Exhaling, Sophia slumped back in her seat and looked out the window. 'Yes.' Her eyes went distant, and I wondered where she went.

I reached out and touched her hand. 'I'm just saying I can't handle that.'

Sophia looked at me, letting her eyes clear. 'That's fair enough. I'm sorry I pushed.'

I smiled. 'No, you're allowed to push. I'm glad you do.'

Chapter 35

Jack

After going camping with Michael, we went to pick up the keys for my new flat. Then Michael helped me move my things out whilst my parents were at church.

It was a relief to move out of my parents' house, as it meant I could avoid answering any of the questions they would have if they saw me now, and I didn't have to worry about running into Miranda.

Mum texted me asking if she could come see the flat, and I told her to hold off for a few days. If she came over, she would take one look at me and start asking questions.

I wasn't at a point yet where I had any answers that I wanted to share with anyone.

I spent the next few days in a fog. It hurt that Miranda hadn't let me be part of our baby's life – short as it was – and that I hadn't been allowed to mourn the death of our baby with her. But most of all it hurt to know she didn't trust me enough to tell me.

The logical part of me understood why she hadn't told me back then. But I had been back for several months, and I had tried hard in that time to show her that I was different – trustworthy and stable – now.

And still she hadn't told me until she felt she absolutely had to.

Now I agreed that there was no way Miranda and I could have a romantic relationship again. Relationships were overrated. Being that open with another person just led to heartache and I didn't want to have any more of that. I would rather be strong and alone than weak and in pain.

No, it was better that Miranda and I went our separate ways.

Still, it felt like I was stumbling round in a perpetual fog. I missed her in ways I could never have imagined. I missed how she would say she wasn't adventurous, but then push herself to do things she was afraid of – just because. I missed the way she wasn't into drama but made decisions based on careful evaluation of how any potential outcome aligned with her values and principles. I missed the way she was committed to caring for people around her, and how she was steady and committed even when it meant having to deal with awful circumstances. And, maybe most of all, I missed her smile and the way she would look at me when she thought I didn't know she was looking at me.

Whenever I heard something funny, I would go to text her, before I realised what I was doing and put the phone away. Or Oasis would come on the radio, and instead of turning up the volume, I would change the station so I wouldn't have to remember all the times we had listened to them together.

I wondered if I would always feel a pang of grief whenever I heard a song by Oasis, or The Arctic Monkeys, or even David Bowie and Queen. And if I would forever be stuck listening to classical music from now on? My guitar sat in its box – I couldn't bear to play anything.

As I wasn't spending my free time at Miranda's any longer, I got myself a gym membership, and started getting up early every morning to go to the gym. I spent hours every week punching the boxing bags until every muscle ached and I couldn't take it anymore. The boxing helped me handle the anger – and I found there was a lot of anger – but it also helped me think more clearly.

In the evenings, I stayed late at work so I wouldn't have to do much more than heat a microwave meal before dropping into bed.

A few weeks later, Michael and I met at the pub to watch a Sunday night football match. It was a big game, but I was too distracted to get into it properly.

'You still stewing over Miranda?' Michael asked over his beer as the game went to half time.

I looked away.

'Do you still feel betrayed?'

'I don't know.' I shrugged. Maybe I felt less betrayed now, but I felt sadder than I had before. 'She should have told me – both back then and when I came back. But I'm starting to feel less angry at her. I've been thinking more about why she didn't tell me, and I guess there's a part of me that's thankful she didn't.'

He narrowed his eyes. 'Why?'

'If she'd told me back then, I would have made it all worse.'

Michael gave a wry smile. 'How?'

'If I'd found out about the baby before the miscarriage, I would have come home, and I would have married her. But...' I looked at him. 'Do you remember when Lisa got sick? Remember how sad everyone was?'

He nodded.

'Well, the reason I left then was that I couldn't handle how everybody hurt over what she was going through. It made me feel so powerless that I couldn't fix Lisa, and so I left. First, I tried to avoid talking about it, and whenever I couldn't avoid hearing about it, I was cold and distant. Emotionally unavailable. And I could tell it was hurtful towards Miranda, but I couldn't handle it.' I ran my hands across my face and sighed. 'I would have ended up hurting Miranda worse if I'd stayed than I did by leaving her. It was the same when my sister, Josie, died.'

Michael set his drink down. 'Uh-huh?'

'I was sad about Josie dying, but I think the worst bit was that there was nothing I could do to fix it. Everyone was hurting, and there was nothing I could do about it. I *hate* feeling powerless. So, that's why I went to counselling.'

'Oh, yeah?' Michael looked up from peeling the sticker off his beer bottle.

'Yeah.' I shrugged. 'I figured it was time I dealt with it, and I hoped that would make me a better person.'

'Yeah, you said about how you thought you'd become a good person.' Michael gave a wry smile. 'And how did it help?'

'My counsellor told me I needed to face my own pain in order to be able to handle other people's emotions. So I processed Josie's death and things like that, and I felt like I came to a place where I dealt with my grief over Josie, and I can handle being around other people that are in pain now. I never used to be able to handle other people's emotions at all before.' I shook my head. 'But now, I don't know that I even want to care at all. I think I'm better off just avoiding all this rubbish. I mean, how is this fair?'

'I don't reckon it's fair at all.' Michael studied me for a while before saying, 'Have you asked yourself what God might think of all this?'

I flinched. 'Um, no.'

'Well, what do you think he thinks?'

'Mum would say something like, God never gives us more suffering than we can handle.'

Michael snorted. 'Yeah well, that's a load of rubbish. Even Paul, in one of the letters to the Corinthians, talks about how he's been under "great pressure, far beyond our ability to endure".' He made quotation marks with his fingers and went on. 'But people like to say that, don't they?'

'Uh-huh.' I took a sip of my beer. 'They also like to say that God is all-powerful, and that's why we can trust him. But if God is so powerful, then why doesn't he stop all this suffering? Why would he think it's reasonable that Miranda would have to go through all of that? Sophia was saying, even on Christmas Day, about how God is good, but how is it *good* to inflict all this suffering on anyone?'

Michael bit the inside of his cheek as if to keep from speaking. Then he looked me in the eye. 'Let's do a thought experiment.'

I sighed. 'Okay?'

'Say God wanted to have real relationship with people. What would be the better way of going about getting that: predestining their lives and controlling them, or giving them free will and allowing them to make real choices that have real consequences?'

I narrowed my eyes at him. 'But God *has* predestined our lives. He is all-powerful and is fully in control.'

'Uh-huh. What if God, who is all-powerful, placed some restrictions on how he were to use his power?'

I huffed. 'Why would he do that?'

'To allow people to make real choices, so they could choose to have *real* relationship with God. If he didn't allow people to make real choices, God would have had to settle for a robotic relationship where all the choices were really made by God.' There was a hint of a smile on his face. 'Kind of like playing chess against yourself. If you know exactly what move you will make when you turn the board around, then the fun of playing chess goes out the window. But if the other player is making their own real choices about what moves to make, even if you know all the possibilities of what the other player might do, suddenly chess can be interesting.'

I smirked. 'I thought you said board games are for boring people?'

'Uh-huh.' He tilted his head. 'But what if it was bigger than chess?'

'Yeah, I see that it would be more interesting for God if we have free will. But that would mean that God *isn't* in control of everything.'

'Exactly.' Michael nodded, then held up his hands. 'Don't get me wrong – I think there's a lot that God is perfectly in control over. But perhaps God *isn't* in control of our choices. Paul says that love "is not self-seeking" – so God doesn't demand that things be done in his own way. Even when people make stupid choices, he won't force his will on them. Perhaps God is just very much in control when it comes to how he responds to us. He will always, *always* respond to us in love and compassion, never insisting or forcing himself on us, but letting us choose freely.'

'It sounds like you're saying that God isn't all-powerful.'

'No, I'm saying maybe he puts some restrictions on his power, in order to allow us to make real choices that have real consequences. For us to be able to have real relationship with him. And if all our choices lead to everything being fun, then they aren't real choices. And then we can't have real relationship'

'Ok, then are you saying God doesn't make suffering happen, but he has to allow it as otherwise we don't have real choices?'

'Sure.' Michael leaned back in his chair.

'Yeah, ok, but Josie dying? Miranda's miscarriage? Lisa dying? None of that happened because anyone chose for it to happen.'

'No, and I don't know *why* any of it happened, but I do know that, though God didn't *cause* any of it, God can be found at the centre of it all. Because he is always looking for ways to bring good out of evil, and he wants us to know his love in *everything* we're going through.'

The game had started again, and Michael went back to watching it. I kept my eyes on the screen, but my attention wasn't on the game. Instead, I thought about the concept of free will.

Could it be that God didn't make suffering happen? And that he wasn't in control? That he allowed suffering because otherwise we would not have free will? But couldn't he stop all this? Couldn't he have some mercy?

And if he did, would he lose the possibility of having real relationship with us?

Chapter 36

Miranda

A week or so later, Sophia and I were sitting at my kitchen table with our laptops open. Sophia was working on marketing for Project Cup, and I was doing the accounts. We hadn't been working for long, when Julia knocked on the front door. 'Miranda? Are you in?'

'In the kitchen,' I called out, making sure to save the spreadsheet before closing my laptop.

Sophia and I both got up as Julia burst into the kitchen wearing the biggest grin. 'Guess what?'

'What?' Sophia asked.

Julia held her left hand up and I saw what looked like a Haribo ring on her ring finger.

I frowned. 'Are you playing the Haribo ring game-'

'Nick and I got engaged!' She jumped up and down and threw herself into hugging Sophia, who froze before seeming to make a conscious decision to engage in the hug.

'What?!' Sophia and I squealed as Julia pulled back, and I caught her hand to get a closer look at her ring. I raised an eyebrow. 'This is a Haribo ring, though. Are you sure you're engaged?'

Eyes wide, she nodded frantically. 'He bought a ring in October that he's going to give me, but he didn't bring it to Kenya, so he gave me a Haribo ring for now instead.'

Sophia smiled and I put on a syrupy voice and said, 'How sweet.'

She sighed, gazing at her ring. 'I know. He is-' Startled, the lights went on in her eyes and she snorted. 'Ha-ha.'

We all laughed, and I caught her in a hug. 'Congrats! I always hoped you guys would end up together.' I motioned to the sink. 'I'll put the kettle on, and you can tell us all about it.'

'Yes.' Sophia nodded decisively and grinned. 'We need all the details.'

That night, I struggled to fall asleep. Julia had told us all about how she and Nick got back together and filled us in on what they had done in Kenya. She had made some interesting contacts, and now there was a greater demand for funding.

It looked to me as though Project Cup was at a critical point. We had to decide whether to invest and consider how we could make the company grow, or to close it all down and be satisfied with what we had accomplished. I knew Julia and Sophia were both wanting to invest more, but I wasn't so sure.

Our success was largely due to the sales at the Christmas market, and I wasn't sure how we would be able to sell a significant number of cups without it. I had told them I would make a spreadsheet and look at the cost/benefit ratio, and we could make decisions next time we talked.

Then Julia had asked what we had been up to in Edinburgh, and Sophia and I looked at each other. Nothing much had changed for either of us, and yet it *felt* like everything had changed. For the better.

Definitely for the better.

It was *definitely* much better that Jack wasn't coming round all the time anymore.

Still, as I struggled to get to sleep that night, I did feel lonely. I was thrilled for Julia. I knew what it felt like to be engaged to the person you loved, and I couldn't have been happier for them.

Nick and Julia had been circling each other for a long time, and though I hadn't expected them to come back from Kenya engaged, I had expected them to at least be dating again after spending the month together.

Still, why would God predestine some people to fall in love and have happy lives together, but predestine others to fall in love just to have their hearts broken? What I had done to deserve all the heartbreak I had been through?

What was wrong with me that God didn't think I deserved happiness?

Julia moved back in with me over the next few days, claiming that living with Nick would be too much of a temptation as they wanted to save sex for marriage. I didn't see much of her, though, as she still spent most of her free time at Nick's flat.

A few weeks later, it was the beginning of March, and we were all hanging out at John and Karen's. They had made Sunday lunch for the usuals to celebrate Nick and Julia's engagement.

Since my last conversation with Jack, I still hadn't been over there, as I figured I would only be a reminder to him of all the things that couldn't be. But I couldn't not go to Julia's engagement dinner, so there I was.

'Miranda, dear! Long time no see.' Karen greeted me when I arrived, giving me a hug before pulling back, and framing my face with her hands as she searched my face. 'Where have you been?'

I gave her an awkward smile and cleared my throat as my eyes found Jack's on the other side of the living room. 'Ah, I've been around. Just busy.' I nodded as she pulled her hands away from my face and stepped back. 'Super busy with, uh... work. You know?'

Her eyes clouded with concern. 'Hmm...'

I pulled my lips into a smile that felt weird on my face. 'Isn't it exciting about Julia and Nick though?'

She clapped her hands together and smiled so wide I felt my own smile grow. 'Yes, isn't it great!' She gave me a conspiratorial look and lowered her voice. 'Of course, my children know how to pick the best people to marry. They get it from their father.' She laughed.

I laughed, too, to cover how utterly awkward I felt. She must have either forgotten Jack had once been engaged to me, or she was trying to give me a compliment. Either way, awkward.

'Not that Jack had the sense to hold on to you, but we'll put that down to him being immature at the time.' She scrunched her nose, and I wished for a sink hole to open and swallow me whole.

Thankfully, Sophia arrived then, and Karen went to say hi.

I took a glass of something bubbly off the table and took a deep sip, expecting alcohol, but was surprised – given Karen's awkward comments – to find it was non-alcoholic. Maybe she was drinking something different.

During dinner I sat next to Sophia and Michael and we talked politics. I had never been that interested in politics, but Sophia and

Michael were going on about an upcoming election in Canada, and I tried to seem interested in order to avoid speaking to other people. Jack was at the other end of the table, seemingly avoiding me as much as I was avoiding him. Thankfully nobody commented, although Julia gave me a few questioning looks.

Chapter 37

Miranda

After dinner, Sophia, Julia and I were sitting in the living room with cups of tea.

'I'm so full.' Julia groaned.

'I know. Me too.' I relaxed into the couch and put my feet up next to Sophia's.

'Let's see your ring, again.' Sophia stretched her hand out to look at Julia's. 'What kind of stone is that?'

'It's a Morganite, or some people call it a pink Emerald.'

'It's gorgeous. I love the rose gold as well.'

'Yeah, me too.' Julia pulled her hand back to look at the ring. 'Nick bought it months ago because it reminded him of me, and just kept it. At the time he never intended on giving it to me, but he bought it because he didn't want anyone else to have it.' She sighed. 'Almost like it was God's plan all along, right?'

I nodded. 'Sure sounds like. I mean, we've all been waiting for you guys to-'

'What did you say?' Sophia sat up properly, tilting her head to one side.

Julia frowned. 'I just meant it feels like God had it all planned out all along. There I was, heartbroken when Nick broke up with me, but God knew we'd get back together. And now, here we are!'

'*No!*' Sophia burst out. 'I know you believe in predestination, but there are too many things wrong with seeing things that way.'

I cleared my throat and tried to catch Sophia's eyes to stop her getting onto her soapbox. 'Sophia-' I started, but it was too late.

'I'm sorry, I don't want to rain on your parade, but I really think you're wrong about God planning our lives like that.'

'What are you saying now, Soph?' Michael sat down next to me and set his coffee on the table.

'She's starting a fight.' I muttered, and he smiled at me. It was a shame he was fake married to one of my best friends. He had the nicest smiles when he gave them out, and I thought maybe if I found somebody like him to spend my life with, then things would be ok. Michael wasn't boring in any way, we would have lots of fun together, and my heart would be entirely safe from falling in love with him.

Nick came in and sat down next to Julia, taking her hand in his, as Jack sat down in the armchair next to them.

I sipped my tea and avoided looking at him, so I didn't have to deal with the assault of attraction I felt for him

'What are we fighting about?' said Nick.

'I'm not fighting. I'm just objecting to how Julia thinks God planned for her and you to be together, and all that happened leading up to this point was part of his plan for you guys.' She frowned. 'That's not fighting. I'm just saying I disagree.'

'Uh-huh.'

'No,' she shook her head. 'I don't just disagree. I most vehemently disagree.'

'There you go.' I glanced at Michael. 'Fighting.'

'What?' Nick asked. 'What do you disagree with? Do you not believe in God now?'

Sophia shook her head again in irritation at him. 'No, of course I believe in God. I just don't believe he plans our lives like that. I don't believe he predestines us to go through hard shit, and I don't think he watches us as we go through that pain with an amused smile on his face, knowing we'll end up coming through it to experience good things in the end.'

'No?'

'No!' Sophia cleared her throat and seemed to realise she was coming across a bit strong. 'Don't get me wrong, I'm thrilled for you guys. I think it's great you've found each other. Finally.' Her lips pulled up as she looked at them, as though she had reminded herself that she should be more personable and not just confrontational. 'I just don't believe you were predestined to end up here in this way. Or at all.'

'Why not?' Nick asked.

Julia and I looked at each other and groaned. 'Really?' Julia said. 'Ask her questions like that and she'll keep going.'

Nick frowned. 'Good. I want to understand how she thinks it works if she doesn't think God has good plans for us.'

'That's just the thing!' Sophia said, excitement visibly running through her as she raised her hands. 'I believe God *has* good plans for us because he is a good God. But they are plans, *plural*. Not *one* plan that we're then stuck with.'

'Same difference, isn't it?' Jack asked.

I couldn't help looking at him, but I didn't like the feelings that rose at the sight of his unshaven face and circles under his eyes. He looked like he hadn't slept in a month. Like he was lonely and sad.

I wished I could have reached out and stroked his face or taken his hand in mine.

'Not at all. If there's *a* plan that determines what happens in life, then God plans for evil. He doesn't just allow it, but he plans it out. And I can't accept that to be true, because that makes him the author of evil, which cannot be because the Bible calls God kind, loving and good.'

'Uh-huh, and if there are many plans?' Jack raised his eyebrows.

I tore my eyes away from him and focused on Sophia.

'Well, that implies the future isn't set, but no matter what happens, God has thought of the possibility of that happening, and he has good intentions for us as we make choices to live a specific future.'

'Huh.' Nick nodded. 'Actually, that's kind of beautiful. It implies Julia and I are together because we *want* to be together, not because we've just gone through the motions of a set plan God came up with.'

Julia looked at him and sighed. 'Yes, that maybe beautiful, but it also means she doesn't believe God knows what will happen.'

Nick looked at Sophia in question.

'Exactly.' Sophia nodded.

'But the Bible says he is all-knowing,' said Julia. 'In which case, he's got to know.'

'I think he is all-knowing in that he knows everything there is to know.' Sophia said, tea forgotten. 'But even God can't know things that aren't knowable.'

I put my empty cup on the table and leaned back against the couch. 'I honestly don't see what difference it makes what God knows or what he doesn't know. Why can't we just agree it sounds like God had a good plan for Julia and Nick, and leave it at that?'

Sophia was having none of it though. 'Because.' She pulled her hands though her hair in frustration. 'Because it makes a difference what you believe about who God is. And he isn't a sadist with evil plans for us to go through trauma. He isn't the author of evil.'

'Ok.' I shrugged. 'So maybe he didn't *plan* for what they went through, but he *knew* about it before it happened.'

'No!' Sophia was getting more and more agitated. 'He didn't know-'

'Yes, because if he didn't know, then he isn't all-knowing!' Julia cut in.

Sophia took a deep breath, and Michael cut in. 'I think what Sophia is trying to say is that God knew all the possibilities of what might happen, and that's why there is no way of coming up with a scenario that he won't have thought of. But he didn't know with one hundred percent's certainty which scenario would be the one they picked. Although, as he knows everything there is to know about both of you, he probably could have guessed at roughly what you might end up doing.' He shrugged. 'And the way we think around how much God knows makes a difference to how we understand him.'

'Right.' Sophia nodded. 'And if God knows we're going to go through something awful but does nothing to stop it, it's like if I know Nick is about to go kill Jack. If I don't try to stop him, or notify the police, and I'm later found to have known, I could be considered an accomplice and equally responsible for the murder.'

Nick's eyes narrowed as he looked at her, 'Are you saying that if God *knows* something will happen, it means he would be, at least partly, *responsible* for whatever happens?'

'Yes.' She tilted her head and held out her hand to rest in the air. 'But there is no evil in God. He is love, and there is no room for even a shadow of evil to exist in his plans for us. That's why it is impossible for him to set a future where we choose to do things that don't align with his love, and it's impossible for him to know a set future.'

'What do you believe then?' Jack asked, and my heart stung as I looked at him.

Would I ever stop missing him?

'I think God knows all the possibilities, but he leaves it up to us to choose.' She smiled. 'But then – like Michael said – he knows us very well, so I'd expect he'd be able to make a very educated guess as to which choices we're more likely to make.'

'But isn't that kind of like him knowing what will happen?'

'No, because he can't know with a hundred percent certainty what we will choose. And if there is even the smallest chance that we'll choose another possibility, then the future must be considered open.'

'I don't see how God can be considered sovereign if he doesn't know the future.' Julia shook her head.

Sophia put her hands out and lifted her shoulders. 'What is harder: deciding the future and then being the puppet master, or thinking of every kind of possibility for every choice every person has ever had to make and will ever have to make, and allowing us the freedom to make the choices we want?'

Nick's eyes narrowed. 'It sounds awfully complicated, though, don't you think?'

'Yes, exactly.' Sophia's eyebrows lifted and she gave him a satisfied smile. 'God can handle complicated, though. That's what I mean.'

Chapter 38

Miranda
It was late that night when I got a call from John.

I had gone to bed, exhausted after the conversation about predestination. I couldn't help but feel that the implications of believing the future wasn't set would be overwhelming. Too tired to think more about it, I had fallen asleep with my Kindle.

When the phone rang, I reached for my phone and hit *accept*.

'H'lo?' I pushed the hair out of my face and yawned, still half-asleep.

'Miranda? It's John.' I sat up straight, all sleepiness gone. A call from John in the middle of the night meant something had happened with Dad.

'Hi, John.'

'I've got some bad news.'

I cleared my throat. 'Ok?'

'Seems your dad's been in a fight, and he's been taken to hospital.'

'What?' Dad wasn't the kind of person to get in a fight.

'I'm going to the hospital. Do you want to come with me?'

'Yes.' I looked down at the tank top and pyjama bottoms I was wearing to sleep in. 'I'll just pull on some clothes.'

My heart was in my throat as I scrambled to find some jeans and a jumper. I was in the hallway, pulling my boots on, when Julia appeared.

'Hey, what's going on?' Her hair was a mess and she squinted through her fingers as if the light was too bright.

'Dad's in hospital.'

'What?' More awake now, she pushed her hair away from her face. 'Is he ok?'

'I don't know.' My voice was shrill even to my own ears. I took a deep breath and pulled on my coat. 'I don't know anything yet.'

She frowned. 'I'll come with you.'

I sighed, overwhelmed at the kindness she was showing me. 'Thank you, Jules, but it's okay. You should go back to bed.'

'Don't be silly; of course I'm coming. I'm just going to pull some jeans on.' She turned to go back to her bedroom. 'Don't leave without me.'

I nodded and pulled on a coat.

There was a knock on the door just as she came back. I opened it to find John on the doorstep. 'Ready?' he asked me.

'Uh-huh, yeah.' I nodded.

'Oh, hi, Julia,' John smiled at his daughter. 'You coming, too?'

We got in the car and I buckled up as John pulled out of the drive.

'You ok?' He looked at me, and I nodded.

'Yeah.' My voice sounded strange… weak. Reminding myself I wasn't a weak person, I cleared my throat. 'What happened?'

'I don't know all the details, but he was in a knife fight, and it sounded bad. They took him straight to surgery.' He glanced at me when we stopped at a red light. He was taking us the back way, past Craigmillar castle, to get there as quickly as possible. 'They said he was still alive, but it sounded like it was a severe injury.'

I nodded and looked out the window, seeing nothing in the darkness. Julia put her hand on my shoulder from behind. She didn't say anything, and I was thankful. I couldn't handle anyone telling me empty words right now.

He was still alive. That sounded ominous. Dad had been in hospital a few years ago, but that was for a persistent pneumonia – not for injuries caused by a fight. How did things get to the point of him being in a fight?

Sober, Dad would never hurt a fly, but things were different when he was on the drink. He had told me violence came closer when he had been drinking, and though he rarely ended up fighting, I knew a lot of his friends had been in and out of jail for assault.

Why hadn't I asked John for help with getting him into rehab? I had known he was drinking for months now.

I cleared my throat. 'I think Dad needs to go to rehab again, John.' Hearing the anxiety in my voice, I made myself take a deep breath. I was *not* a weak person.

He glanced at me as he found us a parking spot. 'Let's see how he's doing, and we'll see what we can arrange once he's better.'

I nodded.

'Miranda.' John parked the car and unbuckled his seatbelt. I felt his hand on my shoulder and turned to him. 'Whatever happens in there, you know we're always going to be here for you.'

My heart sank even as I wanted to lean into the comfort of his hand. Those words were eerily close to those Jack had sent me when he broke up with me.

I forced my face to smile and must have failed badly as he shook his head at me.

'Come on. Let's go see what's what.'

***

A few hours later we were still waiting at A&E. John and Julia were sitting on either side of me, and I don't know what I might have done if they hadn't been there. When we had arrived, John had been to the vending machine and bought coffee for him and Julia, and a decaf tea for me.

Dad had been in surgery for hours, and with every minute my anxiety grew.

Being in the hospital brought back memories of waiting for Mum when she was being treated for her cancer, and the increasing hopelessness as it became clear she wasn't getting better. We kept praying she would be healed, but with every test result my faith grew weaker and weaker.

Had Mum's illness had been God's way of testing my endurance, or giving me an opportunity to grow as a person so I might be able to help others later? The whole thing confused me, because I had felt further away from God than I ever had, and powerless against the cancer. If Mum's sickness was God's idea, I was sure I didn't want to know him.

As I sat waiting for Dad to come out of surgery, I wondered if he would die too. Everything seemed unfair. Why would God inflict awful illnesses on people and allow good people to be injured or killed in senseless knife fights?

I didn't bother trying to bargain with God — there was no point. But as I sat there this time, Sophia's voice sounded in my head. *'There is no evil in God. He is love, and there is no room for even a shadow of evil to exist in his plans for us, so it is impossible for him to set a future where we choose to do things that don't align with his love, and it's impossible for him to know a set future.'*

I had been adamant that she was wrong, but now, for the first time, I wondered if maybe she wasn't as wrong as I had thought. What consequences would her ideas have on my life if I changed my thinking?

I was startled out of my thoughts by a doctor in green scrubs asking if we were James Grant's next of kin.

'Yes,' John answered, standing up. 'Miranda is Jimmy's daughter and we're close friends.'

I stood up, too, and shook the doctor's hand. 'Hi.'

'I'm Dr Cormack, and I've just stitched your dad up. He was in pretty bad shape when he came in. We were concerned about his brain, but we were able to limit the haemorrhaging early on.'

'Thank you,' I said around the lump in my throat. 'Will he be ok?'

'I expect so. Apart from some numbness to parts of the face, I think he'll be able to make a full recovery, although I can't say for certain if he'll be able to keep his ear.' He shrugged. 'There'll be some scarring on his face, but I've done my best. He's still asleep, and is bandaged up, so you can go sit with him if you want.'

I breathed a sigh of relief.

'He'll need to take antibiotics, and paracetamol if he's in pain,' Dr Cormack continued. 'I don't want to prescribe anything stronger, considering his background.'

I nodded. 'Good.'

'He'll be in some pain over the next few days, and he'll need somebody to look after him.'

'Of course.'

'Great. I'll check on him once he's awake, and – if there are no complications – we'll probably be able to discharge him around dinnertime.'

Dr Cormack showed us to where Dad was sleeping, and I sat down next to him, taking his hand in mine. His head was bandaged up, but his eyes and mouth were visible. I didn't want to think about what the face looked like under the bandages.

Looking up at John, I thanked him for taking me to the hospital and waiting with me. He looked so much like an older version of Jack, and I felt a sharp stab as I thought of Jack and his messy hair and beautiful blue eyes.

John looked at me, kindness shining from his eyes. 'No need to thank me, deary.'

My breath caught, and I struggled to speak around the lump in my throat. 'Well, I appreciate it. And you, Julia.'

She hadn't said much but having her there had made me feel less alone.

'I'm happy to stay.'

Judging by how dishevelled she looked, though, she could do with going back to bed.

I gave a weak smile. 'I know. But we're ok. I'll let you know when he's woken up and what happens.'

Julia bit the inside of her lip, and her eyes narrowed as she looked at me, as though deciding what to do. 'You call or text me when he wakes up, you hear?'

I squeezed her hand. 'Uh-huh.'

'And me. I'll be back in a few hours to check on you both.' John stroked the top of my head before looking at Julia and nodding towards the door. 'Let's go, Jules.'

Chapter 39

Miranda

Whilst Dad slept peacefully, I struggled to keep my emotions under control. The severity of Dad's injuries, the hopelessness of his addiction, and the loneliness in it all threatened to overwhelm me. I didn't know how to deal with all this.

Then there were the waves of grief over losing Mum that kept hitting me. I missed the way she would have come in and taken charge of the situation, and how she knew Dad. I felt sure she would have known what to do and how to sort him out now.

The more I thought about it all, the more overwhelmed I felt, and my thoughts drifted back to what Sophia had said about what God knows. Where was God in all this? Had he predestined Dad to end up in hospital tonight? Or was this just one possible outcome of the millions of possible choices? And if God wasn't the brain behind the night's events, then what was he?

Checking my watch, I noted that it was five twenty in the morning. Much too early to text Sophia for some answers. I sat back in the uncomfortable hospital chair and sighed.

I needed answers, though.

I got my phone out and downloaded a Bible app. I remembered how Karen would tell people to start with John's Gospel, so I brought it up and started reading. I had one burning question in my mind: who was God, really?

It was midmorning by the time Dad stirred. Still holding on to his hand, I watched as he opened his eyes. He cleared his throat, but his voice was still hoarse when he said, 'Alright?'

I gave a startled laugh. How this situation could ever be considered alright was beyond me. 'You will be,' I said, trying to seem reassuring.

'Right.' He closed his eyes again and sighed.

I wondered if he had gone back to sleep, but his thumb kept stroking my hand – like he used to do when I was a little girl and woke up after a nightmare. 'Do you remember what happened?'

'Not much.' He cleared his throat again, and I got up and got him some water from the sink. 'You ok?'

'I am now. Scared me, though.' I passed him the plastic cup, then threw my hands in the air. 'What do you think you're doing, getting knifed?'

He startled but managed not to spill his drink. 'Miranda darling, I'm in some pain here. Maybe you could keep your voice down just a wee bit, so my head doesn't explode?'

I narrowed my eyes. 'Mmm. Don't think we're not going to have words about this later, though.'

Dad emptied the cup and wiped his hands over his mouth. 'Oh, I wouldn't dream of it.' His eye twinkled as he looked at me before closing his eyes again.

How could he be lying here bantering with me when he had just been through a drunken knife fight and hours of surgery? I took a breath and relaxed back in my chair as he fell asleep again.

Dad slept for most of the morning, which was reassuring.

I kept reading the Bible. Though I had read some of the Bible before, it struck me now how John kept saying that God was explained through Jesus. So, I figured if I wanted to know who God was, I would have to find out who Jesus was. And as I read about Jesus, I struggled not to like him.

John described him as the light, and already in the first chapter it said that grace and truth came through him. In all his dealings with people, it appeared as though he was kind and loving, especially to people on the fringes of society. I wondered if John's Gospel really was a true representation of Jesus, and how it compared to other books?

Surely God wasn't as good as he came across from reading John?

By midday, Dad was sitting up eating lunch. A couple of hours later, they removed the bandages to check his face.

Though the doctors seemed pleased, I found it difficult to look at him. There were stitches along Dad's eyebrow, down his cheek and along the side of his head, and his face was swollen and red. The right ear was stitched back on, but the doctor frowned at the sight of it, and suggested I keep an eye on it, as it may need to come off again. The other side of his face was bruised as though he had taken a fist to it, and his neck bore bruises as though someone had tried to strangle him. Looking at it all, I felt like being sick. Dad was lucky not to be in the morgue.

After redressing the wounds, Dr Cormack discharged him, and John came to collect us. Julia stayed with her parents so I could stay in her room, and I made up my bed for Dad in order to be able to keep an eye on him. I found him some old clothes I still had from when he used to live with us.

As both of us struggled to stay awake, we had an early night, and even though I wasn't in my own bed, I fell asleep as my head hit the pillow.

***

The next morning, we were having breakfast when the doorbell rang, and John and Karen came over.

I glanced at Dad. He had taken his paracetamol and antibiotics, and the swelling had come down some, but he was still bruised and sore. He was also jittery, something I put down to him going through withdrawal from the alcohol. He looked like he would rather be anywhere else but did his best to put on a smile. His face looked like most children's idea of what a monster looks like, and his smile didn't reach his eyes.

'Morning,' Dad said as John and Karen came in the kitchen. He struggled to meet John's eyes, and shame was written all over him.

Karen put two carrier bags on the counter and hugged me as John sat down at the table next to Dad and they started talking.

Still tense after all the stress of the last few days, I struggled not to fall apart as Karen's hug made me feel a little less alone. She had always been quirky in the best ways, but also, she was kind and sincere and she exuded comfort.

'Now, then. We need to make some tea,' she said, and went to fill the kettle.

I got some cups out and helped her put away the food she had brought.

'I know you don't eat meat, but I brought over some bolognaise for Jimmy, and there's a pork stew in there as well. I'll just pop them in the fridge, and you can heat them later.'

'Thank you.' I nodded gratefully and sat down as she finished making the tea.

'You look like you've seen better days,' Karen said to Dad as she put a big tea pot and a milk jug on the table.

Dad gave her a wry smile. 'You should've seen the other guy.'

I froze. 'What?'

'Miranda, I'm only having a laugh.' Dad's smile slid off his face as he looked at me. 'Don't worry, darling.'

I didn't see anything funny with this situation. At all. 'But do you remember what happened?'

Dad winced. 'Bits and pieces. Mostly it's just black.'

I shook my head and drank the tea Karen had poured for me as John and Karen picked up the conversation. I felt increasingly angry by the whole situation. Angry and unsure of how to handle everything. If Dad could make jokes about it already, he couldn't see how serious it all was. I wanted to bang my head against the wall and scream.

'Miranda?' Karen's voice brought me out of my thoughts.

'Sorry, what?' I raised my head to find her gaze.

'I was just asking about the stitches.'

'Uh-huh. The doctor said we have to go back in a week.'

'They had to sew part of my ear back on.' Dad touched the bandage on his ear. 'They said there's a fifty-fifty chance it'll take. Otherwise, they'll have to take it back off again.'

Karen frowned. 'It sounds as though you need-'

'I need to go for a run.' I cut in and stood up abruptly. I couldn't take it anymore. 'Can you stay with him?'

I put my running clothes on and left the house to the sound of Dad insisting he didn't need a babysitter. I didn't need to stay to know John would be agreeing with him but that they would stay anyway.

Thankfully there were still *some* people in my life with a lick of sense.

Chapter 40

Jack

Though I had expected Miranda to show up for Julia and Nick's engagement dinner at my parents' house, I felt insufficiently prepared for seeing her again.

It had been two months since she had told me about the miscarriage, and I had successfully avoided her since then. In that time, I had been through a rollercoaster of emotions, and I still struggled to know what to think or feel about the whole situation.

As she sat at the other end of the table, avoiding my eyes at all cost, I tried to engage in the conversation about Nick getting malaria in Kenya that Julia and Mum were having. I didn't contribute much to the conversation, and Julia kept giving me funny looks, as though she knew there was something going on, but she wasn't sure what.

I ignored her.

I wished for things with Miranda to be different. My sore heart ached at the sight of her avoiding me. There were only a few metres between us, but it felt like I might as well have been in Hong Kong, as the distance between us felt so great.

What would it take for us to put the past behind us?

Then we ended up discussing what God knows. It struck me that between the conversation I had had with Michael about God possibly restricting his power, and the conversation we had that afternoon about there being restrictions on God's knowledge, there appeared to be a theme. Maybe there really were restrictions on God in order for him to be able have real relationship with us?

The whole concept confused me, as it made for a rather weak God. If God had such restrictions on his power, and on his knowledge, and on his ability to control things, then what made him God?

Wasn't the whole point of him being God that he could do whatever he wanted?

But then again, if God was all-powerful and he predestined people to go through horrendous things, then he wasn't a God I wanted anything to do with either.

That night, I couldn't sleep. Seeing Miranda again combined with all the questions I had about God made me feel restless. Nothing in my life made sense anymore.

The next day, I went to work and tried to concentrate, but I found myself staring off into space. When Liz, the secretary I had struggled with when I first started at the office, asked if I was having a rough day, I shrugged. 'It's been two months of rough days.'

'Huh.' She tilted her head. 'This smells of heart break.'

I gave a weak laugh. 'Maybe.'

'Is it that girl you used to have a picture of on your desk?' She was referring to a picture I had taken on the train in China of the two of us.

I had spent hours looking at the way Miranda's eyes seemed to shine in the photo. She hadn't let me post it to Instagram, so instead I had got it printed, and it had been on my desk until I came back from Michael's and my camping trip. 'Uh-huh.'

'She looked like a nice girl.' She sat down and winked at me. Her voice was hoarse from smoking her whole life, but her smile was warm. 'Tell Auntie Liz what happened.'

I snorted and shook my head. 'I don't even know.'

Liz reached out and patted a hand on my arm in a rare display of affection. 'I don't know much about love, except that it takes a strong heart to love, but it takes an even stronger heart to continue to love after it's been hurt.'

I pushed my other hand through my hair. 'Yeah, maybe.'

She watched me for a moment, before standing up. 'I think you should take a couple of days off. Think through what you want your life to be like. You've spent so much time at the office over the last few months, I'm sure we can spare you a few days.'

'Not sure Euan would agree with that.' Euan was the manager of our department.

Liz snorted. 'You leave Euan to me. Don't you worry about him.' She patted my arm again and stood up. 'Now pack up your things and get out of here. I don't want to see you back before Thursday.'

I sighed. Taking time off wouldn't fix things, but it might give me a chance to get some rest so I could concentrate. I didn't have any pressing meetings in the next couple of days, and I was useless at the office when I was this tired.

So, I packed up my things and went home. And though it was only three o'clock, I went to bed and slept for two hours.

I woke up when my phone rang.

'Hello?' I rubbed at my face as I answered the phone.

'Jack? It's Mum.'

'Uh-huh.' My eyes seemed to be glued closed, and my limbs were still heavy. I yawned.

'Are you ok?'

'Mhm. I just woke up.'

'Oh? Never mind. I just wanted to let you know that Jimmy's back from hospital now.'

'What?' I sat up, tiredness forgotten. 'Jimmy was in hospital?'

'Oh, you didn't know?'

'No. What happened?'

'Oh. I thought Miranda would have told you.' She cleared her throat. 'He was in a fight and was cut rather badly. He'll be okay, though. Miranda's got him home now.'

As I got out of bed, I wondered how Jimmy had ended up in a fight. I tried to recall every interaction I had had with him, and every time Miranda had talked about him. I remembered going fishing with Dad and Jimmy as a child, going swimming in the sea, and going for walks in the Pentland hills. In all my memories of him, he was a gentle and kind man, so him being in a fight seemed out of character.

The next morning, I went to see Miranda. Though I was clear on all the reasons for why we wouldn't be getting back together, and all the reasons for why I couldn't afford to care about her, I found myself knocking on her front door. I figured it would all be awkward, but she was going through a hard time, and I could at least be kind.

Mum opened the door, and Dad and Jimmy were having coffee in the kitchen.

I struggled to keep from grimacing when I saw Jimmy's face. It did not look good. Stitches ran across his cheek and down his neck, and there was still a lot of swelling. He moved as though it hurt, but he smiled when he saw me.

'Long time, no see.' He said and shook my hand.

'Yeah. I hear you're lucky to be able to see at all just now, eh?'

He snorted. 'Takes more than a knife to take out old Jimmy.'

'Uh-huh.' I said. 'Is Miranda around?'

'She went for a run,' Mum said. 'Probably won't be long. You can wait for her here if you want.'

'Sure.' I went to put the kettle on and busied myself making tea. Mum and Dad soon left, and Jimmy and I were alone.

'How long have you been back for, son?'

I took a deep breath as I thought about it. 'About six months now, I think.'

'Huh. Do you miss it?'

'Yeah, sometimes I miss it. Hong Kong is beautiful, and the food amazing.' I thought about how less tangled my life had been in Hong Kong. 'And I guess I miss the lifestyle I had out there.'

Jimmy narrowed his eyes. 'Uh-huh. And what's it been like to be back?'

I wondered what he knew and how much he remembered from when I left. He had been drinking hard then. 'I guess it's been good. And hard. And surprising.'

'Mhm.' Jimmy went to scratch his chin but thought better of it and pulled his hand through his hair instead. 'So, are you back with Miranda, then?'

'Nah.' I gave a wry smile. 'She wouldn't have me back, and it's for the best.'

Jimmy shook his head. 'She's always been too smart for her own good, my lass.'

'No, I think she's right about this. We would just hurt each other, you know?'

Jimmy snorted. 'Oh, I know. I've spent my life trying to avoid hurting people and being hurt. I'll tell you, it doesn't do a man much good.'

I frowned.

'You know, I am probably God's favourite person in the whole world.' He smiled.

Considering the life he had led, I struggled to see how he could have come to that conclusion. 'How do you figure that?'

'Because no matter how stupid I've been – and I've been plenty stupid – he gave me Lisa, and then Miranda.' He looked out the window, as though deep in thought. 'And though I've caused the both of them a whole lot of hurt, they've always cared for me.'

'Well that's good, but…'

'I couldn't accept it, though. Can't handle people caring about me when I'm like this.' He pinned me with his eyes. 'Don't be like me, Jack. Don't throw love away if you've found it.'

'Um…' I swallowed. 'Well, as I said: Miranda won't have me, so…'

'Will she not, now?' Jimmy's eyes twinkled as though he found it all amusing. He shrugged. 'Oh well, I guess that's it, then. She's a stubborn one, my Miranda is.'

'Uh-huh.' I nodded. Unsure of where to go from here, I decided to change the subject. 'Do you remember that time when we went camping up by Glencoe?'

Chapter 41

Miranda

I set my phone to record my run but didn't bother with music. There was enough noise in my head as it was. It was my first run of the year, and I headed toward Arthur's Seat, setting a pace that left me having to focus on my breathing instead of on the warring thoughts in my head.

By the time I got to the steps at the car park by Duddingston Loch, my lungs were gasping for air and I had to slow down. Though slower, I pushed myself to run up the steps to Queen's Drive, the road that circled the hill. Muscles burning, I slowed to a walk and looked toward the sea.

The view of the sea meeting the sky was soothing, and though I was in the centre of the city, the air smelled different up there. It was fresher somehow.

I shivered. It was also windier.

I pushed some hair out of my face, took a deep breath and set off again, this time at a more reasonable pace. Following the road round the hill, I stretched my legs as I passed Dunsapie Loch and the road started sloping downward. Though it was only February, and Monday morning, there were plenty of people on the hill – though nowhere near as many as during the summer months.

My runs had started getting longer back when Jack had left for Hong Kong, Mum was sick, and I had miscarried. Though there were weeks after Mum died where I struggled to get out of bed, I soon found that the only way to put life together again was by making sure I kept running. Running meant I had to eat properly, and the days I ran I found sleep came easier. It also helped me think, and it let me feel all the pain of the losses I was experiencing, and I found I was able to somehow go on.

The following summer, I ran a half-marathon, which seemed like a massive win for me. God had just dealt me the shittiest year, but I had survived. Running was how I dealt with sadness, and I reminded myself now that though I was sad, I could handle it. I thought about how I was going to broach the idea of rehab with Dad. And how I was going to pay for it.

But most of all, I thought about God.

Reading John's Gospel at the hospital the previous day had stirred a hunger inside me, and now I wanted answers. If God wasn't some old man on a cloud with a stick out to get me – if I had been wrong about him all this time – what was he really like? The more I thought about it, the more I felt something on the inside grow. It felt like spring, but on the inside of me.

When I came home, I found Jack at the kitchen table with Dad. He hadn't been over since the night I told him about the miscarriage and seeing him there startled me and made my pulse race again. 'Hello.'

'Hello, darling.' Dad's eyes sparkled as he looked from me to Jack and back again.

Jack set his cup down and pushed his chair back. 'Hi. I'll get out of your hair.'

I frowned. 'No, it's okay. You're welcome to stay.'

He looked at me as though he wasn't sure what to think but stayed in his seat.

Ignoring all the feelings of seeing him at my table again, I went to get a glass of water, and drank it all in one go.

'Nice run?' Dad asked.

'Uh-huh.' I wiped at my face, conscious of how sweaty I was. 'I'm going to shower.' I wondered what had brought Jack over. He used to avoid any sign of Dad being in a rough place – to find them chatting over coffee seemed weird.

When I came out of the shower, Jack was pulling hummus and vegetables out of my fridge, making lunch for us, and again I wondered why. He seemed comfortable in my kitchen, and despite my questions as to why he was there or what he wanted, I liked that he was there. His presence soothed me, even as it raised questions.

I decided to leave the questions for another time and gave him a tentative smile as I went to put out new cups for tea to go with lunch. 'This is nice. Thank you.'

He put some pita breads in the toaster and shook his head. 'It's no problem.'

Lunch was awkward. There were loads of questions I wanted to ask, both of Dad and of Jack, but none of my questions seemed appropriate to ask either of them when the other was there. I let them talk to each other, instead, and listened as they told me a story of when they had gone fishing together with John many years ago. It must have happened before Josie died, and it made me try to remember what those years had been like. It seemed Jack and Dad had several memories together – none of which I was part of – and they were having a nice stroll down memory lane together.

I recalled Mum saying that Dad would need me to remember and remind him of who he was. That he wasn't just some alcoholic, but a kind person who was creative, and fun, and caring. And it struck me that Jack was doing exactly that: reminding Dad of who he was even as his jittery hands and the stitches and swelling on his face wanted to label him a drunk.

After lunch, Dad took his pills and went to sit down in the living room.

Jack stayed in the kitchen, helping me clear the table.

'Thanks for staying with Dad when I was out.' I stepped around him where he was putting things back into the fridge. I felt clumsy and unsure of how to handle having him back in my kitchen after so long. What did it mean that he was here?

Jack shrugged. 'It was nice to catch up with Jimmy. Haven't seen him in years.'

'Uh-huh.' I rinsed the kitchen cloth out and went to wipe the table down. Not knowing how to ask how he was doing, I decided to avoid the whole question of why he was here and what it all meant. 'I didn't realise you guys had hung out that much before.'

'It's a long time ago.' He said in a distracted voice as he looked around the kitchen as if to check everything was put away. 'I'll be on my way, then. Thanks for lunch.'

I followed him to the hallway and watched as he shrugged into his coat. His hair was a mess and I wanted to run my fingers through it to fix it. Or ask how he was doing. Or invite him to stay longer – have a cup of tea with me and catch up. But I knew I didn't have the right to do any of that. Instead, I kept my hands to myself and stayed quiet.

'I'll see you later.'

'Uh-huh,' I said, not knowing what he meant. Later when? Shaking my head, I went to talk to Dad in the living room. His legs twitched as he sat on my couch pretending to read a book, and I knew it wouldn't be long before he left.

'Dad, do you need a drink?'

He looked at me, then quickly away, and I kicked myself for not being more specific. Of course he wanted a drink. He was an alcoholic.

I sighed and gentled my voice, 'I meant I was going to make some tea. Would you like some too?'

He cleared his throat and said yes, even though tea was probably last on his list of preferred beverages.

The kettle had just boiled when I heard the front door close. I watched through the window as Dad sat down on the front step and took out his cigarettes. He seemed so jittery, and it struck me he was nervous.

Everything in me wanted to yell at him, but maybe that would do more harm than good, even if it might make *me* feel better. Deciding on a softer approach, I finished making the tea, and took it out and sat down next to him.

'You know Miranda, I've been thinking.' He took a last pull on the cigarette before putting it out on the doorstep.

'Not too hard, I hope,' I said and winked.

He snorted and it was good to see his eyes light up, however briefly. The last few days had been rough for both of us.

'I haven't got many brain cells left after the life I've lived, but I rubbed the ones I still have together, and I thought perhaps there are a few things we need to talk about.' He bit the inside of his cheek as he waited for me to respond. He saw my raised eyebrows and lifted chin and took it as a sign to keep going. 'You know I loved your mother.'

'Are you sure you want to talk about this now?' It had been six years since Mum died, and we still hadn't talked about it. I hadn't wanted to bring it up, as I wasn't sure if the topic would make his drinking worse, but part of me had longed to talk with him about her.

He gave a sharp nod. 'From the time I met your mother, I fell in love. She lit up the room, and life seemed just a little golden when she was around. She made me believe there were things in life worth living for, you know?'

I nodded.

'I didn't have an easy life, and I got into my fair share of trouble. There were drugs and alcohol, and I did things I shouldn't have done. And then when I met her, I realised life didn't have to be like that.' He narrowed his eyes. 'There were other options. And when I was around her, changing the way I lived wasn't even hard. And then you came along, and I had another reason to live.'

I rested my head against his shoulder, huddling closer to fend off the cold, and let him keep talking. He smelled of smoke, and I made a mental note to make sure I washed his clothes before he went back home again.

'The thing with life, though, is that things don't always go the way you want them to. And after a while, I thought I could go out with some friends and have a drink. Only, when they went home, I kept drinking. It was like I couldn't stop. The next morning, I felt terrible and I didn't know what to tell your mum. I knew she'd be disappointed. So, I decided I would have another beer to make the headache go away. Just so I could think clearly again. But again, I couldn't stop. That time I was away for a month.' He sighed. 'And when I finally came back, your Mum looked at me, asked me if I was done, and took me back.'

He bit the inside of his cheek. 'She was like that. She always believed the best about me – even when I showed her there was no *good* in me. When my mood swung, she took me to the doctor, and I was given pills to help stabilise me. But living with someone so good, someone who has such high expectations for me, was exhausting, and over and over again I slipped back to the alcohol.' He gave me a wry smile. 'I know I am a failure, and in the end, it became easier to accept that than to continuously push it all away.'

I sighed as my heart ached for him. He had failed himself, Mum, and me in loads of ways, but it hurt to hear him talk of himself as a failure.

'I will always wish I had been there for you and Lisa when she was sick.' He shook his head. 'At the time, though, I couldn't. Being sober then was torture. And though I've had some sober periods since then, it's been a long time since I've been properly sober.'

I reached out and touched his arm. 'I've been thinking about that. Can we talk about what happened?'

'Aye.' He went to run his hand through his hair but remembered about the stitches and stopped himself with a sigh.

'You know I love you, Dad, eh?' I waited and gave him a gentle smile when his eyes met mine.

'I know, Mir-maid,' he said gruffly. 'And I love you, too.'

I sharpened my eyes, and struggled to keep my voice in a nice tone as I said, 'How on *earth* did you end up in a knife fight?'

He snorted and looked away. 'Ah, Mir, you know what it's like… violence comes closer once there's alcohol involved.'

'So, you're saying you sat around drinking, and all of a sudden someone takes out a knife?'

'No, not exactly.' He gave a dry chuckle. 'Matty was there, and he's been being harassed by this guy, Raz.'

'Raz is the scary guy with the tattoos and the glass eye, right?' Some of Dad's friends had been around for a long time.

'Uh-huh.' A twinkle came into his eye. 'I wouldn't call him scary, exactly.'

'What would you call him, then?'

He sniggered to himself. 'I think I might have called him a wimpy bully.'

I stared at him. 'You called him a *what?*'

'He was putting Matty down. Again. And Matty's only little. Can't defend himself.' He shrugged. 'So, when he started calling Matty's girlfriend names, I called him out.'

I took a deep breath. 'And then what happened?'

'Nothing happened then. He laughed and then left a few minutes later. But then he came back later in the evening. He knocked on the door, and this time he wasn't laughing. He got me to come out, and then it's all black.'

'Uh-huh.' I put my head in my hands, rubbing my forehead as I tried to process the situation.

'But the police got him, didn't they, and I'll be fine.' He smiled and wiggled his eyebrows. 'Might even get some compensation.'

I squeezed my eyes shut, hoping the situation would have changed when I opened them again. It hadn't. Dad still seemed pleased with himself, and I couldn't take it anymore. I stood up and turned on him, gesturing in the air and raising my voice. 'Your face looks like a patchwork quilt, and you might lose your ear. You're lucky to be alive! But sure, you might get some compensation, so it's all worth it?'

He winced. He seemed smaller than before when he looked at me with kind, remorseful eyes. Eyes that wouldn't hurt a fly. 'I'm sorry Miranda.' He held a hand up and tilted his head. 'I don't mean to make light of it. But what's the point in dwelling on all that?'

'The point is that you can't keep living like that.' I took a few steps away and tried to calm down. It was like he didn't realise how much it hurt me to watch him go through all this. Part of me wanted to tell him, but the other part knew it would only heap shame onto him. And shame had never helped anyone get their life sorted out. I took a deep breath and tried to soften my voice. 'What are you going to do with whatever compensation you might get?'

He shrugged. 'Well I have a bit of debt, so…'

'Yeah, so you settle your debts.' I nodded. 'And if there's any money left over, I want you to consider going to rehab. If you don't get any compensation, or there isn't enough money, I'll work out how to pay for it.'

'Yeah, maybe. I spoke to John about it earlier.' A small laugh escaped, but he quenched it before looking at me again. 'Being knifed has a way of jarring you awake, and I've been thinking that maybe I need to sort myself out a bit again.'

'This whole situation is exasperating.' I sat down and reached for his hand. 'But most of all, it scared me. I don't want to lose you, you know?'

'I don't want you scared.' Eyes sad now, he gave my hand a squeeze. 'I can't stay here much longer, Miranda. But you can speak to John, and we'll talk about what's next.'

I bored my eyes into him. 'You're staying here another night, and don't you even try to say otherwise. You've got to keep taking your medicine, so you're staying. Next week I'll come collect you from your flat, and we'll go to the doctor to check your ear together. You're going to be sober for that appointment, you hear?'

'Uh-huh.'

His legs twitched, and I knew I was pushing too hard. I reminded myself that he was an adult and had to be allowed to make his own choices. Softening my tone, I said, 'I mean, it would make me feel better if you would please do those things for me.'

He gave a wry smile and put his arm around my shoulders. 'I'll do my best.'

Chapter 42

Miranda

Dad stayed that night but left after breakfast. He told me he wanted to go back and sort things out at home, and as much as I wanted him to stay, I knew he had to make his own choices. I sent food home with him, and he told me he would make sure to take his medicine.

'You keep your phone on so I can reach you, and…'

'Aye, don't you worry about me. I'll be staying in my flat, keeping away from people.' He sniggered. 'Wouldn't want to scare any children with this face of mine.'

'Well.' I grimaced. 'I wouldn't enter any beauty contests just now if I were you.'

He grinned as he put his arm around me and squeezed.

I hugged him back, careful not to hurt him. 'Be safe, okay?'

'Ha. Safety is overrated.' He winked at me and opened the door, raising his hand as he stepped outside. 'See you next week, Mir-maid.'

Once Dad had left, I considered going in to work, but decided I could do with another day off to recover from the emotional upheaval I had just been through. So, I spent the rest of the morning cleaning, and had just started pulling vegetables and hummus out of the fridge for lunch when Jack knocked on the door.

'Hey?' I answered. He looked like he hadn't slept in days, but still he looked so… *good*. His hair was ruffled, but his blue eyes were sharp. His collar was turned up to his ears, but his coat was open, as were the top few buttons of his shirt.

'Hey.' Jack said, and I felt how his eyes swept over my face. 'Um… Is Jimmy here?'

I shook my head and tried to find my voice. 'He left this morning.'

'Oh.'

'Do you want to come in? I was just about to have lunch.' I stepped back from the door and gestured toward the kitchen.

He looked away and shifted his weight from one foot to the other. I thought he was about to tell me he had to go when he said, 'Yeah, okay. I could eat.' Toeing his shoes off, he followed me into the kitchen, shrugging out of his coat and hanging it over a chair.

I got out a plate for him, put another pita bread in the toaster, and cut up more vegetables. 'You not at work?'

'Huh?' He seemed confused, then shook his head as he sat down at the table. 'I had some annual leave to take before the end of the tax year.'

'Oh.' I brought the last bits to the table and sat down. 'So… what have you been up to?'

'Not much.' He reached for some food and dipped his pita bread in the hummus. Looking up at me, he said, 'You?'

His eyes seemed to pierce my soul today. I cleared my throat. 'Just working on Project Cup stuff.'

He nodded and kept eating.

Not sure what to say, I put food in my mouth too. I glanced at him and noticed his hair was longer than usual. Also, if the size of his shoulders was anything to go by, I guessed he had made use of his gym membership in the last couple of months.

'… okay?' Jack's question broke through my thoughts.

'Uh… Yes.' I squeezed my eyes shut as I tried to shove my speculations about Jack's muscles out of my mind. *What was the question?* 'I mean, no.'

He frowned. 'Right?'

'Right.' I nodded decisively, still having no clue what I had just said an adamant no to.

'No?' Jack seemed confused. 'I mean, which is it? Is he okay or not?'

'Oh!' I smiled with relief as I gathered Jack had asked about my dad. 'I mean yes, *he* thinks he's okay.'

He raised his eyebrows and looked at me expectantly. 'Okay…'

'But he clearly isn't okay. He'll be drinking again by tonight, forget to take his medicine, and end up losing that ear.' I shrugged as though it was no big deal. 'We talked about him going to rehab again, though, and he said he is open to that, so…'

'I guess that's positive, right?' Jack bit the inside of his cheek as he studied me.

'Right.' I avoided his eyes and kept eating as the silence stretched out between us. When I couldn't handle it any longer, I said, 'I don't know if I said, but thank you for staying with Dad yesterday when I was out.'

'No problem. I haven't seen him in ages; it was nice to catch up with him.'

I glanced at him. 'Before Mum died, she told me Dad would need me to remember who he is, and to remind him. Most people look at Dad and see a drunk – and he *is* a drunk – but there's more to him than that. And it meant a lot that you spoke to Dad the person, instead of Jimmy the drunk.'

Jack nodded. 'I wonder how life would be different if we gave up pegging people as drunks, or mentally ill, or whatever job we have, or whatever bad decisions we once made, and instead thought of ourselves and others as people.'

I studied him. 'Yeah…'

Jack's eyes were determined as they fixed on me. 'I reckon pegging people as only being one thing is the lazy way out.'

He wasn't talking about Dad anymore, but I wasn't sure what he was getting at. 'Sure…'

Squeezing his eyes shut, his thumb and index finger pressed at the bridge of his nose. Then he shook his head. 'Never mind.' He had finished eating and took his plate to the counter.

Watching him, I gave a weak smile. 'Are you okay?'

He glanced at me. 'Sure. You?'

I gave a quick nod. 'Uh-huh. Yeah, of course.'

'Of course.' Jack snorted. He stared at me as though he wanted to say more, but held back. Reaching for his coat, he seemed sad as he said, 'I'll be going, then. Thanks for lunch.'

'Right.' I stood up and followed him into the hall. He was pulling his shoes back on and my heart lurched as I realised that he had come to see Dad, and now that Dad wasn't here, there was no knowing when Jack might come back again. When I might see him again.

When he stood up, he was closer than I had anticipated, and, drawn by something I wasn't comfortable defining, I stepped in even closer and pressed a kiss to his cheek.

Taken off guard, he let one hand fall around my waist, and I dropped my forehead on his shoulder as his other hand stroked my head. His smell was both a comfort and a reminder that he wasn't mine.

Realising what I was doing, I pulled back and cleared my throat as I ran my fingers over my face. 'I'm sorry.'

He pulled a hand through his hair as the other reached for the door. 'Right.' Opening the door, he glanced at me. 'I'll see you around, I guess.'

The door closed behind him, and he was gone, and I was left alone to work out what had just happened.

Chapter 43

Jack

After leaving Miranda's, I wasn't sure what to think. Everything inside was in knots and nothing made sense. After wandering around the flat aimlessly, my guitar seemed to call my name, so I took it out for the first time in months. I had never been good with lyrics, but the music came back to me as I played, and though it brought me no answers, I found there was something comforting about playing. Hours passed as I let the music flow out of and into me – the old familiar melodies soon giving way to new tunes that seemed to come from somewhere within me.

I went for a run that evening – my first one outside that year. It was cold and dark and wet, but the icy rain on my cheeks made me feel alive, so on I ran. I thought about how awkward lunch with Miranda had been. I had wanted to see Jimmy again, and I should have left when she had told me he wasn't there. I wondered briefly why I had stayed, but all the reasons that came to mind made me feel uncomfortable.

Instead, I wondered how Miranda had handled all the awful things she had been through. Jimmy being an alcoholic, Lisa dying from cancer, and being all alone with it and having a miscarriage – it seemed like too much for one person to bear. And now she was caring for her dad, who she had almost lost in a fight.

None of it seemed fair, and as my anger rose inside my chest, my instinct was to blame God. But after my recent conversations with my counsellor and other people about God, I wasn't sure I could blame him for any of it any longer.

And that annoyed me, too. It might be nice for God if he weren't to blame, but if he was powerless and out of control in these kinds of situations, then what was he good for?

Liz's words came back to me: *I don't know much about love, except that it takes a strong heart to love, but it takes an even stronger heart to continue to love after it's been hurt.*

Had I been looking at it all wrong? Was God powerful not because he could do anything he wanted, but because he would keep on loving no matter what?

I slowed down as I reached the beach at Portobello. Though it was dark and raining, there were people walking their dogs on the beach and children riding their bikes along the prom. It was too cold to stop, so I ran down the prom towards Joppa. I filled my lungs with the sharply cold sea air, and I felt my head clear as I ran.

When I had started going to counselling in January, I had told my psychologist, Alison, that I didn't have a handle on my life. I needed to work out how to live again. Over the following weeks, I had shared about how powerless I had felt when Josie died. I had felt so out of control as I watched the world crumble around my family. Nothing I did could bring Josie back, and the more I cared, the harder it was to handle my powerlessness.

I had shared about my teenage relationship with Miranda. We had been in love, but I hadn't been able to let myself care about the things she went through, because if I did, then I would feel powerless again. And when Lisa got her terminal diagnosis, I panicked and left the country because I couldn't handle the feeling of being out of control and powerless.

And I had told Alison about how if Miranda would have told me about the miscarriage back when it happened, it would have been more of the same. I would have felt so out of control and powerless when faced with Miranda's sadness and the grief of losing the baby. I would have closed myself off to her, and maybe even blamed her.

Alison was probably the least judgemental person I had ever met. Nothing I had shared with her seemed to phase her, yet shame still filled me as I came to realise that I had spent my life trying to protect myself from feeling powerless and out of control. I had put distance between myself and others, thereby hurting them. And by sheltering myself from other people's feelings, I had become an island. I had decided that relationships weren't worth the pain they caused.

Alison had pointed out that maybe I was a little risk averse.

That had surprised me at first. I had thought of myself as a risk-taking adventurer. I moved to Hong Kong and lived there for several years. I had travelled all over the world on my own. I took big risks at work. But as I thought about it, I had come to see that she was right. My time in Asia had been more about avoiding the people and possible hurt at home than it had been about throwing myself into an adventure.

'It's okay to be risk averse,' Alison had said, looking me straight in the eye. 'But if you want to live a life where you're not afraid of the possible hurt you might experience, then you might want to consider taking a different approach.'

As my feet pounded the pavement now, it struck me that God's approach was the opposite of mine. Where I avoided people to protect myself, and tried to care less about people, he continued to choose to put himself into the mess of the consequences of our choices, and to love us even though our pain must be almost unbearable for him. Even though it technically could be within his power to take charge and force his will on people, he chose the messy, loving way of respecting people's choices.

Liz's words, *I don't know much about love, except that it takes a strong heart to love, but it takes an even stronger heart to continue to love after it's been hurt*, ran across my mind again as I turned around and ran in the direction of home.

Maybe she was right. Maybe God's strength was that he continued to love, even when it hurt him.

When I had been in counselling in Hong Kong, the psychologist had asked me why I thought I would be more able to handle life if I never felt powerless and out of control. At the time, I hadn't understood the question. But now, I wondered if he had had a point. Maybe the way out of the mess with Miranda was to face the pain instead of running from it. And maybe it wasn't just about facing the pain and suffering that life brought, but also about facing the powerlessness that came along with it.

Don't throw love away if you've found it. Jimmy's words echoed in my head. Choosing love appeared to be equal to surrendering to being powerless. But if God and Jimmy were to be believed, it might be worth it.

Chapter 44

Miranda

I had sent enough food with Dad that he should have had enough to eat for the week, but I knew he would forget about food if he was drinking. Therefore, I made a point to text him at lunchtime every day. The evening before he was due to go back to hospital, I called him.

'I'll come for you at ten tomorrow,' I said.

'Tha's g'd,' he slurred. 'Wha's t'morro'?'

'I'm taking you to the hospital because the doctor needs to have a look at your ear.'

'Ma ear, y'hear?' He giggled at his joke.

'Uh-huh.' I sighed. 'Maybe it's time to have a glass of water, or a cup of coffee?'

'Y'alway' say tha'.' He laughed harder. I imagined him shaking his head as he said, 'A glass o' wa'er,' as though it was the funniest thing he had heard all day.

'Right. Look, I'll call you tomorrow morning so you have time to get ready. You've got to be sober for your appointment, you hear?'

'I hear, m'dear.' More giggles.

'Okay, well, I'll talk to you tomorrow morning, then.' I hung up and rubbed my face. Why did he have to make loving him this difficult?

Then next morning, I called at seven. When he didn't pick up, I decided I would have to go early, as otherwise we might miss the appointment.

When I showed up at eight thirty, I was expecting to have to drag him out of bed, so I was surprised to find him dressed and sitting on the front step of the house waiting for me. I suspected he didn't want me to see the state of his flat, and that's why he was waiting for me outside, but at least he was ready.

His face looked less swollen, even though I doubted he had taken care of the wounds.

'Do you want to have breakfast before we go?' I hugged him. His jacket was too big and smelled of smoke, but Dad smelled nice. Like he had showered. 'We have time.'

He gave a weak smile. 'I'll maybe stick to coffee this morning, but I'm happy if you want to eat.'

'Sure.' We got in the car, and I handed him my phone open to my music app. He browsed through my music before putting on some Jimi Hendrix as I drove through town. I smiled as he relaxed back in his seat.

As it turned out, Dad got to keep his ear, and the doctor was satisfied the rest of his wounds were healing up nicely. Afterwards, I took him out for lunch before dropping him off again. As I drove away, I wondered when I would see him next – and what state he would be in then.

That night, I researched rehab options again, and emailed a few places. The likelihood of getting funding for him to go to rehab again was low, which was why I was looking at the private options. They all seemed to cost a lot, or they were faith-based. I wanted Dad to get better, but I wasn't sure brainwashing would be a good idea, so I made a note to speak to John about the options. He had mentioned a rehab before which had sounded okay.

Putting my laptop away, I pulled out my Bible. Ever since Dad had been in hospital, I had read the Bible every day. When I was a teenager and a youth leader had suggested I try reading the Bible, I had laughed. Whenever I would try, I would get to somewhere in Leviticus and give up. It was too dry to keep my attention. But as I read the Bible now, I found it was actually quite interesting.

I didn't read it in order, but picked books at random, and Sophia had suggested I read five Psalms each day – that way I could read through the book of Psalms in a month.

I didn't understand everything I read. Instead, I had a list of questions on my phone, which I would bring out whenever I saw anyone I thought might be able to answer any of them. My questions ranged from what the heckerino Revelations was all about, to what "promise" they kept referring to. Or what Jesus meant when he talked about taking the children's bread and giving it to the dogs when he spoke to the Syrophoenician woman. Or whether I would have to believe in the six-day creation as described in Genesis in order to be a Christian. And though I had more questions than answers, I found that it was okay to have questions and doubts – even Jesus' disciples had doubted him.

Still, the most pressing questions – who was God really, and what consequences did that have for me? – were questions I couldn't let go of. Consequently, I kept reading.

The following Saturday, Sophia, Julia and I met up to talk about Project Cup.

On the way there, I went window shopping in town. I tried on a pair of running shoes but decided my old ones would have to do for a while longer when I considered the price. I couldn't afford to spend money on nonessentials. Maybe if I re-mortgaged the house, I would be able to pay for Dad's rehab. That's what Mum had done last time he went.

By the time I got to the coffee shop by the Meadows, Sophia and Julia were already seated with their drinks, so I ordered a ginger tea and joined them.

'When can Michael apply for indefinite leave to remain, again?' Julia was asking Sophia as I sat down.

Sophia shook her head. 'He has indefinite leave to remain already, but when you get that, you still have to intend to stay married to your spouse if you've been on a spouse visa before. We don't want anyone to suspects anything, so we decided we'd stay married until he has his British citizenship.'

'Uh-huh.' Julia smirked and stirred her coffee. 'And when is that?'

'I think he can apply in June.'

'Oh, wow. That's soon. Are you getting divorced then?'

Sophia shrugged. 'Probably.'

'Really?' I asked. I knew Sophia and Michael's marriage was a sham, but did it have to be?

'Well, there's no reason to stay married once he's got his passport, right?' Julia pushed.

Sophia cleared her throat. 'Right.'

'Huh.' Julia caught my eyes and struggled to hide her grin at how Sophia's head appeared to be firmly stuck in the sand. 'Anyway...'

'Yes, let's talk about your numbers for Project Cup, Miranda.' Sophia said, and looked at me hopefully.

'Okay, but for the record: I think you should let him bring up the question of divorce. I mean, you proposed. Let him end it.'

'You think?' Sophia frowned.

'Well, unless you're in a hurry to move on...' I had a feeling pigs might fly before Michael suggested they get a divorce.

'No, there's no stress.' She pursed her lips.

'Uh-huh.' Julia sent me a knowing look. 'No stress.'

Sophia looked at her and frowned. 'No, I mean, I wouldn't want him to feel pressure.'

'Right. No pressure.' Julia couldn't contain her smile anymore, and it spread across her face.

'Oh, stop.' Sophia threw a serviette at her.

Julia caught it, laughing now. 'What do you mean *stop*? I'm not doing anything.'

Sophia tilted her head and raised her hands. 'Whatever. Think what you want.'

Julia kept laughing. 'Mhm.'

'Anyway,' I said, and pulled out my laptop. Sophia seemed conflicted enough without us stirring the pot. 'I've been crunching some numbers...'

'Uh-huh.' Sophia sat up straight, ignoring Julia.

'And now that we're almost out of stock, we need to decide what to do about Project Cup.'

Julia sobered and sat up, too. 'What do you mean *decide*?'

'Yeah, well, this was a pilot project, right? Therefore, we need to evaluate the outcome and then make decisions as to whether it is something we want to take forward.'

'Oh.' Julia frowned. 'Well, of course we want to keep going. It's been a great success.'

'Okay. You say that because you saw how we were able to support the girls in the school in Mombasa, but I think we need to look at a few more things before we can say *it's been a great success*.'

'Like what?'

'Well, I think we need to evaluate what we've learned about the market for period cups in Scotland, and look at our sales figures, and so on.' I said. 'Don't you think?'

Sophia nodded. 'Uh-huh, I agree.'

'Okay, fine.' Julia relaxed back in her seat. 'One thing that's working well is the web shop, isn't it, Sophia?'

'Yeah.' Sophia moved some coffee cups on the table to set her laptop down. 'We've spent a bit on advertising, and we're growing our social media presence, which has led to our web shop is getting more and more traffic.'

'I think the website and our social media accounts look great.' Julia smiled.

'Considering that's what my real job is, that's a relief,' Sophia said wryly.

'Uh-huh, and that's great,' I agreed. 'There seems to be a market for period cups.'

'Right. If you can sell them at the Christmas Market, then they'll sell anywhere,' Julia said.

'The thing is,' I cut in. 'We've spent most of our earnings on cups for the girls in Kenya, and that means we haven't got much money to put toward new cups, should we decide to keep going-'

'Should we decide,' Julia set her drink down. 'What do you mean *should we decide to keep going?* We've come this far, haven't we?'

'Sure, but if we do want to keep going, we would need to buy new cups, and that costs money. Money which we haven't got.' I looked at her, trying to gather my patience and exercise it. My head hurt, and my neck was all stiff from spending the last couple of weeks worrying, and I didn't really have the energy for a fight. 'And though Angus and I would be happy to do a race to raise money, I doubt we could raise enough to cover what it would cost. And then it might be better if we commit to fundraising every year. That way we can support girls in Kenya directly, without having to spend all our time selling period cups here?'

'I'm getting some bad vibes off you, Miranda,' Julia said. 'What is going on?'

I shrugged. 'I'm just saying if the goal is to support girls in Kenya, then maybe there are easier ways that don't require as much of us?'

'*What?*'

'Well, let's be honest. If instead of spending the amount of money we've spent on making Project Cup happen, we would have just given that amount straight to the school in Kenya. We would have made a bigger difference than we were able to do by doing it this way.'

'Really?' Julia winced. 'But we worked *hard*.'

'Yeah, but we've got to be real here.' I held up my hands. It bothered me when people tried to make up a reality that wasn't actually based on evidence.

Sophia looked at me. 'Give it to us straight – what are you actually saying?'

'I'm saying that if we really want for Project Cup to make a bigger difference than our occasional raising funds might do, then we would have to invest ourselves a lot more and build the business side of this up to be a proper, growing business. And we do have the skeleton in place so we could do that. But in order to do that, we would have to give more of our time.' Waving my hand in the air, I continued, 'I don't want to come across as stingy here, but I don't know that I could afford to cut my hours, or give up my job, in order to invest in a way that would really make this a viable business.'

'Uh-huh. I take it you've run the numbers?' Sophia asked.

'Yeah.' Of course I had. I went on to tell them how many cups we would have to sell to make our profit bigger than our spending. 'And that's not impossible, but…'

Sophia sucked in a breath and winced. 'Not impossible, but it would take a heck of a lot of work.'

'Well, I'm not afraid of hard work.' Julia said in a belligerent tone.

'Uh-huh,' I rolled my eyes. Julia's endless optimism was starting to wear on my nerves. 'But what I'm saying is that we probably can't do it unless we put in more hours. And where are those hours going to come from?'

'Well, we each give a couple of days a week.' Julia held out her hands. 'How hard is that?'

'Mhm, and that would be great, but I don't know that I could afford to do that.' If I had to pay for Dad to go to rehab, I would be strapped for cash, even working full time.

'At what point would it become feasible to pay someone to do the work here?' Sophia asked.

'I looked at that too, and – bearing in mind that paying a salary would cut into the profit – if we were to go ahead now and things were to take off, I reckon we could maybe pay a small salary to someone in about a year.'

Julia brightened. 'That's good. A year isn't that long.'

A year was an eternity if you had to pay for your Dad to be in rehab for that long. 'Well, that's if everything goes according to a best-case scenario.' I leaned back in my chair. 'And it is my experience that most things don't tend to.'

Julia huffed. 'Of course they would. This is a fantastic business. It will take off soon enough and then we'll be laughing. Think of how many girls we're going to be able to help. I've been thinking about refugee camps, and how much of a difference period cups might make there, too.'

'Uh-huh, and I would love to help more people, too.' I held up a hand and tried giving a smile. 'Like I said, I don't want to be stingy, but I think we need to think about this some more.'

'Okay, that's fair,' Sophia said. 'Let's take a week, and then we can take it to the board and make some decisions at our next board meeting on Saturday.'

Chapter 45

Miranda

The following morning, I was having breakfast when Sophia texted to ask if I was going to the Reids' for lunch.

I wasn't.

But after spending the morning looking for ways of raising funds for Project Cup, I found myself getting dressed and putting makeup on. Though I told myself seeing Jack again would just be awkward, my feet had other ideas. A few minutes later, I had been to the shop, and was knocking on John and Karen's door and letting myself in.

The house was already full of people, and I said hi to Sophia and Michael as I passed them on my way to the kitchen, where Karen was pouring vinaigrette over a salad.

'Hey, Karen.' I gestured at the bunch of tulips I had brought. 'Where do I find a vase for these?'

'Aw, you shouldn't have brought me flowers.' Karen smiled, and pulled me in for a hug.

I took a deep breath and relaxed. I had been concerned about Karen's reaction to hearing about the miscarriage, but it appeared Jack hadn't told her.

She pulled back, stroking her hands over my hair as she studied my face. 'You look tired, dear.'

I snorted. 'It's been a couple of rough weeks.' More like months, but who was counting?

Karen stepped back and went back to mixing her salad, as I went through her cupboards in search of a vase for the flowers.

'I hear Jimmy got to keep his ear?'

'Yes. He'll have some scars, but otherwise he'll be fine.'

'Sounds like God was watching out for him that night.' She smiled. 'Those tulips are lovely.'

'Yeah, they reminded me of you.' I busied myself with arranging the flowers for her. Karen's comment about God watching out for Dad grated at me.

'Did you know tulips are my favourite?' Karen asked.

Pushing my thoughts about God aside, I smiled. 'Maybe.'

She laughed. 'They remind me of spring and new beginnings. It's never too late to start again. You know?'

I shook my head and laughed at her obvious hint for me and Jack to get back together. Playing dumb, I asked, 'Are you referring to anything in particular, now?'

She raised her hands, looking all innocent. 'Surely not.'

'I didn't think so.' I put the vase on the dinner table and came back to see if I could help with anything.

'It's nice, though, isn't it, how spring offers a new start?' She tried again.

'Uh-huh.' Not taking the bait, I took a stack of plates and said, 'It looks like dinner's almost ready. I'll set the table.'

In the dining room, Michael and Nick were finding enough chairs for everyone to sit around the table.

I set the plates down. 'Does God protect people?'

Nick glanced at me. 'Sure. He protects and takes care of people. Like how it says in Matthew about how we don't need to worry about anything because God takes care of us.'

'Hmm…' Michael gave me a pensive look. 'I don't think it's quite as simple as that. What are you really asking, though?'

'Well, if God protected Dad when he was in this knife fight the other day, then that seems like a rather arbitrary choice. Why protect Dad from a knife, but let Mum die of cancer? Does God have favourites? But if God didn't protect Dad, then that seems uncaring. So, I guess I wondered how it works?' I looked at my hands as I held them in the air. 'Does God have favourites, or is he uncaring?'

Michael looked as though he was trying to hide a smile. 'What do you think?'

'Gah…' I shook my hand at him in frustration. 'I wasn't asking what I think, but what *you* think.'

'But what *do* you think?' He pushed.

'Neither option seems to line up with the Jesus I've been reading about in the Bible.' I sat down on a chair and pulled my hands through my hair. 'I'm so confused.'

'Uh-huh.' Michael grabbed a chair and sat down too. 'What if God does care and protect, but it mostly doesn't look like a physical thing. What if God caring and protecting us looks like our *souls* being safe in him?'

'What?' Nick frowned. 'But what about how it says about the flowers or the birds and how they don't want for anything because God takes care of them?'

Michael shrugged. 'Uh-huh, but sometimes there are droughts and flowers die. Or birds can't find food, or they eat plastic stuff they find and die.'

'Go on...' Nick went into the kitchen and grabbed a bunch of cutlery and started putting them out.

Jack and Julia came in with potholders and the salad and set them on the table. Julia found matches and lit the candles in the centre of the table.

'Yeah,' Michael continued. 'Sometimes there's war, or drought, or terrible poverty, and if that verse was talking about God providing materially for us, then I think there are big questions around if God plays favourites. So maybe Jesus isn't referring to a physical need, but to our spiritual need. Maybe what he means is that we don't need to worry about the only thing that really matters.'

'Which is...?'

'Whether God will continue to love us whatever our circumstances are.'

'Huh.' I bit my lip as I thought about it. Could it be as simple as that?

'Yeah, I've been thinking more and more that that's right.' Jack spoke up.

I turned toward him in surprise. 'I didn't think you believed in God?' Looking at him brought back the memory of the cheek kiss I had given him when I last saw him, and the way he had stroked my hair, and how he smelled so good.

I felt my cheeks heat, and quickly looked away.

Michael rolled his eyes. 'Honestly, this not believing in God thing is such a ridiculous concept. Most people believe in God – people just struggle to define what God is.'

'Sure.' Jack started pouring water into the glasses on the table. 'I believe in God, but I think my view of him has changed a bit recently.'

Intrigued, I wondered what that meant, but I didn't get a chance to ask, as it was time to eat.

That night, I looked up the passage in Matthew which Nick had referred to about how we didn't have to worry about anything, because look at the flowers and birds. It came just after Jesus saying things like there was comfort for those that mourn, and mercy for the merciful, and that those that were pure in heart would see God. And then, at the end of that chapter, he went on to encourage his listeners to love not only their friends, but their enemies, because that was what God did.

I put my Bible on my bedside table and turned the light off. It struck me that maybe this love was the essence of what God was. What would my life be like if I was to live it as though God was really loving?

I remembered the youth weekend I had been on in Oban as a teenager, and the YWAM team member who had talked about how committing a whole life to God might seem daunting, but it was okay to try it out for a little while.

And I remembered how Mum used to have a cross stitch hanging in the kitchen, which I took down when I redecorated after she had died. It said *Taste and See That the Lord is Good*. I smiled as I remembered how Dad used to look at me when I was little and Mum had cooked something new that didn't look appetising to me. Replacing *the Lord* with *the food*, he would use his most dramatic voice – as though he was reciting Shakespeare – and say, 'Taste… and see… that the *food* is… good!'

Maybe it was time to taste and see for myself whether God really was good or not.

That night, as I pulled up the duvet and snuggled in, I closed my eyes and whispered, 'God. If you are as loving as some people say you are, then maybe I would like to work out how to follow you?'

Chapter 46

Miranda

The next day, I was in the lunchroom at work when Angus came in with his sandwich.

After the almost kiss back in January, I spent several weeks trying hard to avoid him. It turned out it was all for nothing, though, as the next time I saw him everything was back to normal. As though that awkwardness had never happened. He was one of those good people who were awkward enough as they were, and therefore couldn't be bothered to make things more awkward if they could avoid it.

'Hey,' I said.

He shook himself, as though he had been deep in thought. 'Hi.' He smiled when he saw me, showing off his dimples. 'You having soup?'

'No.' I held up the container with my salad. 'It's Salad Monday today.'

'Oh.' He frowned. 'I didn't realise that was a thing.'

I smiled and got my fork out. 'It isn't. I just made it up.'

He relaxed and unwrapped his sandwich. 'I see. It seems most days are soup days for the ladies here, otherwise.'

I nodded. 'I think some people think soup will help them stay in shape. I can't do it, though. Whenever I have soup for lunch, I feel like killing someone by the end of the day.'

'Yes, it's a mystery to me.' He shook his head and I got the feeling it was just one of a long list of mysteries he had observed women do. 'I signed us up for the race I was talking about. Are you still up for it?'

'Uh-huh. Although we haven't decided whether we're going to continue with Project Cup yet.'

'Why not?'

I grimaced and looked down at my salad. It was a good idea, and between the three of us I was sure we could make it work. So why did I hesitate? 'I don't know,' I muttered.

He studied me for what felt like a long time. 'Huh.' He leaned back in his chair. 'You're chickening out.'

I put my fork down and threw him a glare. 'It's not chickening out if it's based on data.'

'Really?' He shrugged. 'Sounds like an excuse to me.'

'Some of us have bills to pay. You know.'

'Excuses, excuses. I'll help you raise the money you need to employ someone.'

I narrowed my eyes at him, communicating my suspicion. 'Why would you do that?'

'I don't know. Maybe some things are worth taking some risks on.' He shot me a wry smile. 'When I'm old, I don't want to look back on my life and think *huh, I've lived a safe life*, you know? We've got to approach – not avoid – our fears.' He leaned forward and squeezed my hand across the table. Lowering his voice as though he was telling me a secret, he continued, 'I know that in this field, safety and risk management is everything, but real life happens when there's some risk involved.' He grinned and pulled his hand back, waving it toward me. 'Like, you've got to ask the beautiful accountant out for a date to see if there's any possibility of more there.'

My cheeks grew hot and felt my shoulders tense. 'Umm…'

'And sometimes it's a dead end.' He shrugged. 'But who knows what risk might end up paying off in the end?'

'Yeah, about that…' I started, intending to explain my behaviour after our awkward cheek kiss, but struggling to find the words.

'Don't worry about it. I took a risk and gained a friend.' He smiled a reassuring smile. 'Think of all the things we might miss out on if we live life the safe way.'

'But the data…' I tried.

'Data, shmata.' He seemed to catch himself. 'At least that's how I want to live my life. But you do you.'

I huffed. 'Right.' We ate in silence as I pondered his words. 'Are you saying you really think you can help with getting funding?'

His mouth widened, showing his dimples off as he said, 'I don't know if it's possible, but I'd be happy to give it a go.'

Something inside me felt taunted by his optimism. Maybe because it revealed that my hesitation to take risks was less about being responsible and more about how cynical I had become. I sighed. 'Maybe you should come to our next board meeting. Julia would like you.'

'This Julia sounds like a wise person.'

I snorted. 'She's annoying, and her head's in the clouds – always coming up with new lofty ideas – but sure.'

I spent the rest of the afternoon trying to focus on work but found myself mostly staring out the window thinking about anything other than work. When I was old and looked back on my life, what would I see? What did I want my life to look like?

I tried to put my attention back on the spreadsheet in front of me. I was good at spreadsheets and risk calculations, and I normally enjoyed doing it. But maybe that was my way of avoiding the things I feared? Maybe it was time for me to take a few risks. Even if I ended up losing out. Maybe taking a risk on Project Cup would be like tasting to see if God was good.

I reminded myself that God being good didn't mean my bills would miraculously be paid. And I still didn't have a solution for Dad's possible rehab bills.

But maybe I could step out of my comfort zone and see what might happen? Maybe I could try to trust that God would still love me and be kind to me, no matter what happened? Maybe it was time I trusted that God would still love Dad whether I could afford rehab for him or not?

Yes. It was time I made some changes to my life.

***

The following Saturday morning, Julia helped me make a big salad to go with the fresh bread rolls I had put in the oven for lunch.

'I think I'm getting the hang of this cooking thing, don't you?' Julia asked as she put the salad in the fridge.

'Uh-huh.' I smirked. 'As long as there is no actual cooking involved, and you stick to doing what you've been told to do, then you definitely do great in the kitchen. For sure.'

'Haha.' She threw me a glare and muttered, 'Well, we can't all be Nigella freaking Lawson.'

I laughed. 'Don't be so hard on yourself. Nick likes cooking, so you won't starve.'

'I guess.' Her shoulders slumped. 'I burned a boiled egg a few days ago at Nick's.'

'Huh.' I bit my lip and tried to keep the laughter from slipping out. 'How did you manage that?'

'I left it boiling and forgot about it.' She wrung her hands and lifted them to her lips as she winced. 'All of a sudden, there was a loud bang, and when I got there, the egg had exploded and the whole pot was black. I couldn't get the pot clean and had to bin it.'

I shook my head and got some cups out and set them on a tray for making drinks later. 'I didn't know it was possible to burn a boiled egg. What did Nick say?'

'Last night he asked if I'd seen the pot. I told him a neighbour had asked to borrow a pot, so I had given it to them.' She closed her eyes, as though she was too embarrassed to keep them open. 'But he didn't buy it, because the only neighbours in the house are a seventy-five-year-old Iranian man who is away visiting his nephew in Germany, and an arrogant man in his mid-thirties who yells at kids and drives a leased car, which he inspects every Saturday morning to make sure it hasn't got any new scratches before he goes golfing. And then there's an older lady who is always cooking – you can smell it in the hallway all the time. Hence, when Nick asked who I'd lent the pot to, Kevin or Janette, I froze. Neither of them would ever come asking to borrow a pot.' She grimaced. 'I ended up confessing and told him I'd replace the pot.'

I tried to keep my smile from spreading too wide. 'What did he say then?'

'He laughed, and he told me he wasn't laughing *with* me, but *at* me.' She shook her head and held up a hand in the air. 'As if he's so cool, just because he happens to be good at cooking.'

'Uh-oh.'

'I know! I've told him nobody likes a know-it-all, but he doesn't seem to care.' She shrugged. 'And then he went on to make me pancakes, and they were amazing. I guess he's a know-it-all with some redeeming qualities.'

I snorted. 'Oh. I'm glad he's forgiven.'

Julia laughed as there was a knock at the door. 'I know; I'm such a generous person sometimes.' She went to answer the door as I counted out cutlery to go with the plates I had put out on the counter.

'Miranda?' Julia hollered from the hallway. I went over and found Angus on the front step. He gave a stiff smile and held his hand up in a little awkward wave when he saw me.

'Hi, Angus, come on in.' I introduced him to Julia, and he held out his hand to shake hers.

'Oh, so *you're* Angus.' Her lips pulled up, and her eyes sparkled as she shook his hand and glanced at me. When he turned to take his coat and shoes off, she mouthed, 'Interesting.'

I pressed my hand to my stomach to ward off the sinking feeling at seeing the glee on her face. Maybe it hadn't been a great idea to invite Angus to come to the board meeting without explaining it to everyone first.

Julia went about trying to find out every piece of interesting information about Angus as we went back to the kitchen, where the timer for the bread in the oven went off.

'Don't feel you have to answer all her questions,' I said, as I searched for my oven mitts.

'Oh, it's all fine.' Angus said as though trying to reassure both me and himself that he was okay.

'Yeah,' Julia said as she threw me a pointed look. 'Angus says it's all fine.' Turning back to him, she nodded approvingly. 'And, how long have you guys known each other for?'

I snorted and turned to take the bread out of the oven when Michael and Sophia arrived. As they came in, Julia introduced Angus to them. He seemed to visibly relax when Michael rescued him from Julia's interrogation by asking, 'Was that your bike out front?'

Michael and Angus went to sit down in the living room, and Sophia turned to me. 'He's fit.'

I felt my cheeks heat and tossed my oven mitt at her as I busied myself with transferring the rolls onto the cooling rack. 'He's a *friend.*'

'Of course.' She agreed too easily. 'A very fit friend.'

Angus had kind eyes, and he was intelligent, and talented. And good looking. His lean muscles, dimples and symmetrical face were very attractive. 'I have eyes,' I agreed, and met her eyes. The laughter in mine must have satisfied the question in hers. There was no spark between Angus and me. There was only one person I had ever found any spark with.

I glanced at the doorway of the kitchen when I heard Nick and Jack arrive, and winced as Julia said, 'Have you guys met Angus, Miranda's *friend?*'

My stomach felt like I was on a rollercoaster as Jack cleared his throat and held out his hand to shake Angus's. 'No, I don't think so. I'm Jack.'

When I had invited Angus to join our board meeting, it had been a spur of the moment thing. And when I had thought about it afterwards, I had thought it was a great idea. He was well connected and understood the vision and – most importantly – he wanted to help. It had seemed practical for him to come along. But as I watched as Angus and Jack shook hands and realised who the other was, my stomach felt as though it were in freefall. I realised now how stupid an idea it had been.

Jack knew I had gone out with an Angus the evening before I told him about the miscarriage, consequently Angus being here now made it look like we were a thing, and like I was trying to show everyone that I had moved on from Jack.

When Jack looked at me, a question in his eyes, my world stood still. Part of me wanted to tell him Angus was just a friend – nothing more. But the other (more selfish) part of me wondered why I should explain anything at all. We had both agreed there was no future for Jack and me, so why should Angus be any of Jack's concern?

I knew the answer to that question, and maybe I hoped – just a wee bit – that Jack would be jealous. It wasn't rational or very mature of me – I know – but there was a part of me that just wanted what it wanted.

And it wanted Jack.

That part of me found it hard to breathe when he looked at me like I was the only person in the world. It made the rest of the world seem out of focus, and all I could see was him.

Only him.

'Mir?' Sophia cleared her throat loudly and ran her hand down my arm to get my attention.

I gave my head a shake and tried to focus on her. 'What?'

'Should we eat here, or in the living room?'

'Um...' My brain wasn't working properly. 'Whichever.'

'Are you okay?' She whispered.

I nodded sharply. I was fine. I would be fine.

Her eyebrows lifted, and her eyes told me she knew. 'Let's eat in the living room,' she said. 'We'll fit better there.'

'Sure.' I glanced toward Jack, who was talking to Nick and Angus. He seemed... relaxed. I wiped my hands on my jeans as I battled the confusion at his lack of reaction to Angus being here. Maybe it would all be okay? I took a deep breath and tried to apply myself to making sure everyone had what they needed for lunch.

An hour later it was clear that bringing Angus along to the board meeting like this had not been a good idea. At all.

Jack was being perfectly appropriate – almost too friendly – to Angus, and it was rattling me. *I* knew I had no romantic interest in Angus, but *Jack* didn't. Still, Angus being there didn't seem to bother Jack one bit. And Jack's apparent indifference irked me. Did he not care at all if I moved on? Had our relationship been worth so little to him?

I tried to tell myself it was a good thing. It meant Jack had come to terms with the fact that we weren't right for each other. But it stung that he didn't seem the least bit jealous. We might never be together again, but there would never be anyone else for me. Still, he had clearly moved on.

Julia offered to make teas and coffees before we started the board meeting and took Nick along to the kitchen. Jack was chatting away with Angus, Sophia and Michael, all of them getting on like a house on fire.

Which was great. Really great.

Still, the longer I watched, the more depressed I felt.

'Miranda?'

I was startled out of my thoughts as Sophia put a hand over my hands, which were wringing each other. 'Yes?'

She stood up and motioned toward the door. 'I need a word outside.'

I followed her onto the front step, and she closed the door behind us.

'What's going on?' She asked.

'Nothing.' I answered too fast, and I could tell she didn't buy it.

'Don't be silly. You look like you're thinking of killing someone.' She gestured toward my face.

'Yeah, well, maybe I'm a little annoyed.'

When I didn't continue, she said, 'With…?'

'With *Jack*,' I whisper shouted. 'I've just brought a guy to the meeting, and Jack hasn't even batted an eye.' I waved my hands in the air. 'How could he move on this fast? He's not even a little bit jealous.'

Sophia took my hand. 'That's good, though, right?'

'What? No! It's like he never cared about me at all.'

'But you said you guys will never be together again. This is what you want, isn't it?'

I took a deep breath and tried to collect myself.

'You want him to move on, and maybe one day you can be friends again, remember?' Sophia pressed.

'Right.' I croaked around the big stone which had lodged itself in my throat and looked away. 'Still, it would be nice if he hadn't erased me entirely so soon.'

'Let him forget. And you forget him, too.' Sophia squeezed my hand gently. Then she smirked. 'Or do something about it.'

My eyes flew to hers. Do something about it? 'No, you're right. Of course.' I gave a shaky laugh and shook my head. *What was I thinking?* 'Of course.'

'Great. Then let's go back in there and work out the future of Project Cup.'

I nodded decisively. 'Right.'

I followed Sophia back inside, my eyes automatically finding Jack's as I entered the living room. He was whistling that song I couldn't place as he leaned back in his chair. Though I had just agreed with Sophia that it was best for both of us to move on, I found myself wondering if maybe, *maybe*, I had it all wrong. Still, I sat down as Nick and Julia brought our drinks and got my notebook out.

Chapter 47

Jack

Ever since Miranda told me about the miscarriage and I stopped seeing her all the time, I had felt conflicted about Project Cup board meetings. Board meetings meant I had to see Miranda again, and that was painful. But also, they meant I got to see Miranda again, and there was really nowhere I would rather be than next to her. So, yes. Conflicted.

When I had first arrived and understood who Angus was, I had experienced a flicker of jealousy. Not because I thought she had moved on – I wasn't sure that was possible for either of us at this point – but because Angus could hang out with her without a whole lifetime of unprocessed pain getting in the way. As I recognised my jealousy for what it was, I realised I had some decisions to make.

After my run the other night, I had been back to see my counsellor, Alison, twice. When I had told her that I wanted to try to change, she had looked me in the eye and said, 'Changing might hurt. At times, it might hurt a lot.'

'Yeah. I'm hoping it will be worth the pain.' My laugh felt awkward, or maybe I laughed to cover how awkward and utterly out of my depth I felt. 'It will be worth it, right?'

Alison smiled. 'Only one way to find out, I suppose.'

'Uh-huh, and what is that one way?'

'Well, seeing as you have gotten to where you are by avoiding anything that might be painful, maybe you would like to consider doing the opposite for a while. Try to approach the kinds of things you would otherwise avoid.'

'Approach, don't avoid.' I nodded. 'Where do I begin?'

'Well, if this was about you just being generally risk averse, then you could go take a financial risk, or do some extreme sport, or something.' She twisted her lip. 'But I reckon you'd feel quite comfortable with those kinds of things.'

I gave a wry smile. 'Yeah, I think I've done those kinds of things in the past to appear confident and adventurous. I'm not afraid of losing money or injuring myself physically. I'm scared of feeling powerless in the face of other people's feelings. I'm afraid of not being able to fix people that matter when they hurt. So, I've tried to live as though they don't matter. As though I don't care.'

Alison nodded. 'And for you to approach these things now, it would look like...'

I closed my eyes and lean my head backwards against the chair. 'It would look like caring.'

After actively choosing not to care about things for so long, it had become a habit to shrug things off. And being able to shrug things off had been an asset in many ways – it had made me able to climb the career ladder quickly. But as I looked at my life now, I saw it as a false strength. To care wasn't the same as being weak. Really caring and being able to handle the disappointments and hurts in life was *real* strength.

As I talked to Angus in Miranda's hallway, I went through a whole range of emotions, the first being an intense flicker of jealousy. And because the jealousy was uncomfortable, my initial reaction had been to shrug it off. But then I had looked at Miranda, and as her eyes met mine, I found in myself a new determination not to settle for being okay with our relationship being broken. A determination never to settle for less than *everything* with her ever again.

I did my best to get to know Angus, so I would experience the jealousy until it hurt beyond what I could handle. He turned out to be a really nice guy, and part of me was thankful Miranda had a good guy in her life that evidently cared about her. The other part of me struggled to contain the emotions that warred within me. And as I sat there, eating some food she had made that probably would have tasted lovely had I been able to taste anything other than my own emotions, I decided that enough was enough. I wasn't going to let pain and hurt dictate my life anymore. Despite the pain and the feeling of powerlessness screaming at me to get up and leave, I stayed, and wondered what I needed to do to get Miranda back.

'Has everyone had a chance to look at the numbers I sent out?' Miranda asked, once everyone had a drink and had sat down. She looked around the room, meeting everybody's eyes except mine. Was she annoyed with me?

The Arctic Monkeys' *Baby I'm Yours* had been running through my mind ever since I had come back to Scotland and seen Miranda again, and I whistled it softly to myself as I got my phone. We had spent hours listening to The Arctic Monkeys together in our teens, and though this wasn't a song that well defined the Arctic Monkeys – it was probably a cover – it well defined my state. I would belong to Miranda until the end of time.

I pulled up my emails to find the document she was referring to. When I had first seen the email, I had looked at the numbers, and they didn't look great. I mean, it was great that they had been able to fund the distribution of period cups to that high school in Kenya, but I wasn't convinced it was a cost-effective model in the long term. I sipped my coffee as everyone started talking over each other, asking questions about particular numbers. To me it seemed obvious that it had been a good pilot project. But if it was to be continued as a serious social enterprise, some major investment would be required for it to be viable in the long-term.

'If everyone understands where the numbers come from now, then I'd like to give you my interpretation of them,' Miranda said, glancing at Julia, who was already frowning. 'I think this has been a good project, but honestly, if we had just spent the money we invested in having period cups shipped to the high school in Kenya straight away, we would have been able to give out a similar amount of period cups.'

'Yes, but...' Julia tried cutting in.

'However,' Miranda kept going. 'By selling period cups in Scotland, we have also raised awareness of period poverty, and those that have bought a period cup have obviously cut down their period waste massively. As far as awareness and environmental impact goes, we've done some good.'

Julia looked pleased, elbowing Nick in the side as her smile widened. 'Exactly.'

'On the other hand, though…' Miranda waved her finger in the air, pointing at Julia and herself. 'Julia and I have both taken long haul flights, which obviously isn't great from an environmental perspective.'

Julia frowned again. 'Uh-huh. But…'

'Let me finish.' Miranda held up her hand. 'What I'm saying is, there are pros and cons to how we've carried out this project. And when I look at these figures and weigh everything up, then I think we now stand with a choice of three options. We could say we've done a good thing and wrap it up now. Or we could keep this up on a project kind of basis. That would mean we would work like we have been, and in the end, we could have made a similar amount of difference by just giving the money straight to the organisations or schools that we want to help. And in my view, that isn't really an option as it seems a rather inefficient way to make a difference.'

'Gah!' Julia couldn't keep it in any longer. 'Why are you being so negative, Miranda?'

'I'm not-' Miranda tried to say.

'Why can you not see that as we keep going, this whole project will take off?'

'Julia, hold on-' Nick ran a hand down her arm, trying to get her attention.

'No, I've got to say this.' Julia shook her head and looked at Miranda, waving her hands in the air as she spoke. 'There are loads of possibilities of things we could do with this. But you refuse to see any of them. Why does everything have to come down to a balance sheet?'

'I don't-' Miranda tried again, but Julia wasn't listening.

'Not everything can be measured-'

'Julia, hold on.' Nick took her hand. 'Take a breath.'

Sophia and I winced at each other as Julia slowly turned to face Nick. 'Take a *breath*?'

Nick's smiled apologetically at her. 'Yeah?' He shrugged as he said, 'Miranda isn't out to get you. It's okay.'

I rubbed my hands over my face and snorted as I thanked God I wasn't Nick.

'I *know* she isn't *out to get me.*' Julia's eyes took on that rather agitated edge that meant she thought she was being pushed just beyond what she considered reasonable, and she didn't like it. Having been on the receiving end of that look plenty growing up, I shook my head and hoped Nick knew what he was getting himself in to. She went on, 'I *know* it's bloomin' *okay*. We're just having a *disagreement* is all.' She looked at Miranda. 'Right?'

Miranda cleared her throat. 'Sure.'

Nick held his hands up and sank back into the couch. 'Sure. Great! Good.'

I avoided looking at anyone to keep from laughing at him.

'Look, I get it,' Miranda looked Julia in the eye. 'You're right that there is much more to be done here. I feel strongly about period poverty, too, but we need to look at the facts. And considering the facts, those are two of our options.'

'But these are not *facts*, as much as they are your interpretation of the data,' Julia insisted.

Miranda held a hand up, her eyes exasperated, and I hid a smile as I imagined the mess this whole project would have been without Miranda's sense and determination to live in reality. It took courage to step out of the dream, take a hard look at reality, and choose to live in it even when it didn't measure up to the dream. 'If you would let me *finish*, I'd like to say that a third option would be to invest properly in Project Cup so that it can become a viable social enterprise.'

'Oh. Okay.' Julia nodded. 'Go on.'

'Right.' Miranda gave her a wry smile. 'If we want to do this properly, then Project Cup has to go from being a nice hobby to being something we treat as a business – investing ourselves in it more fully.'

'Yeah, I've been thinking about business start-ups, and how they tend to fail,' Sophia cut in. 'I've never seen Project Cup as a business, but as a movement. Or a revolution. We want to see an end to period poverty. Imagine the impact all those girls who are dropping out of school could have on the world if they were to get their education. But this isn't just a *job* – it's a calling. You know?'

'That's what I'm *saying!*' Julia raised her hands in the air.

'Uh-huh, and rah-rah and all that,' Miranda seemed to struggle not to laugh. 'I agree – it's great that we have dedication. But I'm trying to say that there's *risk* involved. And that risk is something we should all weigh up before we go any further. What will the actual cost be? Will we quit our jobs and immerse ourselves in selling period cups?'

'Sure!' Julia lit up at the thought. She had always jumped first and thought later. 'That's a great idea.'

'And how are we going to pay our bills? How will we eat? Look Julia, it's great you're enthusiastic, but can we be a little realistic here too? You love teaching – are you really going to give that up?' Miranda looked defeated, and my heart sank as she said, 'I wish we could have a *real* conversation about this.'

'Yeah, okay, you might have a point there.' Julia smiled and took a deep breath. 'Okay, but maybe I could come down in hours, though.'

'Uh-huh, and is that something you can afford to do?'

'Of course. I can turn the heating down, and eat porridge and boiled eggs.' Julia nodded and Miranda looked like she was counting to ten.

'Okay, great, but isn't that a conversation you want to have with Nick, considering you guys are getting married and will be living together?'

Julia clearly hadn't thought of that, but she played it off as though it wasn't a big deal. 'Oh, well, Nick's onboard. I'm sure he doesn't mind.' She turned toward him. 'You like porridge and boiled eggs, don't you?'

'Um...' Nick looked like a deer in headlights. He looked at me as though he was asking for help, and I could only shake my head and bite my lips to keep from laughing at his prospects of freezing at home and having burned porridge for the foreseeable future.

'Sophia, say something!' Miranda gave Sophia an expectant look.

'Well, I don't think it's any of our business how Julia and Nick decide to structure their finances.' Sophia rubbed the back of her neck. She seemed unsure of what Miranda was asking her to comment on. 'But if it was me, I wouldn't think Nick has much say in how Julia wants to spend her money. Do you?'

Michael shook his head at Sophia and tried to hide his smile. 'I don't think that's what Miranda meant.'

'No! *Obviously*, that's not what I meant.' Miranda's eyes were wide, and her voice rose as she said, 'I don't *care* how they structure their finances. I care that we make calculated *choices*. If I am going to risk my job and my house, then I want to know that you guys have thought through your own commitment, too. I don't want to jump into this if you guys are going to change your mind when you realise that there's actual cost involved.'

'Oh, right,' Sophia said quietly with a nod. 'Of course.'

'Yeah, okay.' Julia cleared her throat. 'That makes sense.'

'*Thank* you.' Miranda said in an exasperated tone. She took a deep breath.

'I'm sorry,' Julia said quickly, scrunching her face up as though embarrassed. 'I didn't realise you were seriously considering this as an option. I thought you had made your mind up that it wasn't worth it to keep going. So I came ready to fight.'

'Yeah, I know. It's okay.' Miranda ran her hands through her hair, leaving them at the top of her head as she said, 'I'm still not decided either way, but I think we need to properly explore all options before we make a decision.'

'Right. We should definitely do that.' Sophia nodded.

Julia's eyes sparkled. 'What do we do next?'

'Okay.' Miranda smiled and pushed the sleeves of her shirt up. 'Next we look at what it would look like to take the third option. I've looked at a few scenarios and costed them out.'

'Okay, great.' Julia relaxed back in her seat and motioned for Miranda to continue.

Miranda went on to paint a picture of what the social enterprise could look like in five years, and then passed around papers with a potential budget for the first year. Her vision was inspiring, but after glancing at the budget it was clear to me that there were some real hurdles. I wondered if all this was just an elaborate way for Miranda to explain to everyone why she wanted to close it all down, or if she really thought it was worth investing in. And I couldn't help but think of how, for so long, I had thought we had a chance to make our relationship work, but in her mind, it had been doomed from the start.

'As you can see, this budget doesn't balance, and that's due to a few things, but one of the major reasons is that I've included a paid position. That's because I'm not in a financial position to quit my job and work for free right now. And Julia isn't going to quit her job either, and I bet you're not either, Soph. Right?'

'I wish I could just quit.' Sophia looked up from the budget and grimaced.

'Mhm.' Miranda nodded. 'That's why I've included a paid position which we could share. That way, we could all come down in hours at our real jobs, but also work and get paid a little here. I mean, it's not a massive salary, but it's something.'

'That sounds great,' Michael said. 'But where is the money to balance the deficit going to come from?'

'That's what I'm saying. I don't *know*.' Miranda threw her hands in the air. 'That's why we're having this conversation, 'cause how on earth am I meant to know how to find this kind of money?'

'Then, you *have* made your mind up already.' Julia said disappointedly. 'I thought you said you were open-'

'I was telling Angus all this over lunch the other day, and he had some thoughts.' Miranda went on as though Julia hadn't spoken. She gestured towards Angus and winked. 'He's not just a pretty face, you know.'

Angus flushed and gave an awkward laugh.

I reminded myself I was thankful that Miranda had good friends, even as I wished that I, rather than pretty-faced Angus, could be the one to fix her problems.

'Okay, all I said was I have some contacts, and I think it wouldn't be impossible to raise that kind of money for a year,' Angus said. 'By the end of the first year, I think you should be able to cover this position by your sales, and if you can't, then you would need to have another conversation as to where this is all going. But for now, I think it's a great idea and I would love to help you make it work.'

Julia clapped her hands, and Miranda grimaced at Angus before giving Julia a patient smile. 'Yeah, yeah, so there are ways of making it work.'

Angus coming in as a white knight stung a little before I realised that Miranda's problem was never the money. The deficit was big considering the size of the project, but in the big scheme of things it wasn't a huge amount of money we were talking about. No, Miranda's problem wasn't money. Miranda's problem was that she wasn't sure she could trust the rest of us not to leave her alone and sinking.

As this dawned on me, I felt hope stir for the first time in months.

Miranda hadn't called us together to tell us she wanted out. She had called us together to see if we were willing to give it a real go. To see if we were in it together. She wanted to make this work, maybe more than anyone else in the room. But she didn't want to do it alone.

I rubbed a hand over my face as I wondered if maybe that was the reason that she had ruled out being in a relationship with me again. Did she think she would end up alone in it? That I would leave when things got hard?

Well, if that was the case, I knew what to do.

Chapter 48

Miranda

'Angus, where have you been all my life?' Julia said, after Angus finished talking about some of his ideas for how we could raise the money we would need.

Angus ran his hands down his jeans, looking every kind of uncomfortable as Nick scowled at Julia.

'What?' Julia asked.

Nick raised his eyebrows and said in his most dry tone, 'Angus, *where have you been all my life? * Are you for real? *I'm* sitting *right here.*'

Julia stroked his cheek with a smile and shrugged. 'I'm just saying it's nice to hear something positive. For once. I didn't mean it like that.'

'Yeah, yeah.' Nick smirked and shook his head.

Sophia snorted. 'Uh-huh. Is that it then? We're doing this?'

'Um…' I still felt a bit overwhelmed by it all.

'What is it now?' Julia sighed as she looked at me. 'Miranda, what more do you need? It will be a tough year, but we're all in this together. Let's live a little!'

My eyes flashed to Jack's. He was studying me intently, as though trying to work me out.

Live a little. Julia's words echoed in my head.

Part of me wanted to take offence at them, but the other part knew too well that if there was one thing which I was an expert at, it was how to avoid living. Ever since the year when Jack's and my relationship ended, I miscarried, Mum died, and Dad went off the rails with the alcohol, I had kept existing, but I had done my best to avoid life. Some verse I had read in John's Gospel came back to me: *The thief comes only to steal and kill and destroy; I have come that they may have life, and have it to the full.* I had underlined that verse several times. It had seemed an important one.

Fine. I had chosen to try to follow Jesus, and he seemed keen on living.

I straightened my back and nodded. 'Well, if you guys are sure you're all in, then I guess I'll speak to my boss tomorrow to let him know I'll need to come down in hours.'

'Yes!' Julia shrieked as she leapt across the coffee table and swept me up and into a hug. Not able to stand still, she rocked us from side to side and beamed at me. 'You're not going to regret this!'

A laugh escaped. 'I sure hope not!'

Sophia stood up too and held her hand up for a high five. Julia ignored it and went to hug her, too. Sophia stiffened, her smile frozen on her face as she tapped Julia's back awkwardly. 'Yay…'

I shrugged and smiled at her. 'Yeah. Yay… I hope.' I glanced at Jack again. He winked at me, causing a tingle to run up my spine. I quickly turned away, and we sat down to iron out the details of what was next for Project Cup.

As our meeting had taken so long, I sent Julia and Jack to get some nacho crisps, salsa and ice cream, and the rest of us made vegan chilli for dinner. We all ate together, and though I was still unsure of the wisdom of continuing Project Cup, I felt myself relax as the dinner conversation went into more casual territory. Soon everyone was sharing stories and laughing. Our social enterprise might crash and burn, but at least we would have fun trying to make it work.

I glanced at Jack to find him looking at me.

Again.

He gave me a soft smile. I wasn't sure what his smile meant, but I couldn't look away, and soon my stupid heart wished for things it couldn't have. Or maybe it could?

'Miranda?' Julia cleared her throat loudly to get my attention.

'Uh, yeah?' I pulled my eyes away from Jack's and put my hands over my cheeks to cover the blush I felt rising.

'Are you having any more ice cream, or can I take your bowl?'

Everyone helped clean the kitchen before they all left me alone with my thoughts. I made myself a cup of tea and sat at my kitchen table as I tried to process my feelings after the board meeting. The anxiety I had felt about going all in hadn't vanished completely. I still dreaded the thought of not having enough money, and I wasn't sure we could actually make it work. But it was a risk I had to take. As soon as Monday came around, I would speak to my boss about working less at the bank – before I chickened out.

When there was a knock at the door, I glanced at the time. It was after eleven and pitch-black outside. The only person that would ever show up at this time of the day was my Dad. The cool air hit me in the face as I opened the door, and I pulled my cardigan closer to stop from shivering.

'Hello?' I pushed the door open wider so he could step inside, doing a double take when I saw it wasn't Dad standing on the front step, but Jack. 'Oh, it's you.' Self-conscious, I ran a hand through my hair. 'Did you forget something?'

'You could say that.' He shut the door behind him, and his eyes scanned my face. 'Are you okay?'

I nodded. 'Is that why you came over? To ask if I'm okay?'

Jack's lip tugged to the side. 'No.' He stepped closer and held up a shoebox. 'I came to give you this.'

I swallowed as awareness of how close he was flooded me. I had to look up to see his eyes, which were set on mine. I could reach out and touch him if I wanted to. I closed my eyes and reminded myself that I *didn't* want to. 'What is it?'

'It's for you.' He cleared his throat, and his eyes roamed my face as he held the box out to me.

Taking it from him, I avoided his eyes. 'Okay.'

'Let me know what you think. Okay?'

I didn't trust my voice but gave a sharp nod.

'Great.' He shot me a nervous smile before turning and opening the door. 'Good night,' he said as he left, closing the door behind him.

'Good night,' I echoed at the closed door.

Once I had made another up of camomile tea, I sat back down at the kitchen table and glanced at the shoebox. Not sure what to expect, I opened it and found a stack of letters. The first one was written on the day he had left Scotland for Hong Kong, and the last tonight. Deciding to go read them in chronological order, I reached for the first one.

My dearest Miranda,
Today I left my heart in Edinburgh and left for the other side of the world. Because I can't handle not being able to fix your problems. There, I told the truth for once. Not that you will ever read this, but still. I told you I'm coming back soon, but the truth is I may never come back. Not unless I can find a way to handle all these feelings. I know I should have let you go, but I couldn't do it. Not today. For a little longer, I will let myself live in the fantasy that one day we will be together again.
I tell myself I'm looking forward to being in Hong Kong, and that this is some great adventure I'm living. But the truth is that life feels bleak without you – like watered down lukewarm tea without any caffeine. Like I'm missing a limb. Maybe I'll get used to this ache someday. I don't know.
All I know is I miss you.
Your Jack xx

I read the letter again as tears filled my eyes. If only he had told me these things at the time. I put the letter aside and took out the next one.

Dearest Miranda,
I dreamed of you tonight. We were walking down the beach at Portobello with a baby girl – our baby girl – strapped to your chest in one of those baby carriers. You were beautiful in the sun as you nuzzled the baby's head, your eyes shining as you looked at me. The baby was still tiny, and fast asleep as we walked along the water's edge discussing what to name her. You were keen on Morven after your Grandma, but I wanted to call her Mabel. We weren't about to come to an agreement anytime soon, so we were throwing around all kinds of other names we could think of. I suggested Sue, but that reminded you of Ruby Sue in the Griswold family Christmas, and then you couldn't stop quoting the film and laughing to yourself. 'Remember when they go to chop the Christmas tree down?' you said and then did the voices: 'Isn't it a beaut, Audrey?',

'She'll see it later honey. Her eyes are frozen.'
Your laughter woke me up with a smile on my face, and I never found out what name we decided on in the end.
But as the dream faded, so did the happiness I had felt, and instead panic filled me. I can't be a dad when I can't even be there for you.
That's why I sent you an email and ended our relationship for real.
And though I knew it had to be done, I wish I'd had the guts to do it better. You deserve better than a stilted email. I'll call a counsellor today – I need to change.
I don't expect you to wait for me, but I hope to the God I don't believe in that one day I will learn to handle all these feelings and you'll give me another chance.
In the meantime, don't miss me.
Forever your Jack x

The tears were flowing freely now. I had been pregnant when Jack had written this letter, although I hadn't known it yet. Whenever we had spoken about children as teenagers, it had been in a joking way, always in a distant future kind of way. But Jack's dream made me think the jokes had been a cover, hiding his true thoughts and feelings. He had always come across as such a cool guy, hardly ever letting on he was affected by anything. Life might have been difficult for other people, but Jack would shrug off problems like they weren't significant at all. I had loved that about him, even as I found the way he would dismiss my problems frustrating. I had seen glimpses of his feelings from time to time though. There had always been more to Jack than his coolness.

I laughed through my tears as I read the part about National Lampoons Christmas Vacation. Such a good film that would never grow old.

Wiping at my cheeks, I read letter after letter, each deeper than the previous one and full of his agony at being away. He wrote when my mother died, and his letter was so different than the polite note of condolences I had received back then. He shared his favourite memories of my mum, and as I read them, I was reminded of things I had forgotten about her. And he wrote about how he had almost stopped seeing his counsellor, but when my mum had died, his inability to go home and face the loss made him realise he had only peeled a couple of the layers off the onion, and there were more layers to peel. He said they had made a plan to process some more, and then he would go home and see me when he felt more able to handle things. So, he had sent me a note, which he had written about twenty drafts of before googling what to put into it and sending it off with the intention to fix everything when he next saw me.

I remembered how I had planned an impromptu visit to London once I found out he was coming home for a visit. I hadn't felt able to deal with the hurt that seeing him again would cause.

He wrote about what he had learned as he went through therapy in Hong Kong, and how he was processing his sister Josie's death.

As I read letter after letter, I cried for me and I cried for him.

The letter before he finally left Hong Kong and moved back to Edinburgh was filled with determination to live his life without hiding from his feelings and hope that I would see the real him and be willing to try again.

There was another letter from when we were travelling in China, wishing it would never end. Another from after we came back, filled with disappointment, questions, and hope that we might still work out.

And then there was a letter from a couple of days after I had told him about the miscarriage.

Miranda,
I don't know how to breathe with knowing you never felt you could tell me about the miscarriage.
I don't blame you – I wasn't the kind of person you could tell things like that back then. I wish I was. I wish I was the kind of person you could have shared your grief with. The kind of person you could have talked to about all the broken dreams and all the disappointment and despair you must have felt. The kind of person who could have grieved with you and been there for you.

But I wasn't. And no matter how much I wish otherwise, I can't change the past. I can only acknowledge that I was highhanded, arrogant, stupid, broken and unable. And for all the ways that my brokenness made you feel, I am sorry.
I know it was too early to know whether it was a boy or a girl, but I wish I could have told you how our baby would have been the most loved little girl or boy in the world. You told me that you didn't name him or her, but if it was a girl maybe we could have called her Mabel. It means lovely and beautiful. She would have been gentle and kind and determined and strong and beautiful – I know that because you are all those things and I'm sure you would have rubbed off on her. And it would have been a privilege to be her dad.
I know that now.
And as I grieve over our baby and over the past, I also grieve over the future. Over every day that we will exist on this earth without each other.
I wish I could tell you how I love you. How I still carry a picture of you in my wallet. I probably always will. But I think you're right – you're better off without me.
Forever your Jack xx

After reading letter after letter all night, I wouldn't have thought there were any tears left, but as Jack's words of grief and hopelessness pierced my soul, all I could do was succumb to the sobs that took over.

The next letter was written only a few days ago.

Miranda,
I had a few conversations that led me to believe I have been wrong about some things.
I realised recently that I've been pretty angry at God. First for my sister's death, and later for things like your Dad's alcoholism, Lisa's death, the miscarriage, and so on. People talk about God as being loving and kind, but then they pray to God because they think he's in control, and you know how I feel that's just crazy. If God's in control, then how come all

these bad things happen? Is he making them happen? Did he kill my sister, or our baby? Because if Him being in control means he makes bad things happen, then he's not good, or kind, or loving.
But I'm starting to think I've been wrong.
Sure, there are things God is in control of, but if he's given us free will, then there are a bunch of things he's not in control of.
At all.
Like our choices.
Because God is good, and kind, and loving. Therefore, it must be utterly impossible for him to orchestrate evil. And he allows us to have real choices with real consequences, and he grieves with us when those choices lead to suffering. He doesn't insist on his own way, even when he knows his way is best.
I've been doing everything all wrong. I came home from Hong Kong intending to show you that we should get back together. And every time you said no, I found a way to work around it.
And then you told me about our miscarriage, and I understood how damaging my making all the decisions for us has been to you. Love doesn't insist on its own way, and I'm sorry for every time I decided that I knew best. You had every right to push me away after the way I behaved back when I first left. You have every right never to trust me again.
And I didn't think you ever would. Until tonight.
Tonight *you* kissed *me*. On the cheek, but still. Then you let me hold you. I guess it made me wonder if maybe, maybe you'll be willing to give us another chance someday.
I will always, always, always love you.
Forever your Jack xx

Finally, there was the last letter.

Miranda,
When I came back from Hong Kong, it was because I felt I

had changed. I had learned to handle my emotions and I wanted a second chance with you. I wasn't going to shy away from suffering anymore, and I was going to show you that I could be there for you when things got hard.

And as good as my intentions were, I hadn't yet understood that you didn't need or trust anyone to handle things for you, to fix your problems, or to lean on. You are smart and capable and can handle anything life throws at you alone.

Still, I wonder if sometimes you feel lonely and wish you had a companion. Someone willing to jump into life's adventures together with you. Someone to mutually share life's joys and horrors with. Someone to laugh with and to grieve with.

I never intended for you to read any of these letters. But now I wish I had shared them with you earlier. Maybe then you would have known how much I feel and think about you. Maybe then you would have known that you were not alone in our relationship.

I don't get to go back and do things differently, and if you give me another chance I will let you down again from time to time. I *have* changed, but I'm still a work in progress. Despite all that, I hope as you read, you'll hear my heart.

I love you. I always will.

Forever your Jack xx

Something deep inside me awakened as I read his last letter. Sophia's suggestion to forget Jack and let him forget me, or to do something about it rang in my mind. There was no forgetting Jack. There never would be. And from reading his letters I knew he would never forget me either.

Though it was five o'clock in the morning and I knew Jack was probably asleep, I took out my phone and sent him a text.

Me: Can we talk?

As soon as the message was sent my determination gave way to doubt. *Can we talk??* Why had I sent that text without thinking it through first? What was I going to say to him?

It wasn't two minutes before my phone lit up with a message back from him.

Jack: Meet me at the beach in an hour

An hour was no time at all. My nerves rattled almost audibly and made me feel queasy. Why had I thought this would be a good idea? Was I really going to do this?

I rubbed my stomach and glanced at the wall where I had hung Mum's embroidered verse again. *Taste and See that the Lord is Good.*

I swallowed my doubt and went to wash my face.

Chapter 49

Miranda

It was starting to get light outside by the time I got to the beach at Portobello. Sitting down on the wall between the prom and the beach, I watched as the waves licked the sand in the dim light. Spring was on its way, and it had started to get a little warmer in the last week, but it was still cold before the sun was up. It was the perfect morning to watch the sun rise. Everything was peaceful and calm. The sun was on fire on the horizon, painting the sky in light pinks and oranges as the waves swept in over the sand.

'Miranda?'

I turned toward him and watched as he approached me. Despite the cold, I felt my hands get clammy. 'Jack.' I nodded and wiped my hands on my jeans.

Closer now, he stopped and sat down next to me on the wall, and I felt his gaze on my face, which made it harder to hold on to the blush that was breaking out. Taking him in, I noticed that his hair was a mess, there were dark circles under his eyes, and his cheeks were scruffy. He looked as tired and nervous as I felt.

'Are you ok?' I asked when he had sat down beside me.

He flashed me a self-conscious smile. 'Uh, I'd like to say yes, but that would be a lie. I'm nervous.' His eyes roamed my face. 'You?'

My head felt as though it might come off, it was nodding so hard. 'Me too.'

His smile softened. 'We can be nervous together then.'

I laughed awkwardly. 'Yes.'

Jumping down into the sand, he said, 'Come, let's walk. I can't sit still when I feel like this.'

I jumped down too, and we walked down toward the water in a silence that stretched so long it was painful, before I cleared my throat. 'I read your letters.'

'I figured.' His eyes narrowed as though he was bracing himself. 'What did you think?'

Breaking eye contact with him in order to be able to think, I turned toward the sea again, rubbing my sore neck as I searched for words. 'I feel... honoured that you would share your thoughts and feelings with me like that.'

He grimaced. 'I should have been open with you about it all from the start.'

I shrugged. 'Shoulda, woulda, coulda... The past is the past.'

'Aye, but from now, on things will be different.' He bit the inside of his lip before continuing, 'I want to be open and real with you.'

'Thank you.' Hearing how stilted it sounded, I winced. 'About the kiss...'

Jack glanced at me before looking away, and we kept walking towards Joppa.

I cleared my throat and without thinking the words poured out of me. 'I kissed you because I didn't want you to leave thinking I didn't care about you. And I wanted to thank you for everything you had done for me and Dad, but-'

Jack hung his head as he shook it. 'There was never a need to thank me.'

'I-'

'No, listen.' He rubbed his hands over his face. 'It was nice to see Jimmy again, although I hope he'll feel better next time I see him.'

'Still, I'm grateful. I know I could have done it alone, but it was nice of you to be there.'

'I know you can do *anything* alone, but you shouldn't have to.' His eyes met mine, and I noticed they were wet. It struck me that I had never seen as much emotion in his eyes as I did then. He shook his head and took a deep breath. 'I wish I was there for you when you miscarried, and when Lisa died. You have no idea how sorry I am that you were alone in all that.'

I nodded. 'Yeah, it sucked.' I glanced at him. 'I missed you.' I wasn't going to make light of the worst time of my life. But he wasn't the only one that had made decisions out of brokenness. 'The way I thought about things didn't help, though. If you'd been here, I probably would have pushed you away, because I was afraid that I might come to rely on you too much. I'd seen how Mum relied on Dad, and over and over again he failed her. So, I decided I wouldn't be like Mum. I'd be fine on my own. And I was angry with God for putting me through all that.' I frowned as I thought about it. 'I've come to realise I got it wrong, though. God didn't make me miscarry, and he didn't kill Mum, or make Dad an alcoholic, or make you break up with me. But God knows all the possibilities, and he isn't surprised when shit happens.'

Jack smirked at me. 'Oh no?'

'No! He's not there like, *oh no, what will I do now?*' I waved my hands in the air. 'I've come to think that God is able, and he wants to take the shitty circumstances and turn things around. He's able to find solutions and ways even where I can't see them.'

We kept walking, but the silence wasn't awkward now. I didn't feel unsure anymore. Instead I felt like, no matter where the pieces fell, it was right to have it all out with him. It wasn't *easy* to trust him with the vulnerable places in me, but it felt *right*.

I cleared my throat. 'You were right in your letter when you said about me feeling lonely and wishing for a companion. Not relying on anyone other than myself meant I feel lonely a lot. And it meant losing you. Again.' I sighed and pulled my hands through my hair. 'Gah! This is hard.'

The corners of his lips pulled up slightly as he stretched out a hand to me. I took it, and felt a shiver go up my arm. His hand was big compared to mine, and warm, and strong.

'I've decided I don't want to only rely on myself for everything anymore. I'd rather trust that, through all the shit, God has good things for me, and when I'm unable to cope, his love will still be there for me.' I looked up at Jack, deciding to lay it all out there for him. 'I think I misunderstood Mum too. I thought she kept looking to Dad to fix things for her, and he could never be steady or safe enough for her. It angered me that she would continue to take him back when he'd hurt us over and over again. But I didn't understand that she didn't need him to be any different, because she trusted that God would be there for us no matter what choices Dad made. You know?'

He gave me a lopsided grin. 'I always thought Lisa was kinder than most people.'

I snorted. 'Uh-huh. I used to think she was weak, the way she kept taking him back. But now I think she was a pretty amazing person. She didn't see herself as a victim, and she wasn't threatened by Dad's dysfunction. Instead she chose to love him, even as it hurt, and she trusted God to still love her when she hurt.'

Jack sat down in the sand, so I sat down next to him and stared at the sea. The waves were lapping the beach and the sun was lying above the horizon now. 'I was wrong not to tell you about the baby.'

'If you'd told me back then–'

I shook my head. 'I *should* have told you when I first found out I was pregnant. You had a right to know. And we should definitely have talked about it when you came back.' Running my fingers through my hair, I continued, 'I shouldn't have closed down on you like I did. I forgave you for leaving a long time ago.' I gave him a wry smile. 'It would have been hypocritical not to forgive you, because I often wished I had left too.'

Jack swallowed, but his voice was hoarse when he spoke. 'Do you ever wonder what life would be like if you hadn't miscarried?'

'Of course.' I leaned toward him and let him wrap his arm around me. 'Do you?'

'Yeah.' He frowned. 'Honestly, I don't think I would have handled it well, considering the place I was in at the time. I wasn't able to handle much back then.'

I nodded. It meant a lot to me that he was honest with me. 'Isn't it strange that you had that dream about us arguing about baby names before I found out I was pregnant?'

'Yeah.' Jack shrugged. 'I've dreamed of having children with you for a long time, though. I still do.'

I looked up at him and decided to go all in. 'Me too. I never stopped loving you, and I should have sorted things out with you and trusted God to take care of me whatever happened.'

Jack tucked some of my hair behind my ear, causing my ear, and cheek to tingle with excitement. He was close enough that I could see my reflection in his eyes. He bit the inside of his cheek as if to stop from saying something.

'I'm sorry I pushed you away.' I braced myself before saying, 'Do you think we could try again?'

Chapter 50

Jack

The hope I had felt since the board meeting now exploded in my chest like fireworks. For years, I had dreamed of the day when we would get back together. And now it seemed those dreams were on the cusp of coming true.

That was what she meant, right? She did want to get back together, didn't she? I tried to reign in my hopes. She probably wanted to be friends again – at least to begin with.

'Miranda…' I swallowed, feeling unsure of myself. *Don't mess this up, don't mess this up.* 'Just to clarify, what do you mean when you say *try again*?'

She frowned. 'I mean, I'd like to have you in my life again.'

Dread filled me, and all the fireworks fell flat in my stomach like a big rock. 'In your life again?'

'Yeah.'

'Like as a… what? A neighbour? A friend? A partner? A husband? A what?'

'Yeah…' She nodded. 'Like all of that.'

'Oh, yeah?' Not able to believe what she was saying, I said, 'Are you sure?'

Pulling her hand to herself, she glanced at me before looking toward the sea. 'Are you not?'

'No, no!' I reached for her again, but she avoided my hand, and my heart lurched at how she was pulling away from me. 'Mir, you're misunderstanding me.'

She pushed some hair out of her face. 'Am I?'

'Yes!' I ran my hand over her soft hair and reached for her hand again. 'Listen, I want to be all those things to you. I just don't want you to feel pressured, or like you're making a decision you're not sure of.'

'I don't feel pressured.' Miranda gave a shy smile and squeezed my hand. 'I've let my fears run my life for long enough. I want to *live* my life. And I want to live it with you.'

The fireworks in me were back – this time bigger and more electric than ever before. I grinned. 'Great. Me too.'

She grinned back at me. 'Great.'

'Great.'

She laughed softly, as though unable to contain her delight. Pulling her hand to my lips, I kissed her knuckles. She leaned forward, letting her nose brush my cheek, and I tilted my face towards hers as she pressed her lips to mine.

Time stood still and sped up all at once.

She pulled back a little, still smiling.

I wrapped my arm around her, brushing my hand down her hair and let myself breathe her in as she nuzzled into my neck. I wanted to stay there for the rest of my life. Never let go of her. Never stop feeling her breath on my neck.

But there were still things to talk about.

Still holding on to her, I leaned back so I could see her face. 'As much as I want to get back together with you, and as much as I'm working on changing, I need you to know that I don't trust myself on how to deal with suffering of any kind right now. The way I handled finding out about the miscarriage tells me I've still got stuff to work out.'

'That's ok. I don't need to trust you to deal with my pain, or anyone else's.' She gave me a reassuring smile. 'You can fail as much as you need to – I will fail too. But I want to trust that in our failures, God is big enough to still offer us his love. And if he loves us, then I want to trust that, whatever happens, I'm going to be safe in his love.'

I slid my hand under the hair behind her neck and tilted her head toward me. Her face shone with delight. I was pretty sure my face matched hers, because I was delighted too. The over the moon kind of delighted, where I wasn't sure I would be able to ever express just how delighted I was.

Pulling at her shoulders, I relaxed back onto the sand until we were lying there, side by side, her head resting on my shoulder, and her arm splayed across my chest. Matching my breath to hers, I wrapped my arm around her and felt as though all was right with the world.

'There is one thing you should know…' I said, placing a kiss into her hair. I felt her stiffen, as though unsure of what I might say next.

'Uh-huh?' She tilted her head so she could see me.

'I have no intention of failing at another engagement.'

Her eyes narrowed. 'What are you saying?'

'I'm saying, I don't want to mess around. This will be a short engagement with a wedding date which we're not cancelling. We should start to plan the wedding straight away.'

She relaxed back, snuffling her face into my shirt as though hiding a smile. 'Huh.'

'Do you still have your ring?'

She sat up, pushing her hair away from her neck to pull out a long necklace I'd seen her wear tucked into her shirt from time to time. At the end of it was the ring. 'I almost threw it in the sea at one point. And I considered pawning it.' She pulled the chain over her head and gave me a wry smile. 'Couldn't do it, though.'

I nodded. 'Do you still want to wear it, or should we get a different one?'

'I don't want a different one.' She frowned as she undid the necklace and pulled the ring off. 'I kept it to remind myself of how hopeful I was back then, and how I shouldn't have trusted you, and how I shouldn't trust anyone again.'

I snorted. 'Then maybe a different one would be a good idea?'

'No.' She shook her head. 'Now it reminds me that though we have ups and downs, I can trust that God's love covers us. Besides, it's a beautiful ring.'

I took the ring from her and put it back on her finger. 'Then let it also remind you that I will always love you. And for as long as I have life in my body, I want that life to be intertwined with yours.' Pulling her hand close, I kissed her palm.

Her eyes glimmered with hope and love. 'Okay.' She leaned forward to meet my lips, and everything was alright with the world.

Epilogue

Miranda

We sat on the beach, talking and listening and snuggling, until Portobello's dog owners were awake and walking their dogs on the beach. I didn't want to leave the cocoon of love we were creating, and at the same time I couldn't wait to get on with our life together.

When my stomach growled, Jack laughed. 'Let's go home and make breakfast.' He pulled me up, threading his fingers through mine as we walked.

Jack had walked down to the beach, so we took my car back home. There, we had eggs on toast for breakfast, before snuggling up next to each other on the couch and falling asleep. I woke up when Jack's phone rang on the coffee table.

'Let it go to voicemail,' he muttered as he pulled me close.

'It's your mum, though.'

'What time is it?' He squinted at the phone with one eye. 'Really? One o'clock?'

I stretched my sore back and yawned. 'She's probably wondering why you're not at lunch.'

Though I would happily have stayed on the lumpy couch, snuggled up with Jack for the rest of the day, we ended up going to Sunday lunch at the Reid's. We crossed the lawn and went up the stairs, Jack's arm wrapped around my shoulders and the ring firmly back on my finger again.

'Are we telling everyone now, then?' I asked.

'I think we'd struggle to keep it a secret, don't you?' Jack smiled as he scanned my face, stopping to peck my cheek before opening the door and pulling me inside.

'Hi,' Jack said as we walked into the dining room. 'Sorry we're late.'

Five pairs of eyes looked up from where they were dishing out food, and I smiled shyly. I still felt uncomfortable coming to lunch. John nodded and went back to his conversation with Michael. Nick and Julia were making eyes at each other, but Sophia gave us a once over through narrowed eyes, and a questioning smile as she saw our joined hands.

'That's okay, dear.' Karen looked up from where she was dishing up beef stew onto someone's plate. 'Oh good, Miranda. I wasn't sure if you were coming, but I made you a veggie stew just in case. It's still in the kitchen, I'll just get it now.'

Jack sat down and pulled out a chair for me next to him.

'Ah, thank you. It's okay, I'll get it,' I said, and turned to the kitchen instead of sitting down. I took a deep breath, to settle the nervous feeling I had going on, and went to find my food. When I came back, I sat down next to Jack, and he took my hand under the table. I smiled at him before looking down to find my fork.

'How's it going?' Sophia raised her eyebrow at me.

I cleared my throat and avoided her eyes. 'Fine. You alright?' I pulled at my hand, but Jack wouldn't let go, squeezing it gently and stroking his thumb across my ring and knuckles. Giving up on the idea of getting my hand back, I started eating my food with my right hand only.

'Uh-huh.' She smiled at me. 'Fine.'

I nodded. 'Good.' Biting my lip, I tried to hide my smile, but it was futile. The happiness in my heart had to express itself on my face and wouldn't let me hide it. Not even a little bit.

Sophia's smile widened, and soon we were laughing out loud.

'What's so funny?' Julia asked.

Jack bit his cheek. 'Yeah Mir, what's so funny?'

I shook my head and turned my face toward Jack to hide it from everyone's eyes. 'Nothing.'

Jack smiled and let go of my hand, wrapping his arm around me and giving my head a soft kiss. 'I asked Miranda to marry me this morning, and she said yes.'

I breathed him in, before turning back to everyone. They were smiling and cheering, and Karen held her hands to her mouth as though stopping her internal squeal of glee from escaping.

'Are you for real?' Julia stood up, her chair falling on the floor behind her as she ran to me, pulling me out of my seat to hug me.

She squealed and jumped up and down as she found the ring on my hand and held it up for everyone to see.

All the years of feeling unsure of where things stood, all the years of feeling uncomfortable as the ex-fiancée of the son in the family, all the years of wishing for something that couldn't be real. They all fell away as we were embraced and congratulated by everyone.

'Well isn't that funny: I felt led to make a fancy dessert.' Karen sighed. 'There you go; God knew all along, didn't he?' Karen started clearing the table.

'I think that's what's called *confirmation bias*,' Michael muttered.

'What's that, Michael dear?' Karen asked.

'Nothing.' Michael sighed, and opted not to rock the boat. 'It was nothing.'

Later that afternoon, John pulled me aside to tell me he had a plan for getting Dad into a free rehab. It felt like a stone fell off my shoulders and I could breathe again. It was a Christian rehab, and John knew of other people that had gone through their intense but good program. There was a waiting list, but until there was an opening for Dad, John would meet with him every week, and Dad had agreed to go to AA with John again. This time I knew rehab wasn't going to be a magic cure; there would continue to be ups and downs in his journey. But I hoped Dad would get better and be able to straighten out his life some.

And I would trust that, whatever happened, God's love was deep enough, thick enough, wide enough, to cover us all.

Acknowledgements

Thank you for reading Miranda and Jack's story. I still struggle to believe there are people that want to read my weird stories, but I'm thankful for every one of you. I hope Cross My Heart has inspired you to ask new questions and to not settle until you find answers that align with the character of God as revealed in Jesus.

It is my aim whenever I write not to preach – I want to leave room for the questions to grow, rather than to give answers – but I recognise that in this book I come awfully close. This is because I do have strong beliefs about God being good and loving. The Russian writer Leo Tolstoy said: '*It is terrible when people do not know God, but it is worse when people identify as God what is not God.*' So, in this story, there are a few conclusions. Sorry about that.

And thank you to all who contributed to making this story happen:

Thank you to Ernest for pushing me to think outside of the box and for challenging me not to settle. Thank you for being so patient with me, and for walking alongside me through the highs and lows of life. I love you.

Thank you to my children. You guys inspire me, widen my horizons and push me out of my comfort zone, and I'm so utterly blessed to be your mum.

David: thank you for challenging me and championing me to know Jesus more. And thank you for reading my manuscripts and being real with me.

Samuel: thank you for your honesty and for your kindness.

Mary: thank you for being an inspiration to so many and for giving of yourself to champion young people to know Jesus more. Thank you for all the hours of editing and for continuously finding ways of encouraging me to write better. And thank you for all the input and for letting me ask a million questions.

Becky: thank you for catching the annoying repetitions, for the tweaks (all of them, but particularly the New Year's awkwardness), and for pushing me to do better. And most of all – thank you for your friendship.

You guys are all amazing and I wish you all lived closer.

Thank you also to Youth With A Mission. I'm so thankful for the thirteen years I got to work with you all.

Thank you to Jesus for showing me what love is.

If you enjoyed Miranda and Jack's story, I would appreciate it if you would leave a review on Amazon or GoodReads – or recommend 'Heart of Us' to all your friends!

Much love,

Emma Browne

Other Books by Emma Browne

Cross My Heart
Julia comes home to her flat in Edinburgh, Scotland, to find her brother's annoying friend Nick is living in her flat. Nick won't go away, and soon their frenemy relationship turns into friendship, and attraction turns into... love.

But Julia's guilty conscience and Nick's broken background put up hurdles for their relationship, and they soon find themselves questioning the beliefs they've held as true for as long as they can remember.
A contemporary romance with Christian themes.

Sophia and Michael's book is currently being written. For news about when to expect it, sign up to Emma's newsletter: eepurl.com/dmvk0H
Or follow on Instagram: @romancebyemmab

Printed in Great Britain
by Amazon